A
Perfect
Husband

Hilary Boyd trained as a nurse at Great Ormond Street Hospital, then as a marriage guidance counsellor. After a degree in English Literature at London University in her thirties, she moved into health journalism, writing a Mind, Body, Spirit column for the *Daily Express*. She published six non-fiction books on health-related subjects before turning to fiction and writing a string of bestsellers, starting with *Thursdays in the Park*. Hilary is married to film director/producer Don Boyd.

ALSO BY HILARY BOYD

Thursdays in the Park
Tangled Lives
When You Walked Back Into My Life
A Most Desirable Marriage
Meet Me on the Beach
The Lavender House

A Perfect Husband

Hilary Boyd

Quercus

First published in Great Britain in 2017 by Quercus
This paperback edition published in 2017 by

Quercus Editions Ltd
Carmelite House
50 Victoria Embankment
London EC4Y 0DZ

An Hachette UK company

A CIP catalogue record for this book
is available from the British Library

PB ISBN 978 1 78429 418 2

10 9 8 7 6 5 4 3 2 1

Typeset by CC Book Production

Printed and bound in Great Britain by Clays Ltd, St Ives plc

'Women's total instinct for gambling is satisfied by marriage'

Gloria Steinem

PART I

CHAPTER 1

Freddy gazed unseeingly at the pretty Chinese girl in the sleeveless black dress on the other side of the roulette table, aware that he was doing so only when she smiled at him, giving a coy wave with a delicate, manicured hand. He smiled back, although it was a purely reflexive twitch of his mouth, never reaching his eyes. He was in the zone.

He'd been feeling sick all day, his nerves wired to the point where he felt as if he'd been flayed, the skin literally scraped from his flesh. His body smarted each time someone bumped into him, brushed against him or ran into him – heads down on their screens – on the narrow, crowded Soho pavements near the recording studio he owned. Every sound, even Lily's worried goodbye this morning, had set his teeth on edge so that he was barely able to respond with the grace he knew she deserved. She wasn't stupid: she knew something was up. But there was a way out of this crisis – he never questioned it. It had just eluded him recently, a run of bad luck – which he sensed would change tonight.

Now he sat in his favourite casino, embraced by the elegance of another era: warm wood-panelled walls, high ceilings, solid chandeliers, long windows looking out towards the darkness of the night-time park. It was a hushed, padded, cosseting environment, the croupiers and pit bosses polite and well trained, the clientele rich – or, at least, having the appearance of wealth. As had Freddy, of course. Most importantly, the club still used the European wheel, only one zero, not the American version so popular these days in the London gambling clubs. Popular because of the added double-zero pocket, giving a house advantage – small though it was at five and a quarter per cent – on straight bets of almost double the European system. Which mattered to Freddy. Although Fish, his cynical, world-weary American gambling crony, laughed every time he mentioned his preference, saying, 'It's not the house you have to worry about, buddy.' Fish was in California tonight, thank goodness. He would only have been a distraction.

Numbers flashed through his mind like a mantra as he silently chanted the clockwise sequence: 0, 32, 15, 19, 4, 21, 2, 25 . . . He sat and watched the ivory ball's trajectory through one, two, three and more spins of the wheel, scrutinizing the frets between the pockets to check for nicks or irregularities, assessing the twist in the croupier's throw, before finally placing his first bet. He gave in to the mounting anticipation. His hands, meanwhile, played with the piles of black one-hundred-pound chips in front of him, the smooth clay surface like worry beads through his fingers. The satisfying click as they fell back on each other was reassuringly familiar. And, of course, a tantalizing precursor to the hit.

He selected five from the stack, placed two on 23 red, straight up, two on a 'street', laying his chips at the end of the line containing 7, 8 and 9, and the last on 0. The croupier was a tall, olive-skinned man, in his late thirties, Freddy judged, with dark, blank eyes and slicked-back hair, maroon waistcoat, white shirt, black tie – Eastern European would be a predictable guess despite the 'Tom' on his name-tag. He called, '*Rien ne va plus*,' in a bored monotone and Freddy's heart closed down, his breath held, his mind still, completely without thought.

This was the hit. Unconnected to the outcome, it existed entirely in and of itself, a silent, intimate realm of intense, glorious, terrifying anticipation that sent shivers up his spine and wound his body to fever pitch. No drug he'd ever taken came anywhere close, and he'd tried a few. Mere seconds it lasted as the wheel spun, the ball careened around the top space in the opposite direction, dropped, bounced the frets, dropped again, found the pocket. But it was no less powerful for its brevity. And this was only the first time: there would be more, always more . . . minutes away, anywhere, anytime.

'Nine, red,' the croupier intoned, placing the chunky, bevelled glass dolly on the winning square with a flourish, then quickly sweeping the losing chips from the green baize with his shiny gold-metal rake, stacking them deftly and with awesome speed in their allocated space on the table beside his station.

Freddy came out of his trance. *He'd won*. He took a deep breath as he watched Tom stack the round flat black chips on top of the two he'd put down, then start a new column, and a third, all even in height, sliding them towards him with his rake, barely glancing at him, uninvolved. The Chinese girl across the table raised an elegant eyebrow at him, nodded her congratulations. He clicked automatically through his chips, calculating his win. No big deal – less than two and a half thousand, not even a minute dent in the mess – but a start nonetheless, a real start, a feel for things to come. It was definitely his lucky night.

It was still dark, although the sky to the east was lightening, clouds streaking the horizon in what would be a beautiful spring dawn, when Freddy emerged, exhausted, from the womb world of the tables. The nightmare of his real life hit him with force, like a ball kicked at his chest, as he stepped onto the cold London pavement. Across the night hours he had won, he had lost, won again, lost again. An exhilarating ride. He had drunk a lot of coffee, eaten an indigestible burger and chips at some stage, chatted aimlessly with the girl in the black dress – who seemed to get off on watching other people lose their money rather than losing her own – and now he had close to twenty-one thousand pounds in his pocket. Good, but no good. No good at all. In fact, in the scheme of things, pretty bloody pointless.

CHAPTER 2

Meanwhile, Lily waited by the open doors of the West End theatre, clutching two programmes, her eyes scanning the street, filtering the crowds drifting in as she waited for her friend. It was freezing, raining, blustery, a generally vile March evening. She had come by taxi from the flat she shared with her husband, Freddy, in Sussex Square, and she wasn't dressed warmly enough, wanting to show off the gorgeous richly coloured wool jacket Freddy had brought back from Italy a month before. She longed to get inside to the stuffy warmth of the theatre. But Prem was always late. The warning bell hadn't gone yet, but it soon would – she wondered if she should go in now and leave her friend's ticket at the box office.

Lily loved the theatre, loved the excitement of a live performance, the sense of anticipation as the lights went down, the absorption in another world. But she wasn't in the mood tonight. She'd have much preferred to have a large glass of wine somewhere with Prem and spill out her worries. But the play lasted nearly three hours and it would be too late afterwards. Her friend worked long days at the shop she owned in Marylebone, selling ergonomic chairs and desks, and was always exhausted.

'Lil!' Prem was by her side, breathless, her beautiful face alive with amusement. 'I've been shouting at you.' She gave Lily a hug. 'Always away with the fairies, you.'

Lily laughed, handing Prem a programme as she dug the tickets from her Chloé bag – another gift from her husband. They made their way into the bowels of the building, almost the last to do so, the bell ringing insistently now, to the house seats Freddy had been given by a client currently working at his studio. The client, Asif somebody, happened to be the star of the play. Their seats were in the middle of the row, the rest of the audience already settled and tutting irritably as Lily and Prem squeezed past the knees and feet, coats, bags and briefcases that obstructed their progress between the cramped old rows, muttering 'Sorry' and 'Thank you' as they went. But Prem was always forgiven: even at fifty-two her dark-eyed, natural beauty and the dramatic sweep of glossy hair down her back turned heads wherever she went. She didn't seem to notice the attention, however, which always endeared her to Lily, living as she now did in Freddy's self-conscious, privileged world where image counted for so much.

Lily did not consider herself beautiful – although Freddy often insisted she was. Her sister, Helen, had been the one with the looks. But with her floppy brown hair shining auburn in sunlight, her large hazel eyes, strong nose and slim figure,

8

Lily possessed a diffident grace. And coupled with her restrained bohemian style and wide, forthright smile, she was a woman who caught the eye in any gathering. It sometimes brought her up short to realize she was now part of Freddy's glamorous milieu, no longer the life-or-death theatre of brain surgery – her first husband's profession. In fact, she'd never felt entirely part of either, her own world more solitary and internal, her comfort zone the smooth, blank paper upon which she loved to draw.

'Go back and say hi to Asif,' Freddy had instructed earlier. 'I told him you'd be in tonight.'

'Do I have to? I barely know him,' Lily had protested. She always felt awkward hanging around in those small, stuffy West End dressing rooms, the actor half clothed, high from the performance, eyes dark with mascara, skin thick with greasepaint, searching her face to see whether she'd *really* liked it or was lying through her teeth to protect his or her ego. It was another world backstage, a private club from which ordinary mortals like herself were excluded, always tense with an unsettling mix of insecurity, competition and hubris. If Freddy were there, it would be fine. He always knew what to say, how to make everyone feel good, but Lily just felt stupid and out of place.

Freddy had kissed her, running his finger down her nose, smiling the loving smile that never failed to melt her heart. 'Don't be such a wimp, Lily. He'll think you hated it if you don't go back. All you need do is pop in for ten seconds, say how simply marvellous it all was, gush a bit. How hard can that be?'

She nodded. 'I'll see,' she said, knowing she wouldn't. She would make up some excuse about Prem needing to rush off. Freddy could text Asif tomorrow, gush all he liked. And anyway, he was in such a strange mood at the moment. The thought made her stomach twist and she pushed it away, opening the programme and pretending to be interested in what she was about to see.

'Where's Freddy tonight?' Prem asked, leaning towards Lily as the lights in the auditorium faded.

'Umm . . . work, the usual,' she replied. But something in her tone must have alerted her sensitive friend.

'You okay?' she whispered, as Asif Baka wandered barefoot onto the stage in tracksuit bottoms and a frayed white T-shirt, which showed off his suitably toned biceps, reading a book upside down. Not a promising start.

In Lily's opinion the play was dreadful – overacted and pretentious. Prem agreed. Lily noticed she had nodded off for a while in the first act and envied her ability to switch off like that.

'Do you have to stay?' Prem asked as they hovered uncertainly in the corridor by the entrance to the bar, standing back from the press of people eager for a half-time drink.

'Freddy would say I should. But I can always tell him you weren't feeling well or something. And if Asif is pissed off, then I'm sure he'll get over it. It's not as if we're all best mates. He's just a client of Freddy's.'

'Clients are important.' Prem's business mind kicked in. 'I'll do the second half if you want me to.'

Lily laughed. 'No, let's get out of here. It's ridiculous sitting through something neither of us is enjoying just so we can go backstage and be fake to someone who probably won't even register who we are.'

'Put like that . . .' Prem grinned and took her friend's arm.

'So what are you saying?' Prem asked. They were sitting in the basement of a restaurant/bar just yards from the St Martin's Lane theatre, in William IV Street. Set out on the rough wooden table between them were a bottle of Bordeaux, olives, Italian salami, chilli-garlic prawns, strips of toasted sourdough and a small terracotta bowl of *cervelle de canut* – a soft creamy cheese dip with shallots and chives. 'You think Freddy's having a thing with someone?'

Lily felt close to tears at the idea, although it was what she'd been silently thinking for weeks. 'Well, what else can it be? He's tense, distracted all the time, constantly checking his phone – not that he doesn't always – coming in at God knows what time . . .'

'Freddy's never kept normal hours, though. Don't musicians record all night sometimes?'

Lily nodded. 'They do, but Freddy doesn't have to be there all the time – he has people to do that. And he never used to, not night after night. I don't know . . .' She gazed at her friend. 'It's different. I can't explain how, but he's acting strangely, even for Freddy.'

Prem reached across the table and laid her hand over Lily's. 'God, you're freezing.' She patted her and withdrew. 'Have you asked him about it?'

'Yes. He just says he's really busy, he's sorry, things will improve shortly. He says to stop worrying.' She gave a short laugh. 'Which is exactly what he'd say if he was having an affair, right?'

Prem sighed, and raised her eyebrows slightly. 'I suppose . . . It's just . . . Freddy adores you, Lily, you know he does. I realize he's gorgeous and out there and every woman on the planet envies you for being married to him. But honestly, I've never taken him for a flirt. Whenever I see him, he just seems totally into you. I mean, you've only been married . . . What is it? Three years? Surely it takes longer than that to stray.'

Lily didn't reply, just picked with her nail at a warm drop of candle wax solidifying on the table. She noticed that some saffron ink from a drawing she was doing of a girl's face she'd studied on the Tube a few weeks ago had stained the inside of her second finger and rubbed at it absentmindedly with her thumb.

'Don't you think?' Prem was asking.

'That's what I tell myself. But I just know something's up, and what else could it be?'

There was silence between the two women. Then Prem, her voice tentative, asked, 'Are you still having sex?'

After a very long pause, Lily answered, 'No.'

She saw her friend's mouth twist. 'How long?'

'Weeks.'

'And this isn't usual?'

Lily shook her head. For her and Freddy, not usual at all. She and Prem did not normally talk about their sex lives. She had no idea if Prem and her husband, Anthony, had a good sex life, a bad one or a non-existent one. She had never asked and didn't want to know. She'd had other friends who went into lurid detail – one in particular who'd talked at length once about a strap-on penis, which had left seriously unwanted images in Lily's head that were hard to dispel when next she met the couple over spaghetti bolognese. So it struck home that Prem was even asking.

'You think that proves it?' Lily asked, her stomach turning on the red wine she had being gulping down too fast.

'It probably indicates he's under some sort of stress. But maybe it's just business. Maybe the studio isn't doing so well, or a client has kicked off about something. It could be a host of things to do with work or money that he doesn't want to worry you about.'

Nothing Prem had said comforted Lily. Freddy was a great businessman. He'd had his recording studio for years now and it was highly respected in the industry. It had made him rich. If there were problems he'd share them with her as he always did, giving her the lowdown on which artist was in and what they were recording and whether he thought the work was any good. He had his hand in everything.

When Lily didn't reply, Prem went on, 'I absolutely refuse to believe Freddy is having an affair. I just can't see it.' She eyed her friend for a long moment. 'Go home and ask him. Don't let him wriggle off the hook this time, Lil. Keep on at him till you have a proper answer. Otherwise you'll drive yourself mad, probably over something quite trivial that's nothing at all to do with you.'

Lily sighed, trying her best to accept what Prem had said. She was so grounded, so practical, and mostly right. She was an amazing friend. Lily thought back ten years. News of her first husband Garret's death – so sudden, so shocking, so completely unbelievable – making Lily's head spin so hard she could hardly breathe. Prem hadn't made a fuss, just scooped up Lily's then teenaged twins, Dillon and Sara, and taken them back to her house. Sara was friends with Prem's only daughter, Aisha, at the Fulham secondary school they both attended. She'd fed them, comforted them, brought wine and groceries round to Lily's house, while Anthony temporarily palmed off his divorce clients to deal with the bureaucratic nightmare involved in bringing Garret's body back from Switzerland. She'd been more of a sister to Lily than her actual sister, Helen.

'You trust Freddy, don't you?' Lily asked, her heart beating uncomfortably fast when Prem didn't reply at once.

'I don't know him that well but, yes . . . yes, I trust him.'

'Like you trusted Garret?'

Prem hesitated again, frowning. 'I knew Garret from when he trained with Raj at Guy's – twenty years at least. And he was . . . he was one of those people you'd trust with your life, literally.' She laughed. 'That's the point of a brain surgeon, I suppose.' Raj was Prem's older brother. He and his partner, Hal, lived in Minnesota, where Raj worked at the Mayo Clinic, doing research on genetic sequencing.

Lily gave a rueful smile. 'And you don't feel like that about Freddy?' She shrugged. 'No reason why you should.'

'As I said,' Prem replied, 'I've only known him for such a short time. And we don't see him much – he's always working.'

*

14

Lily got home late – the two women had sat for hours over the wine and then some fresh mint tea. She was fired up by Prem's insistence she get the truth from her husband. He wouldn't be asleep – Freddy seldom went to bed before midnight, often considerably later. She realized she was nervous, almost frightened, as she let herself into their sixth-floor penthouse in the smart block set back from Bayswater Road, minutes from Lancaster Gate. Did she really want to know what was making him so edgy, so distant? Shouldn't she just do as he'd suggested and stop worrying, let it pass, whatever it was?

She pictured him lounging on the sofa in the soft light of their large, luxurious sitting room, probably in his habitual jeans and untucked shirt, bare feet propped on the low oak coffee table, his handsome face, framed by thick, dark wavy hair, looking up at her with its perfect light-olive complexion and those large brown eyes, which could switch from being charmingly social, to tender and so loving, to something much darker and unfathomable, all within seconds. 'Mercurial': that was the word someone had once used to describe Freddy March.

But the flat was dark and silent. Lily slipped her heels off – they were stupidly high and her feet had been aching almost since she'd put them on – and left them in the hall, padding over the polished floorboards in her stockinged feet to the bedroom at the end of the corridor. Maybe he was asleep after all. The door was open, though, just as she had left it hours before, the smooth, expensive white bed linen untouched, except for a sea-green cardigan she had failed to put away

15

earlier. She glanced at the bedside clock: 1:05 a.m. *Where is he?* She reached for her phone to check if he had called, and rang his mobile when it was clear that he hadn't. It went straight to voicemail: 'Freddy March's phone. Leave a message and I'll get back to you.' His voice was warm and strong, confident. She loved him so much.

Where are you? she texted him. *I'm not asleep. Pls call when you get this. xxx*

Then she wandered back to the sitting room and went to stand by the glass doors onto the balcony, staring across the roofs at the city, the lights still dotted randomly over the floors in the hotel nearby, the dark patch of Hyde Park behind. She heard a police siren in the distance, over the constant background growl of traffic which never stopped and which she barely noticed after so many years in London. Her head was thick with the tension she knew she'd been hanging onto for weeks now, and also, no doubt, from too much red wine. There was no point in waiting up, she decided. If Freddy were involved in an all-night session at the studio, he'd have his phone turned off anyway. Better to talk to him in the morning. If she confronted him when she was so tired, she'd probably accuse him of all sorts of ridiculous stuff and they'd have a row.

CHAPTER 3

When she jerked awake around five it was to an empty bed. She sat up, heart racing. It was chilly in the room, the heating not yet triggered. Quickly, she wrapped her naked body in the pale blue soft-wool dressing-gown Freddy had given her for her recent birthday and walked through to the sitting room, hoping her husband had crashed on the sofa, not wanting to wake her. But it was dark and empty, the dawn barely breaking outside the uncurtained glass. The previous night's rain had blown over, and it looked clear on the horizon as Lily glanced out of the window, shivering.

Where the hell are you? she wondered, turning to curl up on the sofa, her cold feet tucked under her. She checked her phone, which she'd left charging on the glass side table by the door to the hall. No message. The flutter of anxiety grew in her gut, making her feel sick and even colder. *He's at the studio*, she thought, trying to be firm with herself. Where else could he be till this time? But he always told her if he might have to do an all-nighter. And it usually meant till about four thirty, latest – even the keenest musicians ran out of fuel. So the answer seemed obvious: in someone else's bed. She tried to picture it. Maybe they'd had sex and he'd fallen asleep by mistake. Or maybe she – whoever 'she' was – had insisted he stay, insisted he make a decision, forcing his hand so that he would have to confess the affair to Lily.

Her thoughts were almost detached, as if it were someone else's husband she was picturing *in flagrante*. Because it was impossible for her to believe her Freddy might, right at this moment, be kissing another woman, stroking his finger down her nose as he did Lily's, muttering his love for her, despite the tensions of the past month.

Lily reached for her sketchbook, her love of drawing a lifelong comfort and distraction since childhood when severe, life-threatening asthma had restricted her physical freedom, pinning her to her bed or, swathed in blankets – like a precious artwork – propped up on the sofa. Her wispy, anxious mother would hover over her, while her sister and friends were out in the fresh air, riding bikes, swimming, playing sport, *free*. She could not imagine surviving those early years without pencil and paper.

As she waited, she found herself unthinkingly sketching Garret's face on the thick cream paper in front of her. It was strange how her hand remembered things her brain did not. She still had photos of her first husband, of course, but since her marriage to Freddy they had been shut away in albums at the top of one of the wardrobes in the bedroom. Lily had not thought it fair to Freddy to have daily reminders of a man she had once loved. A man who had acquired the inconvenient halo of those who die young. These days, she recalled Garret's essence more than his actual features, remembered the feel of him more than his physical form. But her hand still knew every line.

Like Prem, she had trusted her first husband implicitly. Although he was just as much of a workaholic as Freddy, his job as a leading neurosurgeon in a busy London hospital taking up all hours, Lily had never for a single minute worried he wasn't where he said he'd be. Garret was like Freddy in that he was charismatic, unconsciously seductive, someone who could command the room, his charming smile effortlessly drawing people into his circle of admirers. A big, broad-shouldered Irishman, he was warm and very physical, someone who had made her feel safe.

But Lily had often felt she was part of 'Garret Tierney Inc'. There was no exclusivity with him, no special place where she felt she alone occupied his affections. He loved her, she thought, enormously, but only as much as he loved his children, his friends, his work, his colleagues and the beleaguered victims of the Iraqi war, one of whom he'd operated on with remarkable success – a seven-year-old child with terrible brain injuries who'd been flown to Britain by a charity.

Her second husband, although similarly warm and physical, and equally able to charm the birds from the trees, seemed to have eyes only for Lily. He made her feel as if she were the entire centre of his world, despite his moods being sometimes difficult to predict, his sudden need to be alone disconcerting. She had thought her new marriage would mirror the uncomplicated friendship she'd shared with Garret. But Freddy's love for her was a far more exclusive, more intense, more unpredictable thing. Lily felt he understood her on a deep soul level in a way no one else in her life ever had.

But as she waited in the early spring morning for him to return, she wondered how well she really knew him. Their first meeting, four years ago in Prem's shop, had been what her friend later termed a *coup de foudre*. The instant, irrefutable connection was like fitting the final, long-lost piece into a jigsaw puzzle.

Prem had bamboozled Lily into working for her after the twins had left home to go to college: Dillon to Bristol, Sara to medical school in Nottingham. Lily, two and a half years widowed at the time, had sunk into a dull despair at the lonely, empty days stretching ahead of her. Days she couldn't find the energy to fill. She had, by absolute choice, been a full-time mother since the twins were born.

She was not ambitious, had never had a burning desire for a career. In fact, she had never wanted to do anything but be left alone to draw the small, detailed, brightly coloured pen-and-ink portraits at which she was so good. Although no one could ever convince her of this because her going to art school had broken her father Roy's heart. 'That's a bloody stupid waste of a life,' he'd told her, tugging on his bushy auburn beard as he always did when upset, his fit, wiry body rigid with outrage. 'You have to be brilliant to make it as an artist, and you're not brilliant, Lillian, not by a long chalk.'

He was not being intentionally unkind, Lily had thought

later. He just assumed that everything in the world was black and white, categorized by a straightforward rule, like a try or a penalty. Rugby was Roy Yeats's passion, his obsession, his *raison d'être*; the family came a poor second. His day job was as a tough – and, by all accounts, inspirational – games teacher at a secondary school near Potter's Bar, where Lily had grown up. He also refereed club rugby matches all over the country, and there wasn't a detail of any game ever played that he couldn't instantly recall.

Lily remembered his voice, always so confident and loud, ricocheting round the house after she'd told him about her offered place at Byam Shaw in north London, broadcasting his dissent in no uncertain terms to his cowering family. But Lily had quietly gone ahead anyway, side-stepping her mother's spurious worries – or manipulations – that college would bring back the asthma and make her ill. She was sick to the back teeth of being thought weak, an invalid, and she told no one at college about her childhood condition.

But after Garret died, her drawing hand had become paralysed. Every image she saw around her echoed with the past, every room in the house a scene set for those times when her family had been whole, when her world had seemed perfect. It had panicked her that she couldn't draw. Her pencil hovered above the blank page, but her hand was unable to commit to the lines and shapes that were normally hardwired to her brain, as if her hand had been disconnected.

So, although she had no need to work – her husband had left her well provided for – over time Lily came to enjoy her job and the interaction with Prem's clients in the shop. It was better than sitting at home, moping. And buying a desk chair seemed to open up in the clients a wealth of personal disclosures. She listened while they told her about back problems, injuries, operations, fitness challenges, worries about their business and their family. They had filled her loneliness to a degree, enough to make her feel, as the years passed, that there were still pleasures to be had. She had never imagined falling in love again, despite Prem's dismal parade of potential suitors.

Then one Monday morning – nearly six years after Lily had been widowed – a tall, confident figure, well-dressed in expensive jeans, white shirt and a tailored black corduroy jacket, with indigo trim to the turned-up collar, had pushed open the shop door and strode straight to where Lily was standing. Smiling at her, he had thrust out his hand and introduced himself as if he had been expecting to meet her his whole life.

Lily, surprised by his forthrightness, had looked into his face as he said 'Freddy March' and felt a small shock of recognition, not based on any known previous acquaintance. Freddy had continued to stand close to her, engaging her with a vivid tale of a homeless man he'd met on the walk from his Soho studio, who had told him his life was about to change – she'd never asked him if the story was an invention, a handy chat-up line. Prem told her later that she'd been certain they were old friends as she watched them from across the shop floor.

Their courtship had been swift and unchallenged. He wasn't married, just a couple of long-term relationships he said hadn't worked out, and had no family, except a father suffering from dementia in a Nottinghamshire care home – whom she'd yet to meet. Freddy had said he'd rather visit him alone, his dad at the stage where he got upset at new faces. Lily was a widow and the twins had left home. No one, except her older sister, Helen, seemed anything but pleased at the union: two single people, turning fifty, finding love . . . What was not to like?

Within three months they were living together in Freddy's glamorous Sussex Square penthouse. Another three and Lily had sold the family home in Fulham, given money to her children and kept a fair chunk of security, which she'd invested with one of Freddy's banker friends. Within another three they had announced their wedding, which took place the July after they'd met, a swish affair in a famous restaurant in the South of France, with fifty friends and family.

'Fairytale', 'whirlwind', 'magic': her friends had applied all the clichés and Lily understood why. But to her Freddy was bones-and-flesh real, not some fantasy Disney prince. She loved him from deep in her soul. More passionately than she'd ever loved Garret Tierney. Freddy had awakened things in Lily she still didn't understand: a restiveness, a need, an almost painful yearning. She felt slightly obsessed at times. And with that obsession came the nightmare ache of jealousy.

Lily came out of her daydream to the sound of a key in the lock. Freddy entered the room slowly, not seeing her at first as she lay curled up on the sofa, clutching her sketchbook, and she had time to scrutinize his face in the seconds before he did. A person used to studying faces carefully, what she

23

saw shocked her. He looked devastated, exhausted, blank, as she imagined people look when someone they love has died. Then he noticed her and adjusted his expression to a slow, tired smile.

She jumped up, not going to him, as she normally would, to throw herself into his embrace, but standing behind the coffee-table on the grey-and-cream-patterned rug in front of the gas-log fireplace, arms folded tight across her chest.

Freddy attempted another grin, this one slightly more successful than the first, and came round the end of the sofa, rubbing his dark, stubbly chin. But she backed away. 'Where have you been?' she asked, all the pent-up tension of the previous few hours – it was now nearly seven o'clock – making her words sting as they whipped across the room.

They rarely argued. It was only at the start of their relationship, when Freddy thought Lily was pulling back from social events he was sure she would enjoy, that they'd sometimes wrangled. He saying it would be fun, she saying she wasn't in the mood, not admitting she was shy and felt intimidated by his myriad high-profile friends, many of whom were in the public eye. Lily had never been much of a socializer.

She still had not got used to the fact that they might start the evening having a drink at an opening, launch or private view, move on to someone's house for dinner, leave late and go to a club, leave even later and grab an espresso at Bar Italia in Frith Street, Soho, finally making it home in the small hours. Freddy would have his arm round her most of the night, or be pulling her along by her hand, his pleasure and pride in her company obvious to all. She did enjoy herself when she began to know his friends better, but she would have been just as happy with one of those events in an evening, not all. Or not even one: supper alone with her new husband was Lily's idea of heaven. Freddy, however, was insatiable. 'It's part of my business, Lily,' he told her. But she knew it was more than that.

Now he sighed and collapsed heavily onto the sofa in front of her. 'God, Lily, I'm so sorry. I got stuck with this maniac Ukrainian producer, Borys, who says he's going to put all sorts of business my way. He's clearly filthy rich, got a massive film studio in Kiev and a mansion on the Embankment ...' He yawned. 'Anyway, he was coked up to the eyeballs from the off, wanted non-stop action, wouldn't let me go. We did the King's Road Ivy, then Annabel's, Hertford Street and Loulou's – loathe that place ...' He yawned again, his face stretched to what looked like breaking point. But Lily was able to focus only on her husband's bloodshot eyes, his scratchy chin, his sweaty shirt, not on what he was saying. 'Then, just when I thought I was home free, he insisted I take him fucking gambling. I've only just got rid of the man.'

'Why didn't you phone me, text me, something, so I didn't lie awake worrying about you all night? I've been up since five, imagining what you were up to ...'

Freddy raised his eyebrows, a sudden tension in his face, brown eyes unfathomable, as he waited for her to go on.

'I finally came to the conclusion you were in the arms of some horrible girl, sleeping it off after a night of unbridled passion. Sabrine, I thought. Or – or that dreadful Emily.' On

25

the verge of tears, she heard the brittle note in her voice as she named a couple of socialites she was sure lusted after Freddy: beautiful girls and at least twenty years younger than Lily, who was fifty-four. They had the easy, proprietorial intimacy she so envied. Girls who would hang on Freddy's arm, make effortless small talk with him in sexy whispers, giggle a lot . . . Manage to imply they had some sort of special relationship based on knowing him longer than Lily had, while at the same time being patronizingly friendly to Lily herself.

At Lily's suggestion, Freddy looked aghast, then threw back his head and roared with laughter, so clearly amazed that Lily was taken aback.

'*Sabrine?* Really? Christ, Lily, I do hope not.' He continued laughing, a genuine, almost out-of-control giggle – tiredness a contributory factor, no doubt – only stopping to draw breath before starting all over again. 'And Emily? Blimey, I wouldn't trust my body to her cold-eyed scrutiny. Anyway, her bottom line is a Learjet. She wouldn't drop her drawers for anything less.'

Lily, despite her genuine annoyance with him, couldn't resist a smile.

'*Seriously?* You thought that?' Freddy was on his feet and had her wrapped in his arms before she had a chance to change her mind. Looking into her eyes, his own suddenly intense, he said, 'I don't fancy those women, Lily, honestly I don't. I wouldn't touch them with a bargepole. You need never, *ever* worry about my screwing another woman. I just wouldn't.'

Scooping her up in her dressing-gown, he carried Lily to

26

the bedroom and laid her on the bed, leaning over her and gently running his fingers through her short, satiny-brown crop. Freddy said the colour was 'truffle' – he loved the softness of her hair, although she despaired of its fineness. He brushed the long fringe off her forehead, slowly bending to kiss her mouth as he slipped his hand inside her robe and found her small, naked breast.

It was only much later, after they had made love, slept a bit, woken and showered, made coffee and scrambled eggs, only after Freddy had gone off to the studio, that Lily had time to think. Although she was totally convinced he was telling the truth about last night, she still didn't understand what was really bothering him. She couldn't forget the look on his face when he'd walked through the door that morning. It wasn't the look of a man who'd just had a tedious night with a Ukrainian producer – bonding was par for the course with Freddy. It was the look of a man in complete despair. But the lovemaking, especially after so long, had soothed her. She hadn't wanted to spoil the moment.

CHAPTER 4

Freddy did not go to his studio. As he was leaving the block of flats, his phone rang. Staring at the screen, he bit his lip, hesitated, then reluctantly answered. The call lasted barely ten seconds. Apart from 'Hi', the only words Freddy uttered were 'Fifteen minutes', before he clicked off, striding purposefully towards Lancaster Gate Tube.

Lau Heng's office was two floors above a shiny red and gold Chinese restaurant on the corner of Soho's Gerrard Street and Newport Place, facing the entrance to what is generally referred to as the 'Chinese car-park'. It was an unimpressive place for such a successful man: Mr Lau – Freddy had learned the Chinese surname comes first – owned numerous restaurants in Chinatown, a casino and properties all over Soho. The two rooms were dingy white, worn brown carpet tiles underfoot, grey metal filing cabinets lining the walls, the

28

glass in the windows dull with city grime. There was no computer on Heng's desk, just a tidy pile of stacked letters, a red lacquer cup holding a clutch of new-looking biros, pencils, a pair of black-handled scissors, and three identical mobile phones in a neat line on the leather desk surface. It was Lin, his assistant, dwarfed by the wide-screen desktop in the outer office, who apparently held the reins of the online environment.

When Lin saw Freddy she nodded briefly. 'Go in,' she said, indicating her boss's door. Freddy had long since stopped trying to charm the severe middle-aged woman, always dressed in black, her dark fringe low over wary eyes.

Freddy knocked and tentatively pushed open the door, forcing himself to breathe slowly to maintain the appearance of calm. Lau Heng would immediately scent any iota of fear.

'Freddy!' He was seated behind his desk, beaming broadly. He managed to look pleasantly surprised to see Freddy, although he'd summoned him to his office not half an hour before. He was a small round man in his fifties, grey hair brush-cut short, smartly dressed in a dark tailored suit and open-necked white shirt. His heavy black-rimmed glasses gave him an air of seriousness, belied by his almost permanent grin. 'Come in, come in. Take a seat.' He indicated the only other chair in the room, a treacherous blue swivel number with chrome feet that had sent Freddy sliding across the carpet tiles on a previous visit. But today he did as Lau Heng asked and perched gingerly on the padded seat.

Mr Lau continued to beam, small hands placed on the desk in front of him, palms down, waiting.

Freddy took a breath. 'You wanted to see me.' There wasn't anything else he could think of to say: the loan the Chinese man had given him was so long overdue, the conversation they were about to have so painfully familiar.

'I am hoping you have some good news for me.' His accent was almost entirely English – Lau Heng had come to London from Hong Kong when he was twelve; only his slightly sing-song intonation was Chinese.

'It's been a bit of a rough time,' Freddy said, after a pause that he hoped might indicate the huge pressure he was under and elicit some sympathy. 'But I intend to pay back at least half by the end of the month.'

It was bollocks, of course, and Lau Heng knew it. On pre-vious occasions, however, he'd nodded and pretended to believe Freddy. Not so today.

'Hmm . . . half. I'm afraid we have come to the end of that road, Mr March.' He lifted his hands towards him as if to say 'Over to you', and waited, his dark eyes behind his spectacles never leaving Freddy's face.

Freddy squirmed. *'Mr March', is it? Not the usual 'Freddy'.* Of course he felt bad about the debt – or 'loan', as he preferred to call it – but not very bad. Lau Heng wasn't short of a bob or two and Freddy would repay it as soon as he could lay his hands on it. 'You know I'm good for it, Mr Lau.'

The businessman raised his eyebrows slightly, said nothing.

'I take this very seriously,' Freddy went on, lowering his eyes to show respect. 'But I've got clients who owe me a shedload of money and they're dragging their feet, so I haven't been paid myself for months. I know they've got it, so it won't be a problem in the long term. I just need a few more weeks.'

Saying it made part of him believe the lie. Why not? There *were* always clients who hadn't paid. Freddy conveniently skated over the fact that, even if they did, it wouldn't scratch the surface of his debt to Lau Heng. And he had paid himself his salary, regularly and in full, plus the odd bonus he never really justified.

The man on the other side of the desk shook his head very slightly. The beam, however, still seemed perfectly genuine – the sort of smile to which it was hard not to respond. And he liked Lau Heng. They had always got on well when they had met in his casino, years ago now, before Freddy had made the rash decision to borrow money from the man.

'I'm sorry, Mr March. I hear what you are saying, but I don't feel it would help either of us to let this situation slide.'

Freddy noted the tone and gave up being bullish. 'I need more time. Please, just four weeks, Mr Lau.' He cast himself on the man's mercy, his brown eyes imploring.

After a long moment, during which Lau Heng's mouth tightened, he said, 'The first of April. No more time.'

'Thank you. I absolutely promise you will have your money by then.'

Freddy felt almost faint with exhilaration. Nearly sixty thousand pounds and three weeks to find it might not have sounded so thrilling to most people, but the important thing was that he had bought time. Lau Heng would not send round his terrifying gang of enforcers. Not yet, anyway.

He tripped on the step into the street and nearly went

flying, his heart racing in his chest, so keen was he to get away from that smile and all it implied. Crossing Shaftesbury Avenue, he strode at a fast pace along Frith Street, cut through Soho Square gardens, past Govinda's and the Hari Krishna temple, navigated Oxford Street and into Rathbone Place, heading for one of his favourite coffee shops. He ordered a double espresso and sat at one of the narrow wooden tables, which was riveted to the floor, gazing out of the plate-glass windows onto the street. It was thronged with young, *über-cool* advertising people, disgorged from a number of high-end agencies in the surrounding streets.

I have been here before, he thought. *I've wriggled out of worse than this.*

But the time he was remembering was not the same, not worse by any means. Back then, he'd been younger and with no ties. He'd basically had nothing to lose. Now he had so much. He cursed himself, realizing what a fool he'd been for thinking he could lead a normal life, for believing he could have a business and a wife, even a family, her children becoming his.

Lily. He inhaled slowly, his thoughts returning painfully to the moment this morning when he'd kissed her. The anxiety in those clear hazel eyes, the way his kisses had gradually dispelled her fear. She had slipped under the wire that very first morning he'd set eyes on her in the Marylebone shop. Not a beautiful woman in the accepted sense, she had none-theless stopped his breath, the frail quality in her slim figure belying a steady, thoughtful expression and poise. She looked like someone who would know how to listen. And however unexpected and bizarre, it was a soul connection. He couldn't have ignored it if he'd tried. She seemed to complete his life, make him see what he'd been missing all these years. He had been so sure he could clean up his act for her. And at first he had. Months had gone by after he'd met Lily without a single flutter.

Freddy shook his head, trying to focus on the current problem. No point dwelling on what might have been. But his normally quick brain seemed unable to come up with a plan. The situation had burgeoned to such chaotic levels that every way his thoughts led they skidded to a halt. So absorbed had he been in his habit that he'd taken his eye off the ball. Deals he should have clinched, he'd messed up, his head elsewhere. Extravagances such as the improvements to the studio equipment, the state-of-the-art soundproofing, taking on too many staff, were way beyond budget and mostly unnecessary for a small business like his. But gambling was not just a roulette habit: it was intrinsic to Freddy's personality. He would always, *always* assume that he would find the money, the deal would be done and things would turn out exactly as he dreamed they would.

The pending court judgement on the company would kick in any day now: next month's salaries were in jeopardy; the bank was screaming, daily, for resolution of the overdraft; Lau had given him three weeks; and Barney, his endlessly accommodating bookie, had cancelled his account and was not returning his calls. Not a good sign: Barney was a mate. And HMRC . . . He couldn't even think about them. This was just the sharp end of his nightmare.

The final straw was the overdue rent on the penthouse. Every time he went home he expected the locks would have been changed, expected to find Lily sobbing in a heap by the front door, expected to see someone's muscle waiting by the lift to break his kneecaps.

He could have dealt with all of that, though, if it hadn't been for Lily. She believed in him. Nobody in his life ever had before. Sure, he was always able to charm people into doing what he wanted, but he sensed they did it *despite* their better judgement, because they *wanted* to trust him, not because they actually did. But Lily got him. She loved him for being Freddy, not for his superficial charms. The thought of her finding out the scale of his financial meltdown made the coffee he'd just swallowed rise in his throat.

Fingering the bundles of cash in his coat pockets from last night's casino win, and knowing that any payment had to be in cash from now on – his credit lines were all shot – he made a calculation of priorities. Rent. That would take half of it. He had to leave himself enough of a stake to win more, but Lily's security must come first. If the penthouse went, the game would be up.

Horses? he wondered, calculating how to make the most of the remaining money. The payback on just one bet *could* be huge. Freddy, a solidly loyal roulette man now, had neverthe-less made a lot of money on the nags – and occasionally the dogs – over the years. And lost a lot too. But he always felt the track was his father's domain. He experienced a sudden flashback of the sleazy betting shop in Fosse Road South, Leicester, glimpsed, as a boy, when his mother had dispatched him to fetch Vinnie home. He would put his head round the door to be confronted by the familiar shuffling desperation of a room full of no-hopers, the pungent miasma of booze and fags, the despair – almost tangible, even to a child – in the litter of discarded betting slips. Then his father's sullen pretence that he couldn't hear Freddy's call. Freddy had vowed, back then, that he would never, ever gamble a single penny of his money. It was so bloody dumb.

But twenty-five to one, ten thousand on the nose? Quarter of a million, plus the ten thousand stake: two hundred and sixty thousand pounds. Even half that, twelve to one – more likely odds for a potential winner – would net a hundred and twenty, plus stake. Freddy allowed himself a moment to imagine the thrill of winning that amount.

It would sort some of it. Shut Mr Lau up, sub the wages for a month. The bank and the taxman would have to wait, but he could throw them a small bone. There wouldn't be enough to cover the County Court Judgement against the studio: that was those bloody accountants who seemed to think he owed them a mint. *Christ, they've waited for years, why go for me now?* But the court had not yet set a date; it would probably be months before he even had to appear. By which time . . .

Problem was, which bookie would take the bet? He needed someone absolutely reliable. Barney was a genius, but he would want his money back first. He did a mental trawl through the options and settled on Jansen Cole, commonly known as JC, a young guy, very ambitious, he'd met through his friend Fish. JC seemed impressed by the famous people Freddy knew. And horses were his thing. He'd said a number

35

of times that if ever Freddy needed help . . . He leaned back on the stool and dug out his mobile from his jeans pocket. He was feeling slightly better now he had a plan. He did not even entertain the possibility that the horse might lose.

CHAPTER 5

Dillon watched his mother push open the heavy glass door of the café. He saw the face of the maître d' light up as he welcomed her. Business-like to the point of rudeness, the man, in his trendy suit – which looked deliberately two sizes too small – with his flicked-back fringe, designer stubble and pointed black lace-ups, took no prisoners when it came to the average customer. But for his mother his face softened as he kissed her on both cheeks. Everyone loved his mum.

Dillon rose from his seat to welcome her.

'This is a treat,' she said, sliding into the leather banquette opposite him.

He smiled. 'Got to be allowed the occasional skive.'

Dillon was the spit of his dead father: tall, broad-shouldered and athletic, with clear blue eyes in a strong face, his dark hair rumpled from the cycling helmet that sat on the seat beside him – he biked everywhere. But he had none of his father's drive. His current job was as an editorial assistant for a small academic publisher in Islington. The salary was rubbish, but he loved the team. And the low-pressure, although still diligent, approach to the work suited him. Dillon hated stress.

'How's Gaby?' his mother asked.

'Yeah, good. Crazy busy as usual. I hardly see her.' His Brazilian fiancée was the ambitious one of the two, her small theatre company, always on the verge of extinction from lack of funds, demanding every minute God sent, with almost no financial reward and, as yet, no critical acclaim either.

'Doesn't that bother you?' Lily asked.

'Sometimes, I suppose. But she loves it, Mum. I either accept her as she is, or get out.' He chuckled. 'You know her. Can you imagine the fallout if I tried to control her?' Gabriela was feisty, vibrant, full of energy – it was what he loved about her.

His mum smiled. 'Not a pretty sight, I'd imagine.'

Dillon was never quite sure if his mother approved of his girlfriend. She was always kind and welcoming to her – and never criticized her to him – but he felt they had little in common, except himself. The clue was the odd remark, such as 'She obviously makes you happy', which implied reservations.

He fell silent as the waiter brought two chef's salads, laid a round tin of mini-baguettes on the table, a saucer of butter wrapped in waxed paper, then topped up the Badoit they were drinking. He was desperate to broach the subject of the wedding money, but there was an unusual weariness about his mother today, a distracted air, which gave him pause. 'How's Freddy?' he asked.

'Busy,' she said, without her usual enthusiasm.

It had been a painful revelation, seeing his mother fall in love. As it had never occurred to him that she might find another husband, he had been unthinkingly hostile to the very idea of Freddy. Hostile to Freddy as well, in the first months of their acquaintance. Even though, when they'd first met, it had been six years since his father's death, the sight of his mother being held and kissed, however chastely, in front of him and his sister had made his stomach turn.

But Sara had told him scornfully that he was an 'Oedipal cliché', the son who is in love with his mother and jealous of his father. Or stepfather, in this case. Which had brought him up short and forced him to soften his hostility, because it was so clear that the man made his mum happy. And when he finally allowed himself to like Freddy, he found he liked him a lot. Freddy, wisely, had never tried to be a substitute father to the twins.

'I suppose neither of us would have been happy with a layabout,' he commented wryly, as they began to eat.

It wasn't till coffee and an extensive chat about books – both of them devoted readers and always storing up recommendations for each other – that Dillon spoke about what was really on his mind. 'Mum, I don't want to bother you with this, because Freddy said he's on it, but the Roof Gardens is hassling for the balance and Freddy did offer . . .'

'Have you spoken to him?'

'I tried. I've emailed and texted a few times, and he says

39

not to worry, he's got all the details.' Dillon took a sip of his *macchiato*, not looking at his mother. 'But they rang again this morning and said that if they don't get it by the end of the week we'll lose the booking.'

He saw the puzzlement in his mother's eyes.

'It's only five weeks away, Mum. I'm sure they can sell the slot three times over if we don't cough up.'

That wasn't the only problem. The expensive venue was one thing, but all the other costs that went with it – invitations, cake, dress, cars – were eye-watering. And Dillon was too embarrassed to keep asking for more money. He wished he'd turned down his stepfather's offer and gone for something smaller, more low-key. It would have suited him far better, but he'd wanted the best for his fiancée and Gabriela was so excited.

His mother was frowning. 'I'm sure he's just forgotten. He's been putting in such long hours at the studio, and with these idiotic networking evenings he insists on doing, I don't think he can remember his own name at the moment.' She put a hand reassuringly over his. 'I'll talk to him tonight.'

Dillon breathed a sigh of relief. 'Thanks, Mum. That'd be great.' He didn't add that his friend Josh, who was flat-sharing with Samuel, one of Freddy's sound engineers, said Samuel hadn't been paid last month.

It's probably nothing, he told himself as he said goodbye to his mother, thanking her for lunch, then twisted open the D-lock securing his bike. *An admin error or something.* Freddy was loaded, that much was clear, and he'd been the one pushing for the Roof Gardens. The studio was always incredibly busy, too, according to Samuel. But the uneasiness he'd felt since he'd seen his mother's expression when he'd told her about the wedding money would not go away. Something was up: his mother was not a worrier by nature. She was more a dreamer, someone who often didn't seem properly attached to real life, with a calm, almost fatalistic outlook – a trait he envied. But she had appeared distinctly tense today, no question.

CHAPTER 6

'Ha! Rent-a-mob.' A deep male voice made Lily turn. Joe Tarrant, a middle-aged music producer and one-time client of her husband, laid a hand on her bare arm and reached forward to set his heavy, sweating jowls briefly against her cheek. He smelt end-of-the-day rank, of stale aftershave and cigarettes. Brushing his thinning grey hair back from his forehead, he took a large gulp of champagne and raised his eyebrows at Lily. 'Where's Fred, then?' he asked, although he didn't seem too interested in Lily's response, his pale shark-eyes darting back and forth across the crowd, presumably hoping to spot someone more interesting than herself.

Lily hated going to these openings without Freddy, but he had texted her only as she got out of the cab, saying he'd been held up and wouldn't be able to get there for another half an hour. She hadn't fancied wandering around Leicester Square in her dangerously high heels while she waited, so she'd decided to brave the scary PR girl with the platinum crop and lime green micro-dress alone, then negotiate the gang of black-clad minders hovering at the entrance to the new restaurant with as much nonchalance as she could muster.

'This opening is unmissable,' Freddy had told her. A new dim-sum restaurant – Freddy loved Chinese food – with the most extraordinary interior. 'Everyone is talking about it,' he said. 'We can check out what all the fuss is about, grab a glass of free bubbly, then go and get some supper, just the two of us.'

Lily had smiled her agreement, but she had known that would not happen. Her husband, inevitably, would bump into an acquaintance – someone who might be helpful with clients, Freddy would insist – so they'd stay, and when they did go, it would be with a whole gang in tow. The evening would be fluid, messy, drunken. Freddy wouldn't leave her side, but they would have no chance of a private conversation. And that was all Lily wanted to do: sit down and talk things through with him, ask why he hadn't paid the wedding money as he'd promised, finally find out what was wrong.

The interior was as spectacular as the press had insisted, the suspended ceiling of wide bamboo mesh swooping across the cavernous space all the way down to the pale marble floor. It created a grotto effect, within which curved bamboo screens and backlit bamboo sheets on the walls provided smaller pockets of more intimate dining space. To Lily it had a modern, slightly futuristic atmosphere, with the huge round saucer-lights above the bamboo mesh providing a garish yellow glow over the assembled first-nighters below. Stylish, she decided, but not cosy: the room was too high, the marble too chilly, the bamboo somehow impersonal. It reminded her of a restaurant in Hong Kong, where Freddy had taken her a couple of years ago, and she wondered if the same designer had done the job.

There must have been around sixty people in the room, the babble of conversation and the odd shout of laughter echoing as it disappeared up into the roof. She spotted a few celebrities: a glamorous presenter, an actor in a recent television drama – for whom Sara claimed to have the hots – a tall blonde with a familiar face she couldn't quite place.

'On his way,' she said to Joe now, preferring to stand alone with her pleasantly cold champagne flute and watch the people than make small talk with a man she barely knew and was aware Freddy did not particularly like.

'Hear he's having some trouble with Jerome. I did warn him.' He suddenly grabbed the arm of a slim dark-haired girl in a long patterned dress, high wedge-heeled sandals, and an oversized leather jacket which made her look even more waifish than she already was.

'Hey, Suki, you trying to avoid me?'

Suki twitched her arm free. 'I certainly was, Joe. Seems not very successfully.'

The hollow smile she flashed made her words, spoken in a south London accent, sound more truthful than Joe obviously chose to believe, because he laughed and said, 'Ooh, we're on form tonight!'

She tossed her hair back and waved at him dismissively as she strode into the crowd.

'Going to find another drink,' Joe muttered, not bothering to ask Lily if she might also like her glass topped up.

Freddy was suddenly by her side, scooping her into his arms, lifting her off her feet as he dropped a kiss on her cheek. 'Sorry. Got caught up.'

He put her down and gazed around, taking in the woven ceiling, the bamboo screens. 'Hmm, think I like it . . . different anyway.' Then she saw him searching the crowd. 'Talk to anyone interesting?'

'Only Joe Tarrant.'

Freddy pulled a face. 'That's a no, then.' He grabbed two sticks pierced through breaded balls of something from a passing tray, held one out to Lily. 'Let's do a quick circuit, see if there's anyone I need to bond with, then we'll go. Fancy Hakkasan? Keep in the spirit of the evening? I know it's usually a bit of a zoo, but it's Tuesday night, shouldn't be too manic.'

He began to push through the crowd, clutching her hand in his, stopping frequently to say hello to someone and introduce Lily if she didn't already know them. Lily was content to be by his side. He seemed happier this evening, more relaxed, and she began to enjoy herself as the second glass of champagne hit the spot. It was always the same when she was with Freddy: nothing else seemed to matter.

They got separated and Lily found herself talking to Suki, who turned out to be a witty, no-bullshit singer, currently freaking out about finishing her next album. She thought she would have liked to draw the girl's face, which held a raw edginess, all monochrome angles and hollows.

But Lily did not have a chance to study Suki's face further, because Freddy interrupted. 'Got to go, Lily.'

She raised an eyebrow at his brusqueness.

'Now. Please, come on.'

His arm slung round her waist, he waved an apologetic hand at Suki, and hustled Lily towards the stairs and out past the minders into Leicester Square.

'What on earth's the matter?' she asked, breathless. But he didn't reply. His face set, he took her hand and began to sprint towards Charing Cross Road, past the slot-machine arcade and the Hippodrome's timeless exterior.

'Wait, please! I can't run in these shoes – I'll break my neck.'

He glanced impatiently at her feet and slowed his pace a bit, turning to cast an anxious look back towards the restaurant.

When they reached the edge of the square, he left her on the busy pavement and ran to the middle of the road, traffic pouring past in both directions, twisting this way and that in his effort to find a cab. He finally flagged one down on the opposite pavement and yelled to Lily, holding the door open and ushering her inside.

'Are we going to Hakkasan?'

'I'd rather go home, if you don't mind.' Freddy clutched her hand so tightly as they sat in the dark of the taxi that she thought she'd lose the circulation in her fingers. She didn't question him further, though, aware of the tension coming off him in waves. Once at home, he went immediately to the kitchen and opened a bottle of red wine, the sharp, metallic grinding as he unscrewed the top the only sound in the room. He poured two large glasses and handed one to Lily.

'What was that about?'

'Sorry,' was all he said, taking a gulp of the wine and not looking at her, resting one hand on the gleaming white marble island in the middle of the room as if he needed support.

Lily sat down on one of the pale beechwood chairs that stood around the kitchen table. The room was almost entirely white, which Lily had thought ridiculously impractical when she first saw it, but had come to love. It was a light, restful space in which they both enjoyed cooking and eating, the view across the rooftops mesmerizing from the wide wall of window.

Freddy was acknowledged between them as the better cook – Italian his food of choice, although he was capable of turning his hand to any country's cuisine. Unlike many men he was fanatically tidy, setting out his ingredients in neat rows, tidying away each pot or pan as he went, wiping the marble clean of any spills. Lily's cooking, by comparison, was hit-and-miss, even after years of family meals still unconfident – but then she'd never had much interest in it beyond feeding Garret and the twins.

Lily took a deep breath. 'Sit down. Tell me what's bothering you, right now. I can't stand the tension a moment longer, Freddy.'

The look he gave her was veiled, unseeing. She waited. He put his glass down on the marble top, resting both hands on the surface now, bowing his head. But still he remained silent.

'Dillon says the Roof Gardens is yelling for the final payment and you haven't been returning his calls. Joe said you were having trouble with someone called Jerome. You look like someone's died. You stay out all night. Then running from that party tonight as if you were being chased by Mad Max ...' She stopped, feeling the familiar tightness in her chest, and tried to steady her breathing. She always carried her blue inhaler wherever she went, but it had been months since she'd needed it.

Freddy sighed, raised his face to look at her, then came slowly over to the table and dropped into another of the beech-wood chairs, pulling it sideways and stretching out his long legs, crossing his feet at the ankles. He rested his elbow on the table, his fingers still clutching the stem of his wine glass.

'Okay.' He stopped again. 'Okay, well, the truth is that one of my clients hasn't paid up, and it's a lot, and it was money earmarked for the salaries.' He shrugged. 'I've been really worried, although I know this guy's good for it . . . or at least I assume he is. But cash flow is an issue and the bloody man won't return my calls.'

'Is this Jerome?' Lily felt his anxiety, but was aware that she was partly relieved. Surely this was par for the course with any business. Prem had frequently been in a similar situation, clients taking it to the wire before coughing up, sometimes leaving it till they were threatened with legal action.

Freddy nodded.

'When was the money due?'

'Nearly six weeks ago.' He ran his hand through his dark wavy hair, shaking his head as if trying to rid himself of his problem.

'What are you going to do?'

He frowned. 'I honestly don't know. This is a very successful producer. He's absolutely minted. I just don't understand what game he's playing.' He paused. 'He lives in sodding Frankfurt, so I can't even go and doorstep him.'

'Does this mean you can't pay the wedding money? I'm sure I can find it, if not. It was good of you to offer in the first place.'

Freddy looked momentarily alarmed. 'No, no, it's not a problem. I'll drop it in tomorrow. I'm sorry, I've had so much going on. I keep meaning to speak to Dill.'

She nodded. 'So you haven't paid the February salaries?'

'Nope.'

'Won't the bank sub you for a few weeks?'

'Not on a potentially bad debt, no.'

She fell silent.

'Everyone's being very understanding at the studio, but they all have mortgages, rent, the usual shit to cover. They won't be understanding if I don't come up with something pretty damn soon.' He drained his glass, gave her a weary grin. 'But, hey, I'm sure I'll find it somehow. I always do.'

He got up, stretched his arms to the ceiling, cracking his knuckles as he bent back his interlaced fingers.

'So why did we have to leave the party in such a hurry?' She knew there was more he wasn't telling her.

Freddy yawned. 'Oh, just someone I really didn't want to talk to . . . You know how it is.'

Lily didn't know. Nor did she think this explained her husband's excessive anxiety to flee, but she could see he was tired and when he reached for his phone and asked, 'Chinese or Indian?' she chose Chinese and left it at that.

CHAPTER 7

With every foot the plane rose in the sky, Freddy's heartbeat slowed. The anonymous, womb-like interior; the constant hum of the engines; the low light; the chilly air tinged with a faint scent of fabric freshener; safety in the company of hundreds of fellow passengers, none of whom knew Freddy or his problems . . . He loved flying. Best of all, no one could contact him in this blessed lacuna: no threats, no pleading, no harassment. For the next few hours – he changed planes in Detroit, then another hour and a half to Las Vegas – he was safe, real life slipping from him like a discarded cloak.

Fish had insisted. 'This guy could be the answer,' he'd told Freddy the previous morning, his voice on the phone unusually excited. 'Don't know where the fuck he gets his money, maybe nowhere honest, but he's up for serious investment in the UK, he claims . . . and he *loves* show business. You only have to throw him a few famous names and he'll be eating out of your goddamn hand.'

'Money-laundering?' Freddy had asked.

'Didn't ask and I suggest you don't either.' His friend had let out a low hum, a familiar sound that meant Fish was thinking. 'You're not going to go all virtuous on me, are you, buddy? The guy could be perfectly legit.'

'It's worth a meeting,' Freddy had replied cautiously. He had no desire to get himself embroiled with some Vegas gangster who wouldn't just break his kneecaps when things didn't go well. But if it meant saving the company . . .

'So get your ass on a plane and I'll set something up with Larry tomorrow,' Fish had said.

Aaron Fishley III was a rich Californian in his sixties who'd spent his life – and the immense fortune from his father's furniture empire – occupying a stool around the curved black-jack tables of the world's casinos, gambling away his inheritance. Which, as luck would have it, was immense enough to accommodate even Fish's ongoing extravagances. Tall and lean, his long, impassive face, handsome nose and small black-dark eyes reminded Freddy of an ageing Mr Spock. No pointy ears, but his tidy cap of greying hair also strongly resembled Leonard Nimoy's.

Fish had picked Freddy up a decade ago at a casino in Cannes, while Freddy was networking at the Marché du Film – the business side of the more glamorous festival. Listening to the story of his life, Freddy had assumed his new friend would be cynical and world-weary, exhausted by the struggle to break free from such a wasted existence. But the opposite

51

was true. Fish loved his life – or professed to, most convincingly – and was endearingly naive. He considered himself an excellent card player; he claimed to have become a people-watcher, an amateur philosopher, a mentor for younger gamblers, advising them when to quit, providing a shoulder to cry on when they ignored his advice. He balked strongly at Freddy's suggestion, made early on in their friendship, that he find more gainful employment.

'I don't drink excessively, I don't whore around, I'm kind to my old mother. I've chosen my path, same as you. Who's to say yours is worthier than mine?'

Who indeed? Freddy had thought at the time, an uncomfortable flash of memory reminding him of his own father and how far from 'kind' his feelings were for him.

But now Freddy had stopped thinking about Fish, his gangster investor, even Lily and the money he'd forgotten to pay to Dillon's wedding venue before he left for the airport. 'Forgotten' being the word he chose: it was less pejorative than any of the more truthful ones. He was too tired to think at all. He ordered a whisky-no-ice from the sharp-faced blonde behind the drinks cart, knocked it back, ordered another, then slid almost instantly into a dead, dreamless sleep.

'D'you gamble, Mr March?'

Larry Hedstrom was not what Freddy had expected. An etiolated figure in beige chinos and a short-sleeved white shirt, probably Fish's age, with skin that looked as if it had never seen the light of day and washed-out blond hair cut neatly like a banker's, he spoke softly. They sat in his vast air-conditioned lounge in a sprawling bungalow next to an exclusive golf course to the west of the city. Through the plate-glass window, past the still, glinting surface of the blue-tiled pool, there were stunning views over the flat plain. The foreground was dotted with the improbably green grass and palm trees of the course, then miles of sandy scrub desert stretching towards the distant ring of the blue-grey Spring Mountains.

It was very quiet, just the soft hiss of a sprinkler arching back and forth across the stubby grass outside the open doors, the sharp *ki-ki-ki* of a large black bird perched on the edge of a terracotta planter holding a prickly cactus, the sun burning everything else to silence.

They settled on the chilly cream-leather sofas, coffee in white bone china cups on the long glass coffee table between them. There was little sign of habitation, not even a cushion, or a rug on the pale-wood floor. Magazines lay in a precisely overlapping line at the far end of the table – exclusively motor-racing glossies, as far as Freddy could see. A milk-glass bowl of potpourri sat alone on a slender chrome stand by the doors onto the terrace, while the lighting was entirely from discreet spots in the ceiling.

Freddy shot a quick glance at Fish, sitting at the other end of the sofa, but his friend's face was carefully noncommittal.

'Call me Freddy . . . I've been known to have the odd flutter,' Freddy said, hoping he was holding the right line between prude and renegade.

Larry smiled. His pale eyes seemed to be appraising Freddy, but their expression was not unfriendly. He wondered what Fish had told Larry about him.

'I'm in the programme,' Larry said. 'Have been for sixteen years and twenty-four days now.' A brief smile flitted across his face as he spread his arms to indicate the near-empty room. 'All this came to me when I looked my addiction in the face,' Larry rolled his eyes heavenward, 'and took hold of the Almighty's open hand.' His accent was soft and politely southern.

Freddy looked at his friend. *Is he joking?* But Fish was innocently sipping his coffee, not looking his way. *Obviously not, then.* Maybe Fish had told the American that Freddy had a problem. 'That's a hard thing to do,' he said to Larry. 'I congratulate you.'

The American's face took on a slightly smug air. 'Salvation is open to everyone, son.'

The man's a loony, Freddy thought. *And don't call me 'son'. Fish has brought him in to save me. What a waste of fucking time.* He'd have some sharp words for his friend later.

'So tell me something about yourself, Freddy. Something personal so I can get a hold of who you are.'

Freddy didn't want to tell the man anything, certainly nothing personal. The room, for all its cool air and space, felt suffocating, the man opposite like some knowing preceptor who could see straight into Freddy's damaged heart and was intent on setting him on the path to righteousness. But taking a deep breath, he played along. The last-minute flight had cost him too much of his precious cash and he had to get his money's worth. So he told Larry about Lily and her children, the only good things in his life. And in the telling, he felt tears gathering behind his eyes.

'Family keeps a man honest,' Larry was saying, nodding approvingly. 'Family and God.' He paused, eyebrows raised a fraction, perhaps waiting for Freddy to declare his own love for the Almighty. But Freddy had been brought up in a godless house, where the idea of the Church had been rudely sneered at as a middle-class weakness, his mother's Catholicism carefully kept private from his brutal father. He had been too young when she died to have thought to ask her if she secretly attended church behind Vinnie's back, maybe went to confession on the way to the shops. He hoped for her sake that she had.

'I'm not a religious man, I'm afraid,' Freddy declared, not having any desire to take money from the man under false pretences.

Larry smiled. '"Who through faith conquered kingdoms, enforced justice, obtained promises, stopped the mouths of lions." Y'know that quote, Freddy? Hebrews eleven, thirty-three.'

Freddy heard the squeak of Fish shifting on the sofa's leather surface.

'Hey, Larry, cut it out, will you? You make us all feel bad for being so ungodly.'

Freddy was surprised by Fish's directness.

'I don't mean to do that, son,' Larry, ignoring Fish, replied to Freddy. 'Seeing a soul in torment, it's my duty to respond.'

There was an awkward silence. Freddy wondered if the multi-millionaire considered Fish's soul equally at risk, or just his own.

'Tell him about the studio, Freddy,' Fish encouraged.

*

'He liked you,' Fish insisted later, as they sat in the pleasantly quiet, blissfully cool, dark-wood low-lit bar of the hotel in which Freddy was staying, sipping double gins and tonic.

Freddy used the puce napkin to hold the cut-glass tumbler, slippery with condensation from the ice, the bubbles soft in his throat, as he waited for the kick of alcohol to work its magic. It had been a long, tense day.

Larry had insisted they take a tour of the golf course, then ordered Kobe steak tartare for them all, which Freddy hated – he liked his meat thoroughly incinerated – followed by warm, sugary *zeppole* at his special table on the exclusive club's shaded terrace. The waiters – mostly Mexican, Freddy decided – wore white gloves and spoke in low, respectful tones, anticipating Larry Hedstrom's every whim and virtually tugging their forelocks at him.

He must be bloody rolling, he had thought, *if he attracts this level of fawning in a club only open to multi-millionaires.*

'Rubbish. He pitied me, thought I was "a soul in torment".' Freddy sighed. The armchair was so comfortable he wanted to fall asleep that instant as the jetlag kicked in.

'Well, he got that right. But he'd never have bothered with lunch and the tour if he hadn't liked you.'

'That was just showing off. And why do very rich people always order for you? Like being broke prevents you understanding a menu.' He pulled a face. 'Raw meat makes me retch.'

Fish shook his head slowly. 'The guy treats you to literally the most expensive dish on the planet and you're insulted?'

Which was almost true. Freddy had certainly felt belittled, as if his character had somehow come up short in the meeting

56

with Hedstrom. 'You were very personal with him,' he said, a note of accusation in his voice he didn't bother to check. 'Like you knew him way better than you let on.'

'Used to.' Fish was not offended; it was hard to offend Fish. 'We were in high school together, Inglewood, but I haven't seen him since, not till he pitched up at this New York gallery opening. Then our paths have crossed the odd time I'm in Vegas. Never liked him at school either. He was kinda creepy even as a kid. Just thought he might be useful to you.'

'Yeah, thanks for that.' Freddy realized he was being ungrateful. 'Sorry, I do appreciate your help.' He thought for a moment. 'You said he loved show business . . . didn't seem the type to approve of such frivolity.'

Fish nodded, whether in agreement about Larry loving show business or not approving of it, Freddy couldn't tell.

'What'll you do if he doesn't come through?'

'Shoot myself, I suppose.'

Fish stared at him, his dark eyes beady, as if he wasn't entirely sure Freddy was joking. Freddy wasn't either. 'You could always allow him to save you,' Fish suggested, his half-smile indicating he thought this rather a cunning plan. 'Claim a moment of epiphany and credit Larry with it. His ego wouldn't be able to resist.'

'Who knows? I might even *be* saved,' Freddy said morosely.

Fish pulled himself to his feet. 'Better get some drinks in before that happens. Salvation won't come with a double gin.'

For the first time since he'd got off the plane, Freddy began to relax. It was gone three in the morning, and Fish had long

57

since retired to the one-bedroom apartment he owned in a high-rise near the south end of the Strip. The roulette table was still crowded though: people did not come to Vegas to sleep. They were mostly middle-aged American tourists except for a young Japanese couple – badly dressed and clearly not regular gamblers from their childish shrieks of mock-despair as they lost.

Freddy felt lightheaded and slightly mad. It was Vegas. Cruel desert sun and the natural beauty of Mount Charleston versus gaudy fantasy constructions depicting real places like the Eiffel Tower; piped music even outside on the Strip itself; retail to satisfy even the most extreme shopaholics; shows to die for. Then the noisy, clanging, over-lit dens of slot machines, the quieter, cooler, more seductive aura of the blackjack and roulette tables. A tawdry unreality. But this city-plonked-on-the-sand required – almost compelled – its visitors to be hedonistic, irresponsible, wild.

He had barely slept and downed too many gins with Fish, who seemed to have an infinite capacity, never appearing drunk. Hedstrom's perspicacity about his troubled soul had disturbed him in ways he didn't really understand. Freddy did not believe in God, but he was superstitious, like any gambler. Was he worried the guy would put a hex on him, make him lose so badly that he had no option but to turn to God? A ridiculous notion, but he felt uncharacteristically vulnerable. He'd been cap in hand to investors for various projects many times, put up with all sorts of rich-man capricious bullshit to get what he wanted, but this time felt different. It was as if Larry could see right through him, as if he were holding a mirror up, insisting Freddy gaze at his soul. And Freddy had no desire whatsoever to do that.

Casinos the world over are basically all the same, he thought, as he waited for the croupiers' slick shift change. The tables, the room, the clients, the casino staff around him could equally have been situated in London or Kuala Lumpur. Even the virtual-roulette environment, which Freddy had tried in the past and rejected – no atmosphere, just hard-core, anonymous online betting with a facility that scared even him – unimaginatively mimicked the real-life establishments.

'Place your bets.' The new croupier's voice was fresh and enthusiastically American. But after all the weeks of fear, the constant pressure stabbing like a sharp pain through his body, Freddy knew he no longer had the energy to care what happened. A sudden restlessness, an unprecedented waft of boredom overcame him as he mechanically pushed his chips to rest straight up on 32 and 18, a split on 14 and 17 and a colour bet on red – which had only a one to one payout, but obviously a better chance of success.

But the anticipation that always drove him into the zone as the croupier spun the wheel and dropped the ball was uniquely absent tonight. No buzz, no thrill at all. He watched listlessly as the ball came to rest on 22 black. He knew he had come to put a lot of reliance on the high. It bolstered him, protected him, took away the need to think. But all he could do now was think, as if Hedstrom had unlocked a carefully bolted door, behind which were such painful memories that Freddy felt agonizing tears pricking behind his eyes. He just wanted to lay his head down on the green baize and sleep, never wake up.

CHAPTER 8

Lily hugged Sara close, enjoying the rare sighting of her daughter. She thought she looked unusually well. Tall and athletic like her brother, she frequently appeared physically worn down by her life as a medical student – currently in her sixth year of training and working as an F2 (Foundation Year 2) at Kingston Hospital. Mentally she clearly thrived on the pressure, but the gruelling hours and snatched ready-meals, lack of sleep and proper time off did not allow for the cycling, climbing and swimming she loved.

A good-looking girl, with an open face and generous mouth, Sara's green knitted hat was pulled down at a comical angle over her wild, dark-brown curls. Lily saw a spark in her blue eyes today, a glow to her pale cheeks that made her wonder. Sara was the more outgoing and gregarious of the twins, and had, in Lily and Garret's opinion, seemed like an older sister to Dillon, even though she had been born second.

They set off briskly along the Broadwalk, a wide ribbon of path that runs north–south across Kensington Gardens, towards the Round Pond. It was cold, a vicious March wind sending the already low temperature plummeting. Lily brought her dusty-pink pashmina up around her face, thrust her gloved hands into the pockets of her black hooded parka.

'It's bloody freezing,' she complained. 'Are you sure you want to walk?'

But Sara gave a small leap of exuberance, held her arms out to the wind, closed her eyes like a child. 'This is great. I'm cooped up in that hospital twenty-four/seven – I feel as if I never see the light of day any more.'

Lily smiled at seeing her so happy. Even as a child Sara was focused and independent, had her own agenda. But she and Lily were close, always on the same page when it came to values. They linked arms, striding out under the watery spring sunshine towards the pond.

Once there they chose a bench, old and rickety, with a curved wrought-iron frame, the wood slats blistered and grey from years of exposure. Sitting close, their backs to the wind, they watched the ducks and geese waddle about the newly surfaced area beside the water, being fed by a small child let loose from her buggy. Her little hand was now held out for more chunks of bread, but the request was being ignored by the bored foreign au pair texting on her phone.

Lily waited for her daughter to speak. She knew she had something to tell her: she could feel the repressed energy in the small talk they'd exchanged on the short walk over the hill. *Have she and Stan finally set a wedding date?* she wondered.

61

But Sara said nothing, just sat as if she were in a world of her own, wrapped in her navy Uniqlo down jacket, hands wedged under her thighs, one brown-booted foot absently kicking the metal leg of the bench.

'How's Stan?' Lily asked eventually.

The silence was electric now, and suddenly Lily knew what Sara was going to say before she said it.

'Mum . . . Mum, I've met this guy . . .' She shot her a guilty look, but couldn't help a small smile escaping at the same time.

'Sara!'

'I know, I know . . .'

'Tell me.'

Sara's face spread into a broad, if slightly apologetic, grin. 'He's amazing, Mum. He's American, his name's Ted and he's an anaesthetist at Kingston. And, well, we just . . . It was—'

'Wait. You're telling me you're cheating on Stan?'

Her daughter nodded. Then her expression turned to one of genuine anguish. 'I don't know what to do. I love Stan, but Ted . . . Ted is something else.'

Shocked by what she was hearing, Lily asked, 'Does Stan know?'

Sara screwed her face up exactly as she had as a child. 'No.'

Lily was dismayed. She loved Stan too. He'd been little more than a gangly, clever teenager when she'd first met him – a student in the same year as her daughter at Nottingham Medical School.

'Isn't this just a sex thing? A fling? You've been with Stan since you were kids.'

Sara sat, head bent, hands twisting. 'I don't know, Mum. I hardly see him these days. He's at Guy's, I'm in Kingston. We're almost never at home at the same time.'

Lily didn't reply at once. She'd always thought of Stan as a young Garret. He and Sara were particularly well suited to each other in her opinion – both ambitious, both driven, both wanting to save the world.

'Don't ruin what you have with Stan,' she begged Sara, moving round on the bench until she was face to face with her daughter, who was doing everything possible to avoid her eye. 'Have a fling if you must. But please, please, don't break up with Stan. If you do, you'll regret it for the rest of your life.'

Her daughter looked stricken. 'Don't say that, Mum!'

'Well, it's true. You and Stan are meant for each other.' Lily didn't know why she felt so angry. It was Sara's life, but she felt as if her daughter were rejecting her own father and all he'd stood for by dumping Stan. The thought was intensely painful.

'Ted makes me feel like I can conquer the world,' Sara said softly into the silence.

Lily remembered the feeling well. When she and Freddy had got together it was as if she'd been given a special power, as if anything she wished for she could make happen. 'That's the phenomenon of being in love. It doesn't last, and it certainly doesn't mean that Ted is The One.'

Sara frowned. 'That's a bit cynical, isn't it, Mum? Wasn't it like that with Freddy? And that turned out to be true love. Stan and I . . . It was different.' She let out a long sigh. 'This feels so good – I can't stop thinking about Ted.' She sighed as if she'd suddenly come down to earth. 'You said you knew the very first second you saw Freddy.'

'I suppose, yes, there was something . . .'

'That's what happened with me and Ted.'

'But I wasn't in a relationship at the time. We were both free.'

Her daughter shrugged. 'You never doubted he was right for you, though. I remember you saying. I thought you were mad – you didn't know Freddy from a hole in the wall.'

'I was mad.' Lily couldn't help smiling at the memory. So mad that she had been instantly consumed by the unknown Freddy March. His lifestyle was not really compatible with who Lily was; they had no friends for context, no structure to support them. Yet she had felt this absolute certainty about him. It was like a solid thing that sat at the very centre of her being.

'Well, so am I,' Sara said, a blissful smile spreading over her face.

Lily was blindsided by her daughter's elation. 'Are you going to tell Stan before the wedding? He and Dillon are so close.'

Sara groaned. 'I know, I know. God, what shall I do? I can't keep pretending.' Then all the ebullience disappeared, her eyes suddenly filling with tears. 'What if I'm making a terrible mistake, Mum?'

'You'll just have to suck it up,' Lily said unsympathetically. She watched her daughter's face fall. But if she wanted Lily's approval, she wasn't going to get it. They seldom argued, and she felt miserable as Sara got up off the bench in silence, hands buried in her pockets, shoulders hunched in anger. But she was not going to condone something she was sure would be a terrible mistake.

The trip to the shops to find some shoes to go with Sara's dress for the wedding was a tense affair, neither woman's heart in it. Lily cursed herself. It wasn't her business. She had moved past Garret, after all. Wasn't it fair that Sara also let go a love affair begun when she and Stan were almost children, when Sara was still grieving and uncertain after her adored father's death? But however much she rationalized her daughter's behaviour, she still felt the shadow of Garret Tierney slipping into history, between the covers of the family album.

Weddings, she thought, after she'd seen her daughter off at the Tube station. *They always stir things up.* And, not for the first time, she felt tears prick behind her eyes that Garret would not see his beautiful son get married.

It was midday before Freddy arrived at the flat the following morning – rumpled and exhausted from the red-eye. He let out a long breath of relief as he dropped his leather holdall on the polished wooden floor, striding over and burying his face in Lily's hair, hugging her so tightly she feared she would snap. He smelt of coffee, his skin astringent with plane wet-wipes.

Freddy drew back and looked into her eyes. 'Hello,' he said, grinning, before kissing her gently on the lips.

'How did it go?' she asked, hopeful. Because beyond the tiredness there seemed a new atmosphere about her husband. Was it relief? Reprieve?

He let her go and sighed. 'Well, I think it went rather well,

Lil. The man was a serious weirdo, some school friend of Fish's made good. His main concern was saving my soul. But he seemed to like the idea of the studio. Fish was sure he'd cough up.'

'That's fantastic. When will you know?'

'Oh . . .' Freddy waved his hand in the air. 'He's going to get back to me this week, when he's had time to check out all the paperwork I sent him. Bastard made me eat raw meat so he'd better invest.'

Lily laughed, her spirits lightening. 'Worth the trip, then. I'm so happy for you.'

Freddy yawned and stretched his tall body upwards. 'I think I'll go and lie down for a couple of hours. I haven't really slept much since I left.'

'You don't want something to eat? A cup of tea?'

For a moment he just stared blankly at her, as if he hadn't heard. Then he said, 'Not really. I'd love it if you'd come and lie down with me for a while, though.'

Freddy showered, then they both undressed and got into bed. The linen sheets were cool and clean – Lily had changed them that morning – and she heard him let out a sigh of pleasure as he took her in his arms. They didn't make love, just luxuriated in being close again.

'You know I love you, Lily,' Freddy said.

'I love you too.'

'You can't imagine how good that makes me feel, being loved by you.'

Lily wondered at his words. Freddy wasn't one for sentimentality.

'You're the first person in my life I feel loves me for who I am,' he went on, his words spoken softly as she lay with her head on his chest, 'not who I pretend to be.'

She glanced up at him, but he was gazing at the ceiling.

'Me . . .' he finished.

Then he rolled over to face her, their heads on the same pillow, inches apart. He brushed her hair off her face, tucked a strand behind her ear. 'Remember what I said, Lil. Promise?'

She didn't understand what he was talking about, but she nodded anyway and he smiled.

'Love you so much,' he said. Then his drawn features relaxed and his eyes closed. Within a minute he was asleep.

For a while she lay beside him and watched him, taking in every contour of his face, the dark lashes resting on his cheek, his full mouth twitching in sleep. She reached up and touched her finger to the wide, triangular scar above his left eyebrow – a bike accident as a kid, he'd told her. She felt a surge of happiness, knowing that they had each other, knowing that things were going to be all right.

Slowly she began to extricate herself from his embrace. Pushing back the duvet, she slid out of bed, tiptoed across the room to gather up her clothes and left her husband to sleep.

CHAPTER 9

Gabriela's eyes were flashing, her body buzzing with tension as she stood before him, arms akimbo. 'He hasn't paid? Freddy hasn't paid?'

Dillon took a deep breath. 'Appears not. They want the money by tomorrow.'

His fiancée threw her arms into the air. 'Why not? Why hasn't he paid? How can he do this to us?' She turned and stamped her bare feet over to the kitchenette of their one-bedroom second-floor conversion just behind Holloway Road in north London. The back window looked onto an adventure playground, but it was Monday and it was closed, Dillon knew. The noise of the children's shouts when it wasn't could be deafening.

Gabriela grabbed a blue plastic tumbler from the open wooden shelf in the corner and ran the cold tap, gulped down the contents, then wiped her mouth with the back of her hand before turning to Dillon. Her wide-set dark eyes and full lips – now drawn down in a pout – were framed by light-brown hair, currently highlighted with blonde streaks, which fell down her back in a curtain when it wasn't pinioned in a plait or a ponytail, as now. She was petite, trim from the dance classes she took, her breasts high and rounded. Dillon thought she was the most beautiful girl he'd ever seen.

'Well?' she demanded, holding her hands out, palms up, as if expecting Dillon to produce a rabbit out of a hat. 'What are you going to do about it?'

'I've tried calling Freddy so many times, it's getting embar-rassing—'

'You're *embarrassed*? Oh, *meu Deus* . . . It's him who should be embarrassed. Call your mother.' And when Dillon didn't immediately reach for his phone, as he'd already left two messages for her, she added, her voice urgent, 'Now, call her *now*, *querido*, before those bastards cancel our wedding.'

Dillon felt a sense of doom as he clicked on his mother's number.

She picked up on the second ring. 'Sorry, I've just seen your calls – we've been at a screening all morning. Is everything all right?'

'Yeah . . . is Freddy with you?'

'Sure. Do you want a word?'

'Please.'

After a second he heard his stepfather's voice, 'Hi, Dillon. I know why you're ringing. The Roof Gardens.'

'Um, yeah. They want the money by tomorrow, absolute latest, or we'll lose our deposit and the venue.' He hesitated.

'I hate to hassle you, Freddy. It's just ... I mean, if it's a problem ... I'm sure we could scrape together something ...' That wasn't true, but Dillon hoped his mother would come through. She had offered.

'No. No. They'll have the money, Dillon – please don't fret. It's my fault, I got hijacked by this trip to Vegas. It sent everything else out of my head. I'm so sorry. Please apologize to Gabriela.' He gave a rueful laugh. 'Just what you both need with all the other strains of a wedding.'

Dillon laughed too. 'Has been a bit tense this end.'

'Your mother is more worried about the seating plan,' Freddy went on cheerfully. 'She's saying she doesn't want to sit next to Uncle Frank.'

'Really?' Dillon feigned surprise. This was a family joke. Uncle Frank, Lily's father's brother, was one of those people who, through no fault of their own, start boring you even before they've opened their mouth. Frank Yeats was in his early eighties now, but his mind was still sharp and he liked to talk ... and talk, and talk. Mainly – after a long career as a civil engineer – about sewer systems, past and present, locally and globally. He was fascinated by them, each and every one.

He heard his mother saying something in the background, then her laugh.

'Your mum says it's Aunty Helen's turn.'

As Dillon ended the call, after some more banter about annoying relatives, and glanced at his fiancée – whose eyes were fixed on him, their expression tense and almost threatening – he tried to feel relief. Forcing himself to smile at her,

70

he said, 'Freddy's sorting it. He said to tell you he's very sorry. His trip to Vegas made him forget.'

He did sound as if he was telling the truth, Dillon told himself. He hadn't detected any sliding or evasion in Freddy's words. *In fact*, he thought, *he sounded more cheerful than he had in a while. Perhaps the trip was a good one.*

'But has he paid?' Gabriela demanded, her expression far from relieved. 'Has he actually put the money down on the table?'

'He says they'll have it by tomorrow,' he said, but clearly his fiancée was picking up on his doubts.

She dropped her hands from where they'd been resting on her hips and came to sit beside him on the sofa, curling her legs under her, taking his large hand in her own small one, stroking his skin with her thumb absentmindedly. 'I have a bad feeling, *querido*,' she said. 'About everything.'

They sat in silence.

'And Mamãe is going to drive us both mad,' Gabriela said. 'You have no idea. Your mum is so reasonable, so . . . quiet.'

'It'll be fine,' Dillon assured her, hoping that by saying it often enough it would become true, because she was getting more anxious by the minute about her mother's arrival from São Paulo. And ten days squashed together in this tiny flat, with a person whom Dillon had not met and even Gabriela described as 'crazy bad', was a daunting prospect. They would give Renata their room, of course, and sleep on the new Ikea sofa bed, which was supposedly arriving this afternoon. He was waiting for it right now, working from home today, because his fiancée was scheduled to teach a children's drama club over in Highgate. But he was not looking forward to his prospective mother-in-law's visit.

'I love you,' he said, drawing Gabriela into his arms, rubbing his palm down the soft skin of her bare arm. Not for the first time, and not without a good measure of guilt, he allowed himself to imagine the bliss of being on the other side of their wedding day, to imagine a morning when they could sit having a restful conversation that didn't involve how to survive Renata, or which relative could best withstand two hours' listening to Great Uncle Frank ... Or if Freddy would come up with the money.

CHAPTER 10

Freddy had twenty-four hours and a stake of five thousand. The landlord had been sorted, Freddy handing over the money in cash to a surprised letting agent on the afternoon of the previous day. Now the Roof Gardens was his top priority. Dillon's wedding must go ahead at all costs. He needed seventeen for that, more to survive on for the next few weeks, his target twenty-five grand. Although twenty would do. Luckily it wasn't more. Feeling flush at the time, he'd given a larger deposit to the Roof Gardens than they'd asked for last year, when the venue was booked.

'I've got to work late tonight,' he told Lily, as they stood on the busy pavement in Wardour Street after the morning screening. 'I don't want you worrying that I'm getting my end away with the lovely Sabrine.'

It had begun to rain, a cold and depressing March drizzle, and they instinctively moved against the building, Freddy waving to various industry mates who had also watched the painful documentary about a Syrian doctor's family living in Lebanon.

He took Lily's hand and leaned down to kiss her. She looked tired, he thought, although he'd done his best to make the two days he'd been home as carefree as possible. They'd had Sunday lunch at the Delaunay, one of Lily's favourite restaurants. They'd bumped into some friends there and sat for a long time, sharing a mellow red, just talking and laughing. Then they'd gone for a walk in a welcome burst of spring sunshine along the South Bank, enjoying the colourful stalls and throngs of people, general hubbub and music from the many buskers. They'd held hands, saying little.

Freddy had felt as if he were in a bubble: a fragile, perfect, transient thing that would pop and disappear at any second. It was like an advert for his life, the way he wished things were, the way he *claimed* they were, the way they could have been, if only ... And, as such, he tried to switch off from reality, just live in the moment and savour every sight, sound and touch as if it were his last.

Lily had been very gentle with him, as if she knew he was hurting, and they had made love long into the night, an ebb and flow of lust and tenderness, soft kisses and caresses that seemed intensely satisfying in and of themselves, followed by a sudden crescendo of desire, sinking once again into a sleepy, sensual warmth. Freddy, as he stood there on the wet pavement, heard in his head an echo of Lily's soft cry as she came. He wanted to be in that place again, just the two of them, where nothing bad could ever happen.

74

But she knew him too well. Whether she believed his lie that Larry Hedstrom would come through, he wasn't sure, but the worried frown he'd caught a couple of times, when she thought he wasn't looking, told him she did not. And it wasn't actually a lie. He had sent the documents to Hedstrom, as requested, and there might be a miracle: the man might decide the studio – which, until recently, had been a thriving concern – was a good investment. But he doubted very much that he would. *If he's after my soul*, Freddy thought, *he can have it, tattered as it is. But he'll have to pay.*

The night started well: up three grand in less than an hour. The buzz was back and Freddy, after an initial nervousness, was beginning to enjoy himself. He was secure in his favourite Hyde Park haunt, the casino employees welcoming him affectionately, like a trusted family member.

It was around midnight, after he'd availed himself of a club sandwich, sent it back because the toast was soggy, then lost his appetite in his eagerness to get back to the tables, when he returned to find an old casino acquaintance in his seat: Cosmo Gough-Browne.

'Freddy, old chap,' Cosmo greeted him, his jowly face, red from all the country sports he pursued in lieu of employment, breaking into a drunken grin. 'Long time no see.'

Freddy's heart sank. It was imperative he keep focus tonight. He was on a mission. He didn't dislike Cosmo, who was affable at best, thick and narrow-minded at worst, but he didn't have time for banter. For Cosmo, dressed tonight in a dinner jacket from some earlier event, gambling was merely a hobby. He could lose what he liked and still go home to his magnificent Dorset pile without breaking a sweat. Not just that, but Cosmo was in his seat, his lucky seat. He could ask him to move and the man, polite to the last, would probably do so. But had he jinxed his winning position?

'Come on, Fred, get those chips out,' Cosmo was urging, pushing a huge pile of his own towards 19 red.

There was only one other person at the table now, the previous group of noisy French footballers having gone to the bar. He was a slim Middle Eastern youth in a black suit and navy shirt, who looked too young to gamble and seemed nervous, holding a handful of chips tightly in one hand and shaking his head when the croupier glanced at him, eyebrows raised, before stating, '*Rien ne va plus.*'

Freddy waited, watched Cosmo lose about a thousand pounds.

'Bad luck,' Cosmo said loudly, as if referring to someone other than himself, then prepared another hill of chips for the next spin of the wheel.

Freddy, trying to concentrate, eyed the green baize as the croupier flicked Cosmo's chips off the cloth and quickly stacked them.

'*Faites vos jeux* . . .' the mechanical chant rang out.

'Not having a punt?' Cosmo asked Freddy, nudging him playfully. 'Come on.' He lowered his voice: casinos didn't take kindly to side bets. 'Let's make this between us. I'll bet you a bag I win more than you on the next spin.'

Freddy thought about this. A thousand – 'bag' being short for 'bag of sand' in money slang – seemed a fair punt. Cosmo was famous for his reckless dislike of anything but a straight bet, liking to win big or not at all.

The footballers were back and the table noisy, the croupier distracted.

'Done.' Freddy nodded his agreement and was rewarded by a slap on the back from Cosmo's meaty fist.

'Splendid.'

'If neither of us wins it's a wash, agreed?'

Cosmo nodded. 'No outside bets, that's too easy. Has to be a straight, split or street. No corners, no six-liners.'

In the event, both men lost. Freddy, egged on by Cosmo's presence, was down fifteen hundred on the night. He'd seen it as only risking five hundred; the rest he'd wrongly assumed he would get back from the side bet with his friend.

'Go again?' Cosmo wasn't really asking as he slid the chips onto 21 and 19 red again. 'This time make it two bags, eh?'

The croupier slung the ball round the rim of the wheel. Freddy pushed a conservative five hundred onto the table, a split on 17 and 20 black, then held his breath. He felt discombobulated, out of control. Cosmo was ruining everything with his careless rivalry. Freddy knew he should leave, wait in the bar till the man had gone home and start again. But time was running out. He had to have the money by morning; he couldn't afford to wait.

When the ivory ball finally settled in 17, Freddy felt his heart somersault. He'd won! *Nine grand and two from Cosmo. Plus what I already had. That's seventeen five. Nearly there*, he whispered to himself.

'Lucky bugger,' Cosmo said cheerfully, counting out two

thousand in chips and pushing them across to Freddy. The piles were mounting in front of him in a very satisfactory way. Just a few more punts to get the cushion he needed and he was out of there. He saw the floor manager – a small, neat Algerian called Abdullah – out of the corner of his eye and knew he was watching Freddy, as he would anyone making a substantial win. Freddy waved and grinned and received a small raise of the eyebrows in return.

'Right, now you're so bloody rich, let's make it three bags.'

'Sorry,' Freddy said, pushing back his chair and standing up. 'Need a break.'

But Cosmo grabbed his arm. 'Hey, you can't quit before I've had a chance to get my money back, my friend. That'd be a very poor show.'

Freddy watched the previous bonhomie evaporate from Cosmo's bloodshot gaze. He was looking at Freddy imperiously now, a man used to getting his own way. Freddy twitched his arm free. 'I need to pee,' he said.

Cosmo eyed him suspiciously, pulling his mouth down at the corners. 'No arguing with that,' he said finally, turning back to the table at the croupier's request for bets, as if responding to a siren call.

Freddy, relieved, made his way slowly across the thick carpet to the Gents, where he shut himself into a stall in the empty room and sat on the closed lid of the toilet, his face sunk in his hands, suddenly overwhelmed by tiredness. He could go home now, safe in the knowledge that Lily's son could get married in four weeks' time, his responsibilities met. He would have five hundred in cash, enough for a few days, by which time something would have turned up.

Freddy nodded off for a few minutes, waking disoriented and in a panic, his mouth dry. Go home, a voice was telling him. Go home *now*. Go home, go home. It felt as if his life depended on it. As if some terrible, unnamed thing would destroy him if he didn't. It did have a name, of course, and the name was Freddy March, but Freddy couldn't see that.

Jerking up from the seat, he went over to the basins and rinsed his face in cold water, washed his hands with the Molton Brown liquid soap, dried them on the small white towel taken from the neatly folded pile in the corner and reviewed his reflection in the mirror. What he saw shocked him. A man with tension lines and dark circles about his tired, hunted eyes, hair dishevelled, skin sallow, lips dry. *I look ill*, he thought, attempting to brush some order into his hair with his fingers. He heard the warning echo in his head again: Go home.

'Three bags?' Cosmo asked, round about two thirty in the morning.

Freddy shook his head. 'Can't.'

'You chicken?'

'Yeah.'

Cosmo shook his head in disbelief. 'Freddy March refusing a bet? Never been heard in the history of the world.'

'First time for everything,' Freddy said tiredly.

'Come on, man. One more and I'll let you go home. Marina will be white-facing at the window by now, so I should be getting off myself in a mo.'

Freddy thought this was highly unlikely. Cosmo's wife was a hard case. She had few illusions and even less interest in her husband's many foibles. In fact, she'd probably be quite glad if Cosmo didn't come home ever again. Freddy had met her only once, years ago, at a weekend party at an acquaintance's stately home in Yorkshire, and she'd terrified the life out of him with her cold eyes and disparaging comments about everyone in the room.

'Okay . . . one more. But only one, Cosmo. I mean it.'

'Aah,' Cosmo's sigh of satisfaction had a knowing tinge, which irritated Freddy. Was he so predictable?

But he couldn't think about that now. He was still up on the night over all, but down on his previous high by nearly six grand. He didn't even bother to ask himself why he hadn't gone home when he was up, because he rarely ever did, despite that bloody voice in his head. Being up gave you confidence: you knew you were on a winning streak so it was hard to resist another punt. And being down meant you were desperate to be up again, so you needed to punt then too. There were really only two reasons why Freddy left the tables: exhaustion and an absence of stake money.

'Two, not three,' he told Cosmo, who shrugged his agreement.

But the ball decided neither would win and their chips were briskly swept up by the croupier's shiny rake. *Shit, shit, shit.* Freddy cursed himself for allowing Cosmo to bully him. The man was bad luck.

Cosmo yawned and stretched his chubby body. 'Good fun, old chap. Glad I bumped into you. Went to a God-awful charity bash earlier and got saddled with a shoot at Balfour's place in the autumn. His birds are so small I never manage to hit the buggers. Stingy bastard. Can't stand the fellow.'

'You won it?'

'Won it? No such luck. Marina made me bid for it, said she'd promised her pal Julia I would. Cost twice as much as it should have.' He shook his head in mock-despair. 'Life's a bitch and then you marry one, eh?'

Freddy could hardly keep his eyes open. The group of Chinese businessmen who had joined the table half an hour before were noisily egging each other on, their shouts grating on his already tender nerves. *Okay*, he thought. *I'll give it till four, and limit myself to a thousand. When that's gone, I'll go home.*

CHAPTER 11

'I'm furious with him,' Lily heard her sister, Helen, say on the other end of the phone. 'He's known the wedding date for over a year and he should have finished the chair months ago. But no. Always the same with my dear husband. *Mañana, mañana*, always *mañana*. God knows when they'll get their present now.'

'I'm sure it's fine, Helen. They'll just be thrilled to get it whenever. I know how busy he is.' Lily spoke quickly. She didn't want a long phone call, even though she and her sister rarely spoke. She was at Evelina Children's Hospital, part of St Thomas's on the South Bank, where she had been a children's play volunteer two mornings a week since she'd stopped working for Prem. A sleeveless volunteer's jerkin over her jeans and T-shirt, she had been drawing a cartoon story for a four-year-old girl called Marley, whose eczema had made her whole body red, cracked and flaky, bleeding in places.

It looked agony, but the child had been laughing at Lily's drawings and was now happily absorbed in painting over Lily's figures with some dirty red poster paint while her mother went for a coffee. The huge play area in the outpatients' department, with a towering shiny blue and pink slide in the centre, wasn't yet busy, so Yolanda, another volunteer, had taken her place with Marley while she talked to her sister over by the plate glass windows.

But Helen wasn't to be easily placated. 'David's always busy because he's so bloody slow. If he just got a move on, there wouldn't be a backlog of impatient clients waiting for their stuff to arrive.'

'He's painstaking rather than slow, I'd say. I mean, his work is so beautiful, he can't cut corners.'

'Yes, well, I wouldn't expect you to understand, Lily. You have no idea how frustrating it is living with David because you've been married to two men who know how to earn a living. You don't have to worry about mundane things like mortgages and money. Rich people always admire artisans. The ones who visit David's workshop love poking around, oohing and aahing at all his half-finished rubbish. They think it's so "real"—'

'I wasn't saying that,' Lily interrupted, the 'rich people' grudge boringly familiar. 'But David wouldn't be so sought after as a furniture maker if he was slapdash and just thought of the money.'

There was a sigh at the other end of the phone. 'I'm not asking him to be "slapdash", as you put it, just to get a move on, not take six months to make one small cabinet.' Another sigh. 'Anyway, how are the preparations going?'

Lily knew Helen didn't really want to hear the details. Her sister was always so busy, so determined not to have a moment to indulge in frivolous chit-chat, so she said, 'Fine. I'm keeping out of the way unless I'm asked.'

'I'm not wearing anything grand, by the way,' Helen went on. 'I can't afford the time or money to buy something new so it'll have to be the navy dress I bought for Dad's funeral.'

Lily almost laughed, but managed to control herself. Only Helen could come to her nephew's wedding in a funeral dress. Their father had died nearly seven years ago, from a huge stroke while he was sleeping. He had just never woken up. Lily had been impressed that anyone had managed to slip away so neatly, so painlessly. 'Fit as a butcher's dog', Roy Yeats had liked to describe himself. Gone in a second. But his death had fitted in with his no-nonsense life. Had Helen really had no cause to buy a new dress for seven years?

She hadn't come to Lily and Freddy's wedding in the South of France, of course. 'I can't possibly take the time off,' was her excuse, but Helen was an academic – teaching business management at Oxford Brookes University – and the term had finished by the beginning of July. Lily knew the real reason was that she did not feel comfortable with Freddy's friends. She understood – her own reservations, when she'd first met her husband, had not been dissimilar – so she hadn't pressed her to come. In fact, Lily was relieved she hadn't, knowing she would have sat on the sidelines looking on disapprovingly at the fancy dresses, designer sunglasses and clear display of wealth on the exclusive sunbaked terrace. She would have made it her mission to feel out of place, on principle. But, God, she was so tired of the competition.

It's not Helen's fault, Lily told herself – not for the first time. It had started the moment Lily was born, six weeks premature. Helen had been three and was, according to her mother's stories later in life, virtually ignored. They sent her away to stay in Norwich with Grandma Irene, whom she had barely met, for the two months Lily had spent in a hospital incubator.

It had been touch and go as to whether she would survive. The severe respiratory problems she suffered from, her lungs being so immature, were life-threatening on a daily basis, especially back in the sixties, when neonatal medicine was not very advanced. And it didn't stop there. The damage to her lungs as a newborn had made her a victim of the crippling asthma she had suffered during her childhood, which on occasion required urgent hospital treatment. So the attention had been relentlessly on Lily from day one. Helen knew she had to be good and quiet, and always take second place.

To Lily, her parents had not appeared to love her more because she was sickly. In fact Marion, her timid mother, with her powdery skin and fluffy, almost see-through hair, seemed almost scared of her much of the time, as if she were constantly terrified she might have another asthma attack. She fussed endlessly, drove Lily crazy. And her father gave the impression of controlled irritation on their many trips to Barnet General, as if Lily might avoid the attacks if she chose. He had, she thought, favoured Helen, for her diligence and robust approach to life. His elder daughter was the nearest thing to a rugby-playing son he was likely to get. But Helen could never see it like that.

'That'll be great. It doesn't matter what you wear,' Lily said, unable to remember much about the dress other than that it was as dreary and plain as all her sister's clothes.

'I can't compete with your glamorous friends, anyway. No point in trying.' Lily gritted her teeth and didn't reply as Helen went on, 'But I've never been bothered about what I look like – it's not a priority in my world. I just want to see dear Dillon married.'

'And you'll stay with us? You don't want to be driving back to Oxford in the small hours.' Lily kept her tone as light as she was able.

'Oh, goodness, no. I don't drink, so it's not a problem.'

'Will Kit be coming with you?'

There was a tense silence at the other end of the phone. 'I don't expect so.'

Lily wished she hadn't asked, her heart breaking for her sister on the subject of her only child. Kit was a drug addict. In and out of rehab, at thirty-one he was unemployed and unemployable. A brilliant, charming boy, he'd been offered a place at Magdalen College to study biochemistry at the age of seventeen, then, at only twenty, had gone on to do a doctorate. But something had happened to him during that time and he had gone off the rails. Now he could be found in a miserable flat in one of the concrete sixties high rises on the infamous Blackbird Leys estate. Helen refused to see him; David drove over every week to check on his son. The last time Lily had talked to Helen, Kit had just done a stint in rehab.

86

Lily thought guiltily of Dillon and Sara, their comparatively happy lives, then about her own good fortune with Freddy. The gulf between her and Helen couldn't be breached. How painful it must be to come to your nephew's wedding and remember the times Kit and Dillon had played together as boys in their Oxford garden, racing round the lawn, making camps under the magnolia, coming into tea, faces flushed and happy. Kit was always in charge, Dillon, four years younger, his willing and adoring foot soldier.

'How is he?' she asked tentatively, not wanting to ignore the situation, but glancing over at her co-worker as another two children joined the play area with their mothers.

'Oh, nothing changes. He checked himself out of the clinic after barely a week. He was completely out of it last time David visited, didn't even acknowledge his father. The flat was a tip as usual, stinking, David said, full of rubbish, needles, empty cans, fag butts, some girl – presumably another addict – passed out on the sofa. I . . . I don't know how much longer he can go on like this . . .'

Lily heard the break in her sister's normally brusque voice. 'It must be such hell for you.'

'And Kit too,' Helen said, after a moment.

'Isn't there anything—'

'Don't go there, Lily.' Her voice was hardly above a tired whisper. 'David does his best every time he sees him, but . . .'

'No, I'm sure. I didn't mean—'

'There isn't a night goes by,' Helen interrupted her again, 'when I don't lie there expecting the police to phone and tell me he's dead.'

87

Lily swallowed. The image was so terrible.

'There's not a damn thing any of us can do about it, unless Kit comes to his senses.'

'Please stay with us after the wedding, Helen. Make a night of it. We could debrief, sleep in, go somewhere for a slap-up brunch in the morning. It'd be fun.'

Lily knew her suggestion would be met with refusal, but she had nothing else to offer her sister.

'No . . . thanks, but no. I don't like being away from home . . . in case something happens.'

'Okay, well, you don't need to decide now. Listen, I have to go – I'm at the hospital.'

CHAPTER 12

Freddy hadn't slept, just come straight to the Berwick Street studio from the club, deliberately arriving very early, before the others. He didn't want to face his employees if he could help it, but facing Lily seemed the worse option.

His office was on the first floor. Studio 1, for dubbing, took up the ground floor, while Studio 2, the music-recording area, was in the basement. An editing company rented the attic space. It wasn't grand, but his clients seemed to enjoy the more intimate surroundings.

Wired from the long and stressful night, Freddy badly needed diversion from his problems. He decided to test the recently installed multi-track mixing and recording software, get his head around it. He was no longer actively involved in the recording and dubbing process – hadn't been for nearly a decade now, his job being to bring in clients and run the business side of the company – but he wanted to know he could still do it. And check that he'd got his money's worth from the shysters who'd installed the equipment.

Glyn, Freddy's senior sound engineer, had taken time to adjust to the swish new panel, preferring the old-fashioned desk where he controlled every knob and slider himself to create the mix. 'The whole thing's too bloody automated. I don't feel like I'm in charge,' he had complained.

Freddy had silently thought the same. But he refused to be the cliché of the older person with his head stubbornly stuck in yesterday's sand. The computerized desk could create way more tracks than the old system; the sound was supposedly pinpoint clear; the feed coming from the microphones was potentially more precise. Finally, it didn't matter whether it was better or not – there were probably very few people who could tell the difference. It was the future and every artist booking the studio would expect a state-of-the-art system for their dollar.

Samuel, the flat-mate of Dillon's friend Josh, was already at the desk in Studio 2 when Freddy arrived in the basement. And he seemed to have an impressively good grasp of the system. They spent the next hour or so putting the software through its paces. It was a welcome break for Freddy. Real work.

By ten o'clock, Freddy was back in his office. The room looked out onto the street and the stalls of the busy food market. He loved the shouts of the Cockney fruit and veg sellers, the clatter of crates, the hubbub of the jostling crowds. It had changed so much in the thirty years he'd been hanging about

Soho, and even more in the nine years since he'd built his studio. And, like everywhere else in Soho, it had been gentrified.

When he'd first been to the market there was a tall, broad-chested chicken seller called Ernie, who would gut the chickens and throw the innards, feet and all onto the striped red and white canopy, shouting as he did it, then scrape them off at the end of the morning. But he had packed it in years ago – nobbled by Health and Safety, no doubt – to be replaced by more sophisticated traders: there was now a falafel stall, a salad bar with kale a prominent ingredient, and a bakery company with fancy cupcakes and gluten-free chocolate brownies nestling in greaseproof paper. Freddy often bought one for his lunch.

Pale-wood venetian blinds covered the glass between him and his assistant, Isla-Mae, the daughter of Max Blackstone, Freddy's entrepreneur friend and multi-millionaire, and this morning he had closed them against the girl's inquisitive stare. He liked Isla-Mae, who was a hard worker despite her spoiled upbringing, but she was nosy, always wanting to find out what was going on and having an opinion on everything that passed through her hands.

His phone buzzed and he picked up the receiver.

'Glyn's here, Freddy.'

'Thanks. Send him in.'

Freddy took a deep breath, came out of the document he'd been perusing on his laptop and closed the lid.

Glyn had been with the company since its inception. A genius, in Freddy's opinion, at nurturing the artist, not letting his mix drown and dominate the original style, Glyn was hugely sought after by those in the know. Joachim – almost equally respected – was in charge of the dubbing studio. Overweight, late forties, with small, bright eyes, Glyn had a mess of thinning curls and a beard, shot through with grey, which looked as if it were an oversight rather than a style decision. Freddy had never seen him in anything but T-shirt and jeans.

'Hi, Glyn, have a seat.'

Glyn, normally easy-going and cheerful, looked solemn, awkwardly rubbing his hands together and staring past Freddy towards the window. His expression showed both embarrassment and vexation. 'Wondered how it was going on the salary front.' And before Freddy had had a chance to speak, he went on, in a rush, 'See, Angus keeps telling us we're just about to be paid, but nothing happens. Then I catch him this morning and he says the exact same thing: "It's imminent, I promise. Just waiting for the bank." And, well, here's me thinking that can't still be the case.' His soft Welsh intonation was apologetic, but Freddy knew the man to be tough and forthright, not someone you could palm off with half-truths.

Freddy sighed, feeling the painful drawing in his guts. His vision was suddenly blurred and he rubbed his eyes, stretched them open. 'It's been a bit of a tricky time, Glyn, I won't lie to you.'

The man on the opposite side of the desk looked at him steadily, waiting, Freddy was sure, for him to say it would, nonetheless, be all right.

'We've had some bad debts recently, and—'

'Who?' Glyn interrupted him.

'Umm, there's been a few ... I'm too soft, people take advantage. Jerome Kant, for a start ...'

'But he only booked a week.'

'This time, but he hasn't paid us for that massive chunk he did before Christmas.' Freddy winced at the lie, hoped Glyn didn't have any contacts in Jerome's camp who would question his exaggeration. Because Jerome did owe them money, but, as his engineer had pointed out, only for a week's worth of studio time.

'You're kidding me.' Glyn gave a soft harrumph of indignation, and Freddy hurried on before he could ask for more details.

'Then there was the work done on updating the mixing desks and the software. Those crooks charged me nearly double the estimate, but by the time I found out, it was too late. Angus had paid. I'm fighting them on it, but I don't hold out much hope.' This also was true, but the amount a mere drop in the ocean of the huge company debt. He could tell from Glyn's expression that he was not sounding convincing.

'So, you saying we're not going to get paid? Or what's the plan? I mean, the lads have got rent due, mortgages ... If we knew it was definitely coming ...'

'God, I understand, Glyn. I haven't slept for months worrying about it. But I was in Vegas at the weekend to meet a potential investor, and he seems solid, loved the studio's profile.'

Glyn waited, his mouth twisting as he chewed the inside of his cheek.

'Worst-case scenario, if I haven't got funds from somewhere by the end of the week, I'll put my own cash in till things have settled down.' He threw his hands up in an expansive gesture. 'I won't let you down, Glyn, you know that. What with one thing and another, these last few months have been a bit of a mess, financially. My fault, took my eye off the ball.' He looked earnestly at the man opposite. 'But we've been through lean patches before and come out the other side, right?'

Glyn nodded uncertainly. Freddy had met Glyn when they were both working at De Lane Lea Studios in Wardour Street, when Freddy was still a sound engineer. When he had taken the leap and got his own place, he had poached Glyn, much to the irritation of their former boss.

'And we will again. Your salaries will be paid, one hundred per cent, by next Monday. You have my word.'

Glyn finally grinned, relief flooding his round face, and Freddy felt utterly ashamed at the faith the man placed in him. Not that he'd let him or the seven other employees down, even once, in the nine years they had worked together. And Freddy *would* find the money by Monday, he absolutely would.

'Thanks, appreciate it. The lads'll be mightily relieved. And I must say, it's taken a weight off my own mind. The missus hasn't been too well recently – I think I told you about the ME? They don't think she'll be back at work for a while yet.' Glyn pushed on the arms of the chair and rose to his feet, stretching his hand across the desk to shake Freddy's. 'Wish I'd come to see you sooner.'

'Door's always open.' Freddy got up too, waited till the Welshman had gone, then turned to stare out of the window, down onto the busy market.

The universe is pitiless, he thought. *It just goes on in exactly the same way, day in, day out, regardless of the train wrecks happening in people's lives. A man could lose his wife to cancer, but the postman still delivers letters, the supermarket stays open, cars pile up and down his street, flowers bloom, the man still breathes and shits and thinks, however much he doesn't want to any more. It doesn't seem right, somehow, such supreme indifference.*

His phone rang. 'Angus wants a word,' Isla-Mae told him.

Max was waiting for him as he left the office around six that evening, standing in the street, his attention, as always, fixed on his large screen iPhone 6. Aware of Freddy standing beside him, he held up a finger for him to wait, then finished an email, his thumbs clicking away at the speed of light.

'Done. Sorry.' He grinned up at his friend. Max was small and solid, with short dark hair framing a face with wide blue eyes and dark lashes. It had the potential to be handsome if the bags beneath his eyes and the skin pasty from too much time working hadn't detracted from that promise. He seemed perpetually on the edge, Freddy thought, despite his millions, his expression intense and questing, as if searching for something that remained for ever out of reach. *If anyone saw the two of us now*, Freddy said to himself, *they would assume Max was the one with the problem, not me.*

'Where's it to be?' Max asked as they strode off towards Broadwick Street. 'American Bar? Hix?'

'American.' Freddy wasn't sure why Max offered a choice, as they both loved the bar in the Parisian-style brasserie, Zédel, and almost always met there. 'Could murder a martini.'

They turned left into Lexington Street, right into Brewer Street – past the rejected Hix – then left into Sherwood Street, making no attempt to talk until they'd arrived in the gorgeous art deco/beaux arts interior, the walls decorated with hundreds of black-and-white photographs and posters of people like the legendary French singer and actress Mistinguett. A series of long flights of stairs led them to the dark basement bar, where an immaculate blonde in a short black dress greeted Freddy and Max each with a kiss on both cheeks.

'Mr March, Mr Blackstone, very good to see you,' she said. 'Is it just the two of you?' The bar was popular and usually packed later in the evening, a booking essential, but Arianna and Chloë, the other maître d', would always accommodate Freddy and Max, however busy.

Installed in a banquette along the wall, Max ordered a beer, Freddy a very dry martini, straight up, with a twist. Only when the drinks were served, the olives and salted almonds placed in the centre of the small table, did they finally speak. Freddy was nervous. Max was his last chance of some instant cash for the salaries, but his friend knew him too well: he would sense immediately why the studio was in trouble.

They went back thirty years, he and Max, becoming friends when both worked in a then-fashionable club in Great Queen Street called Zanzibar, Max as a barman, Freddy a waiter. Neither took his job seriously enough, but both were good at charming the famous clients into thinking they did. And it was at the club that Max had met Stew Kincaid, who had set him off on his path to riches by lending him a small deposit for a flat in Kensal Rise, which Max had done up and sold on, the first of many. He was now, by his own admission, worth around fifty million.

Freddy decided not to beat about the bush. 'I'm in really bad trouble, Max,' he said, fortified by a sip of the cold, nearly neat gin.

His friend nodded, waited for him to go on, leaning back against the dark leather and looking, for the first time, relaxed.

'I should have told you before, as an investor. But it's all been quite sudden. I can't meet the salaries this month, people screaming for loan repayment . . . taxman . . . bank a daily nightmare.' As he went on to detail the true extent of his failure, he felt suddenly on the verge of tears. It was so good to be able to talk about it to someone who wasn't a victim of his recklessness. But Max, he felt, as his only share-holder, had a vested interest in the business staying afloat.

'A proper mess, then,' Max said. Originally from Darlington, his northern accent had softened a little after decades in the south, but the County Durham cadences were still very strong. Freddy, on the other hand, had carefully ironed out his Mid-lands accent and adopted standard English with 'estuary' leanings. He prided himself that only a trained phonetician would be able to pin him to a Leicestershire childhood.

Freddy mentioned the sum he would need to get himself out of trouble. He'd fixed on an amount that he thought might be acceptable, not the amount he really needed.

'Oh, my word.' Max looked aghast. 'How did that happen?'

There was silence as both men sipped their drinks. The bar had filled up, the noise level now high, but Freddy liked that: it gave them the illusion of privacy. He waited for Max to say something, but his friend was just frowning at him.

'I was wondering . . . hate to ask . . . you know I never have before . . . well, only once . . . twice if you count that time in Spain . . .' He looked at the ceiling to stop his tears, swallowed hard. He absolutely could not break down. 'I'm on the ropes, mate. The whole thing's going to collapse like a house of bloody cards if I don't find some money soon. Lily has no idea, Dillon's wedding is at stake . . . I don't need it all . . . just enough to pay the salaries and the wedding venue, get by until I can get the studio refinanced.'

Max liked his wife, Freddy knew that, and he was shameless in playing the Lily card.

His friend took a long breath, sucked his bottom lip under his top teeth in a familiar gesture. Then shook his head. 'Is this the usual?' His tone was sympathetic. It gave Freddy some hope.

'What do you mean?'

'You know exactly what I mean, Freddy. Are you in this mess because you're gambling again?'

Again? thought Freddy. *When have I ever not?* But of course he'd told his friend that he had stopped after the time, about six years ago now, when Max had bailed him out to the tune of thousands, all of which Freddy had paid back. He had often quit, but only for short periods, the longest being when he met Lily. And he always meant to stop – every day of his life he meant to stop. But the 'meaning to' feeling, based more on guilt than resolve, only lasted till the much more powerful lure of the hit kicked in, and he told himself he would stop tomorrow.

'No,' Freddy said, looking him straight in the eye.

But Max, from his sceptically raised eyebrow, clearly didn't buy it. 'Come on, Freddy, this is me you're talking to.'

Freddy lifted his glass and gulped the rest of his martini. He weighed up how much sympathy he'd get if he confessed the real truth, or stuck to a series of scarcely believable hard-luck stories about bad debts and overspends.

'How long?' Max was asking, before Freddy had a chance to decide.

Freddy shrugged. There was no answer.

His friend was leaning forward, elbows on his knees, hands clasped, his intense gaze resting on Freddy, making him squirm. 'Fucking hell, Freddy,' was all he said.

'You don't know how hard it is. I keep thinking . . . hoping . . . I always feel sure I'm going to win. And I do. They say a gambler always loses, but they don't. I don't. I won over twenty thousand the other night.'

'And then lost it, by the sound of things.'

'Not all of it—'

'Please,' Max interrupted. 'No details. You've got a problem, man, a huge, destructive, unmanageable problem. Are you really going to wait till you've lost that fantastic wife of yours, your business, your reputation, before you get help?' He didn't sound angry, just frustrated and a bit bewildered.

Too late, Freddy thought, as he waited for the refusal, which he now saw as inevitable. He didn't want a lecture, didn't need one. He knew all the arguments, knew Max was completely right. And a part of him didn't want his money anyway. He hated being beholden to his old friend, who had started with as little as Freddy – basically nothing – back in the Zanzibar days, and had been so annoyingly sensible in every aspect of his business life since.

'The day you can convince me that you've stopped, and stopped for a decent length of time, Freddy, I'll up my investment in the studio. I believe in you. I hate to see you screw things up, but I'm not going to give you money just so you can lose it.' He threw his hands up in a take-it-or-leave-it gesture.

Too late, Freddy repeated to himself. *You don't understand. That's way, way too late.*

'I'm sorry,' Max said, and Freddy could see that he genuinely was.

CHAPTER 13

Lily was nervous. She had not wanted this meeting with Stan, but he had sounded so upset, so insistent, she hadn't known how to refuse. He had also begged her not to tell Sara, his desperation bouncing her into agreeing. And now she felt horribly disloyal to her daughter. Sara had made the decision – for better or worse – not to tell Stan till after the wedding, so he shouldn't yet know about American Ted. But clearly he sensed something was up.

The café she'd chosen was on the South Bank, near the Globe, roughly halfway between Evelina's and Guy's, where Stan worked. She'd had a tiring morning with the children, one little boy having such a serious tantrum because he wasn't well enough to go on the slide that Lily had thought he had stopped breathing. His little face was suffused with purple and he was rigid with frustration. It had reminded her of how she felt when she couldn't get her breath.

Stan was late, and Lily began to hope he wouldn't show. But then she saw his familiar figure – tall and broad-shouldered, dark hair flying in the wind, always rushing. Like a whirlwind he pirouetted through the crowded lunchtime tables and plonked himself down opposite her, breathing hard, pushing his metal-rimmed glasses up his nose with an exhausted sigh. 'God, I'm so sorry, Lily. I got caught . . .'

She smiled. 'It's okay. I haven't been here long.' That wasn't true, but she was desperate to put him at his ease. They had always had a good relationship, Stan treating Lily like a surrogate mother at times, his own being a high-powered businesswoman in Hong Kong, where Stan had partially grown up.

By the time the waiter had delivered the stand of small plates with the Greek mezze and basket of warm puffed pitta, Stan was already well into a rant about the hours he was expected to work and the toll it was taking on his personal life. He did not find it easy to talk about himself or his emotions – easier, by far, to focus everything on his beloved work. Lily just nodded sympathetically, waiting for him to run out of steam. But when he eventually did, his face fell into lines of such misery, she was shocked.

'What has she told you?' he asked, fixing her with his bright blue eyes, his look tormented.

Lily tried to appear puzzled.

'You must know, Lily. Sas tells you everything.'

Why the hell did I agree to this? Lily asked herself. *I can't lie to him, it's not fair.* But she also knew it wasn't her place to reveal her daughter's secret.

'Know what?' she asked, her voice more irritated than she'd intended, although her annoyance was with herself, not Stan.

Stan raised his eyebrows, his expression cynical. When he answered it was as if he were talking to a halfwit. 'That Sara is having an affair.'

'She told you that?'

'No, she doesn't need to.'

'Stan . . .'

'Please,' he begged, grabbing her hand across the table and squeezing it hard. 'Please, Lily, put me out of my misery. When I ask her she just says I'm being ridiculous, that she's exhausted, that she doesn't have time to bloody think, let alone have an affair. But she's changed. She barely comes home, even though I know she's not on duty. We never make love . . .' He paused. 'And she's being unusually kind to me.'

Lily knew that Stan would find this last transgression the most telling. Sara was tough; she took no prisoners. She and Stan had always had a very straightforward, unsentimental relationship. No frills. But also – until now – no secrets. 'Look, Stan. This is between you and Sara. I met you because you sounded so upset. But it's not fair to ask me stuff you should be asking her.'

Stan let go of her hand and slumped back in his chair, briefly closed his eyes. 'Right. So that's a yes.'

'I didn't say that.'

He looked away, biting his upper lip. 'Who is he?'

Lily sighed. 'Talk to her, Stan. You've got to talk to her.'

'I *have*. I told you. She just denies it.'

Lily thought of Freddy. She had talked to him time and

again, and he always had a plausible answer, one that allayed her fears in the moment. Then his obvious tension would manifest itself again, and she would wonder. He'd been home early last night and they'd had a cosy shepherd's pie in front of the television – a rare event. But then, around ten, he'd checked his phone and cursed, explained that this famous American record producer was in town and was demanding Freddy join him at Annabel's. He hadn't come home at all, just rung to say he was going straight to the studio. Lily didn't have time to question him before he'd said he loved her and clicked off.

'Listen,' Lily said, steering her mind away from thoughts of Freddy. 'You and Sara have been together a long time. There's bound to be the odd glitch, especially when you're both under such pressure at work.' She tried not to think of her daughter's radiant face when she'd been telling her about Ted.

But Stan, after a moment of consideration, seemed slightly mollified. 'You think?'

'Of course.'

'So I should just shut up, let things ride?'

Lily thought about this. Maybe it was the best course. Let Sara have her fling. Get over Ted and realize what a mistake it would be to lose Stan. 'I don't know. I can't tell you what to do. But sometimes badgering people only makes things worse. You know how stubborn Sara is.'

Stan nodded dispiritedly.

'And sometimes it's not important. You don't need to know.' She knew she was talking to herself more than Stan.

His face shut down with a weary acceptance. 'So there is something to know.'

Lily didn't reply and Stan must have taken her silence for agreement. He closed his eyes again.

'Sara loves you, you know that.' Lily spoke sincerely, but felt like a traitor to both him and Sara. She was glad when her daughter's boyfriend pushed back his chair and rose to leave.

CHAPTER 14

At the seventh floor, Freddy exited the lift and wandered outside to gaze at the immaculate roof terrace. The banks of green foliage had the pale translucence of early spring, interspersed with bright splashes of flowers, sky blue benches along the paths and pink and white flamingoes beside the pond. Looking across at the London skyline, he could make out the curved dome of the Royal Albert Hall to the east, bordered by the green swathes of Kensington Gardens, St Mary Abbots church across the high street. He hadn't announced himself yet: he needed to give out an atmosphere of supreme confidence when he met Suzie, the events manager, and he wanted a few minutes to gather his wits. Another long night at the tables had netted a miserable seven grand, which he was sure he could work up to the seventeen required, but he needed more time.

Suzie was small and charming – as you might expect from

someone in her line of work. She shook Freddy's hand warmly and ushered him to a table in the empty restaurant, where a coffee pot and white cups, a plate of mini croissants and another of strawberries, their tips dipped in chocolate, had been carefully laid out.

'If you would prefer something stronger . . .' Suzie said, smiling and indicating the coffee, but Freddy shook his head, gratefully accepting the cup she handed him.

'Right,' he said, straightening up. He'd showered at the studio and changed into a dark suit and white shirt – he kept a selection of clothes at his office, in case of all-nighters – and hoped he looked like someone who had seventeen thousand to spend on a wedding. 'I won't beat about the bush. I spoke to my stepson, Dillon, and he said you were asking for the balance on the wedding by today.'

Suzie picked up her tablet, which had been lying beside her on the white-clothed table, and clicked it open. 'That's right, Mr March. It was actually due last Friday.' Another friendly smile. But Freddy wasn't fooled. This was not a woman to mess with, her dark hair too sleek, makeup too perfect and tastefully understated, her gleaming diamond engagement ring too expensive. *Tiffany's*, he thought.

'Well, I appreciate your giving us some leeway . . . Although the wedding isn't for another four weeks or so.'

Suzie checked her tablet again, although she must have known the date long before the meeting. 'Three weeks on Friday. The fifteenth of April, yes.' She looked up at Freddy. 'But the contract clearly states that the balance is due one calendar month before the event, Mr March.'

'I realize that. But the thing is ...' Freddy leaned a little closer to the table, holding Suzie's eye '. . . it's a little delicate. I don't want to bore you, but my wife is the one paying for the wedding, and she hasn't been well recently ... Things have been tricky . . . with her affairs . . . if you get my meaning.'

Suzie looked as if she wasn't sure she did, but she nodded anyway, and seemed drawn in by Freddy's brown eyes and conspiratorial expression.

'I've taken it in hand,' he went on, after a pause which signified the seriousness of the problem, 'and I can have the money to you, absolutely for certain, by Monday.'

Suzie frowned slightly. 'Well ... the problem is, we have so many people wanting to book with us. And if you were to default – not that I'm saying you will,' she added hastily, as Freddy summoned an indignant look, 'but if you did, it doesn't give us much time to sort out another client. That's why we have the rule.'

Freddy nodded sympathetically. 'Absolutely, I totally see. It could be awkward filling the slot at the last minute. But we have already paid way above the usual deposit, so even in the unlikely event that we were to default – which I assure you we won't – your losses wouldn't be *sooo* great.' He cocked his head to one side, gave one of his famous smiles. 'Would they?'

Suzie gave a short sigh. 'Okay. Let me think about it and get back to you later today, Mr March.' She didn't look happy, but she didn't look too disturbed either. Obviously she had to be seen to be doing her job, but he'd got her, he was sure of that. She just wouldn't want to lose face.

Freddy stood up. 'That's great, Suzie. I can't tell you how

much we all appreciate your help. It's been such a difficult time . . .' He reached over and shook her hand quickly, before she could change her mind. 'I'll look forward to hearing from you. You have my number, I think. Contact me, rather than my stepson. He's very busy at the moment.'

She nodded, smiled. 'I hope things work out for you. Weddings can be so stressful.'

That was generous, Freddy thought, and he immediately felt horribly guilty for his lies – implying Lily was some sort of nutter, unable to manage her affairs. Which he hadn't until now, so intent was he on getting the result he needed.

Once safely outside the building, he wanted to punch the air. It wasn't much of a victory – the money was still due by Monday, but Monday was nearly a week away. A great deal could happen in a week.

He walked across the Gardens, past the Round Pond, up towards home. It was a beautiful spring day and Freddy luxuriated in the warmth of the sun as he found a bench near the Peter Pan statue and sat down to think. His head was spinning from lack of sleep, his mouth dry. The sums going round in his head no longer had any coherence. All he knew was that he needed money, and fast. There were still a couple of options, investor-wise, he hadn't plumbed, but both had major snags.

The first one, Nelson Posner, was basically a gangster, an asset-stripper with no moral conscience. There would be blood – probably Freddy's – on anything he got from him. The second was an unscrupulous trader, one Morgan Weber, who specialized in shorting – short selling – and had made billions thereby, according to various rich lists Freddy had seen. But although at one stage they had been sort of friends, Morgan was highly competitive and a bully – being mean to waiters was one of his specialities. He would revel in Freddy's failure, rub his nose in it, then probably not come through. So he would have humiliated himself for nothing.

This was his problem, Freddy understood. From sheer stupidity he had lain down with dogs and now, inevitably, he risked getting fleas. He brushed the idea of either of these two men from his mind. Better to crash and burn than associate himself with villains like that.

He sat there for a long while, people passing the bench alone and in groups, children circling the statue, squirrels darting among the trees. At one stage he dozed off – he didn't seem to have enough energy to move a muscle. Eventually he decided he would have tea with Lily, then go into town, hole up in one of the establishments he favoured – maybe the Piccadilly Club, he hadn't been there in a while – not stay out all night again. He was completely exhausted and Lily was worrying again. And who knew? He might sort it out this afternoon. If not, he still had five days before Armageddon.

'So you paid them?' Lily's first question, as her husband walked into the penthouse, was laden with anxiety.

He summoned a grin, nodded emphatically. 'Sorted.'

'You went in there?'

'Yup. Saw Miss Suzie Perfect. All done.'

Lily's face broke into a wide smile. 'Oh, Freddy, thanks so much. Dillon and Gaby will be so relieved.'

Freddy took Lily in his arms, kissed the top of her head, held her against him. 'I'm sorry it took so long. I didn't want them to worry.'

'Doesn't matter now.' She raised her head and the love in her eyes made Freddy wince. She was such a good woman – how could he have jeopardized her happiness?

As he held her, he made a fresh vow. As soon as this mess was sorted out, he would get help, start again. There were groups all over London. He had even been to one a couple of years ago with his friend Peter, a reformed gambler who was, like Larry Hedstrom, determined to save Freddy. But the group was so pious and needy, spewing out never-ending tales of self-destruction that he felt bore no relation to himself, he had run a mile. He hadn't spoken to Peter since.

Freddy made loose leaf tea in the red pot, warmed some cheese scones he'd picked up on the way home, laid two chocolate eclairs on a plate, found butter and blackcurrant jam – delicious with cheese scones – in the fridge and poured milk into a small jug. Then he dug out china cups, saucers and tea plates that had belonged to Lily's mother, setting it all on the kitchen table along with two lacy linen napkins – also Lily's mother's.

As he surveyed his handiwork, he thought the presentation worthy of a food magazine, the sun pouring onto the gleaming white surfaces, showing off the pretty blue and white china and silver spoons, the tempting chocolate buns, the crusty scones, yellow slab of butter and rich, dark jam. This was his haven, his bubble. Nothing could touch him here.

They sat in the tranquil kitchen and talked as they ate. Now that Lily thought the wedding money had been paid, she seemed more relaxed and told him about the little boy who had nearly choked on his rage, and her lunch with Stan.

Freddy pulled a face. 'God, Lily, you shouldn't have seen him without telling Sara.'

Clearly irritated, she replied, 'Well, obviously I know that. I feel terrible. But it would have said just as much if I'd refused to meet him, wouldn't it?'

'You didn't tell him about oily Ted?' He'd never met the guy, but he was sure he was a no-good chancer.

'No, but as good as. He was very insistent.'

'Poor bugger. He should know, anyway.'

'Does he have to?' Lily asked. 'If it's not serious?'

He frowned. 'She's taking away his power, not telling him. It's always better to be in possession of the facts.' He had no idea why he'd said that.

'Well, *you*'re not telling me all the facts, Freddy March,' she said after a moment, seeming angry and defiant in the face of Stan's humiliation. And for a split second Freddy had an almost overwhelming desire, a physical compulsion, to tell her everything. But he stopped himself on the brink of confession. Like Stan, did Lily have to know? Might he not save the day, even now, even at this eleventh hour? He'd done it before.

CHAPTER 15

Dillon took the call at work. It was after eight on Tuesday evening and the small office was empty. He had been delayed by some last-minute changes to a book they were publishing on sexuality in nineteenth-century Britain. The author, a highly respected historian, was unable to leave the text alone, making myriad changes up to the very last minute – for which Dillon was responsible.

'Mr Tierney?'

'Yes?' he said distractedly, his eyes still on the screen and the Track Change notes from his author.

'It's Suzie from the Roof Gardens.'

'Hi, Suzie.' He had no sense of premonition, just a weary resignation at having to deal with yet another wedding matter.

'Umm . . . I've left messages for Mr March, but he hasn't got back to me.' A pause. 'I'm afraid we still haven't received the balance of the money. Mr March promised last week in our meeting it would be with us yesterday, Monday, at the very latest. I can't hang on any more, Mr Tierney. I'm sure you understand . . . It's a popular venue . . .'

Dillon, who hadn't really been listening, frowned, swung away from the screen. 'Sorry, what?'

'Mr March hasn't paid the balance.'

'Hasn't paid? But . . .' Dillon's heart jumped in his chest.

'I made an exception and extended the deadline till Monday,' Suzie was saying, her voice sounding genuinely regretful. 'But there's no sign of the money. I've tried a number of times to contact Mr March, but he hasn't returned my calls.'

'Wait. You're saying you're cancelling our wedding?'

There was a sigh at the other end of the phone. 'I'm afraid I have no choice, Mr Tierney. I gather there have been some difficult issues with the family, and I do sympathize. But it clearly states in the contract that the balance is due one calendar month before the event.'

'What issues?' Dillon's head was spinning. His wedding, cancelled?

'Well, Mr March said . . . I realize it's delicate—'

'What's "delicate"?'

'I think you should talk to Mr March about it.' Her tone was flat, as if she were getting impatient with his questions.

'Please, please don't offer our slot to anyone else, Suzie. I'm sure there's been some stupid mix-up. I know he's paid. Can you give me half an hour and I'll sort it? Please.'

Maybe it was his clear desperation, but the events manager hesitated. 'Umm . . . okay, well, half an hour then. But I honestly can't hold it any longer, Mr Tierney. This is a caring company, and the last thing any of us want to do is ruin someone's special day. But I'm sure you can see our point of view. If the money hasn't been transferred by midday tomorrow, I'm afraid I will have to cancel your booking.'

'I'll get back to you as soon as possible. Thanks.'

Dillon clicked off and sat for a moment, stunned, swinging his chair from side to side, trying to work out the ramifications of what Suzie had just said. Then he quickly punched in his mother's number. She didn't pick up. He followed with Freddy's. He didn't pick up either. He tried his mother again. No joy. He left texts for them both, saying, 'Please ring, very urgent.'

Slamming his phone down on the desk, he got up, not knowing what to do next. He felt sick. The thought of telling Gabriela the news made him feel even more nauseous. *I won't call her till I've seen Mum*, he thought, grabbing his jacket from the back of his chair and closing down the document on the screen. The book would just have to wait. He would come back early in the morning and finish it.

Clutching his bike helmet, he vaulted down the dirty brown-carpeted stairs at the back of the building, which was on the first floor of a Regency terrace, above a dry cleaner's in a small road behind Upper Street. Pushing open the rear door to the paved patch of garden where he kept his bike, he unclamped the D-lock and pushed the bike through the very narrow alleyway between the houses – which always smelt of piss – onto the pavement. As he zipped up his hooded blue storm jacket and fastened his helmet in place, he realized that his mother and stepfather could be anywhere. They seemed to be out most nights and there was no guarantee that they would be home if he went all the way to Sussex Square. He hesitated, tried his mother's number for the third time. Just the same irritatingly cheery voice telling him to leave a message. Which he did, again.

In the end he decided to go over to Freddy and his mother's flat. Take the risk. His mother and stepfather checked their phones regularly. In the time it took him to ride to West London – roughly twenty minutes – one of them would have replied and then at least he would be there to talk to them properly.

As Dillon, deciding to avoid the West End, wove in and out of the evening traffic on Euston Road, buses piling past him, the night air cold and reviving after the stuffy office, he thought about his stepfather and began to suspect the worst.

The problem wasn't so much the wedding – his mother had assured him she'd bail them out if there was a problem, and he knew she had the funds, which he would somehow have to pay back – as Freddy's integrity. He had told Lily, *quite specifically*, that he had paid the balance. He'd told her, and she'd told Dillon, a week ago. And he hadn't. So where did that leave them all?

Maybe there genuinely has been a cock-up in the transfer, he told himself, not really believing it. Because how could Freddy lie so blatantly to Mum, knowing so much rested on it? *How could he do that?* He couldn't, was the answer. By the time Dillon arrived in his mother's square, he had almost convinced himself the bank had to be at fault. They didn't always get it right. That, or Freddy was having a nervous breakdown, had completely lost the plot. His mum had been saying for weeks that he was very stressed.

Why, oh why didn't we plump for the Italian restaurant round the corner? Nino is a friend. It would have been perfect, he thought as he arrived at his mother's block, dismounted and chained his bike to a lamppost. Undoing the strap beneath his chin, but keeping the helmet on his head, he rang the penthouse bell. No answer. Neither had there been any response to his urgent calls and texts. He wondered what to do next. It was only nine fifteen – Gabriela was out tonight, with her French partner in the theatre company, Benoît Simon. So he had time before dropping the bombshell.

He was hungry, but he didn't fancy sitting alone in a restaurant. After a few minutes of standing about on the pavement, he decided he had to eat and wandered back onto Sussex Gardens, found a basement Malaysian café and ordered a takeaway beef rendang and rice, which he took back to his mother and stepfather's block in a thin blue plastic carrier bag.

A young couple were leaving and Dillon held the heavy glass door for them, then entered the mirrored, marble-floored foyer. There were two padded black leather chairs flanking a small rectangular glass-and-chrome table. He sank into one and opened the cheap plastic containers of food. The curry was oily and tepid, the beef so tough it threatened to pull out his teeth. He ate it anyway, starving as he was, receiving some disapproving looks from various haughty residents passing him on the way to or from the lift. But no one challenged his presence there.

He must have nodded off, because the next thing he knew, his mother was shaking his shoulder, her look full of concern. 'What are you doing here?' she asked. 'Is everything all right?'

Dillon quickly stood up, trying to collect himself from a vivid anxiety dream about a boat full of people he didn't know powering towards some rocks. He kept shouting, but no one seemed able to hear.

His mother and stepfather were staring at him, waiting for him to respond.

'I'm . . . I needed to catch you. You weren't answering your phones.'

'We were at the National,' his mother said, reaching into her bag for her mobile as she spoke. 'What is it, Dillon?' He thought she looked tired and not entirely pleased to see him.

The lift doors opened and a tall grey-haired man stepped out, giving them a cursory glance.

'Evening, Harrison,' Freddy said, nodding to the man, who nodded back with a half-smile. 'Let's go up,' he added, taking Lily's arm, waving to Dillon to follow.

No one spoke as the lift creaked its way to the top floor. Freddy pulled his keys from his jacket pocket and opened the front door. Dillon could see that his stepfather looked tense, his face unusually pallid and drawn. He wondered if they'd had a row.

'I'll get some wine,' Freddy said.

Dillon didn't stop him, just followed his mother into the sitting room and sat down on the sofa while she stood by the mantelpiece, a hand on it to steady herself as she slipped off her heels one at a time, spreading her manicured toes into the rug with what looked like relief.

'Tell me.'

Raising his eyebrows, he asked, 'So you don't know, Mum?'

'Know what?' Now she was staring at him, a puzzled frown on her face.

'That the wedding money hasn't been paid and they're cancelling the booking if it's not in the bank by tomorrow morning?'

'That's rubbish,' she said, brushing her dark fringe off her forehead with a dismissive gesture. She moved over to the charcoal club chair on the right of the fireplace and sat down with a weary sigh. 'Freddy told me he paid it a week ago. They must have got it wrong, lost the payment or something.'

His stepfather came into the room, holding three glasses upside down by their long stems, a bottle of red wine in the other hand, all of which he put down on the coffee table.

'Dillon says the money hasn't arrived at the Roof Gardens. They must have lost it.'

Dillon watched Freddy closely as he straightened up, shot a glance at his mum. There was no surprise on his face, just a closed, wary expression, as if he were silently calculating something. *Another lie?* Dillon wondered.

Freddy stood looking down at them, both hands now thrust into the pockets of his jeans. He had pulled his blue shirt out of the waistband, taken off his shoes, revealing a pair of bright red socks. Dillon waited.

Addressing Dillon, he said, 'Why didn't they call me?'

'Suzie has, she says, a number of times, but you didn't get back to her.'

Freddy shook his head in apparent despair. 'I gave her both numbers, but she's probably been ringing my other phone. It fell under a bus yesterday, on the Strand. I was taking it out of my top pocket and the damn thing slipped out of my hand and landed in the bus lane just as a number eleven was going past. Smashed to smithereens.'

'Bad luck,' Dillon said, trying to keep the impatience out of his voice, 'but what about the money? Suzie says we've got till midday tomorrow.'

Freddy finally looked concerned. 'Can't think what's gone wrong.' He reached along the sofa and patted Dillon's arm. 'Don't worry. Leave it with me. I'll sort it out in the morning. I asked Angus to do the transfer, so maybe he forgot or something . . . I hope he didn't send it to someone else!' He picked up the wine bottle and unscrewed the top, pouring a small amount into a glass and taking a sniff, a sip. Nodding a little in appreciation, he proceeded to pour wine into each of the glasses, handing one to Lily, one to Dillon, then sat back with his own cradled in his left hand.

Dillon didn't know what to say. But he didn't believe his stepfather.

'Umm, yeah . . . That's great, Freddy . . . Thanks . . . But the thing is . . .' He stopped, having no idea how to phrase his concerns. He could hardly call him a liar to his face with absolutely no proof. A phone under a bus? *Really?*

'You're looking worried, Dillon. Please don't,' his mother chimed in. 'If Freddy says he's paid the money, then there isn't a problem. It'll be some idiot in Admin. They must have hundreds of bookings there. I'm sure stuff goes astray all the time.'

'I promise I'll ring Suzie first thing. They aren't going to cancel a high-profile wedding like ours. It would look terrible.'

Dillon took a deep breath. 'That's exactly what they are

going to do, Freddy. Suzie was quite clear. She says they have people queuing up to book our slot.'

Freddy gave a short laugh. 'Well, she would say that, wouldn't she? She's only winding you up to make sure she gets her cash.'

'So you're saying the wedding is solid?'

'Of course it is,' Freddy said. 'Do you honestly think we'd sit by and let Suzie Cream-cheese cancel your big day?'

His mother shot him a sympathetic look. 'Poor Dillon, she must have really freaked you out to get you rushing over here at this hour.'

He took a large gulp of wine. The taste of that revolting beef still lingered on his tongue and he was only too happy to wash it, and his anxiety, away. He remembered Gabriela and pulled his phone out of his pocket, checked the screen. But there was no message.

'I'd better get home,' he said, finishing the wine and putting the glass down. 'Sorry to have intruded.'

'Stay the night,' his mum said. 'Please. You can't drive home drunk.'

He laughed. 'I'm not drunk. And it's only a bike. I'm not in charge of a lethal weapon.'

Freddy didn't insist and Dillon got the impression he was relieved his stepson was leaving.

As he mounted his bike, his face flushed from the wine, his fingers fumbling with his chin strap, he tried to banish the sense of calamity that still hovered, no matter how much his mother and stepfather assured him that everything was just hunky-dory.

CHAPTER 16

Freddy lay beside his sleeping wife in the darkness and knew that the game was up. It was no longer a case of if he would be discovered but when, and how he should manage it to inflict the least possible damage. His luck had been terrible this past week. The not-inconsiderable chunk of money he'd had – which was almost enough for the wedding – was long gone, although at one stage on Friday night he'd had more than enough for that and a few weeks' living as well. Now he had barely a thousand in cash. Nothing else. His three credit cards were maxed out, his debit card blocked, his phone account cancelled. There was no 'other' phone: he'd had to buy a pay-as-you-go and make up the bus story. *Sometimes*, he thought, *I wish I wasn't such a convincing liar*. He'd never be in this mess, he reckoned, if someone had called him to account sooner. Not that he was blaming anyone else.

In a way, as he lay there, he felt more relaxed than he had

in weeks. Not happy: he was far from happy at the thought of confessing to Lily. In fact he couldn't even go there in his head. But the pressure was off now. The pressure to find money here, there and everywhere, to finagle, screen creditors' calls, lie, lie and lie. He'd failed, and he knew he must take the consequences on the chin. That had been his father's favourite expression: 'Take it on the chin, son.' Which meant, in Vinnie Slater's terms, 'Stand there and let me beat the shit out of you until you scream for me to stop, because it gives me enormous pleasure. But don't blame me: this is all your own fault . . . son.'

Freddy allowed himself to think about his father for a moment. He rarely did, pushing the pain back into the box whenever it threatened his thoughts. The last time he'd seen him was, what, twenty-five years ago? Maybe longer. Vinnie still tried to get in touch, usually around Christmas, probably because he was drunk. But Freddy wasn't tempted. He told everyone his father had Alzheimer's. And who knew? Maybe he did by now – he must be nearly seventy-six.

Turning in the darkness to fit his body against Lily's warm back, he wondered if this was the last time she would let him do so. By tomorrow night she wouldn't be speaking to him, no doubt. But he was too tired even to feel that particular pain. He wanted so badly to sleep and hoped, not for the first time, that he might never wake up.

Almost inevitably, Freddy did wake up, at around six the next morning. He'd slept flat out, no dreams that he could remember, and now, as he looked at his dishevelled reflection in the bathroom mirror, he felt as if he had the worst hangover in the history of the world. But it wasn't a physical hangover. He picked up his shaving bowl, wet his brush and swirled one into the other until he had foaming, soapy bristles to sweep around his chin. This morning he saw his mother's eyes looking back at him. Not only their colouring of deep brown, the thick, dark lashes, but also the expression of hurt and fear that had hung about Maria for as long as he could remember.

Their looks came directly from Maria's Maltese mother, Pina – a beautiful girl who'd turned heads and, as a consequence, had been knocked up as a teenager by an English soldier at the start of the Second World War, then swiftly abandoned. She had brought up Maria in Valletta, the capital, with no help from her shamed family, cleaning for the well-off British administrators and diplomats, enduring the nightmare siege of the island, and coming out skin and bone, all her meagre rations given to her precious baby daughter.

As a child, Freddy had loved those trips to Malta. His grandmother was fierce and uncompromising – she'd had to be to survive – but also kind, and she had adored Freddy. They would sit together, cross-legged, on the cool tiles of the kitchen, in the baking afternoon heat, and she would tell him stories about the island, the war, his mother.

By then Pina lived in a small flat near St Julian's Bay, about twenty minutes north of Valletta. It was five minutes' walk from the sea, where they would swim off the sharp rocks of the bay in the clear, deep, aquamarine water of the Mediterranean. But he'd particularly loved being there because his father had had to stay behind and mind the Leicester pub. It was a month of safety and calm every summer, when his nerves were not raw and jangling at every sound that might signal his father's presence. And each year it became harder for him and his mother to go home.

He went through to the kitchen. Dawn was breaking over the city, the wash of light beautiful and serene. He knew Lily was unlikely to be up for at least an hour, but he quietly laid the table, being careful not to chink the crockery, then broke some eggs into a bowl and put a small pan on the unlit stove with a chunk of butter in the bottom and a wooden spoon, ready to receive the eggs for scrambling. He filled the filter paper with coffee grounds and topped up the water, cut bread from a French sourdough loaf, slotting the slices into the Dualit toaster, poured grapefruit juice from the carton in the door of the fridge into two small blue glasses and finally retrieved the marmalade from the cupboard to put in the centre of the table. The simple preparation stopped him thinking. He refused to think. 'Live in the moment,' people were always smugly insisting these days – as if they did any such thing – and this was the moment he clung to, because it felt like the last moment of his life.

Lily, rumpled and half asleep, her dark hair sticking out at odd angles, smiled as she saw the table.

'Sit,' he said. 'I'll put the coffee on.'

She did as he told her and sipped the juice, watching him as he turned the gas on and ground pepper into the eggs.

'Sleep well?' he asked.

She nodded. 'Like a log. That play was so intense, it exhausted me.'

He laughed, marvelling that he could do so with such ease. 'Bit dark for my taste. There didn't seem any hope, no chink in the despair. Good production, though.'

'Hmm, you know me, I like dark. But I get what you mean. A tad too relentless, maybe.'

Freddy spooned a neat pile of warm egg onto her white china plate, then some on his own, and sat down opposite her.

'Thanks. This is lovely,' she said, as she began to spread her toast.

They discussed the play some more over breakfast. Freddy would have been happy to talk about it till the end of time rather than allow a gap in the conversation through which the chaos might slip. *Just this last minute of peace before Armageddon*, he begged silently to an uncaring universe.

But the bubble of tranquillity could not last. Lily, her meal finished, wiped her fingers on the white cotton napkin Freddy had put beside her plate, pushed back her chair to cross her bare legs and pulled her dressing-gown over her knees. She glanced up at the wall clock beside the fridge and said, 'I suppose it's too early to ring Suzie?'

Freddy felt his body close down, his heart somersaulting, Olympic style. *This is it.*

'I can't pay,' he said simply, unable to sort out the vast jumble of information that it would be necessary, eventually, to impart to his poor wife.

He saw her frown, her face go still.

'What do you mean?'

126

'I've fucked up, Lily. I mean seriously fucked up. I'm broke.'

It seemed such an inadequate description of his situation, but it was the best he could do. Words piled up to be spoken, but he held back the flood for a few moments longer.

Lily, still frowning, leaned towards him. 'Broke?'

He nodded. 'The studio is in the shit, I'm talking receivership, and me, personally . . . I'm bankrupt, Lily. I can't pay for Dillon's wedding.'

Tears welled in his eyes as his wife continued to stare at him, uncomprehending.

'The studio is bankrupt?'

He wished she'd react instead of repeating his words back to him. Wished she would do something, say something, get angry . . . get it over with.

'How did that happen?' she was asking. 'I thought it was so successful . . . You said it was always booked up. What on earth went wrong?'

'Bad decisions . . . bad debts . . . I invested too much in the new mixing desks and software . . .' Even now, when the chips were, literally, down, Freddy found the truth was stuck fast in his throat.

'No! So this is what's been bothering you. Why didn't you tell me, you idiot? I can help out, lend you some money till you get back up and running.' She shook her head at him. 'I'll pay for the wedding. I offered right from the start. He's my son, my responsibility – you didn't have to be so generous.'

She reached across the table and took his hand. 'We can sort this out, Freddy. Is it very bad, the debt? Would my money be enough?'

He couldn't look at her.

'I mean, if necessary, you could sell the flat, couldn't you? We don't need this grand place. We could find something smaller . . . Freddy, speak to me.'

His wife clasped his hand more tightly, then let it go and tried to raise his chin with her fingers, so that he would look at her. But he was crying now, in great breathless gasps, the sheer enormity of the mess only really hitting him at that very minute, as he viewed it through Lily's eyes.

'Freddy?'

She got up and came round the table, sat down beside him and put her arms around his shoulders, dropping a kiss on the side of his head. 'Please, don't . . . Just tell me, tell me exactly what the situation is. I'm sure it's not as bad as you think. We'll figure something out.'

Eyes brimming with tears, he finally turned to her, his fingers tearing at the napkin in his hand. 'No. No, we can't work it out. This is way, way worse than anything you could possibly imagine. So bad that when you hear the full extent of my fuck-up, you'll never speak to me again.'

'Stop it, Freddy. You're frightening me.'

He steadied his breathing, wiped his tears away with his napkin. 'I'm a gambler, Lily. Plain and simple. I've lost it all, gambled it away over the past year or so.' He saw the incomprehension in her face. 'Everything's gone.'

'Everything? What do you mean?' She moved back.

'I mean every single penny . . . gone.'

'But what about this flat? It must be worth millions.' Her voice was still strong, still hopeful.

'It's rented.'

'Rented? But you said . . .'

'I lied to you.'

'Why?'

'I don't know. I suppose I wanted to be someone I'm not, someone you would love.' It sounded pathetic, but it was true.

Lily was silent as she sat beside him, arms now hugging her body, head bent.

'You're a gambler,' she said, as if she'd suddenly heard what he said. She looked up and he saw her eyes were full of disbelief. 'I don't understand. What sort of a gambler? Horses? Cards?'

'Roulette.'

'You've gambled everything you own at a roulette table? Honestly? When? When were you doing this?' And then he saw the penny drop. 'Those nights when you said you were working . . . you were in a *casino*?'

'Sometimes. Not very often until recently . . . This last year, maybe nine months, has been particularly bad.'

'That's ridiculous,' Lily said, almost to herself.

'I always think I'll win,' he said softly.

'But I thought we were happy. Why would you destroy that?'

'I've been happier with you than I've ever been in my whole life.'

Bewilderment filled her eyes. 'So why, Freddy? Why did you need to do it?'

'I don't know.' He didn't, but he was aware his problem had nothing whatsoever to do with Lily or the life they'd shared these last few years.

'How long have you been a gambler?' she asked, after another moment's silence.

He didn't answer, didn't want to face the fact himself.

'What – all your life? Before you met me? After you met me . . . ? God, I can't believe this. Why the hell didn't you tell me? We could have done something. There are hundreds of places you can go to get help.'

She got up, angry now, finally angry. After a few moments' pacing up and down the kitchen, she came back to her chair and plonked herself down. 'Okay . . . listen. This isn't the end of the world. You might have to go bankrupt, but we can survive that. Maybe you'll lose the studio, but we can live on my money, rent somewhere cheaper. I'll pay for the wedding . . . You can get help.' She rubbed his back encouragingly. 'Nobody died, Freddy.'

Not looking up, he said, 'Good as. Your money is gone too.'

Freddy watched the colour drain from his wife's cheeks.

'All of it?'

'All of it.'

'No! No, you can't have . . . You said you'd given it to your broker. You said Jonathan had invested it. You said . . .'

'I lied.' He looked her straight in the eye. 'I lied to you, Lily. Comprehensively lied. I stole your money, literally stole it, from under your nose. There's nothing left.'

'But . . . are you honestly telling me we have nothing – no money, no assets, no investments?' She blinked, her mouth working furiously. 'How much? Tell me how much you've lost.'

He welcomed her anger. Until his last sentence extinguished her hope once and for all, she still seemed intent on being kind, on helping him . . . loving him. He didn't deserve that.

He began to gather up the multiple debts in his head, line them up for inspection, but the task was too great.

'A lot.'

'How much?'

He knew she wasn't going to let it go so he began the dismal litany. 'Sixty to a man called Lau Heng, seventeen for the wedding, two months' salaries at the studio, about fifty. Overdraft, forty odd. Tax . . . God knows. Your money. My bookie, Barney . . . Lost track of how much I owe him.' He saw the shock on her face. 'There are others pending. Our ex-accountants have applied for a County Court Judgement. The studio rent is overdue . . . It must be close to half a million.' He had no idea, in fact, if this was true. The real sum could be twice as much for all he knew.

Her mouth dropped open. 'You've gambled half a million pounds? Half a million of other people's money?'

Freddy tried to take her hands, but she snatched them away, hunched over, swaying slightly back and forth, her bare feet pressed together on the rungs of the chair.

'I don't believe this.'

'I'm so sorry,' he said. 'I know it's pointless to tell you that, because it's beyond sorry, and there's nothing I can do to make it better. But I am sorry.'

'What are we going to do about the wedding?' Lily said

after what seemed a long while, her voice small, her eyes, now raised to his, blank with shock. 'What are we going to do, Freddy?'

He pulled her to him and she buried her head in his shoulder, this time not resisting his embrace. The life seemed to have gone out of him. It was as if his body were not his own. He felt no pain, no sorrow – although he knew he was sorry. Neither was there any urgency to sort things out. For the first time in his life he didn't have a plan. He didn't even feel he had the strength to comfort the woman he held in his arms. Nothing. He felt nothing at all. Freddy March, once revealed in all his true glory, had ceased to exist.

CHAPTER 17

Lily shut herself in their bedroom, leaving Freddy slumped in the kitchen. They had run out of things to say, because Lily didn't know what to ask. The problem seemed so massive, the shock so great, that her mind was blank.

Now she was pacing the large room like the proverbial headless chicken. She didn't know whether to get dressed, fall back into bed and cover her head with the duvet, go out, call someone, cry, beat the life out of her husband. She was shivering, wired to the hilt, and completely baffled.

She thought she should be scared, but she wasn't sure what to be most afraid of. A sudden and complete absence of money? Her husband's lies and secret addiction? Her marriage? Her son's wedding fiasco? How, in God's name, was she going to tell Dillon and Gabriela that the wedding was off? Sitting down on the bed, she realized she was having trouble believing what Freddy had said. The whole thing felt like a hoax, a ridiculous novelizing of their lives, and any minute now he would appear at the bedroom door to tell her it was nothing more than a bad joke.

Just now, in the kitchen, Freddy had kept asking her why she wasn't angrier with him. But how can you be angry with a situation you don't understand? Yes, the facts were there, but getting her head round the destruction of the whole edifice of her life surely took longer to digest than a mere hour. She would be angry; other people would be angry too, she anticipated that. But right now she just felt crazy.

Hating to be alone in the debris of the bomb just detonated, Lily went to find her husband, even though Freddy had been the cause of the explosion. He was exactly where she'd left him, his head sunk on his arms at the kitchen table, eyes shut. *Is he asleep*? she wondered, incredulous that anyone could find even temporary peace in his situation. But he lifted his head when he heard her bare feet on the tiles, staring at her with his dark eyes, now bleak with misery. She wanted to shake him, to make him tell her he was mistaken, that no such preposterous nightmare existed. She waited, absurdly, in vain.

Freddy got up, came round the table and took her in his arms. He was warm and felt safe and strong as always. She allowed herself to wallow in his embrace. They stood pressed together for a long time, neither wanting to let the other go.

When finally they pulled apart, she said, 'We'd better tell Dillon.'

'I'll do it,' he said.

'What about the rest?'

'I don't know, Lily. I don't know.'

She went to sit down, resting her elbows on the table. 'Won't it just mean bankruptcy?' She looked up at him, willing him to engage. 'That's only for a year, I'm sure. We can survive it, can't we?'

Brushing his hair off his face with both hands, combing his fingers through the waves, he shook his head. 'It's not as simple as that. The Chinese guy who lent me the sixty thousand won't be pleased. He's not the type to go for a CCJ. Then there's Barney. I don't know what he'll do, but he has some distinctly villainous sidekicks.'

'What are you saying? That someone will send the heavies round to rough you up?' She was joking, but he raised his eyebrows.

'Something like that.'

'*Seriously?*'

'I owe a lot of money to a lot of people, Lily. They'll be angry. And they'll think I'm hiding stuff, that if they threaten me I'll cough up.' He sighed. 'I get it. How would I feel if someone owed me such a huge amount of money?'

'So . . .'

Freddy, leaning against the work surface, his hands in his pockets, didn't speak for a while. Lily was someone who liked to have a plan. She had always been of the opinion that any problem had a solution if you looked hard enough. And she felt he wasn't looking hard enough. 'For God's sake, Freddy. You must have worked out this would happen sooner or later. Don't you have a Plan B?'

Not looking at her, he said, 'I always thought the next spin would sort things out.'

Throwing her hands into the air, Lily said, 'But that's ludicrous. How could you be so stupid?'

'All I can say is that it felt possible at the time.' He met her eye. 'In fact, it still seems possible. If I had enough stake money, I would try again.'

Lily didn't know how to respond. 'How much have you got left?'

'About a thousand.'

'How long is this flat okay?'

'Till the end of April, but the landlord might kick off once he hears about the bankruptcy.'

Silence.

'What are we going to do?' she asked, for what must have been the tenth time that morning.

Her husband didn't reply at once. Then he said, 'Can you go and stay with someone? Prem, maybe.'

'Me?'

'Lily, look, I'm a liability. You mustn't be around me right now. It not only might be dangerous, but I have to sort this out on my own. You don't deserve any of this. The best plan is that we separate. Let me deal with my appalling mess.' He gave a wry smile. 'Plan B, if you like.'

Lily's heart lurched. Through the gruelling morning of revelations, not once had she imagined that they wouldn't work it out together. 'Separate? You want us to separate?'

Freddy grabbed her hands. 'Listen to me, will you? You need to understand. I don't *want* to. You know the thought of being without you tears my heart out. But it's not fair on you. I can't do what I have to do and expect you to stand by and watch.'

'What *is* it you have to do?'

'I've told you. I don't know exactly, but it won't be pretty. And I don't want you to be part of it.' He looked away. 'Anyway, I can't understand why you'd want to be with someone who's done what I've done to you.'

'I love you?' She gave him a puzzled frown, wondering, after all they'd shared, that she needed to say it.

A look of frustration, presumably at her stubbornness, crossed his face. 'But I've fucked up. I'm not that man you say you love. I'm a fraud, a liar . . . a compulsive gambler. You don't love this version of me, Lily. How could you?'

Lily didn't know how she could either. She only knew that she did.

'It's only bullied politician's wives who stand by the garden gate, holding hands and smiling at their scumbag husbands,' Freddy added. 'You don't have to do that . . . You *mustn't* do that.'

Lily's phone, sitting on the kitchen table, buzzed. It was Dillon. She showed the screen to Freddy, who took the mobile, pressed it to his ear and walked quickly out of the room. She didn't follow, having no desire to hear what was said. She was suddenly overwhelmed by a rare cowardice in the face of her son's inevitable distress. *I'll speak to him later*, she told herself, feeling sick at the thought.

Shut in the bathroom, the shower on full, she crouched in the wide stall hugging her knees, warm water pouring down on her bent head.

Freddy doesn't mean it, she kept telling herself. *He's falling on his sword, trying to protect me after the event. Trying to do the decent thing, even if it's a bit late in the day. Separation would break his heart – he told me that. He just thinks he ought to leave. He's pre-empting what everyone else will say.*

An anguish akin to the grief she remembered after Garret's death assailed her, made her gasp for breath. *No, no, please . . .* Her words were silent. *I can't lose him, please, I can't. Not Freddy as well. Please, not Freddy.* She did not know or care to whom this plea was addressed. Not a believer in the God her parents had introduced her to in Sunday school, and subsequently at the church they attended every week without fail, she found herself, nonetheless, at moments of crisis, reverting to her childhood training and saying prayers to the heavens, putting her fears out there, seeking help from an undefined higher being.

Her hair damp, skin glowing from the heat of the shower, she automatically rubbed cream into her face, spritzed her arms and legs with body oil, as she did every day, pulled on a pair of black jeans and a long-sleeved white T-shirt over her underwear. She opened the bedroom door and listened. Was Freddy still talking to her son? But there was silence in the large flat. She padded along the corridor to the sitting room. Freddy was not there, only her mobile lying on the coffee table.

She called out to him, went back along the passage to the kitchen, called again. She could hear the note of panic in her voice, but the fear that he had already left her dissolved her guts, made her heart wild in her chest. There was a silence in the empty rooms she found eerie and threatening.

With shaking hands, she pressed Prem's number. Her friend answered immediately.

'Hey, you must be psychic, I was just about to phone you. Do you and Freddy fancy supper on Saturday? Raj and Hal are over and I know they'd love to see you. But no doubt you two are gallivanting off somewhere smart, as usual.'

Lily found she couldn't speak.

'Lily? Are you there? Hello?'

A sort of strangled sob escaped her.

'Lily . . . say something, for God's sake. What's happened?'

Words tumbled out through her tears.

'Slow down, take a breath. I can't understand a word you're saying.' Prem's voice was urgent. 'What was that about Freddy?'

'He's . . . he's . . . lost all our money, every . . . penny. Gambled it . . .' Another bout of sobbing drowned out the rest.

'That's insane.' There was a shocked silence. 'Listen, Ian's gone to lunch and I can't leave the shop till he comes back. But—'

'No, it's okay, I know you're busy. I just . . . I just . . .'

Lily had a moment of surprise that it was only lunchtime. It felt as if a whole day, a year, a lifetime had passed since she'd woken that morning, so oblivious to what was about to happen.

'I'll text him right now, get him to come back. Stay where you are. I'll be with you as soon as I can.'

Prem hung up, leaving Lily to give full vent to her tears.

CHAPTER 18

Gabriela had been screaming, cursing, then invoking God and the Devil in a turbulent mix of Portuguese and English, since Dillon had told her about his phone call with Freddy. Now she was just lying on the sofa – the new one, specially bought for them to sleep on when her mother came over for the now non-existent wedding – and sobbing noisily.

He'd gone into the office at six that morning to sort out the edit, having slept barely a wink. The tiresome document was taking for ever and Dillon was sure he was missing stuff, his mind so far from the words on the screen that his normally forensic ability to spot a mistake had all but deserted him.

He hadn't slept because his stepfather's sangfroid in the face of Suzie's threats – supposed to soothe Dillon, no doubt – had been very far from reassuring. Not even his mother's clear belief in every word that came out of her husband's mouth had convinced him. So it hadn't come as a huge surprise when Freddy had finally told him the unpleasant truth.

That it was not a surprise, though, did nothing to diminish the shock – or the dread of telling his fiancée. He knew he couldn't ring her with such bad news: he had to be there for her. So he had told his boss that Gabriela wasn't well. He'd then downloaded the file he needed to finish onto his laptop and biked off home at top speed, his brain whirring as he tried to put together the best words to explain their predicament.

In the end he'd just told her straight out. There was no way he could see of sugaring the pill. 'Freddy can't pay the rest of the money. Nor can Mum. We're fucked.' And the screaming began.

Now she lifted her head from the cushion into which she had been pressing it for the last ten minutes. Puffy-eyed, skin pink, light-brown hair straggling damp around her cheeks, she gave him a furious look as she hurled the cushion onto the floor. 'He's a bastard. A bastard, bastard, bastard.' Her accent made the first syllable short and explosive.

Dillon was sitting uneasily on the edge of the small kitchen table opposite the sofa. 'He didn't seem to believe that Suzie would actually cancel it. He said it would look really bad, that they'd never do it.'

Gabriela sat up, her expression disbelieving. 'Does he think he's the Queen of England? Who lets someone have a wedding they haven't paid for?'

'I know. To be honest, he seems a bit unhinged, as if he's totally lost it. He was rambling on about how it was all his fault, how he'd let us all down, how Mum was a saint . . . How he'd really believed he would win.'

'*Meu Deus*,' she whispered softly. 'Freddy gambled our wedding away. He's a nice man – I don't believe he'd do that.' She bit her lip, a fresh horror obviously presenting itself as her eyes widened. 'Mamãe! Mamãe's coming and there's no wedding? What are we going to do?' She covered her face with her hands, began rocking back and forth on the sofa, small moaning sounds escaping from beneath her fingers.

Dillon came to sit next to her, ignoring the insistent buzz of yet another call from his mother, trying to keep his anger under control in the light of his fiancée's meltdown. He was baffled by Freddy, but found most of his rage directed towards his mother. She must have known what Freddy was doing. How could someone indulge in a habit that extreme and his wife not have a clue? And how could she have given all her own money to him without monitoring it? So bloody naive it took his breath away. She had called him four times now, but Dillon didn't want to talk to her.

He put his arm round Gabriela's shoulders. 'Listen, I've been thinking. It doesn't have to be a disaster. We can still get married, just somewhere else. There are hundreds of restaurants—'

'Nowhere is going to have a place at the last minute for a hundred and fifty peoples.'

'People,' Dillon said automatically. Gaby's English was very good. She had lived in London for nearly ten years now, coming over on a bursary at nineteen to study arts and festival management at South Bank University. But whenever she was upset, her language lapsed.

'That's what I said.' She glared at him and he backed down.

'We can ask Nino. He'd be sympathetic – he might close the place for the night.' He thought for a minute. 'We'd have to cancel most of the guests, just keep it to family and very close friends. Wouldn't be more than, say, twenty-five? Less, even. It might work.'

Gabriela stared at him. 'But we can't get married in his restaurant, can we, Dill? Remember? The place has to be legal for marrying.' Her features tightened. 'Like the Roof Gardens.'

'I know. But we've registered, filled in all the forms, we're officially set up to get married *somewhere*. We just have to tell them we're changing the venue. I can't see why that would be a problem.'

'Really?' Her voice was rising now. 'Okay, so *where do we go*?'

He knew he had to come up with something fast. But he didn't have a clue. 'I'll ring the registrar and ask. They must have a list of designated places. Or I can check it out online.'

She shook her head in frustration. 'God, Dillon, you are living in another world. How do we pay for this new place? Have you forgotten? We don't have money now.'

Dillon had forgotten. Or, at least, he was so used to asking his mother and stepfather to bail him out – not huge amounts, but he only had to hint at something he needed, like a new bike, for one of them to suggest they might help – that he couldn't get his head around the fact that this source, which had been a constant safety net in his life, through his gap year, university and beyond, had suddenly dried up.

For a brief moment he wondered what his mother would

do now. But part of him didn't really believe the two of them had absolutely nothing left. Not wedding money, perhaps, but surely enough to keep going. Freddy had said it was 'disastrous', but his stepfather was not above exaggeration when telling a story, usually for comic effect, although there was no comedy here.

Dillon searched his brain for someone who would stump up, but it would involve a fair amount, even if they scaled it right down. Most of his friends were just scraping by, still employed on short-term contracts, with no guarantee of future employment past a few months.

Getting up from the sofa, he said, 'I'm going to ring Sara.'

Gaby nodded, a spark of hope in her eyes. She was slightly in awe of his sister, whom she saw as so competent, so ambitious, so clever.

Sara's mobile was engaged and he left a message. It was a long ten minutes before she called back.

'Have you heard?' he asked, not even saying hello.

'I've just been talking to Mum. What a nightmare. She said she'd been trying to get hold of you.'

'Huh!' His sister was taking her usual phlegmatic approach to life. Nothing seemed to faze her – normally a trait he admired. Today, however, he was thoroughly irritated. 'I don't want to talk to her.'

'Oh, come on. It's not her fault Freddy's a compulsive gambler, Dill. She sounded in a terrible state.'

'*She*'s in a terrible state. You should see Gaby,' he said.

'Yeah, no, I get that. She must be devastated. What are you going to do about the wedding?'

'I haven't a sodding clue. Maybe you can tell me what you'd do if your wedding was cancelled last minute and you didn't have any money to organize another.' He took an angry breath. 'And you've got your crazy Brazilian mother-in-law coming to stay in your tiny flat for two whole weeks for a wedding that isn't going to take place. Plus a whole raft of equally crazy sisters and aunts and cousins and God knows who else arriving on these shores.' Another breath. 'What would you do, eh, Sas?'

'Hey, don't take it out on me. I've only just heard. It must be a total nightmare for you both.' He heard her say something muffled to someone else. 'But, wow, can you believe Freddy? I mean, I sort of knew he was a player – all those famous people he hangs out with, the parties, the yachts and suchlike. But it never entered my head he was frittering his millions away at a casino. What's poor Mum going to do?'

Dillon didn't want to think about Freddy. Or his mother. He wanted his sister to come up with a plan to save his wedding, and perhaps even his relationship.

'I'm going over to see Mum later, when I've finished here,' Sara was saying. 'She said Prem was there, but Prem has to get back to the shop and I don't want Mum to be on her own. She must be freaking out.'

Dillon felt a brief shaft of guilt. Then the anger returned. 'I'm sure it's not as bad as they're making out. They must have some money left somewhere. I mean, there's the flat—'

'Rented,' Sara interrupted. 'I think it must be serious, Dill. Freddy would never have ruined your wedding if it wasn't. He's not like that.'

'So you say. But obviously neither of us knows even vaguely what our stepfather is like, do we?'

'True.' His sister fell silent. 'Listen, ring Mum. Please. She's got enough on her plate without you kicking off too.'

Dillon didn't answer.

'Gotta go,' she added in a whisper. 'Talk later.'

She hung up and Dillon was left holding his phone, disappointed.

CHAPTER 19

Freddy answered the call from his bookkeeper as he walked away from the flat. He hadn't said goodbye to Lily, or told her where he was going, because he couldn't face her again. The hurt in her eyes, the disbelief, had made him feel as if he'd been scorched all over. Yes, of course he'd known she would be upset – he had gone over the grim scenario a million times in his head. But he hadn't really believed it would ever happen, not really. When he did think about the impact on his wife, he had imagined rage and blame, explosions that would somehow blow him away. He'd expected her to banish him, to tell him, quite reasonably, never to darken her door again. What he hadn't bargained for was her strange desire to see it through together. And her love for him was an agonizing twist of the knife. She wouldn't walk away from him: *he* had to do the walking. Which felt almost too hard.

'Freddy, where are you?' Angus's voice was tense. 'There's

a bit of a situation here. Did you see the winding-up order against the studio in the *Gazette* this morning? All hell's breaking loose. Every creditor on the planet seems to have read the bloody thing. Bank's frozen the account. They're all baying for blood. It's Air-Live who've gone for us, the bastards. But we never got a petition. I'm just about to phone James. They can't advertise the order without serving us first.'

Freddy barely broke step as he walked along Bayswater Road towards Marble Arch. He'd been unable to face the Tube, needing to get some air after the nightmare morning. Astonished it had taken so long for one of them to go for the studio, he nonetheless knew that he had brought every ounce of charm to bear in persuading the other suppliers to whom he owed money to hold off. Air-Live, the company responsible for computerizing the mixing desks, was not the largest creditor by any means.

'They did serve us, Angus. I got the petition over a week ago.'

The bookkeeper was silent at the other end of the phone. He was a novice, Angus. Freddy had hired him only three months before, when Mike Stone from the accountants, Stone, Williams, had begun playing up, and put him in charge of the payroll, sales and purchase invoicing, petty cash and so on. But he had not given him access to the main account.

'Why didn't you tell me?' Angus asked politely – he was barely Dillon's age and this was one of his first jobs. 'Couldn't we have got James to apply for a CVA or something? Bought some time while we sort this out.'

He sounded so keen, Freddy was loath to disappoint him.

'Wouldn't have worked, Angus. The courts would need to be persuaded that the studio is viable for a CVA. And it's gone too far for that.'

Angus went quiet again. 'Okay . . . so . . .'

'Listen, do nothing. I'll be there in about twenty minutes.' He paused. 'And Angus, please don't tell Glyn or Isla-Mae or anyone yet. I want to do that myself.'

It was mild, threatening rain, no sign of spring in the grey London streets as Freddy walked on. He couldn't even muster the energy to get upset, because part of him welcomed the meltdown. It was a blessed relief to stop lying. People would take over his life now, tell him what was required. He wouldn't be able to do what the officials asked, of course – as in, pay up the thousands he owed – but there were reliable systems for dealing with these situations. He didn't care about being a bankrupt. He knew a lot of people in his fickle industry who had gone the same way. And it was the least of his worries, set against the backdrop of losing Lily, putting his workforce out on the street, ruining Dillon's wedding . . . knowing gossip about his gambling habit would be spreading like a virus around London's glitterati by now, his reputation shot.

He stopped in a coffee chain to get a double espresso to take away, and slowed his pace as he approached the Berwick Street building, sipping the hot, strong coffee, savouring it to an unusual degree, as if this day of reckoning had heightened his senses, made him intensely aware of the tiny pleasures in life.

*

149

Isla-Mae's face was noncommittal as she tidied her desk, piling the odd personal item into her capacious leather bag. In went a small cactus plant, an expensive-looking biro, a flower-patterned spiral-backed notebook and a royal blue mug upon which was printed, mysteriously, 'Leeds, born and bred'. Isla-Mae was Notting Hill through and through, her parents' Darlington vowels thoroughly expunged by a boarding school where any deviation from the distinctive slangy drawl adopted by such girls would attract merciless teasing.

Freddy hovered, watching her. The last hour had drained him. He had gathered his employees in the sound studio in the basement, where they perched uneasily among the equipment left by a band who were – or had been until today – recording their first album there. The lights were dim, a faint rubbery smell emanating from the new soundproofing. Freddy could smell coffee as he waited for Angus to arrive. Glyn had barely said good morning to him as he'd opened the heavy door, flanked by Wayne, Joachim, Samuel, Lee and Megan. Not quite the whole crew, but he assumed the other two were not working today.

They won't understand, Freddy thought as he toyed nervously with the cuff buttons of his stupidly expensive Paul Smith shirt. He missed his Rolex, but that had gone long ago – hocked, not stolen from a French hotel as he'd told Lily. *They'll think I'm lying, hiding my money, letting them go to the wall with a rich man's typical lack of concern.* Should he tell them the absolute truth? Or should he fudge it? *Will they be more upset, take longer to get over losing their jobs*, he wondered, *if I admit I gambled away their security? Isn't it better, in this instance, to lie?*

But he knew he couldn't win. They wouldn't believe him whatever he said. The truth, ridiculously enough, was the least believable scenario. It was doubtful that anyone earning what they did could even remotely conceive of gambling away hundreds of thousands of pounds. So he lied. He told them bad debts, bad decisions on his part and not enough financial savvy had led to the company's downfall. He told them he was devastated. He told them he had used every single penny he had to try to salvage the business – which was true, in fact. He told them he hadn't slept for six months worrying about their fate. He told them he was personally bankrupt. He said he was sorry. And again, as it had been with Lily earlier, the word was useless in describing just how penitent he was. A stupid, ineffective word that implied a sort of polite, minor-league transgression. He hated himself for continuing to repeat it in the face of the stony silence. But he didn't know what else to do.

Glyn, inevitably, was the first to speak. 'So that's it, then? We won't get paid?' His normally friendly gaze was shocked and sullen now.

'The receiver will decide who gets what, I'm afraid. It's out of my hands now. But you will all be creditors, obviously. And there's a lot of very expensive equipment to sell.'

'Being a creditor won't pay the mortgage,' Glyn said.

The others were silent, looking at each other, the floor, their mobiles, none of which had any signal in the cell-like studio.

'What are we supposed to do now?' Joachim asked tentatively. He was a first-class technician, a nerdy, pale, mostly silent young man, but always polite and greatly respected for his work. Now Glyn turned to him, his round face red and sweating in the stuffy, enclosed environment – no one had turned on the air-conditioning this morning.

Giving a harsh laugh, he said, 'Haven't you been listening to Mr March, here? Company's gone tits up, boy. We've been sold down the proverbial.'

But even after the baldness of Glyn's statement, his soft Welsh tones flat with anger, the faces bore little comprehension.

'Do we go, then?' Samuel asked.

'Yes,' Glyn replied. '*Yes*, you do bloody go, Samuel. Hoppit, all of you. Fuck off home, if you've still got one to go to. Nothing for you here.' He cast an aggrieved look at Freddy and made for the door, letting a welcome gust of air into the heavy atmosphere.

Freddy was sweating too. The caffeine hadn't helped, his nerves already shredded, and now, as he watched his workforce file out slowly, heads bent, he knew he had to sit, or fall down. Slumping against the wall, he spotted a low, rickety stool, which must have belonged to the drummer of the band using the studio, and lowered himself onto it. Swaying, he tried to take deep breaths, then doubled over as a stabbing cramp racked his guts. *Does it get much worse than this?* he wondered. But he knew the answer was probably a resounding 'yes'.

Now Isla-Mae spoke, her tone not unsympathetic. *But then,* Freddy, thought, *she doesn't have a mortgage, or even rent. She still lives with her parents in the wide, leafy stretches of west London.* 'Did you speak to Dad?'

'I did.'

'And he couldn't help? Really?'

Freddy smiled. 'He knows me too well, Isla-Mae.'

She obviously wasn't sure how to take this, and bent to her task of packing her stuff.

'I'm sorry it had to end like this. You've been really great,' he said, and she smiled up at him, her square, rather plain face registering a mild embarrassment at the compliment.

'Yeah . . . I've enjoyed it.'

He didn't know what else to say, wasn't sure if he should hug her or something. He was fond of her, had known her and her brother, Red, since they were babies. But being her boss was new to him and he'd always felt slightly awkward with it, if he were honest, never knowing what, of his work practices, she was feeding – innocently enough – back to her father. So he turned, with a smile and a wave, went into his office and shut the door behind him.

He thought of Joachim's question, 'What are we supposed to do now?' and felt a chasm opening in front of him. A void. No work, no wife, no home, no family, no money. Probably no friends either – no one wanted to be associated with such spectacular failure in case it proved contagious. His brain knew the truth, but his mind was unable to take in what it really meant.

Feeling a bolus of grief forming in his gut, and worried he would break down, start to howl if he didn't get a grip, he stood up, went over to his favourite spot by the window, his arms raised, hands resting on the wooden frame, and looked down on the busy market. Real life, not his ridiculous version of chaos. It distracted him momentarily.

Then a well of misery bubbled up, unrelenting, until he found his chest heaving silently as he tried to control himself. *Isla-Mae must not hear me cry.* Hand over his mouth, he gulped, tried to breathe, but he was unable to stop the self-pity punching through his lungs, his throat, his whole body now convulsed. And the harder he tried to stop, the worse the constricted sobs became. He ended up crouched beneath the windowsill, clutching his knees to his chest, head buried, rocking back and forth in some attempt to find a modicum of calm.

All he wanted was Lily. He was desperate to feel the comfort of her arms around him. The desire to turn back the clock was agony because nothing, absolutely nothing, would change what he'd done.

Just one more night, he thought. *Please, just one more night with Lily.*

But he hesitated as he reached for the phone, not knowing if she would even speak to him. By now she would have rung someone. Sara, maybe, Dillon undoubtedly, possibly Prem – her go-to friend when she was in trouble. He could imagine the collective shock. The disbelief. He could hear the names they would be calling him: criminal, addict . . . bastard, bastard, bastard. They would have ignited her anger, finally made her hate him. Persuaded her, certainly, that she couldn't associate with him any more. And her deluded determination to stick by him would have been steadily chipped away to nothing.

Not wanting to hear any of this in her voice, he texted her. *We need to talk. Sorting stuff at the office. Could be home later, if you'll have me? xxx*

Almost immediately the reply came: *Please come home. x*

He could hear the tears in Lily's message and he hated himself with a fury that made him want to punch something, do damage in a physical way that would take the pain away. He stood there, crushing his mobile in his hand, his body rigid, shaking, but even in his rage aware that Isla-Mae was just outside.

I must look completely mad, he thought, as the red haze began to subside. *I don't want to scare the girl, on top of everything else.*

Pulling himself together as best he could, he smoothed his hair, rubbed his face briskly with both hands – as if he could wipe off the nightmare – and straightened his shirt. Then he stood, taking long, slow breaths until he felt his heart rate return to some approximation of normal. His watch said two thirty. There would be a hundred emails – none of them pretty – waiting on his laptop, but he wouldn't look at them. What could they do to him now, anyway? There was nothing to save. He would clear out his stuff and go home. No doubt the studio landlords would be organizing a lock-out at any moment. They would have seen the *Gazette* and he was nearly two months behind with the rent.

Isla-Mae knocked, poked her head around the door. 'I'm going, Freddy.'

'Yeah, okay . . .' He put on his best smile. 'Thanks again, Isla-Mae. You've been a star.'

She hovered, clearly uncertain as to what to say next. Then she nodded, smiled back. 'Hope things work out,' she said.

'I'm sure they will.'

CHAPTER 20

It's as if someone's died, Lily thought, watching Prem and Sara muttering to each other across the sitting room, casting surreptitious glances, full of pity, her way. She was sitting sideways on a chair by the doors onto the balcony, gazing at the passing clouds, scudding grey and threatening, yet backlit by a persistent sun. The chair was a trendy wooden upright in bleached sycamore, the back a single plank of knobbly wood, by some famous furniture designer – hideously uncomfortable, for show, not for sitting. But she didn't want to be comfortable. This was not her home any more. None of this stuff – which she now doubted even belonged to her husband – was for her use. She would have to pack her life into a few bags and go.

Losing all your money is not the same as losing a husband, she knew that. But everything about today reminded her of Garret's death. The shock, the disbelief, the almost physical desire to reject the information. That day, ten years ago, had been almost a cliché, a scene Lily had watched play out a million times in TV drama. Bell rings. She opens the door. Two solemn-faced police on the doorstep, one male, one female. The 'May we come in?' request, unlikely to be denied. A silent process through to the kitchen, more silence as they sit, both looking bulky and uneasy in uniforms set about with the clobber necessary to their job.

The twins, was her first thought. It was two in the afternoon: they were at school half a mile away. Her brain refused to go any further, but her body had no such qualms as her heart battered her chest, her stomach turned to water and she gulped hard to stop her recently eaten tuna sandwich returning to her mouth.

'You are Lillian Tierney, Dr Garret Tierney's wife?' the male officer, identified at the front door as Tony, asked, his voice deep and frighteningly kind.

'Mr,' Lily said. 'Garret's a surgeon. Surgeons are called "Mr".' She heard her words from a distance. They were standing in for her, preventing Tony saying any more.

'Sorry . . . Mrs Tierney, I'm afraid there's been a terrible accident.'

Frowning, she stared at them. Rhona, the female officer – who should have been working for her GCSEs, not gazing at her like that, her head on one side – looked as if she wanted to run away. Her knuckles, Lily noticed, were white as she clenched her hands neatly on the wooden tabletop.

'Your husband,' Tony was saying, 'had a very bad fall . . . on the ice. Very bad indeed.' Pause. 'I've been told he died before reaching hospital.'

Lily, not understanding, said, 'But he wasn't skiing. He said he didn't have time to ski. He was speaking at this conference in Geneva. We talked last night.'

Tony and Rhona nodded sympathetically and in unison from the other side of the table.

'I'm sorry, I don't know all the details yet, Mrs Tierney. I was told he was in Geneva at the time of his death.'

'Yes, I spoke to him last night,' she heard herself repeat. The feeling she was keeping at bay was so unbearable that she refused to allow it to come any closer.

'I'm so sorry,' Tony said.

Lily shook her head. 'You're telling me that Garret is dead? That he slipped on the ice and died?'

Both officers nodded.

'But how is that possible? He's so fit. He was a champion skier when he was younger.'

'I think it was a head injury.'

A head injury. How ironic. Garret had spent his life dealing with the after-effects of head injury. But no one had been there when he needed help.

'Where is he?' Lily asked. It seemed vital that she know where her husband was. She felt as if he were adrift, alone somewhere in the frozen wastes of the Swiss Alps. She should go and help him.

'They said he was still at the hospital in Geneva.' Tony paused. Rhona still hadn't said a word. 'Is there someone we can call, Mrs Tierney? Someone who can be with you?'

The rest of the day, the week, the months ahead, settled into a strange pattern which, if charted, Lily had later thought, might look like one of those ECG printouts Garret had shown her years ago when her mother was ill with heart problems. Daily life wobbling along the bottom, but spiked with irregular, unpredictable moments of intense pain. She had been surprised at how much of it she could bear and not die herself.

She jumped now, as Sara put a hand on her shoulder and offered her a mug of tea. 'Come and sit with us.'

For a while she did as Sara asked and perched on the sofa, holding the mug she'd been given, Prem at the other end, her daughter on the grey armchair by the fireplace, all of them silent.

'What are you going to do?' Sara asked.

Lily shrugged.

'Obviously you can't stay with Freddy, Mum.'

'Why not?'

Prem and Sara exchanged glances.

'It sounds as if he's a bit out of control,' her friend said gently.

'To say the least,' her daughter added.

'You make him sound dangerous. He's not dangerous.'

Prem raised her eyebrows. 'Well, depends how you see it, Lily. He's a gambling addict, which makes him totally unpredictable. Even you had no idea what he was doing or how bad it was.'

I know all this, she thought impatiently.

'He took all your money, for God's sake.' Sara's voice was harsh. 'Stole it. Lied to you. Ruined Dill's wedding. He's made you homeless and broke ... I don't understand why you would even contemplate staying with him for another second. Or ever speak to him again, for that matter.'

'No, well . . .'

She knew they had her best interests at heart, but she wished they would all go away. They didn't understand, or know Freddy as she did.

'"No, well" nothing,' her daughter retorted. Lily could tell she was still angry about her unsympathetic reaction to her affair with Ted. It was ironic, her judging Sara about her life then failing so spectacularly at her own. But at least Stan hadn't told her about their lunch together.

'You can come and stay with me,' Prem said, ever practical, ever generous. 'I can't offer you a job in the shop at the moment, but if someone leaves you can come back.'

Lily smiled at her. 'Thanks. Thanks so much, that's very kind. But I'm sure I can sort something out.' She and Freddy would sort something out, was what she meant. But she wasn't going to tell them that, then have to deal with the hysterics that would surely follow.

Sara came over, sat down beside her on the edge of the sofa and picked up her hands, squeezing them firmly in her own. She fixed her blue eyes on her mother as if she could compel her to do what she thought best and said, 'You don't seem to get it, Mum. I know all this must be a shock, but you've got to get real. We all love Freddy, but he really has betrayed you. For whatever reasons – and we all know addicts can't help themselves, they don't deliberately set out to behave badly – he's wrecked your life. If you stay with him, you'll both end up in the gutter.'

The word 'gutter' echoed in the silence.

'I think your mum is having a hard time believing what's happened,' Prem said. 'The trouble with gamblers, I suppose, is that you can't see it on them, in the way you can with drink or drugs.'

'That doesn't make it any more acceptable,' Sara said.

'No, of course not. I didn't mean that. But it makes it harder for your mum to understand.'

Sara let go of Lily's hands and stood up, her slim body wired with frustration, her curls wild from repeated raking with her fingers as she began to pace the rug on the other side of the coffee table, arms folded angrily across her chest. 'Did you really not know, Mum? Weren't there any signs?'

Lily didn't answer at first as she trawled back over the last few months of her life with Freddy. 'He's been very tense recently, as I said. And he's been out a lot . . . but then he always is. His work at the studio is often at night. And Freddy's a networker – he goes to clubs and bars with clients, wines and dines them, generally hangs out. It's his job.'

'And what did he say when you asked him what was wrong?'

'That a client who owed him a lot hadn't paid up.'

Sara snorted. 'See? Another lie. Christ!'

'It wasn't a lie. There is a client who hasn't paid up,' Lily said.

'So he says. But how do you actually know?'

Lily was saved from answering by the beep of her phone, which was lying on the wooden coffee table. She knew it was from Freddy before she even picked it up. He wanted to come home and she wanted him to come home too.

Under the suspicious gaze of the two women, she texted back.

'Freddy?' Sara asked.

'Listen,' Lily got up, 'I really appreciate you both coming to my rescue, but I know you're busy and I'm fine now. Apologies for disrupting your day like this. I just panicked. I'm sure I can work something out. I'll let you know later, okay?'

Prem got up at once at Lily's words, but Sara didn't move. Standing there, a wary frown on her face, she twisted her mouth, looking hard at her mother. 'He's coming back, isn't he? And you don't want us here when he does.'

'Sara, please. I know you mean well, and you're both talking complete sense. But I have to do this my way.'

Her daughter shook her head and didn't reply, just marched over to the chair where she'd left her bag and her jacket and snatched them up. 'Okay, you do it your way. But please, please, don't trust that lunatic again, Mum. Promise? We all know you're a softy, but just remember what he's done.'

Lily wasn't going to promise anything. So she just hugged her daughter and thanked her again for giving up her day. And Sara had to be content with that.

'Come and stay with us,' Prem repeated when the door had shut behind Sara. 'We can help you work out what to do. Raj and Hal are staying till next week, but there's plenty of room.'

When Lily didn't reply, she went on, 'Why don't you pack a bag and come now? I don't have to go back to the shop – Ian's there. You can get the rest another day.'

And when Lily still didn't say anything, she added, 'Lily,

Sara might have come on a bit strong, but she's right. I know how much you love him, but you really can't let Freddy coax you into more chaos. If you stay with us, at least you can let the dust settle, give yourself some breathing space to think.'

Lily smiled at her friend. 'I do hear you both, really I do. But I have to see him, Prem. I have to at least talk to him before I do anything else.' She gave a short laugh. 'Anyway, there's nothing left to lose now, right? Damage is all done.'

Freddy did not come home until late afternoon. Lily, tense and so anxious to see him, heard every sound outside the flat with hope. She couldn't settle to anything. Even sketching didn't work today, the lines blurring in front of her eyes, the scribbles random and meaningless.

By the time he opened the front door, she had fallen into a doze, curled up on the sofa, her cardigan wrapped around her cold limbs.

'Lily?' Freddy lay down next to her and she let herself be taken in his arms, let him pull her close, his head resting against her own, his lips in her hair, kissing her softly. She began to cry.

'Ssh, ssh . . .' He stroked her back, held her tight. Neither spoke for a long time. They lay, rocking slightly, as her sobs quieted. Neither had the strength to move.

Eventually Lily pulled back, looked up into Freddy's troubled face. He didn't smile, his eyes full of guilt. For a moment they gazed at each other. He cupped her cheek with the palm of his hand, ran his thumb across her skin, and she shivered, began to drag herself upright.

As they sat together on the sofa, she said, 'I've had Prem and Sara here for hours, telling me never to speak to you again. Telling me I can't trust a word you say. Telling me you're a worthless bastard, basically. A nice bastard, but a bastard nonetheless.'

A small, hard sound escaped him. Then he turned to face her. 'Prem and Sara are right, Lily. I've fucked up so badly, I don't have a thing to offer you except hassle and more hassle. I have no idea what to do, where to turn, and I'm not dragging you any further down than I have already.' He swallowed hard.

Silence.

'Can't we go away?' she asked. 'Wait for things to settle down . . . We could go to Scotland or somewhere, rent a small croft in the Highlands . . . You could do all the stuff you need to do, sorting things out, online. We could . . . I don't know, find a job up there . . . You could get help.' She stopped, the scenario patently too childish, too ridiculous. How could they rent somewhere with no money? What sort of a job was she qualified to do? And the Highlands would hardly be thick with recording-studio work for a bankrupt . . . Or Gamblers Anonymous meetings.

Freddy just raised his eyebrows. 'Lily . . . Lily, we can't stay together, not at the moment. I'm a mess. I can't look after you.'

'I'm not asking you to look after me. I'm saying let's get through this together. Why should we split up? What's the advantage?'

'The advantage is that you don't get involved in my chaos. Let me deal with things, Lily. It'll only be for a few months. I can do what I have to do, work something out . . .'

'I don't want you to go. We're married . . . I love you.'

Freddy sighed. 'God, I love you too, Lily. But I keep telling you, I'm a mess. You can't be responsible for me when I'm like this.'

'So you're just going to walk away, is that it? Leave me without any means of support? What the hell am I supposed to do? Don't you owe me more than that?'

'I owe you way more. But I'm telling you, I can't deliver right now. You'd be better off without me, much better off.' Freddy was beginning to sound angry in his desire to make her understand.

The conversation went on in this vein, round and round, punctuated with tears on both sides, bursts of anger and frustration, getting nowhere as Lily refused to let Freddy go and Freddy refused to let Lily stay.

Hours later, both on the edge, they resorted to the only thing left that wasn't contentious, that didn't involve their past or their future and which went some way to soothing their battered nerves. They made love, right there on the sofa, their clothes yanked off and thrown to the floor, their bodies drawn together in a mutual attempt at fending off the outside world. As he entered her they both let out a loud groan of relief, never wanting to come, but crazy with the need to do so. The sex was fierce and short, both of them trembling as they flopped back against the cushions, breathing hard. They were both too tired to speak. Huddled together, Freddy pulling the throw from the back of the sofa over their naked bodies, they fell into a deep, exhausted sleep.

When Lily woke, Freddy was gone.

PART II

CHAPTER 21

Lily lay on her back in the single bed, under the stiff hollow-fibre duvet in the spare room of her sister's house. Her eyes were wide open, watching the beams from the occasional car stretch across the ceiling through the spotted blue and white curtains on the wooden pole.

Ten days before, when she'd woken alone on the sofa, the first thing she'd done was call out to her husband. But there was no response. She'd quickly pulled her T-shirt and pants over her nakedness and gone to look for Freddy in the silent flat. There had not only been no sign of him, but no sign that he had gone either. The bags and cases he might have packed his clothes in were all there. His shirts and suits, boxers, socks and shoes looked untouched. He had taken nothing, as far as Lily could see. *He's popped out for some food*, she told herself, as she flopped down on the bed. *He'll be back later*.

When he wasn't, she tried to ring him. But time and time

again she got the same diversion to voicemail. As the evening wore on and he still did not appear, telling herself that he wasn't answering his phone to avoid his creditors, or because it had run out of juice, or because he had lost it, began to hold no water. She lay huddled in bed, her limbs frozen, her body stiff even under the thick duvet, waiting.

It wasn't till around midnight, when she finally dragged herself up to make a cup of tea, that she found the message. Written on a torn-out page from his Moleskine notebook, it was tucked between the apples in the wooden fruit bowl on the kitchen table – almost hidden, as if he didn't want her to find it – and said:

My dearest Lily,
We disagree about how things should go, but I know this is the best way. I'm no bloody use to anyone at the moment.
Love you with all my heart,
F xxxx

She had known, absolutely, that he would leave her. His mind had been made up long before he'd come home to her that afternoon; none of her arguments and pleading had made the slightest difference. The note made her cry, but part of her was relieved that he'd gone, because the pain of waiting for him to do so was almost worse.

He'll ring with a new number, Lily comforted herself. But Freddy didn't ring. Not that night, or any subsequent nights. He had simply vanished.

Initially she had been reluctant to leave the flat, despite the familiar rooms feeling empty and slightly sinister now, no longer a place of safety since her husband's assertion that people who wished them harm might be hovering beyond the front door. Freddy had told her the rent was paid until the end of April, but Prem had warned that the landlord might terminate the lease immediately, once he knew about the bankruptcy. Leaving would mean throwing herself on her friends' charity – Lily hated that thought. And ... Freddy might come back.

She had not been able to sleep that night, having already slept, and the darkness stretched out, lonely and cold. As the hours passed, during which she sat curled up on the sofa, half asleep, her mind whirring, Lily's anxiety mounted. But as soon as she lay down in bed, exhausted, she began to cough, immediately recognizing the return of an age-old foe as her chest tightened.

Sitting up and reaching for the inhaler in the drawer beside the bed, she took two long blasts of Ventolin. The sensation of tightness began to ease, but her anxiety fought against the medication and almost immediately the breathlessness returned, this time with a vengeance. It was as if someone was strangling her, reducing the airways to almost nothing. However much she tried to breathe in, her chest didn't seem to move an inch. No air was getting through – it was like breathing through a straw.

She knew she must not panic. The long years of childhood echoed with the mantra: 'Stay calm, Lily, light breaths, slow breaths, watch the lamp.' Her father's voice rang in her ears, and she could almost feel his firm hands around her shoulders as she sat on the edge of the mattress in the dim light of the penthouse bedroom. There was no lava lamp to watch now. The glowing, sea-green waxy swirls floating up and down the glass cylinder had calmed her, distracted her when she'd felt an attack coming on.

She was shivering and frightened as she stood, still coughing, still snatching at breath. She staggered into the bathroom and turned the shower on full, to the hottest setting, until the room was filled with steam – it sometimes eased her chest – and leaned back against the tiled wall, eyes closed. It was warm, pleasantly womb-like, and after a few minutes she could feel her body begin to relax as her breathing gradually returned to something like normal. But it had frightened her. She knew she should not be alone.

Prem and Anthony, as promised, had taken her in. The morning after Freddy left she had packed two large cases with clothes, sketchbooks, art materials, photo albums, laptop and a couple of books and gone back to Fulham, two roads away from the family house in which she'd lived with Garret for most of their marriage. She felt as if she were stepping back in time, the intervening years washed away, wasted.

But she was the ghost at the feast. Despite her friends' kindness, Prem's brother and his partner were staying for their annual visit and there were dinners planned, the house full, people to catch up with, family visits. Lily knew her gloomy silence, her inability to join in, was casting a pall over proceedings. It wasn't fair on anybody. After three nights, she bit the bullet and rang her sister.

'Oh, my God,' Helen had said, on hearing the news. 'Well, I'm not going to say a word, but—'

'Thanks, I'd appreciate that,' Lily interrupted her. Helen had always been deeply suspicious of Freddy's charm.

Helen's offer of the spare room had been typically grudging. 'It's not what you're used to,' she'd told Lily, 'but you'd be welcome to camp out while you find something better.'

Lily didn't feel welcome at all. It had been a last resort.

The bedroom at her sister and brother-in-law's house was small, up in the eaves of the thirties red-brick semi-detached off north Oxford's Banbury Road. It was painted a neutral cream and minimally furnished. The bed faced the window, with a narrow pine chest of drawers immediately on the right by the door, a free-standing metal rail for hanging clothes crammed next to it and a rug, beige and patterned with thick, ugly circles in primary colours, on the laminate floor by the bed. The only other furniture was a rough, wobbly, unvarnished bedside table – definitely not David's work, perhaps one of Kit's school projects – carrying a small red desk lamp.

It was cold, still only April, and a wet, chilly spring so far. Lily was freezing: the radiator under the windowsill was not working, and every time she moved around the room, she hit her head on the sloping ceiling. But Lily did not complain. She had been in Oxford a week now and, although stunned and thoroughly miserable, was grateful for the shelter her sister had offered.

'Poor Dillon. Poor Gabriela,' Helen had said, the first night of Lily's stay, as she laid the white china dish of macaroni cheese on the kitchen table and dug a serving spoon into the crisp, bubbling cheese topping, directing the handle towards Lily. David had made the supper – he did all the cooking. 'What on earth are they going to do about the wedding now?'

Helen was still in her work clothes: a light grey trouser suit, ill-fitting across her broad bottom, the jacket cut too short for her tall figure, a cheap, plum-coloured crêpe-de-Chine blouse beneath, which did nothing for her pale complexion and greying auburn crop. It was almost, Lily thought, as if she *wanted* to look as unattractive as possible, a two-fingered gesture to a world that had somehow disappointed her. Although she had a PhD, a professorship, had had two books published on business management, was married to one of the best husbands in the world and had all the material things she could wish for, Helen seemed permanently disgruntled. Yes, her son was an ongoing nightmare, but her disgruntlement predated Kit's addiction by twenty years.

Growing up, her sister had been the one with the looks. Lily had ached with envy at Helen's beauty, her ability to attract boys, a string of them beating a path to her door from when she was fifteen. Back then she had been striking: tall, with their father's thick auburn hair worn long down her back, a slim, athletic figure from all the sports she played, and those huge, fierce grey eyes, which seemed to draw the boys in with promises never fulfilled. Helen was not interested. She would cast them off with utter disdain, making Lily and her mother, often witness to these dismissals, wince

174

and beg Helen to be nicer. But Helen, angry, it seemed, from the bottom of her soul, brushed off their pleas with scorn.

Only David, large and bumbling and kind, had managed to get under the wire one very hot day when the inner tube of Helen's front wheel had blown and got stuck in the tyre rim. She couldn't even push the bike without the rubber getting caught in the spokes.

Stranded on the Broad in the centre of Oxford, the rooms she shared with an American student way out in the further reaches of Summertown, she had been cursing under her breath, staring accusingly at the tyre, arms akimbo, when David Herring had stopped and offered to carry the bike home for her. Helen was twenty-four, still a student, doing her PhD in business studies. David was a carpenter, seven years her senior, much in demand with the Oxford professors for his cabinet-making skills. They had, after all, a lot of books.

And strangely, since Helen had rejected half of Oxford by then she had allowed David to court her. It must have been love, Lily always assumed, although Helen had never said as much, making out that David was merely decent and accept-able rather than her knight in shining armour – she hated to be dependent on anyone. But David didn't seem to mind. He clearly adored his wife, even thirty-three years on, her iras-cible temper and bossiness, her put-downs, seeming to go clean over his shaggy head.

'I don't know. Dillon won't talk to me at the moment,' Lily replied. 'He thinks I must have known about Freddy's gam-bling. He blames me.'

Lily had made every effort possible in the days since the

debacle to speak to her son. She knew there would be an enormous amount of hassle associated with a cancelled wedding. Even though much of the preparation was the responsibility of the venue, there would still be guests to inform, the registrar, wedding cars and band to cancel, Gabriela's dress to be returned. She wanted to help. But Dillon had refused to return her calls. Maybe because she kept trying and he'd got sick of it, he had eventually sent a cold one-line text: *We're dealing with everything, Mum.*

No 'love', no kisses. He hadn't told her in so many words to fuck off, but that was the message Lily took from her son's text. She understood his anger, but it cut her to the quick.

Helen raised her eyebrows. 'Hmm . . .' She seemed about to say something, then bit her lip. 'I suppose I can see his point . . . the scale of it. You must have had some inkling, no?'

'No.' She didn't bother to explain further. There was no explanation that people would understand, beyond the weakness of love.

'I always thought there was something . . . sort of *indulgent* about Freddy,' Helen went on, as if Lily hadn't spoken. 'He was too charming, too . . . perfect—'

'They could have it here,' David interrupted, from across the table. His face, as he approached sixty-five, was lined and weather-beaten, his blue eyes faded, his chaotic mane – previously corn-coloured – now almost entirely grey. But there was strength to his physique still, and he had a quiet confidence that Lily had always found reassuring.

She smiled at him. 'That's incredibly kind, David. But

they have to get married in the borough where they registered, which is Islington.' She paused. 'I wish they could come here.'

'Well, I don't,' Helen retorted, thrusting the green plastic salad bowl into Lily's hands. 'I have absolutely no desire to be responsible for a last-minute wedding, even if it is Dillon's.'

David shot a surreptitious grin at Lily, but didn't press the issue.

The kitchen where they sat was a functioning, unremarkable room at the rear of the house, backing onto a strip of paved patio and a square of lawn, surrounded by mature plants and shrubs such as roses, azaleas, sedge grass, potato jasmine along the fence, a large magnolia and a pear tree. David was a diligent, if not a passionate gardener – his passion reserved for his furniture – and the garden was tidy, the plants carefully pruned, the grass unmarked by moles or moss.

They ate in silence, Lily staring ahead at the photographs on the far wall next to the cupboards, mostly of Kit as a child and a young man, back when there had been so much hope. One of the frames contained a pen-and-ink drawing Lily had done when Kit was about ten. His young face, framed by strawberry-blond curls, impish, with his mother's intelligent grey eyes, looked out at her with an unintentional poignancy. She remembered doing the drawing, catching the boy when he was in the garden one summer, trying – unsuccessfully – to get him to sit still for more than a second while she sketched him. She really loved Kit. They'd had a bond when he was growing up. He'd always made her laugh with his crazy inventions and witty responses.

'So where is Freddy now?' Helen was asking.

'He's . . . I don't know.'

Her sister eyed her with disbelief. 'Really? You mean he hasn't told you?'

Lily shook her head, wishing she would shut up.

'I don't understand. Where could he have gone? You don't think he's run away . . . left the country?' Helen's eyes widened in alarm behind her rimless varifocals. 'I certainly hope not, because there are legal obligations attached to bankruptcy. If Freddy doesn't deal with them, he risks being in contempt of court.'

'Of course he's going to deal with it. He told me he would.'

The look on her sister's face implied this was hardly proof. 'So why can't he tell you where he is?'

'He doesn't want me involved, he said.'

'Huh. I'd have thought it was a bit late for that.'

Lily didn't reply. The numb ache that had set in, like bad weather, since Freddy had walked out made it hard for her to concentrate on what her sister was saying. It was as though she were battling through thick fog even to hear the voices around her.

'Well,' Helen said, into the silence, 'you'd better make a plan, I suppose. You'll have to get a job, sort out your finances . . .'

'Leave her alone, Helen.' David, a man of few words who'd been characteristically silent over supper, sounded as if he would brook no argument. 'She's only just got here.'

'Yes, but—'

'You can talk about it another time.'

It was unusual, in Lily's experience, for him to be so firm with his wife. And, maybe because of this, Helen was silenced.

Later, when Lily had made her excuses and gone up early to bed, she'd had a moment on the stairs when she felt like someone else and wondered what on earth she was doing there. It seemed impossible that she was now exiled to this attic room, alone, her family in tatters, her son not speaking to her, totally, utterly broke. And Freddy . . .

CHAPTER 22

'For God's sake, Dillon, I can't help you. I don't know what the fuck to do either.' Sara had met up with her brother in the café round the corner from Dillon's flat. He hadn't wanted to talk in front of Gabriela, who was still alternating between stony silence and bouts of uncontrolled sobbing.

'Yes, but I can't get a straight answer out of Gaby. I don't know what she wants. I think doing it hole-and-corner in some dump we both hate is stupid. We haven't the money for anything decent so it's bound to be a disaster. But Renata's still coming over, then Gaby's sisters and everyone else next week, even though there might not be a wedding now. My instinct is to leave it till next year, plan the whole thing properly. But her family won't be able to afford the tickets again any time soon. And she'll want them at her wedding, obviously.'

He could tell his sister wasn't really listening. She kept

checking her mobile and texting. Bloody Ted, no doubt.

'Sas?'

'Sorry.' She put her mobile into her bag and gave him a deliberately attentive look, moving her coffee cup to the side as if that had been the impediment to her concentration. 'To be honest, Dill, you don't seem to have a choice. If you haven't got the money for a venue then you can't get married. End of. Presumably the town hall is full?'

He nodded. 'For weeks.'

'Well, then, you'll have to let it go, won't you? Think again once the dust has settled.'

'Thanks for stating the bleeding obvious.'

Sara threw her hands into the air. 'Well, what are you asking me for? I can't magic a free wedding out of thin air, Dillon.'

'Maybe I wanted a bit of sympathy. A sympathetic ear, at least.' He sighed martyrishly. 'But, hey, I can see your mind's elsewhere. Have you told poor Stan yet?'

His sister's expression morphed into a frown. '"Poor Stan", as you call him, hasn't been in touch for nearly two days. I haven't had time to go home, been working back-to-back shifts, but he won't return any of my texts. I don't know what his problem is.'

'Hmm, let me think . . . Could it be somehow, I don't know, Ted-related?'

Her eyes widened. 'Really? You think so?'

But Dillon didn't get her sarcasm. 'Christ, Sas. Don't be so fucking naive.'

'No one knows.' Her tone was sullen.

'Ha. Someone always knows.'

'We've been incredibly careful.'

Suddenly Dillon had had enough. 'Whatever. Not my problem. Listen, I'm off.' He made to get up, but his sister reached across and grabbed his wrist, holding tight until he sat down again.

'Sorry, Dill, sorry. I'm as much of a mess as you. I just don't know if Ted is serious . . .'

Now it was Dillon's turn not to listen. He didn't have the will to deal with his sister's affair. From what she'd said, this Ted fellow had always sounded suspect, on course to break her heart, but it would do no good to tell her so now.

They sat in silence, the sky darkening outside the café window.

'God, look at us,' Sara muttered. 'Two months ago Mum and Freddy were blissful, I was nicely engaged to Stan, your super-glam wedding was on track . . . Things were so sorted. And now it's like we've all been fucking shipwrecked.'

Dillon nodded slowly. 'I know, right?' Then a thought struck him. 'Gaby won't leave me if we postpone the wedding till next year, will she?'

Sara considered this. 'If she does, she does. It wasn't meant to be.'

'Always count on you for encouragement.'

His sister gave him an apologetic grin. 'No, well, can't come up with anything better right now.'

'How's Mum?' he asked as they stood on the pavement a few minutes later, giving each other an awkward hug. His mother had been the elephant in the room since the two had

182

sat down earlier. He felt guilty about her, but he wasn't ready to let go of his anger yet. Cowardly as it was, he also didn't want to hear that her life was as shit as his, and have to sympathize.

'Ring her and find out,' was his sister's wafting reply, delivered over her shoulder in a sing-song voice as she strode off towards the Tube, dark coat billowing behind her.

When he got home, Gaby was on the phone, speaking rapidly in Portuguese. When she saw him she turned her back, not even acknowledging his presence and barely pausing in her conversation. The call was interminable. Dillon wanted to wrench the phone from her hand because he needed to talk to her right now, tell her the decision he'd finally settled on. The wedding would not happen this year. He was knocking the whole thing on the head, putting an end to all the uncertainty. It was the best thing for both of them.

When Gabriela finally said goodbye to whoever she was talking to she turned to face him. Her pretty face, normally so expressive, looked oddly blank.

'Who was that?' Dillon asked, a knot of fear forming in his stomach.

Gabriela didn't answer, just shrugged her small shoulders. She was staring at him, phone clutched in her hand, looking as if she wanted to speak, but saying nothing as she stood stock still by the sink. She was dressed in grey sweatpants and a tight, long-sleeved black T-shirt, the neck low, revealing the top of her breasts. Her hair, normally so groomed, was lank around her face, her eyes still retaining puffiness from the days of crying. Dillon wanted to take her in his arms, but something held him back.

'I'm going home,' she said.

'Home?'

She came to him then, took his hands in hers, looked up at him with her large brown eyes. 'Mamãe is very upset, *querido*. I have to go and see her.'

Dillon didn't understand. 'She's not coming tomorrow?'

Gabriela seemed evasive. She dropped his hands. 'No.'

'Is she ill?'

'No, she's not ill, but she's very upset. She thinks . . . she thinks . . .'

'What? What does she think, Gaby?'

His fiancée wouldn't look at him. 'Oh, nothing, it's stupid.'

He pulled on her arm till she met his eyes again. 'What? Tell me what she said.'

After a long pause, she said, 'She thinks you never wanted to marry me. That this is an excuse. She says it's not possible that someone would lose all their money like that.'

Dillon felt himself flushing. 'I don't understand. She thinks I'm *lying* about Freddy?' He was stunned.

She shrugged, said nothing, twisted her arm out of his grasp and turned away.

'Gaby? Come on. You know that's total crap. She – *you* can't honestly believe for a single second that I've made the whole Freddy thing up just to get out of marrying you?'

She swung round to face him, gave him a sad smile. 'No, of course I don't think you made it up, *querido*. My mother is

184

not very sophisticated. She doesn't understand people like your stepfather.'

'She's not the only one.'

'No . . .'

'Please . . . *please* don't go to São Paulo. Not now.'

Another shrug, then Gaby wandered over and sat down on the sofa, drawing her legs up under her, brushing her hair off her face and winding it in a rope behind her head.

Dillon followed her, sat down beside her.

She said, 'Bruna says Mamãe thinks it's a bad omen . . .'

Frustrated, Dillon cursed loudly. 'A bad omen? That's fucking ridiculous. How can Freddy going bankrupt have anything to do with you and me?' He scrutinized her face. 'You don't believe that, Gaby . . . For God's sake, tell me you don't believe that.'

A silence followed that seemed to stretch for ever. Then Gaby said, 'No, of course not. I'm not superstitious like my mother. But things like this make me think.'

'About what?'

'About us.'

Dillon's heart banged in his chest so hard he clutched his crossed hands to his sternum, pressing hard as if to keep it in place. He gasped, then the feeling subsided almost as quickly as it had come. He took a few steadying breaths. 'I love you, Gaby. I love you so much. Don't leave me.' Tears, from the physical effort of keeping himself together, began to spill down his cheeks.

His fiancée saw them and her face filled with pity. 'I love you too.' She wiped his left cheek with her fingertips, a gesture so gentle it only made him cry the more. 'But you are difficult to love sometimes. You seem all closed up. I try to get through to you, but you shut me out.'

Dillon stared at her, baffled. 'I don't know what you're talking about. What's this got to do with the wedding and your mother?'

'It's not. It's to do with us.'

'Are you saying . . . What are you saying?'

Gaby let out a sigh, a sigh of such unhappiness that Dillon embraced her at once. But there was no responding hug: she just lay in his arms like a doll, quite still. Neither moved for a while. Dillon was waiting for her to answer him.

When she finally pulled free, she seemed more distant, more business-like, getting up off the sofa without looking at him, collecting her phone from the table, walking towards the small bedroom at the back of the flat.

'I have to go home,' she said.

CHAPTER 23

The night Freddy had woken naked on the sofa, beside his still-sleeping wife, he had not meant to leave her. Not then, not yet. He wanted more time, just to be with Lily, somehow to imprint upon her how much he loved her, before tearing himself away to put his life in order. But as he'd tiptoed quietly through to the bedroom to get dressed, left the flat to get some supper – *soup and decent bread, maybe, something light* – before Lily woke, he realized he was just prolonging the agony, dragging out the cold inevitability that he couldn't stay with her.

Lily was too generous, too loving. She just didn't seem to fathom the extent to which he'd let her down. But one day she would, and then she would be very angry. *Best to part before that happens*, he told himself. And he hoped, by the time she began seriously to resent him, he would already have shown her his dedication to cleaning up his act, getting his house in order. Then they could be together without having first torn each other to shreds. *It'll only be for a couple of months, max*, he told himself, as he'd walked along Bayswater Road in the darkness, directionless, no plan in mind except a childish need to escape further recriminations, further responsibility.

The person he'd finally phoned, around ten thirty that night, was an old girlfriend. They had been friends first and last, with a brief, ill-judged liaison in between, to which neither of them had been committed, the boredom of a hot summer in London – fifteen years ago now – weakening their resolve. She had since bagged herself a lugubrious Austrian count, and had four blond *Sound of Music*-style children, but they'd remained occasional friends.

Freddy knew Bettina would ask no questions, her house in Belgravia big enough to accommodate him – and half London, indeed – without anyone really noticing. He could hole up for a day or two and avoid all the people baying for his blood, from the Official Receiver to Lau Heng and Barney, his bookie.

It was not so much the liquidation of the company or the inevitable personal bankruptcy that Freddy feared – although he knew he would have to work hard with the Official Receiver to justify some recent accounting lapses. No. That was just a process, he told himself, albeit a tedious and time-consuming one, which would put restrictions on his financial future, his reputation, but wouldn't threaten him personally. It was the other creditors – below the radar – who could make life very unpleasant for him. But he was kidding himself. The whole thing turned out to be much more daunting than he'd expected.

Bettina had disappeared with her brood to Scotland for the last of the Easter holidays, leaving the house silent except for the occasional incursions of Alya, the delightful Malaysian housekeeper, who insisted on making his bed every morning as if he were in a hotel.

He had gone back to Sussex Square two days after he'd left, ringing the bell repeatedly before he went up, to check that Lily had gone. He'd been fairly certain she wouldn't stay there without him, sure that Prem would step in, look after her, give her back her old job, perhaps. And he'd been right. There was no sign of his wife, although her presence lingered painfully, the ginger scent of her body cream pervading the bathroom, a few items of clothing still in her side of the built-in wardrobe.

With an Addison Lee taxi ordered to arrive in half an hour, and spooked by being in the flat, which no longer belonged to him, Freddy had snatched up his stuff as if he were robbing the place. All the furniture, linen, towels and kitchen contents were part of the exorbitant rental, and now seemed like a painful reminder of his careless extravagance. So he took only personal items, things that mattered to him, including his clothes, laptop and tablet, chargers, a box file of papers, their wedding photo – which Lily had ominously left behind – two framed drawings by his wife and some books. He also packed his Canon 5D and high-end Bose sound system, which he intended to trade for cash. The stuff he didn't need for his intended travels he stacked in a corner of the capacious basement storeroom at Bettina's house.

The following week he spent shut away in one of Bettina's spare rooms, amid the most ridiculous luxury of floor-to-ceiling silk Colefax and Fowler curtains, deep-pile wool carpets, cashmere throws in timeless greys, Floris bath oils, and pure Egyptian cotton sheets with a thread count higher than the sum total of his remaining cash.

His time was entirely taken up with clearing out his old life and creating a new, anonymous one. Because the burden of those to whom he owed money lurked like a monkey on his shoulder, he no longer felt safe in the street, although he told himself he was exaggerating, that it was absurd to think he might be physically attacked in broad daylight in the middle of London in the twenty-first century.

He also wanted to avoid a chance encounter with an acquaintance or friend. When he was out and about he felt that everyone was looking at him, as if his shame were burned on his forehead like a branding. It wasn't his imagination either. Tommy Nars, a technician he'd worked with years back, had been approaching him on the Soho pavement the previous day. He'd thought of Tommy as his friend and had employed him in the past. He watched the man swerve when he saw him and cross to the other side of the street. Just the thought of that encounter cemented his desperate need to escape.

So he raked through his emails, answering virtually none, then began the laborious process of saving addresses and other email data before closing the account and setting up a new Hotmail address.

He bought another pay-as-you-go mobile and took a while transferring essential numbers, breaking up his old Sim and flushing it down the loo, like a gangster.

He dug out a credit card in his previous name, Frederick Slater, which had a small borrowing limit that he had kept ticking over since he'd changed his name by deed poll in his twenties, the card replaced every few years but seldom used. He'd forgotten about it until he found it in the bottom of the box file. It wouldn't solve anything for very long, but it might buy a plane ticket or a hotel room . . . rent a car.

He fixed a meeting with James Hardy, his solicitor – James had insisted on seeing him immediately.

It was a nightmare. The man bombarded him with a list of documents as long as your arm that Freddy would have to produce for the receiver, questioning him on every last aspect of his complex finances until Freddy felt like screaming, 'Shut the fuck up!'

He was disoriented. None of it made any sense to him. He had never been good on detail, always leaving it up to others to sort out his financial affairs. But those people were now gone. Even Angus, who had hung on, offering his services – Freddy suspected because he wanted the experience – had backed off when Freddy explained he couldn't pay him even a small amount.

'I need to get away,' Freddy had said to James.

James, a man of Freddy's age, suave and jolly, undoubtedly rich, with a trencherman's paunch and expensive tortoise-shell glasses on his broad nose, looked aghast. 'You can't go anywhere, dear boy. Our receiver friend will demand your presence at a meeting, probably within the next two weeks. You'll have to pitch up. And there's a mass of paperwork to prepare . . .' He stopped, frowned. 'Get away where?'

Freddy shrugged. 'Anywhere. Can't stand it.'

James raised his fair eyebrows. 'No, no, I can see that. Nasty business all round. But once you've got the documents together and had the meeting, things will settle down.'

Freddy nodded as if he were agreeing. James knew nothing about his other debts, or his gambling.

'There were times when I took money from the company . . . not large amounts, but will that be a problem?'

'What do you mean, "took money"?'

'Well, borrowed money from the company . . . personally. I think you call it a "director's loan"?' He didn't really have any idea what it was called.

James was instantly alarmed. 'What are you telling me? You took money from the company you weren't owed?'

Freddy was uncertain.

'That's very serious. How much are we talking? And how often?'

Freddy genuinely had no idea. He remembered five thousand he'd liberated after a client had paid up, gone in one night at the tables. Another two grand the month before. But it could have been a lot more, he knew. Stake money, he'd seen it as, and had been certain he'd return it the following day.

He told James what he could remember, the solicitor giving no sign that the amounts were either better or worse than he'd supposed.

'Hmm ... We'll have to deal with this ASAP, certainly before you see anyone at the Receiver's Office.'

'But I'm the director of the company. I can pay myself what I like, can't I? It's not like I'm embezzling someone else's millions. It wasn't more than a few thousand . . . sort of loans for fundraising, trips to meet investors and stuff. I was trying to save the company.'

James shook his head. 'Fine, if you didn't owe anyone else money and your staff were being paid. But that doesn't appear to be the case. They'll take a dim view about your fitness to be a director, anyway, with this list of transgressions. You'll certainly be disqualified for a while.' He stopped and said nothing more as he chewed his lip, head bent, the bald patch in the middle of his pink scalp suddenly visible. When he looked up, Freddy saw resolve on his plump features.

'Okay . . . listen. Go through your statements and pinpoint when these so-called loans were paid out, then highlight them with a note as to what you needed the money for and send them over to me so that we can see the full extent.' He frowned at Freddy, obviously not sure his client was in complete possession of his faculties. 'Can you do that?'

'I can, I suppose.'

'Then we'll have to come up with a plan PDQ, reasons why these borrowings were legit, find some corresponding expenses, without compounding the problem and getting us both into trouble. By the way, who's been acting for you on the accounts since Mike Stone kicked off? Presumably you told whoever it is about the loans.'

Freddy hadn't told Angus anything, of course, so he replied,

'I just had a trainee guy managing the payroll.' At which the solicitor merely pursed his lips.

'There's a bankruptcy deposit to pay, Freddy, as I'm sure you're aware. Up front. Five hundred and fifty pounds,' James went on.

'*Five hundred and fifty?* I don't have it. Surely nobody does who's going bankrupt.'

His solicitor sighed. 'And an application fee of a hundred and thirty. Altogether six hundred and eighty.'

'But that's ridiculous. Where am I going to get money like that when all my accounts and cards are frozen?'

'Maybe a friend could lend it to you. Your principal shareholder . . .' he consulted his notes '. . . Mr Blackstone. Would he help out? He has a vested interest.' He was looking at Freddy as if he despaired of him, although Freddy was sure he couldn't be the worst offender James had ever dealt with, by a long chalk. 'Where's your wife in all this? Has she got money?'

'She did have,' Freddy muttered darkly. 'No.'

'Well, go away and think about it. It's not a lot of money for some of your friends, I imagine.'

Every day Freddy had been on the verge of calling Max. He was the only person who could save him. But his friend had made it abundantly clear at their last meeting that he wouldn't give Freddy another penny until he was clean and could prove it. 'The day you can convince me that you've stopped for a decent length of time, I'll help out.' Max had said something like that. *How can I ever prove I'm not doing something, anyway?* he asked himself petulantly. *And what is a 'decent' length of time?*

But the truth was that neither the quitting nor the length of time required were criteria met. Freddy had been to the casino every night while he was at Bettina's. He needed cash for his getaway. And over three subsequent nights he had won nearly fifteen hundred pounds – half of which he'd had to hand over to James for the bankruptcy. So he hadn't called Max. What with the money he'd got selling his sound system and camera – ripped off on both counts, inevitably, by the man in the Shepherd's Bush electronics shop because he could smell Freddy's desperation – he had enough, he reckoned, to keep going for a few weeks. Longer, maybe, if he was careful, and if his plan for Malta worked.

Freddy did not sleep the night before he was to meet with the Official Receiver. James had organized all the documentation, then briefed him on what and what not to say. But Freddy was almost shaking with anxiety as he made his way to the Victoria office that morning. His grim mood was not helped by the unlucky coincidence of bumping into Glyn Matthews in Victoria Street.

Freddy had seen the sound engineer out of the corner of his eye – realizing he must just have got off the train from Carshalton, where he lived – and panicked, quickly veering to the right, hoping to escape across the road. But a phalanx of buses was storming down the busy street in both directions, the tyres sending up clouds of spray from the earlier rain, and he was marooned on the pavement as Glyn, breathless, caught up with him.

'Thought it was you.' Glyn, unsmiling, made no attempt to shake his hand. 'Trying to avoid me, I see.'

When Freddy didn't answer, Glyn went on, 'Can't blame you, really. All a bit of a mess.'

Freddy had taken heart from the man's understatement and said, 'Glyn, hi. I'm on my way to see the Official Receiver right now. It's been a nightmare.' He smiled, but Glyn's expression darkened at his words.

'Nightmare, is it? I've been ringing and ringing you, Freddy. Phone's gone dead.'

Freddy squirmed. The man's eyes were like knives to his soul. 'Yeah, had to get a pay-as-you-go. All my accounts are frozen, so the old number's been cut off. I'm skint.'

Glyn's eyebrows went up. 'See, that's what I don't get. Man like you, wife like yours, friends like Isla-Mae's daddy . . . Seems hard to grasp, you running out of money like the rest of us.'

'Seems hard to grasp for me too.' Freddy was trying hard not to resent Glyn's hostile tone. 'Why were you calling me?'

Glyn gave a harsh laugh. 'Funny that. I was ringing to borrow some money. A loan, like. Having trouble with the mortgage, what with Cath not well still.' He shook his head. 'Should've known.'

Freddy just wanted to dissolve into the concrete of the wet pavement. The bleak despair, the disdain in his former friend and colleague's face were devastating. He had known Glyn for more than fifteen years, employed him for nearly ten. They had admired each other, been mates. But now he was looking at Freddy as if he actually hated him. And why not? Glyn had a sick wife, three teenaged children, and was probably having trouble finding another job quickly enough – despite his reputation.

'I'm so sorry, Glyn. I wish with all my heart I could help. You have no idea how terrible it is, knowing I've wrecked so many people's lives . . . People who depended on me.'

At the obvious sincerity in his voice, Glyn's face softened just a little. 'Yeah, well. Don't like asking for money, anyway. Just made me sick to my stomach when I heard Samuel say it's the gambling ruined the business.'

So he knew. Of course he did. Freddy bowed his head. There was nothing to say, no excuses to hide behind with his old friend. Standing there, he felt exposed in a way he never had before – even with Lily – stripped bare by Glyn's contemptuous gaze.

Mr Dubash, assigned to him by the Insolvency Service, was quietly polite, nondescript, not at all the disapproving ogre Freddy had anticipated – he was almost disappointed. Dubash had offered Freddy water in a white plastic cup, settled him at the beige, melamine-topped table in the otherwise bare interview room, and merely got on with the job in hand. Freddy kept waiting for judgement or rebuke, but none was forthcoming from the diffident official.

The meeting went on all morning, however, and Freddy, still distraught from his encounter with Glyn Matthews, had wondered if he would survive it, his head banging with lack of sleep, his whole body rackety with guilt and anxiety. He was sure the questionnaire he was asked to fill in and his answers to Mr Dubash's questions must have seemed confused, almost incoherent, the ravings of a mad man.

Sitting across from him, Mr Dubash did not give any response to the information Freddy offered. He merely listened to his answers with small nods, made his own notes, asked endless, detailed questions and waited patiently while Freddy scrabbled through his paperwork. He was probably used to the gibberish that scared, fractious clients presented to him in his line of work. But when eventually he let him go and Freddy was out on the street again, there was none of the exhilaration he'd expected to feel at getting over the first hurdle. He had merely slunk back to Bettina's mansion, head well down in case another victim of his chaos should pass by.

But now the meeting was over, his resolve to escape was absolute. It was only cowardice in face of the necessary contact with his father that held him back each time he reached for his mobile.

CHAPTER 24

Helen was in no hurry to get home, despite it being a Friday night and the end of a long and tiring week. She dawdled in her office after the others in the department had left, answering emails that did not need answering yet, making tea she had no intention of drinking, skimming a post-grad thesis she didn't have to read for at least another month.

Her reluctance to be home was two-fold: first, her sister's presence. Helen and David had found a rhythm in the years since Kit had left, which worked for them both. They didn't bother each other, David often staying late in his workshop or out in the garden, Helen pottering about, reading or planning the next outing with her birding friends.

She went out most weekends to Farmoor or Otmore in spring and summer, Port Meadow in the winter when it flooded and the over-wintering duck and waders arrived. It was a solitary pursuit, even in a group, most of the day spent outdoors in peaceful contemplation of nature, but Helen felt it saved her sanity. She and David would usually meet for supper, but not always. Sometimes it was a ham sandwich in front of the television – there were no rules. Just two adults with very different interests, living in harmony. Or that was how she chose to view her marriage.

Now her little sister had invaded their space, disrupted the harmony. Lily, to be fair, demanded virtually nothing of either of them, but she was still *there*, and even if Helen did not feel a duty to talk to her, include her in her plans, she was still lurking, a worrying presence Helen was unable to shut out.

And she wanted to help, of course. Although her sister's starry-eyed marriage to the ridiculous Freddy had always smacked of doom in Helen's eyes, being right held no pleasure. She loved her sister dearly, even though they had never really understood each other.

How long will she stay? she wondered anxiously, as she finally packed her laptop and mobile into her black nylon briefcase, switched off the office light and carried her still full mug to the kitchenette at the end of the corridor, where she emptied the contents into the metal sink and rinsed it.

The second reason she did not want to get home today was that David was going to see Kit. He went most Fridays. Helen, as always, felt her heart skitter at the thought of what he might find. She imagined death, certainly, her beautiful son lying in a pool of his own vomit, a needle hanging out of his scrawny arm. She imagined disappearance, Kit taking off, perhaps, to London where he had friends – *Do junkies have friends?* – and never being seen again, the years stretching out with the pain of not knowing. She worried about violence to David, when he pitched up with all good intentions – cleaning the place, bringing tinned soup, stew, beans and fruit, taking the rubbish down to the bins – then being attacked because he wouldn't give Kit or his mates money. But her real dread was hearing the details of what David had found.

He wouldn't tell her unless she asked, and often it took a day before she dared. But in the end she would have to listen and feel the pain all over again, beat herself up for being a coward and not going with her husband, wonder if she should change her mind, if there was something they weren't doing that might save Kit. It was the same sequence each time, and each time she came to the same unsatisfactory conclusion: she could not see him like that. Compared to poor Kit's life, Lily's temporary lack of funds paled into insignificance.

Saturday morning, and Helen had requested a family conference. Lily had been with them nearly two weeks and nothing had been discussed about her sister's future since that first night, when Helen's enquiry had been firmly shut down by her husband. But something had to be done.

Now the three of them sat round the kitchen table, David looking preoccupied as if he were miles away, her sister gazing blankly out at the garden. Helen had a pad of paper in front of her, and a biro which she was clicking impatiently, watching David slowly pour coffee from the cafetière and hand a cup to both her and Lily, stir brown sugar into his own, leave the wet spoon on the wooden table – *men*.

'Right,' Helen said, feeling as she did in one of her first-term seminars, chivvying ten half-asleep nineteen-year-olds texting on their phones. 'Let's start with what you can do, Lily. Skills.'

Lily blinked, turned her attention from the garden, raised her eyebrows very slightly. 'Well . . . I don't really have any.'

'Oh, come on. Of course you do. You can draw. You volunteered at the hospital.' Helen stopped, drew a blank. Her sister had married Garret at twenty-three, just out of art college, then chosen to be a full-time mother, which Helen had never completely understood. The lack of ambition, lack of desire to interact with the world outside her family, baffled her. 'And there's Prem. She employed you for years. Doesn't she have anything she can offer you?'

'Not at the moment. And even if she did, I couldn't afford London rents or the commute. I still had the house when I worked there before.'

She saw Lily's eyes glaze over. Her sister had barely gone out since she arrived, just trailed round the garden, staying up in her bedroom most of the time. Helen was worried: she looked so pale and was even thinner, if it were possible, than usual. And she was making no effort to look nice, or even wash her hair. Those jeans were the ones she'd been wearing all week.

'Okay. Let's think of the options.' She looked at her husband, who was playing with a piece of green twine he must have brought in from the garden, head bent. 'David!'

He jumped. 'Yes. What?'

'Please, we've all got to pull together on this. Lily needs help.'

'Right . . . right. Okay.' He sat up straighter and turned to Lily. 'What do you like doing, Lily?'

She gave him a sad smile. 'Not much, really. Drawing mostly. Reading. Films. Hanging out with the twins. Cooking, sort of, but I'm not very good at it.'

Helen refused to buy into her self-disparagement. 'That profile wouldn't even attract someone on Twitter, let alone an employer,' she said, her tone light, and Lily did smile. 'Do you touch-type?'

'Two fingers, I'm afraid.'

'And you don't cook. Did you do things like spreadsheets or bookkeeping at the chair shop? Logistics, maybe?'

Lily didn't even know what logistics were. 'God, no. Prem handled all the admin. I just dealt with the customers.'

'So retail, then. Perhaps there's a bookshop or one of those design places that sell silk cushions and stuff . . . things that an older person might be good at. Because the fact is that students are so cheap to employ round here.'

When Lily remained silent, the faraway look still in her eye, Helen, frustrated, spoke more sharply than she intended: 'Make an effort, Lily. You have to get work.'

'I know I do. And I appreciate your help, obviously. But I just don't know what I can do. As you point out, I'm not exactly a spring chicken.' She swallowed. 'I suppose I could work in a care home or something.'

'You could. Is that something you'd like?'

Rolling her eyes, Lily answered, 'No, I'd be bloody useless at it. But there doesn't seem much choice, does there?'

'No need to be snippy.'

'Sorry.'

There was silence, just the faint swish of David's

shirtsleeves rubbing across the table as he did cat's cradle with the string, his big hands calloused and scarred, chopped about by the tools he used to make his furniture. 'Why doesn't she just join an agency?' he asked, looking at Helen. 'They'll know what to do with her. Maybe she could be a PA to someone.'

'I am here, you know,' Lily said tartly, which brought a slight frown to David's forehead. 'Sorry, David.' She gave a long sigh. 'I'm being a brat. That's a good idea. I'll look online and find one.'

That seemed to satisfy them both, but Helen was not so easily pleased. 'You'll need some skills, Lily. You can't just sign on at an agency and say you can draw and type with two fingers, then expect to get a job. You'll definitely end up in a care home.'

'You could sketch the inmates in their final days,' David said with a grin. Then, seeing Helen's frown, corrected himself: 'Sorry, "residents". And type up their letters . . . slowly. Two-fingers Lil, the pride of Heaven's Gate,' he added, throwing his arms wide with a flourish and making Lily giggle. 'You've got to create a USP.'

'Oh, very funny. Honestly, I don't know why I bother.' Helen got up. *At least she's smiling*, she thought. It had been a rare event recently.

'Can't you sell your drawings?' David said, serious this time. 'You're good.' He pointed towards the sketch of Kit.

'God, no,' Lily replied, looking horrified at the suggestion. Helen knew she had done many portraits of her friends and their children over the years and thought her sister had talent but, as usual, Lily hadn't bothered to develop it further. It would take too long to build up a client base when she needed money right now, Helen's business brain concluded. But it was something she would talk to her about another time – a sideline for the future, maybe.

'If I were you, I'd go online and find a site that teaches you to touch-type. There are thousands – my students use them all the time. It won't take long to learn if you concentrate. I mean, you haven't got anything else to do at the moment. Then you'll have something to sell.' She knew she sounded prim and bossy, but what else would galvanize the woman?

It was only when she and David got into bed that night that Helen asked her husband about his visit the day before.

'I didn't see him,' he said, leaning back on his pillows with a sigh, holding his reading glasses in one hand, the latest Bill Bryson in the other. Two paragraphs would set him off snoring – no fault of Bill's. 'He wasn't there, I don't think.' He pulled himself up and turned on his side to face her. 'The door is usually snibbed, or even ajar – people wander in and out all the time, it seems. But today it was locked. The bell doesn't work, but I banged on the door and shouted through the letterbox. I couldn't see anyone moving about, but the kitchen has a blind, which is always down, and the letterbox just gives onto the corridor.' He paused. 'It didn't feel as if anyone was there, Helen. You know how you can tell.'

'Did you wait?' Helen saw the usual images looming in her vision with terrifying reality.

'I waited outside for a while, then knocked on the next-door flat. An old boy lives there who can hardly walk, but he usually opens up eventually. He must be away or something, because he didn't yesterday. I sat in the car for an hour at least, watching the entrance to the flats. Kit didn't come back, but he'd probably gone round to someone else's place . . . I don't know, just out looking for more drugs.'

'What should we do?' Helen asked, her nerves jangling. 'Suppose he's in there?'

'I'll go back tomorrow, see if he's about. There's this girl, Kirsty, who's often with him, and there was no sign of her either. The door was locked, as I said, so maybe they've just gone for a trip somewhere.'

'A *trip*? In the state he's in? For God's sake, David! From what you tell me, he wouldn't get to the end of the road. No, there must be something wrong.'

'Maybe he's not taking so much stuff at the moment. Maybe he's a bit better and they went to Scotland or something. The girl's Scottish – she may have relatives up there.'

Helen both loved her husband's optimism and was infuriated by it. David, she thought, made Pollyanna look like a party pooper, always putting a starry gloss on any situation – the exact opposite of herself. 'Shouldn't we phone the police? Get them to check the flat . . . just to make sure.'

'I don't suppose they'd take much notice. He's not a child. He can go out if he likes.'

'He's not a child, but he's a vulnerable adult, David. Doesn't that count?'

'Where drugs are concerned, not really. If they thought he was dealing, well, that's another matter. There'd be a dawn raid and the whole nine yards. Or if he was being violent . . . But an addict who's not home?'

'Yes, but maybe he is at home. Maybe he's lying there, unable to get up, unable to call out, just praying someone will find him and get some help.' An idea came to her. 'We could ring the hospitals, see if he's been admitted.'

David put his glasses down and reached over, put his large hand over hers and gave it a squeeze. 'The police know he's our son. I've told them often enough. They'll inform us if anything happens. They've been round to the flat a few times. But they can't do anything.'

Helen felt her eyes fill and blinked hard. What was the use of crying yet more tears for something she could not change?

CHAPTER 25

Freddy pressed the front door of the Maltese flat and met resistance. It was cool on the dim landing, the polished stone stairs up to the first floor reassuringly swept clean and washed.

He remembered the darkness and the sense of anticipation from his childhood. In those days he and his mother had waited beside their small suitcase for the door to open and the pair of them to be engulfed in his grandmother's fierce embrace. Small and wiry, barely eighteen years his mother's senior – and looking almost younger than her daughter some days – Nanna Pina smelt briny from her daily swim, with a faint tang of sweat and the scent of olive oil, which she rubbed into her skin every night. As Freddy stood there now, his heart faltered with longing, the powerful need for his grandmother to open the door – despite her having been dead thirty-odd years – like an actual pain in his chest.

The door was jammed with junk mail. Freddy had to use the guidebook he'd bought in the airport to push underneath and free enough space to open it a fraction so that he could squeeze through. What he found inside was surprisingly unchanged. The shutters on the Maltese balcony – those colourful, enclosed wooden platforms that graced many houses in Malta, supported by brackets and lined with windows – were closed, so the place was cool and dark, the tiled floor dusty. No one, according to his father, had been in the place for a couple of years, although apparently he paid a pittance to the woman in the flat downstairs to keep it ticking over.

But the same kitchen table – cream-speckled Formica with spindly metal legs – stood in the middle of the room, and the green cupboards, paint faded and chipped, must be the ones he remembered. As were the olive, rust and cream-patterned tiles behind the work surface. The brown leather sofa was a newer addition. Pina had not owned a sofa, just two high-backed beige vinyl chairs with worn, padded arms and wood frames – Freddy remembered the vinyl sticking to his bare back when he came home, all sweaty, from the sea.

The place smelt musty and dank, and he quickly went over to open the shutters onto the street and the afternoon sun. Pina had left the flat to Freddy's mother, and forgotten to change her will after Maria died, six years before she did. So the flat became the property of the man Pina hated more than life itself: Vinnie Slater. Freddy was twenty when Nanna Pina died, but he had never returned to the Maltese apartment after her death, the knowledge that it now belonged to his father souring the happy memories, rendering it no longer a place of safety, even though, by then, he had completely removed himself from Vinnie's abusive clutches.

He walked through to the bedroom at the back of the small flat. His mother had shared his grandmother's bed on their visits, Freddy sleeping on a camp bed in the kitchen. He could still smell the fusty canvas, feel the cold metal of the frame beneath his fingers. The bedroom also seemed unchanged. Pina's mahogany-frame double bed, now stripped bare except for a heavy blue quilt, the bedside table, the cumbrous wardrobe, looked identical, although all his grandmother's trinkets, which had littered every surface of the flat – small Maltese glass vases and paperweights with swirling coloured centres, white porcelain Maltese dogs with cutesy blue bows on their heads – were gone. Freddy had loved them.

He opened the wardrobe to find mouldy pillows and neatly folded linen, the edges yellowed with age and disuse. He closed the door again. Now he was in Nanna Pina's apartment, he didn't know what to do with himself. It had been his goal since the meltdown to escape and now he had. But he had no idea what to do with his freedom.

Turning on the gas – supplied from a canister under the sink – he washed out the kettle, boiled some water, found a lidded metal tin with some dusty teabags and made himself a cup of tea, which tasted surprisingly good. He knew he had to clean the place, get a sleeping bag and pillow – the ones in the wardrobe were beyond salvation – buy something to eat. But instead he lay down on the sofa and fell fast asleep, the relief of finally being there making his body sink into the cushions as if he were a dead weight.

When he woke it was dark, the flat sinister in the shadows, as if it resented Freddy's intrusion on its solitude. He switched on the overhead light, but it shed a dim, sickly glow and the bulb in the fringed table lamp was gone. Freddy sat down again on the sofa, his mouth dry, his head spinning. He was struck by such an overpowering wave of desolation that his whole body went still with it, even his heart slowing almost to nothing, his breath shallow in his lungs. But he didn't dare breathe deeply, in case the feeling, given oxygen, got worse and became even more painful.

He jumped up and went to wash in the sink, sluicing cold water over his head and rubbing his hands hard across his face and hair. Then he grabbed his jacket from the back of the sofa, patted his pockets to check for his money, took the key off the small ledge by the front door and ran down the stairs, out into the Maltese night.

Although it was gone ten, there were people everywhere in Spinola Bay. It was now, to Freddy's consternation, a booming tourist area, construction cranes on every horizon with gleaming new hotels and half-built concrete structures as far as the eye could see. A very different place from the quiet seaside town he'd visited as a boy, the cafés and restaurants along the front packed with holidaymakers, bright lights and loud music.

Breathing a sigh of relief, nonetheless, to be among people again, Freddy slowed his pace, closing his eyes briefly, and laughed at himself for being frightened of his own shadow. He inhaled the familiar smell of the sea, saw the colourful *luzzi* – traditional fishing boats – bobbing on the dark water

211

and the lights of Sliema to the south. Nanna Pina had loved those boats and they often ate their lunch of fresh bread spread with rich *kunserva* (Maltese tomato paste), an orange to peel, on a rickety waterside bench in the hot sun, as they watched them weave in and out of the small bay.

There was a strong breeze tonight, chilly on his skin, but many of the outside tables were occupied. Cold with tiredness, Freddy chose one of the cafés looking onto the harbour, picked an inside table out of the wind and ordered a double gin and tonic. He would buy some *kunserva*, he thought, make himself a lunch like Nanna Pina had. His mouth watered as he remembered the feel of the soft white bread, the tangy sweetness of tomato on his tongue.

But however much his thoughts returned to his beloved grandmother, Freddy could not banish the nerve-jangling sound of his father's voice. He hadn't spoken to Vinnie Slater for, he reckoned, nearly twelve years, and then only to tell him to fuck off. He would not have broken that record if he hadn't been desperate. The only contact had been the curt message his father left every Christmas Eve: 'Happy Christmas, son. You know where I am.' But he had stopped listening, just deleting the most recent unheard.

So each time Freddy had thought about the flat in Malta he had dismissed it, because of the necessity of contacting his father. But he'd run out of options. The place would cost him nothing and was far and away the best place to hide for a few weeks, get his strength back and avoid the fury of his creditors until things had calmed down – or he'd found money somewhere.

Three times he rang his father's number. Three times he clicked off before it was answered. But the third time, Vinnie called back.

'Who is this?' the gravelly voice demanded.

For a moment Freddy didn't reply, then he said, 'It's Fred, Dad.' His father never called him 'Freddy' and yelled at his mother if he heard her use it. 'Makes him sound like a fucking posh jessie,' Vinnie would say.

Now he expected sniping, the usual coldness at least. And even though the voice sounded old, whispery almost, Freddy shuddered.

But Vinnie said, 'Fred?' almost hopefully. 'Is that you, son?'

'Yes, it's me.'

There was a long silence.

'Where are you?' Vinnie asked.

'In London.'

'Oh . . .' The old man sounded disappointed, and Freddy heard the click of a lighter, the draw of a cigarette, the rasp of a chronic cough. 'Long time . . .'

'Yeah.' Freddy was wrong-footed. It felt, for the first time, as if his father actually cared. He immediately regretted calling, an uneasy certainty dawning that he might be sucked back into Vinnie's life if he didn't hang up right now – a prospect that filled him with dread. But he needed the key to the apartment in Malta.

Then there was an intake of breath and the voice recovered some of its strength. 'What do you want? You must want something to be ringing.'

'Need to get away for a month or so. Is Nanna's flat free?'

Freddy refused to recognize his father's ownership of the Maltese property. His grandmother would be rolling in her grave to think that Vinnie had got his hands on it.

Vinnie didn't answer immediately. Then he said, 'Nobody's been in for a while . . . years, maybe. It'll be a mess.'

'Doesn't matter. Can I have the key?' Freddy couldn't keep the impatience out of his voice.

'Must be in some sort of trouble, needing to spend time in a dump like that. What have you gone and done, eh?' The words were followed by a spiteful laugh, which set off another bout of coughing, so savage this time it sounded to Freddy as if his father's lungs must be turned inside out.

'Can you send me the key, Dad? Please.'

Vinnie harrumphed. 'And here was me getting all excited at the prospect of seeing my long-lost son again.'

Ignoring his sarcasm, Freddy repeated his request, trying to summon a modicum of politeness.

'The woman on the ground floor has one. Name's Sinjura Vella – Mrs Vella. If she's not in, the spare's in an envelope in the back office of that Irish place on the corner. Can't remember the bloody name but it's the only one on the street. Bloke called Johnny looked after it, if he's still around.'

'Thanks.'

He was about to hang up, when his father said, 'I'm not so well. Emphysema, they tell me, those bastard croakers. Visit me soon, son . . . There's things need to be said.'

Now, sitting in the bar nursing his second double, Freddy wondered what he would feel if his father died without having seen him again. Relief, he'd always assumed, having wished him dead since he was a child. Also anger, maybe, at the lost opportunity to confront Vinnie with his past sins, to make him squirm, to force him to apologize at last. But that presupposed his father had a conscience, that he was fully aware of the cruelty he'd meted out to his wife and son and was sorry. Could he, Freddy, find the words, in the face of the person who'd terrorized his childhood, to say what he wanted? He wasn't so sure. But seeing Vinnie Slater again, just to test the theory, did not feel like an option right now.

Shaking off thoughts of his father, he got up from the table around midnight and began the short walk back to the apartment, in a side street off the seafront. He felt a sudden return of his optimism, and as he walked he made a firm promise to himself: *I will polish up the flat, buy some books, swim in the pool in Balluta Bay every day, get some proper sleep, eat healthily.* He heard an echo of Lily in his words and smiled to himself. *And absolutely no fucking gambling of any kind. I'll make her proud of me again.*

CHAPTER 26

Today was a glorious early May morning and the four walls of her sister and brother-in-law's house felt like a prison, making Lily gasp for fresh air and freedom. As she walked towards the canal, the warm sun on her face, she felt a sweet, tingling energy rise through her body, which made her want to run like a child. *Things will work out*, she told herself, the first positive thought she'd had in the month since Freddy had left.

Her phone buzzed in her pocket and she was glad to hear her friend's voice.

'How are you?' Prem asked.

'Not bad this morning. It's so beautiful here. I wish you could come and walk in the sunshine with me.'

'I wish I could too. I hate London in the spring.' There was a pause. 'So, tell me, what's going on?'

'Not a lot. Helen's keeps fretting about me finding a job.

But I needed her nagging. And they've both been very tolerant, having me around like this.'

'Remember you can always come to us if it doesn't work out.'

'Thanks, but I'll be fine. I'm learning to type online and then I'll find a job. Not sure what, but Helen seems to think there'll be something.'

'Fantastic. I'm so proud of you, getting your life back on track like this.'

Lily didn't comment, already offended by the implication that her problems were behind her.

'I hope that loser husband of yours has left you alone.'

'Yup.'

'That's a relief.'

Lily said nothing.

'Lily?'

'Yes.'

'Have I upset you? I'm sorry, but Freddy is a loser. And a bastard, for that matter.'

Lily bit her lip. 'Can we not talk about him?'

Now it was Prem's turn to be silent.

'How's the shop?' Lily asked through gritted teeth.

'You still have feelings for him, I understand that,' Prem said, not answering her question. 'I'm only nervous he'll try to worm his way back into your life.'

'Don't worry,' Lily said, more curtly than she intended.

'I have upset you, darling. It's just you have a very kind heart.'

'You make it sound like a defect.'

'No, of course it's not.'

Lily heard her sigh. She didn't know what to say. It felt as if their lifetime of friendship was in jeopardy: they would never agree about Freddy. 'I'm going into the supermarket,' she lied, 'so we might lose connection.'

'Okay, darling.' Her friend sounded resigned. 'Listen, give me a ring and make a date to come and stay, will you? I miss you.'

'I miss you too,' Lily said, and this time she wasn't lying.

Shaken by her conversation, Lily walked on, south along the towpath towards the centre of the city. Even though everything she had once taken for granted about Freddy was in question – his love for her, his integrity, his whereabouts, his intentions, even his sanity – the one thing that was solid, unwavering and *not* open to question, was that she loved Freddy March. It was what had sustained her in those first weeks in Oxford as she battled with loneliness and fear for her future.

He will not let me down, she chanted doggedly to herself as she walked, in the face of the relentless bile directed towards him by Prem and, indeed, everyone else. But she had quickly realized there was no point in defending Freddy or her position with regard to him. She knew Prem was only trying to protect her, and she appreciated that, but her friend didn't know Freddy the way she did.

Now, almost in defiance, she allowed herself to remember his dark eyes when he told her what had gone wrong, so full of sadness and guilt that they could hardly meet hers. She remembered the feel of his skin under her fingers, the way his hair curled away from his forehead so delicately, the dip in his collarbone where she had planted so many kisses. She could smell him, standing there by the still water of the canal, smell him as if he actually lay in her arms, and it made her cry that he might be gone for ever.

David's workshop was a golden, dusty heaven when Lily, still discomposed by Prem's call and tired from her day-long walk and aimless potter in the city centre, dropped by in the early evening. The sun was setting across the meadow behind the small barn, the light pouring through the large, wide-open doors and picking up the tiny flecks of sawdust that swirled through the still air, redolent with the piny scent of new wood.

Her brother-in law was at the large, solid workbench that sat in the middle of the barn, planing, with smooth, rhythmic strokes, a chunk of timber. Fine, milky ribbons of wood curled up from the heavy steel instrument, then dropped softly onto the workbench. The walls were hung about with tools of all sorts, including every gradation of saw, hammer, screwdriver, chisel, and pairs of muffler headphones. There were deep wooden trays filled with widgets, on top of which rested a number of steel rules, a mug, and receipts stuck on a metal spike.

Stacks of timber and unprocessed logs took up much of the space to the right of the workbench, along with the half-finished skeletons of furniture, and on a whiteboard against the far wall, under the pallid glow of a strip light, were displayed complicated-looking diagrams in black felt-tip. The cork board beside it was pinned with overlapping drawings, not just of chairs and tables but of trees, animals, figures

– some naked. Lily hadn't known David could draw so well. Everything was coated with a fine wood-dust, but although the workshop looked messy to the untutored eye, she sensed there was order in the chaos.

David looked up as her shadow fell across the room and grinned. Letting go of the wooden knob of the plane, he waved her inside, brushing away the straggling strands of hair that had fallen over his face as he bent to his task. 'You found me.'

'Nice place.' Suddenly she felt shy as she stood there. They rarely met without the prickly presence of her sister and she had never visited the workshop before.

'Yes.' He looked around, as if seeing the space for the first time. 'I'm lucky.'

'Lucky?'

David shrugged his big shoulders. 'Well, lucky to do what I do in such an ideal place.' He chuckled. 'Sorry, getting a bit carried away, but I love my work.'

'That is lucky.'

He pulled a face. 'Any progress on that front for you?'

Lily shook her head. 'I'm doing what Helen suggested, learning to touch-type. It's not so bad – repetitive, of course, but I'm already getting better.' She paused. 'David, I wanted to talk to you without Helen around.'

He nodded. She had his attention.

'I know it's not easy for you both, having me staying open-ended like this. It would be my worst nightmare: the guest who comes for a week and stays ten years.' She laughed to cover her awkwardness.

'Ten years, is it? Well, at least I can manage my expectations,' he joked.

'I wouldn't impose if I felt I had another option. I just worry, if it goes on too long . . .' She stopped, leaning against the workbench, overwhelmed by her situation. 'You will tell me, won't you, if things are getting too bad? I know Helen'll grin and bear it and say nothing until she actually stabs me. It's not a secret that we've never been particularly close, but I don't want it to get to that point.'

David came round the workbench, resting his bottom against it alongside Lily, both of them looking out towards the setting sun – now a burnished haze on the horizon.

'It's not just you makes her bad-tempered, Lily.'

'Kit, you mean?'

He nodded.

'She never talks about him to me. I feel I can't ask.'

'No, well . . . I wish she'd see him. I know she says she can't, but the guilt of not doing so is eating her up. It's almost as if she resents *me* for going.'

'It's a terrible situation.'

Her brother-in-law didn't reply, and for a while they leaned there together, in companionable silence.

'But you will tell me . . .'

He gave her a wry smile. 'We're not going to chuck you out, Lily.'

Lily, uneasy about everything in her life these days, gave up trying to exact even this small promise. 'Shall we walk back, or do you need to stay and work?' she asked.

CHAPTER 27

Dillon dragged his bike listlessly up the stairs of his house and rested it against the wall in the corridor outside his flat. He dreaded coming home now, knowing that Gabriela wouldn't be there. His fiancée had been gone nearly three weeks, but she was still being evasive about when she might return.

'How is your mum?' he'd asked last night, when she'd finally answered one of his many attempts to get hold of her – he reckoned she picked up on about one in six of his calls. This time there was a lot of noise in the background. It sounded like a bar and Dillon was immediately jealous.

'She's okay,' Gabriela replied noncommittally.

'Where are you?'

'Me and Bruna are meeting friends.'

Did she sound drunk, or was he imagining it? 'Obviously not a good time for a chat, then.'

'Sorry? I can't hear you. Hold on, I'll go outside.' There was a pause, the sound of footsteps, a door opening, then she went on, 'What were you saying?'

The date of their wedding had come and gone, unmarked by any communication from Gabriela. When he couldn't get hold of her, Dillon had got drunk, phoned Freddy's mobile, listened to the disconnected sound, then hurled his own across the room, cracking the screen. He still hadn't forgiven Gabriela for running off like that, for not supporting him. It was as if it were only *her* pain, *her* problem.

'I said it's probably not a good time, if you're with people.'

'It's okay, I'm outside now. Go ahead.'

Dillon hesitated, upset that she didn't seem to want a proper conversation. Like she was waiting for him to get on and explain why he'd rung, impatient to go back to her friends.

'I didn't have anything much to say, just fancied a chat, find out what's going on in your life.' He knew his tone was bordering on snippy, but he didn't care.

'Things are not bad,' she said. But her voice was flat, he felt she was holding back.

'So your mum's calmed down?'

'Mamãe's never calm.' A small laugh. 'Not easy.'

We can't seem to communicate any more, he thought, with despair. *She used to rattle on nineteen to the dozen, never stopped.* 'What's the matter, Gaby?'

'Nothing's the matter. Why do you say that?'

'Sounds like you can't wait to get off the phone.'

He heard an exasperated sigh, 'Oh, for God's sake, Dillon. I'm standing in the middle of a noisy street.'

223

'You said it was okay to talk.'

'I meant if you have something important to say, then I can listen.'

She sounded thoroughly irritated with him. 'Would you rather I didn't call you any more?'

'No. *No*, of course not.'

'So tell me what's happening. I know you're upset about the wedding, but is it more than that? I need to know.'

He waited for her answer in trepidation, instantly regretting his question and wishing he could suck it back from the ether.

'I can't talk now, *querido*, I'll phone you tomorrow,' she said, sounding distracted, and was gone.

Dillon was left, mobile to his ear, feeling almost breathless. He wanted to ring back immediately, but he knew there was no point. Running through their conversation in his head, he tried to pinpoint a moment of real connection between them. But there had been none. She'd called him '*querido*', and that was something, he supposed, but the word had held no warmth.

After gulping down half a bottle of cheap red wine, Dillon brought up his mother's number on his phone and, without thinking twice, pressed the cracked screen – a reminder of all that was wrong with his life. She answered before the second ring.

'Dillon!'

'Hi.'

'How are you, darling? God, I've missed you so much.'

Dillon felt immediately guilty, remembering the huge

number of calls his mother had made in the previous weeks and the curt, angry one-liners he'd texted back in response. 'Gabriela's left me.'

He heard an intake of breath and perversely enjoyed his moment of drama.

'Left you? What do you mean?'

'She's gone back to Brazil, Mum. She seemed to think I'd made the whole thing up about Freddy. Said it reminded her that she found me tricky.'

'That's ridiculous. She'll be back, surely.'

'Really? Doesn't seem like it to me. She's been gone for weeks and now she hardly wants to talk to me. Each time I ask when she's coming home, she avoids the question.'

Despite his resentment towards his mother, he was so happy to be talking to her again. If she had missed him, he had missed her just as much.

'Maybe she just needs to get over the shock. It's a big deal for a girl, having her wedding cancelled. She'll be angry . . .'

'I'm angry too. Everyone seems to think it's just Gaby who's upset, but I'm upset too, really upset. Honestly, Mum, this whole thing is a shambles. How could you let Freddy take all your money like that? Even if you didn't know he was gambling, that was a pretty dumb thing to do.' He paused for breath but couldn't stop the rant, so long stored up. 'I mean, where did you think he was every night? It's like you were playacting this perfect marriage when both of you were on totally different planets.'

His mother went silent for a moment. Then she said, 'I know. I was stupid. I trusted him.'

The wind was taken out of Dillon's sails as he heard the pain in his mother's voice. 'How are you managing?' he asked in a gentler tone.

'Okay. I'm learning to touch-type so I can get a job.'

Dillon had a sudden flashback to his mother walking into that swanky restaurant near where he worked, her clothes designer-expensive, her hair beautifully cut, the maître d' fawning all over her because she was such a good customer. *Touch-typing? God*, he thought, *how the mighty are fallen.* 'Oh, Mum . . .'

'I'm okay, Dillon.' She gave a small laugh. 'I'm resourceful, I'll manage. And . . .'

She stopped and he waited for her to go on.

'And, well, I'm sure things will work out. It's lovely here in the spring. You forget, living in London, how beautiful the countryside is.'

Dillon was quite sure that hadn't been what she'd been about to tell him, and her enthusing about the countryside – a woman who had previously shown little interest in anything beyond the congestion zone? She'd sounded flustered. But he didn't press her.

'I'm so sorry about Gaby,' she was saying, 'but don't hassle her, let her come round. She really loves you.'

'Yeah, well . . . good to talk to you, Mum. Maybe I'll visit one weekend, catch up with Helen and David. Seems like an age since I saw them.'

CHAPTER 28

Freddy turned his head a little, surprised by his darkening tan, which was reflected in the mirror behind the smart apartment-block reception in Portomaso Marina, five minutes north of St Julian's Bay and his grandmother's flat. He was sure the site used to be a beach popular with the locals – sharp rocks and a small strip of sand, if memory served him right. Had Nanna Pina called it 'Shingles' or something like that? He couldn't remember. Anyway, the developers had changed all that.

After only a few weeks in the sun, he looked like a native Maltese. He felt at home on the island, as if part of him had stayed there from his childhood, kept the place warm for him. He liked the people and that odd mix of British and Maltese that the islanders had made into something uniquely their own. He thought he'd muscled up a bit too, repairing the damage from his somewhat degenerate London lifestyle with the daily swimming and walking.

He walked the ten minutes to the open-air pool by the water's edge in Balluta every morning, before he'd even had breakfast, doing a hundred lengths as the sun rose across the sea. Then went back every evening for another hundred, in the setting sun, before supper. It was like meditation, Freddy found – a routine that bookended his days and gave him a sense of purpose.

The rest of his day – after he'd dealt with the endless, irritating emails about his financial affairs – he would fill with activities such as sightseeing in the capital, Valletta, only a cheap bus ride away.

He wandered around the old town, visited the stunning cathedral, sat at a pavement café with a beer or a cup of coffee in the sunshine. Or he might walk up to the seventeenth-century Spinola Palace in St Julian's, take a short ferry ride from the north tip of the island to Gozo, where his great-grandfather had farmed a smallholding. Usually someone who was bored to death at the prospect of a ruin or a museum, Freddy found himself becoming fascinated by this strand of his heritage.

He had to do something to keep busy, because he'd thought that by fleeing to a Mediterranean island, he would be conveniently separated from the snares and temptations of the metropolis. But he was much mistaken. There seemed to be a gambling joint on almost every corner of the island and in all the bigger hotels.

Now, making his way towards the lift in the apartment block, he realized he was looking forward to seeing Shirley again. A social animal and a serial bonder – as Lily liked to call him – Freddy had managed his time so completely alone in Malta only because he'd been in shock. Anyone looking at his current lifestyle might think he was having the time of his life. But he felt like a fraud, a mere shell of a man. He had to wind himself up every morning to go through his daily paces.

He missed Lily so much that he could hardly bear to think about her. When he did, he convinced himself that his course of action in not having any contact with her was for the best. Hearing her voice, listening to her tears and her assertions that she loved him would undo him, of that he was certain. No, he would rehabilitate himself, go back shiny and new, the husband she deserved.

Shirley Solaris opened the door of her third-floor apartment with an anxious frown. 'Oh, Freddy, come in . . . I'm so happy you're here. You'll know what to do.'

The American, a well-preserved woman in her early sixties, was dressed in pristine white Capri pants, a broad-striped, loose blue and white cotton T-shirt, expensive gold chain necklace and patent-leather FitFlops, her toenails painted a bright coral. She dragged Freddy unceremoniously through the spacious sitting room and out onto the balcony, which looked over the marina and the gleaming rows of yachts towards the Hilton on the opposite side of the water.

'You see?' She pointed, squatting down and peering intently into the corner. Freddy, squinting in the bright sun, saw a small bird perched on the limestone floor of the terrace.

'He must be wounded or sick,' Shirley said. 'He's been there all morning. Do you think he's a baby? He can't seem to fly.'

She looked up at Freddy beseechingly, and he thought she might cry. 'What shall I do?'

Freddy, whose knowledge of birds was limited to those he found on his plate, preferably with a sauce, pulled a face. The bird, brown and speckled with a long beak and what Freddy, in his ignorance, considered rather over-large, bright eyes, was darting its head from side to side, clearly extremely nervous of all the attention.

'I called Gori, our shiftless janitor, but he hasn't got back to me.' She stood up. 'We can't just leave him there, Freddy.'

Freddy wasn't sure why not – wouldn't the thing just potter off as soon as Shirley stopped freaking it out? – but he tried to look as if he were considering the options. *Do they have the RSPCA in Malta?* he wondered, deciding the British influence would insist upon it. *But does a bird count as an animal?*

Shirley, with her large, very blue eyes, sunglasses pushed to the top of her smooth, honeycomb-coloured hair, was waiting.

'Is a bird an animal?' he asked, quite keen to know the answer.

Shirley laughed. 'Well, I guess so. Why do you want to know?'

He explained about the RSPCA.

'You're so smart!' She looked delighted with this perfectly obvious piece of wisdom.

'I'll find the number,' Freddy offered, reaching into the back pocket of his jeans for his phone. He'd been hoping for a nice midday gin on the terrace, a bit of lunch, perhaps, in one of the many restaurants – none of which he could afford right now – in the marina complex. Not this palaver over a stupid bird. He'd never seen himself as the knight-in-shining-armour type, far from it, and the way Shirley was waiting eagerly for his next move was positively disconcerting.

Freddy had met her on the ferry to Gozo. He'd been sitting alone at one of the wooden bench tables on the deck, basking in the Mediterranean sun and enjoying the stiff breeze that accompanied the sailing. He hadn't slept well the previous night, anxious to the point of nausea about his future, and was almost dozing, not noticing Shirley among the other passengers until she sat down opposite him and asked him if he knew the ferry times for the returning boats.

Although Freddy had not been in the mood for company, by the time they arrived in Gozo Shirley was his new best friend. She insisted they share a taxi to Mġarr ix-Xini Bay, a peaceful cove she knew, off the tourist map until Brangelina had used it as a location for a film the previous year. How could Freddy refuse? They had swum off the dock in the chilly spring sea, then eaten fresh grilled bream and delicious fried potatoes in the beach café, waiting half the afternoon for the food to arrive, by which time both he and Shirley were thoroughly pissed.

Now, as luck would have it, the apparently feckless concierge pitched up at the door before the SPCA – not royal, obviously – had been summoned.

'I take him,' he said, eyeing Freddy with great suspicion as he scooped up the bird in his big fists, the little thing flapping and struggling inside.

'Where?' demanded Shirley. 'Where will you take him?'

'I take him to the beach.'

'The *beach*?' Shirley screeched.

'Is a rock thrush, Sinjura Solaris. He have many friend on the rocks.'

Freddy didn't take the sullen Gori for a man particularly interested in nature or its inhabitants, or one to put himself out for anyone, let alone a stray bird. He pictured him stomping downstairs and surreptitiously bashing the poor thing – for which Freddy now had great sympathy, having taken an instant dislike to the concierge – on the head and slinging it into the trash before returning to his afternoon bottle of wine and rabbit *ragù*. Shirley obviously thought the same.

'No,' she said firmly. 'I'll take it.'

Gori shrugged, said nothing, just held out his cupped palms to the American. But Shirley blenched and stepped back. 'Freddy, can you? The feel of feathers makes me retch.'

Oh, for God's sake, he thought, reaching out and hoping the same didn't apply to himself – he'd never held a bird. But the little thing felt pitifully small and fragile, fluttery and struggling against his skin. *Much more of this*, he thought, *and it will die of fright.*

The thrush safely delivered to a rock – where it stood twitching uncertainly – Shirley took Freddy, as a reward for his diligence, to a charming waterfront café, which served Italian food and where the maître d' welcomed her with open arms. The prices were eye-watering, the seafood risotto delicious. The second bottle of Soave was well under way when Shirley, seated beside Freddy so that they could both take advantage of the view over the bay, started leaning in towards him, her blue eyes slightly glazed, her hand wandering over the white tablecloth to rest on his. Used as he was to being on the receiving end of harmless flirtation – as Lily had often pointed out – Freddy felt suddenly awkward with this older woman he hardly knew and gently pulled his hand from beneath hers, putting it firmly in his lap.

Shirley gave a sad laugh. 'Oh, no need to get all prim, dear. I won't embarrass you by doing something foolish.' She sat up straighter, very much on her dignity, despite the large amount of wine she'd consumed. 'I just miss being able to touch someone, to get a hug. Chase, my husband, was a big hugger, very physical. He wouldn't let me do a thing in the morning until we'd had a proper hug.' She bit her lip and Freddy could see she was fighting back tears.

Opening his arms, he said, 'Hey, come here,' drawing her against him as they sat on the banquette. She smelt of a floral perfume he thought he recognized, her body tense, her breath trembling. She relaxed as he held her, letting out a small sigh before pulling back.

'Thank you . . . you're a kind man.'

'How long ago did your husband . . .' He was suddenly unsure as to whether Chase Solaris had died or simply defected.

'He passed away two years ago September. We'd barely been here six months.'

'I'm sorry.'

'Me too, Freddy, me too. This was our big adventure. He was older than me by eight years, but he seemed so fit and healthy. When he retired we bought this place so he could sail his boat to his heart's content – he was crazy about boats.'

'Where are you from?'

'Portland, Oregon.'

'Will you go back?'

She shrugged. 'I don't know. My daughter lives in New York and I see her as much here as I did when I was in Portland – which isn't a lot. I have a sister in Montana, but we don't get along . . . I'm not sure what I'd be going home to, except a house where every inch reminds me of dear Chase.'

Shirley's obvious loneliness triggered a corresponding wave of desolation in Freddy. *Is this my fate?* he asked himself. *Hanging out in Malta with a bunch of ex-pats, drinking too much and targeting strays – birds or people – just to plug the hours with a bit of company?* The thought profoundly depressed him.

Shirley was eyeing him, one brow slightly raised. 'And you? Do you have a family?'

Freddy hesitated. 'Yes,' he answered.

She laughed. 'You don't sound too sure.'

'No, of course I'm sure. I have a wife, Lily, and stepchildren back in London.'

'Hmm . . . But there's a problem, no? You looked so sad just then.'

Irritated, he said, 'I'm not sad.'

'Okay, okay.'

They fell silent as the waiter poured more iced water into their glasses.

'So you're here on holiday?'

'Yes . . . no.' He gave up dissembling. What did it matter if this complete stranger knew about the fuck-up that was his life? 'My business went tits up,' he said slowly, carefully stepping over the holes in his story that made him too ashamed. 'Lily and I are taking a break while I sort things out.'

She nodded slowly, 'Looks like we're a bit of a sad pair, hon.' Then her face lightened. 'But, hey, we can have some fun, pass the time together until you have to go home. Better than being alone, I guess.'

And Freddy had to agree.

CHAPTER 29

'I think I've found you a job.' Helen, just in from college, dumped her black briefcase on the kitchen table and stood looking down at Lily, who was at her laptop, diligently typing lesson nineteen on the online touch-typing programme: ... *deposit post wealth our totally tree teeth* ...

'Really?' Lily waited, in a certain amount of trepidation, for her sister to reveal the details.

Helen, clearly pleased with herself, pulled out a kitchen chair and sat down with a sigh. 'I don't know how long it's been up, but there was a notice on the board in the department: someone looking for transcription work.'

'Transcription?'

'Yes, you know, transcribing tapes and stuff.' Helen fished in the pocket of her jacket and held up a card. 'Dr Seth Kramer.' She handed it to Lily. 'I rang him and he says he's writing a book, but he's got a ton of recorded interviews he needs transcribing. I said you'd give him a call.'

Lily looked at the card, which bore nothing except his name, an email address and a mobile phone number.

'He's a shrink,' Helen went on, when Lily didn't reply. 'He sounded really nice.'

Lily was fighting the feeling that her sister was bamboozling her, that she didn't have much choice in the matter. Couldn't Helen have just given her the doctor's card, let her make the phone call? But she knew she couldn't afford to object. 'Wow, thanks . . . Umm, did you tell him I can't type properly yet?'

Helen laughed. 'No, of course not. If he knew that, he'd hardly be likely to employ you, would he?'

'But – but if he's got a lot of work and I take too long . . .'

'Then you'll lose the job, obviously. Don't think like that. Just ring him and convince him that you'll be perfect. Then make sure you are.' Her sister gave her an encouraging smile. 'This is ideal, Lily. You can work from home, do it in your own time. I'm sure the pay is pretty rubbish, but it's a start. It'll give you the chance to build your skill-set, get an employment record going, with references.'

Skill-set? Lily thought. *Employment record?* She knew it was what Helen did best, guiding students into gainful careers, and she knew it was what most of the country had to do to find work. It wasn't that she was work-shy, it just seemed such an uphill struggle at her age, and with her meagre skills, to get herself into the system.

But she wanted to show suitable enthusiasm, and said quickly, 'No, you're right. Thanks, Helen. I'll ring him tomorrow.'

'*No!* Ring him now, for God's sake. Nail it before a million students pip you to the post.'

So Lily, who suddenly felt ridiculously nervous, reached for her mobile and, under the beady eye of her big sister, pressed in the number on the card. She hoped the doctor wouldn't pick up, give her time to think about the whole thing, but after the fourth ring a soft voice said, 'Seth Kramer.'

'Umm, my sister rang earlier . . . about the job?'

There was a pause. 'Helen, is it?'

'That's my sister. I'm Lily. Lily March.'

'Right. Can you come and see me tomorrow, Lily?'

'Yes, what time?'

'Ten would suit. I'm on the canal, just before Aristotle Bridge. Do you know it? The boat's called *Mairzy Doats.*' Lily heard him chuckle. 'Not my choice. She's rust-red and black, just after a bright blue one, if you're coming from town. If you get to the bridge you've gone too far.'

'Thanks,' she said. 'See you tomorrow, then.'

Helen nodded with approval as she clicked off the phone. 'There! Not so difficult. Now you've just got to keep your mouth shut about your typing skills. He's hardly going to test you.'

The boat was easy to find, but Lily was early, worried it would take her longer to walk than Helen had said, worried she might lose her way in the unfamiliar city. Her sister had offered Lily her bike, but she hadn't been on one since childhood and didn't want to end up as roadkill. As it turned out, it took her less than half an hour, a pleasant walk through Summertown.

The canal was peaceful, the boats lined up along the bank reassuringly solid and bright in the drizzly grey May morning. Not sure where to knock, or what boat etiquette required of visitors, Lily hesitated before deciding to brave the rickety strip of wood, cleats nailed at regular intervals to prevent slipping, that stretched from the bank to the stern. The double doors were open, and just as she stepped onto the decking, a head popped out.

Seth Kramer was in his early sixties, Lily decided as he stood beside her, shaking her hand. A stocky man, barely taller than her, he seemed tidy and contained in the open-necked blue cotton shirt tucked into his jeans, the sleeves rolled to just below his elbows, his feet sporting faded tan deck shoes with no socks. Not really a handsome man – his features were too squashed and worn in his square face, his short grey-brown hair and heavy eyebrows too wiry and unruly – but when he smiled, Lily was immediately charmed: his dark eyes behind their tortoiseshell spectacles lit up with real warmth.

'Welcome,' he said. 'Please . . . come in.' He held out his arm, indicating the steps that led down to the interior.

Seeing her looking around – she had never been on a nar-rowboat before – Seth grinned. 'What do you think?' he asked.

'It's . . .'

'Narrow?' he suggested and they both laughed.

It *was* narrow. The ceiling was higher than she'd thought it might be, the light better, despite the venetian blinds half-open on the land side, but the space needed some getting used to. Had she stretched out her arms, she would have been able to touch both walls. Clad in light wood throughout, it wasn't new, but it had obviously been fitted out with care when first built. A galley kitchen area led through to the sitting room, where an L-shaped forest-green sofa with paler green cushions had been built along one wall, opposite a small wood-burning stove – glowing reassuringly on this miserable spring morning – and a drop-down table on which Seth had piled papers, books and an open laptop. A worn black leather desk chair was pushed under the work surface.

At the far end there was a wall across half the width of the boat, behind which, she assumed, were a bathroom and bedroom. A black cast-iron teapot with a frayed wicker handle sat on a shelf – mostly covered with more books – that ran the length of the room, beside it a grey-green Japanese stoneware cup, which Seth now pointed to.

'I've just made some tea – jasmine green. Would you like some?'

Lily said she would, and he went to a small cupboard on the wall above the round metal sink and came back with an identical cup.

'Sit, please.'

Holding the cup by the rim, Lily took a small sip of tea. It was warm, not hot, and fragrant, delicious. Looking around for somewhere to put it down and finding nowhere, she cradled the cup in her lap. The doctor pulled out the desk chair and swivelled it round to face her. As he sat, there was a small puff from the leather seat.

'I should probably ask you about yourself,' he said, smiling. 'My work is quite sensitive.'

Helen had brought up the problem with Lily the night before.

'He'll want references,' she'd told Lily. 'You'll have to ask Prem – she'll give you the necessary.'

'I can send you a reference,' Lily told him now.

'Umm . . . I won't need that,' he said. 'I always feel they're a bit of a waste of time. Since you don't know the referee from Adam, you can't tell if what they're saying about someone is what you would say. And there's no mileage in suing someone when things don't work out.' He paused. 'If we could just talk. Find out a little about each other.'

She had no idea what to say. Should she tell him about Freddy? Should she say she was only in Oxford for a short time? Neither piece of information seemed wise to divulge to a potential employer. And might the taint of Freddy's untrustworthiness rub off on her? Helen had seemed to imply that it would.

'Have you done this sort of work before?' Seth was asking.

Lily hesitated, but she'd always been a hopeless liar. 'No.' Somehow this man seemed too kind, too decent to deceive. *And anyway*, she thought, *he can probably see through people in an instant. Isn't that his job?* She told herself there would be other chances to find work. This was the only the first interview, and her typing was improving all the time. She'd sold her very ancient Golf too, which meant she had a small amount of cash to keep her going, contribute to the household expenses.

'What was your last job?' He was looking at her with those dark eyes of his, which were restful in their gaze.

She took a deep breath. 'The truth is that I'm in a bit of a mess. My husband has . . . We're having a temporary break while he sorts stuff out . . . There's been financial problems.'

He didn't interrupt.

'And I am staying with my sister.' She wasn't sure why she said this. Why would Dr Kramer mind where she was living? 'I haven't been working for the past few years, but I really need a job now.'

'And what did you do for work before?' he asked again.

'I worked in a shop . . . ergonomic chairs and desks. In London. It was owned by a friend. I didn't do admin or anything, just helped the customers find the right chair. It was fun, I loved it.' She was gabbling, telling him stuff in which he would have no possible interest, digging her own employment grave by revealing what she couldn't do, rather than doing what Helen had impressed upon her: 'Only tell him what you *can* do.'

Seth was nodding. 'The right chair is so important.' He patted the leather-clad arms of his own. 'I spent a fortune on this one. I've had it for years and I'm sure without it I'd be a cripple by now, all the hours I spend in front of the computer.'

'You should really have a separate keyboard for your laptop. Otherwise you're bending your head at a bad angle and you'll damage your neck,' she found herself saying, then blushed at her impertinence.

He laughed, a low rumble. 'Good to have an expert's opinion.'

'Sorry.'

There was a silence, during which Lily concentrated on her empty cup. She clung to it like a lifeline, wishing the

242

interview was over. He wasn't going to give her the job. And why should he? She couldn't even type properly.

But he seemed interested enough – or polite enough – to tell her about his work. 'I'm writing a book about how people view the after-effects of therapy.'

She nodded.

'Therapists only hear what's in the room at the time. Then the patient leaves and perhaps doesn't come back. I want to document how a person views their experience of psycho-analysis a year – or even a decade – later. I'm not talking about seriously ill people, who are perhaps medicated and have long-term mental health problems. But a person who has come to me because they are unhappy or depressed ... not functioning well.'

Lily nodded again.

'I want to make the book accessible, not an academic tome. Something the average person can read to find out what this sort of treatment is really about, how much use it might be to them. Case studies, interesting human stories, bit of science ... that sort of thing.'

'And have you found therapy *is* useful?' Lily had met lots of people who were going to analysts in the crowd who inhabited Freddy's world. She wasn't sure it worked particularly well, most of them seeming pretty crazy. But maybe they would have been even crazier without it.

Smiling, he said, 'I have to believe it is, Lily. I've spent the best part of thirty-five years practising it.'

'God, yes, of course. I didn't mean ...' She shut up. Best not to add the other foot.

'It's a valid question. There are probably more detractors than not.' His gaze drifted out of the window.

'You live on the boat?' Lily asked, being polite but suddenly wanting to bring the interview to an end and get out of the hot, stuffy space.

'No, in Jericho. My rooms are there. But I prefer to work on the book away from my patients' space. And I can create mess here.' He cast an amused glance at the desk, the piles of papers and books littered about. 'I didn't want to be constantly clearing my office up, so I bought this old tub a few years back. It's peaceful, I don't get disturbed.'

Lily wondered if he had a wife and children at home, a gang of noisy relatives. Somehow she thought not. Seth Kramer seemed a solitary person.

'Anyway, I have hundreds of hours of interviews. They aren't all *my* ex-patients. I inveigled my colleagues too. Most interviews are inside an hour, some longer, but I just don't have time to transcribe them myself.'

Lily dreaded to think how long it would take her to type up an hour of speech. *Probably a year.*

'I think it would be best to pay you by the interview rather than the hour. Does that suit?'

Is he offering me the job?

She smiled uncertainly. 'Sounds fine.'

'I can give you a few to start with, see if it works out for us both. You could come back in a couple of days – maybe Friday? Then we can discuss how to go forward.' He was giving her a questioning look. 'I really want to get on with it now. This book's been hanging about waiting to be written for far too long. Will you be in Oxford for a while? You said you were staying with your sister.'

'Yes, yes. I'll find somewhere else to live soon, but it'll be here.' Lily wondered why she'd said that. She wouldn't be staying in Oxford when Freddy came back.

'You understand these tapes are highly confidential. The case studies in the book will be mostly anonymous, but the tapes are labelled with real names. I wouldn't want you sharing any of the information you hear, or letting the tapes fall into the wrong hands.'

Lily almost laughed. Dr Kramer was making it sound clandestine, as if she were a spy being entrusted with state secrets. But she kept a straight face. 'No, of course not.'

'If you could do an e-version and also a hard copy? Obviously I'll pay for the printing costs.'

He got up, looking relieved, and went into the prow section of the boat, behind the partition. He came back carrying a cardboard box out of which he picked a handful of small cassette tapes in transparent plastic cases.

'I've been recording these interviews for years now, so I'm afraid it's steam technology . . . I use a Dictaphone. But it works.' He looked around and found a small plastic Boots bag under some books, into which he put the tapes. 'Have you got a machine?'

Lily shook her head.

'I'll give you one of mine.'

When Helen got home from work, she immediately gave her a brief, uncharacteristic hug. 'That's brilliant, Lily, well done.'

'It will be brilliant,' she answered, 'if I can type the bloody things up in time. He wants them back by Friday.'

'Don't be negative. It's only Wednesday. How many are there?'

Lily looked in the bag. 'Four.'

'Only four?' Helen looked disappointed as she turned away to find the kettle and fill it with water.

'How long does it take to transcribe an hour of talking, do you think?' Lily asked. 'If you can type normally.'

Helen shrugged. 'How long is a piece of string? I have no idea ... given that people mumble and talk too quickly so you have to go back and forth ... Maybe two hours?'

Lily very much doubted it would take her only two hours.

'Wasn't that lucky, me spotting his ad on the board? He must have just put it there, or he'd have been inundated with students after the job and you wouldn't have got a look-in.' Helen turned to Lily, leaning her bottom against the worktop as she waited for the kettle to boil. 'And you liked him?'

'I did. He was ... kind. Sort of odd-looking, but he had a nice smile. I thought he seemed a bit sad.'

Her sister laughed. 'As long as he pays you, he can be as miserable as he likes.'

CHAPTER 30

Freddy had stopped swimming in the open-air pool. It was late spring and the sea had warmed up just enough. He would walk down to the water from his grandmother's flat, past the strange cat grotto perched on a rocky knoll – decorated with faded soft toys and bowls of water set out for the strays – at about six every morning. The air was cool then and he would swim off the rocks in the gap between one seafront hotel and another. The sea was still cold, no question, but in his currently Spartan phase Freddy enjoyed the macho glow of stoicism. Then he would reward himself with coffee and a couple of little *pastizzi* – flaky pastries filled with ricotta and mashed peas – in a café on the corner of his street.

While he ate, he checked his emails on his laptop with the café Wi-Fi – there was no connection in the flat. He had to steel himself every morning to face the ongoing mess that constituted his financial affairs. There was invariably a request from James, his solicitor, something from the Official Receiver's office about missing documents or queries about the equipment in the studios, finer points in contracts and statements, invoices to be cleared up.

This particular morning, nearly six weeks since the terrible moment when his world had crashed about him, Freddy was taking stock. It seemed entirely possible to him, as he sat in the warm sun – so far from anyone he knew, his problems muted by distance – that he could stay in Malta for ever. He might drift through his life with a succession of middle-aged women, like Shirley, prepared to bankroll him. He could be wined and dined, sit by swanky pools to work on his tan, visit the odd historic monument or concert … even rescue wounded birds. All in exchange for companionship, for his skills as a professional walker. He knew how to charm people; he wasn't out of place with the rich and famous. *Just a gigolo*, he said to himself, and even that thought didn't upset him as it should, as long as sex didn't enter the equation.

Maybe it was the sun that was making him lazy, or the absolute dread of ever facing Lily and her children again, or the nightmare of setting up a whole new career with his reputation in tatters, but the idea didn't seem such a bad one. Lethargy was new to Freddy: he'd been a lifelong enthusiast and workaholic. These days, though, he felt almost unable to do anything but wander from his bed to the sea, from the sea to the café, from the café to Shirley's condo, from her condo to a local eatery to make the tricky decision of whether to have crab or lobster for lunch. The prospect of anything

248

more strenuous, anything that required his brain to function, his emotions to be engaged, seemed overwhelming.

Lily, Lily, Lily. He repeated her name silently to himself. Where was she? How was she coping? He imagined her back working in Prem's shop, living in Prem and Anthony's comfortable Fulham house. He'd promised her it would be for a few months, their separation, but it was already six weeks and he was nowhere. And despite her assertion that she loved him, she probably wouldn't touch him with a bargepole now – a bankrupt without even a bank account to his name, or the ability to rent a flat, get a mortgage or run a company. The bankruptcy sites even informed him he was no longer eligible to be a postman, which he found almost insulting. He couldn't see himself as one, but still . . .

His phone rang and he answered it with a small sigh, sure, at this time of the morning, it would be James with another tiresome query.

'How's it going, you sad bastard?' Max sounded pleased with himself. 'Thought you'd fuck off and not tell your only friend, did you? Well, I've let you stew in your own juice long enough.'

Freddy laughed. He felt unreasonably glad to hear Max's voice. 'Hey, how are you?'

'Been a bit of a drama with Julie's mum, heart stuff, but she's on the mend now.' He chuckled. 'I had to threaten that James guy so he'd give me your number.'

'Threaten him with what?'

'I told him I knew all sorts of dodgy stuff about you I'd divulge to the authorities pronto unless he coughed up.'

'He must have been terrified.'

His friend laughed again. 'So what the fuck are you doing, Freddy? Is Lily with you? When are you coming home?'

Freddy didn't know where to start. Eventually he mumbled out the details of his life for the last few weeks, trying to detach himself, as he spoke, from the loser about whom he spoke.

'Sounds fucking peachy. All that sea and sunshine. Lucky bugger. Maybe I should go bankrupt.'

Freddy felt a flare of anger in his gut. 'It's about as far from "peachy" as you can get, Max. I'm stranded here. Lily and I have split up. I don't have a job. I have to deal with financial crap all day long. It's shit, despite the bloody sea and sunshine.' He knew he sounded like a whining child, but the implication that he was enjoying himself stung.

But Max didn't do self-pity. 'So what's the plan? You going to hide out in your grandma's flat for ever?'

'No.'

'Well?'

'I don't have a sodding clue what I'm going to do, okay? I just told you, I'm basically fucked.'

His friend was silent. Then: 'Are you gambling?' Max's voice sounded reluctant, as if he were steeling himself for Freddy's response.

'No. Absolutely not.' Freddy felt a surge of pride that he was able to answer with the truth for once.

And Max must have heard it. 'Great. That's great, Freddy.'

'Maybe. But it doesn't solve a single problem.'

'It doesn't create any new ones at least,' his friend replied, then paused and Freddy heard him talking to someone in the background, saying he'd be with him in a minute. 'Listen, now I've got your number, let's keep in touch. You'll have to come back soon, mate. Who the fuck can I go to the American Bar with?'

Freddy ordered another black coffee from the bad-tempered Italian waitress who often served him and tried to think. Max's call had brought back into sharp focus everything he had left behind. *All very well for him to say come home*, he thought, not without a bitterness he knew was unjustified, *but how the hell does he think I'm going to do that?*

'Oh, come on, hon.' Shirley leaned towards him, flashing her most beguiling smile. 'You don't need money. I've got enough for us both. It'll be so much fun.'

They were sitting on the terrace of her apartment, each with a large gin and tonic, watching the sun go down over the sea on the beautiful May evening. Freddy had sidestepped her earlier invitation to lunch. Since speaking to Max, he'd felt as if Shirley were his guilty secret. Real life? He didn't know how to do that any more.

'I'm not taking your money, Shirley. No way.'

Shirley was dressed in a strange black and yellow silk tunic with nautical rope print – it had probably cost a fortune and had been bought in one of the luxury boutiques on the island – and a pair of loose black trousers. Her tanned, perfectly manicured feet were bare, her ankles crossed as she lay back on the cream lounger. She must have been drinking before Freddy arrived, because she was already behaving in a giggly, girly fashion that didn't bode well for the evening.

The American pulled a pouty face at Freddy's refusal. 'Don't be a spoilsport, Freddy. I've made a reservation for dinner anyway, and the food is fabulous there. Then you can watch *me* gamble if you won't do it yourself. How about it?'

Freddy didn't have much choice, but he felt his whole body twitch at the thought of being close to a roulette table again. *This will be the test*, he told himself, suddenly almost relishing the challenge.

The casino – an old converted palace that had been used as a summer residence by some rich Maltese family in the past – perched at the end of a rocky promontory ten minutes' walk north of the marina complex. It was a stunning, neoclassical building in limestone, with a covered terrace stretching round the outside punctuated by curved arches and slim columns. Freddy thought it more like a temple than a gambling joint. He had seen the place often before, but never allowed himself inside. Tonight it glowed a warm, seductive yellow, the word 'CASINO' shimmering on the roof, the light pouring from the interior brilliant against the absolute darkness of the surrounding sea.

There was a brisk wind as they strolled along the walkway, past still, silent swimming-pools and up the curved steps onto the terrace for dinner. Shirley had brought a black cashmere wrap, which she drew round her shoulders as they were seated by the maître d' on padded wrought-iron chairs at a white-clothed table.

'Will you just look at that,' Shirley said, waving her hand towards the view across the sea, lights twinkling along the ribbon of coast as far as the eye could see. 'Isn't it magic?'

Freddy, craning round in his seat, agreed that it was. But he couldn't help feeling anxious. He would not gamble. He could not gamble. But just passing through the huge wooden and glass double doors of the casino as they made their way to the restaurant had been enough to unsettle him.

'Chase hated gambling. He used to say it was the best way to get nothing from something,' Shirley was saying.

Freddy laughed dutifully. He had decided Chase was a smug fuck, the sort of man he'd go out of his way to avoid. But maybe that was only because Shirley was so keen on quoting him. Things like 'If life gives you lemons, make lemonade', and 'Don't *go* through life, *grow* through life'. Although the framed photograph on Shirley's coffee table of Chase Solaris was harmless enough: it showed a bluff, red-faced man standing on the deck of a large yacht, arms folded across his yellow life vest, a contented grin on his face.

'Have you had to step up to the plate since Chase died? Sort of learn to do all the stuff he did before?' Freddy asked when they were well into the second bottle of Côtes du Rhone.

Shirley looked baffled. 'I'm not sure I know what you mean.'

'Traditional man things? Perhaps you used to rely on Chase to book restaurants, for instance, deal with money. If he did that, now you have to.'

Her face softened, 'Oh, I see. Well, yes, I guess I have. Chase spoiled me, Freddy. Never let me lift a finger. "Don't you worry your pretty little head," he used to say.' Tears welled up in her eyes. 'But I find I'm good at all those things too. He'd have been proud of me.'

253

Freddy patted her hand across the table. He'd asked because he was feeling lost, missing so much that Lily provided. But for him it was the intangibles: her quiet common sense, her lack of pretension, an ability to make sense of his world. Things he could never provide for himself in a million years.

'Did she leave you because you lost your money, hon?' Shirley asked, holding his hand rather too tightly.

Freddy shook his head. It felt disloyal even talking about Lily with this woman. *What the fuck am I doing here anyway?*

'Come on.' She threw her napkin on the table and waved at a passing waiter. 'Let's go gamble our worries away.' She gave him a conspiratorial smile. 'Chase wasn't right about everything.'

And Freddy made no effort to resist.

He liked the room: high-ceilinged, the square space was not as big as he'd imagined from the outside; the décor seemed fresh, the rust and gold carpet new. It had a calm atmosphere on this Monday night – no crowds – as he and Shirley pulled themselves up on the black and chrome chairs beside the roulette table.

This is not gambling, Freddy told himself. *It's not my money, not my show.* It was as if Shirley were a Trojan horse, Freddy secreted inside, waiting to explode into the room, to cause mayhem. But as he sat there waiting for the hit, waiting for his old self to surface, he realized there were no fireworks. He was just playing by proxy, the American passing him a pile of chips, both of them discussing where they should be placed, chatting and laughing together as if this were the most mundane pursuit in the world. In his head, during these weeks of abstinence, he had imagined the old familiar feeling of electrification, the palpitations, the few blissful seconds of zoning out. He was both relieved and disappointed it was absent.

Shirley turned out to be a surprisingly reckless player and had won, then lost a fair sum over the hour and a half they sat at the table. But unlike Freddy and his ilk, she knew when to call it a day.

'Those are your winnings,' she said, pushing the chips back towards him. She was ready to cash in what remained of her pile, and he had added his own to hers.

'No. Your money,' he said, sliding them across the baize again.

She laughed. 'Don't argue, Freddy, because, believe me, I'll win.' Her normally breezy delivery suddenly had a touch of metal, backed up by a fierce look from her blue eyes.

What the hell? he thought. He needed the money, so he gave in, thanking her gracefully.

As they walked away from the casino, she linked arms with him. 'What a fabulous evening. Come back for a nightcap?' she asked, looking up at him.

Freddy was tired and discombobulated from the casino experience. He just wanted to fall asleep and forget. But Shirley had paid for everything as usual, even given him money. How churlish it would be to refuse. *This is what it feels like to be a kept man*, he thought sourly. 'Love to,' he found himself saying. He had to walk her home anyway. What harm could come from a quick nightcap? It wasn't as if either of them had anything to get up for in the morning.

CHAPTER 31

Lily was on her way to the narrowboat with the second batch of Seth Kramer's interviews. It was a warm, misty spring morning where the natural world seemed to be quietly alive: silky pink and white apple blossoms, the delicate fairy green of the ancient willow by the bridge, the scent of wild garlic on the breeze, the vibrant yellow of cowslips and purple-blue of bluebells.

She had typed up fifteen tapes in the week since delivering the first batch, sitting at the table with her laptop in the quiet kitchen. It was becoming easier, although some of the interviewees spoke too fast, others mumbled and a few banged on for both sides of the tape. Occasionally she found herself becoming fascinated by what the voice was saying, and forgot to type. She also made a horrible number of typos that she spent hours picking through and correcting. But the psychoanalyst had seemed happy with the work, barely glancing at the printed sheets before handing over another clutch of tapes.

As she paused on the bridge to take in the beautiful day, her phone rang. Sara. It was at least a week since she'd talked to her daughter, and Lily answered with pleasure.

But Sara's voice was frosty. 'Hi, Mum. Where are you?'

'On Aristotle Bridge, going to see Dr Kramer. What's the matter, darling?'

There was a long pause. 'I've split up with Stan.'

'Oh, God. I'm sorry. How did he react?'

'He was angry,' her daughter said, 'but he said he knew, said he'd known for weeks.' A pause. 'He said you'd told him, Mum.'

Lily cringed silently. 'I didn't.'

'He says you did. He says you met for lunch and told him I was having an affair.' Lily could hear the tears in her daughter's words, but before she had a chance to speak, Sara went on. 'How could you go behind my back like that, Mum? Why on earth didn't you say you'd seen him?'

Lily took a deep breath. 'Look, I know I shouldn't have met up with him without telling you, darling, and I'm really sorry. But he was so desperate, he literally begged me to see him, and begged me not to say we'd met. And then . . . well, I suppose he knew when I wouldn't answer his questions properly that I was hiding something.' She stopped, wondering if her babbling was getting through to her daughter. 'But I absolutely swear I didn't tell him about Ted.'

Silence. A sniff. Lily held her breath.

'I knew he was lying.'

'I shouldn't have seen him without telling you. It's been on my conscience ever since. But I wasn't sure this thing with Ted . . .'

There was another silence, then a long sigh at the other end of the phone.

'No, listen, this is all my fault, Mum. I ought to have told him months ago. It's put everyone in a shit position – all my friends were screaming at me to sort it out. But I love Stan. It was so hard.'

'I'm sure.' Lily paused. 'So you and Ted . . . it's serious?'

Another sigh. 'He's wonderful, Mum. I love him so much. I can't wait for you to meet him.' A pause. 'You won't be off with him, will you, because of Stan? It's not Ted's fault.'

'No, of course not. I look forward to meeting him,' Lily said, although she wasn't sure she did. She couldn't imagine Sara with anyone but Stan.

They said goodbye, and Lily had a moment of sadness for the man who had so reminded her of Sara's father. She stood against the warm stone, her phone still in her hand, looking out across the still water of the canal, and remembered the day she and Garret Tierney had met.

It was the end-of-term show at Byam Shaw and she'd been hovering with her friends, nervously checking the reactions of the people peering at their work displayed on the walls. A noisy, swaggering group of men had appeared in the hall – clearly a little the worse for wear – and begun wandering around the exhibits, commenting loudly. Lily and her friends had rolled their eyes, knowing they were probably full-of-themselves medical students because one of them was Vicky's brother – Vicky was an irritatingly pretty and even more annoyingly talented student with whom they all competed. Her brother, Richard, was a boisterous presence at pub outings.

Then a tall, broad-shouldered member of the group had stopped in front of Lily's pen-and-ink portraits – these were her first and she had been experimenting, not sure if the genre suited her style, if the colours were bold enough, if she should have made them bigger, used different paper, if, if, if . . . He had drawn closer, his nose only inches from her work, then grabbed his friend's sleeve and brought him to look.

'Hey, look at these, Raj. Grand, don't you think?' he'd said, his Irish voice warm and admiring. 'I like them.'

Lily, flustered and embarrassed, had held back until her friends pushed her forward and Garret swung round to greet her. He had been overwhelming. Handsome, laughing, his blue eyes gathering her up as if she already belonged to him. Her father and mother had arrived soon afterwards, and Garret had introduced himself, as if he'd been dating Lily for years. That was Garret all over. A man for whom confidence was a given, 'no' not even in his vocabulary.

Now Lily's heart lurched. Garret and his laughing eyes, the father of her children, the man with whom she'd thought she would spend the rest of her life. Her thoughts turned to Freddy, the disquiet she felt at his ongoing silence forcing her to draw a comparison between the two men. But remembering the genuine constancy of her first marriage, she wasn't sure now she would exchange Garret's almost presumptuous love with Freddy's frailer, more sensitive version. His gaze might be less bold than Garret's, his manner less confident against the gold standard of Mr Tierney. He was altogether a gentler person, his vulnerability, in the moments of reflection Lily sometimes caught, glaringly apparent. Still, the love in his eyes for her seemed disarmingly certain, perhaps more ardent than Garret's had ever been. Brushing tears from her eyes, she put her phone away and walked the short distance to the boat.

'Hey, Lily. Come on in.' Seth extended his hand to guide her onto the boat. 'Have you time for coffee? We could sit outside – it's so beautiful.'

They settled in the tatty canvas chairs Seth placed on the decking in the stern of the boat, and Lily accepted the cup of coffee he'd made for her, glad to be distracted from her troubling thoughts.

'I've just got one of these pod machines,' he said. 'I resisted them for an age – it seems such a clinical way to make coffee. Is it okay?' He glanced anxiously at her cup.

'Perfect.'

Neither spoke for a minute, but even though Lily was only meeting the doctor for the third time, the silence didn't feel awkward. She supposed he was used to pockets of silence with his patients.

'How did you get on?' he asked.

'All done. Some of the interviews are so absorbing it's hard not to get involved. Should be an interesting book.'

He pulled a wry face. 'When I finally finish it. But things seem to get in the way, I find.'

There was something so sad in his statement that she found herself asking, 'What sort of things?'

He shot her a surprised glance, and she immediately regretted her question. 'I didn't mean to pry.'

For a moment he didn't respond, his eyes looking out across the canal, blinking hard behind his glasses. 'No . . . no, you're not prying. I'm just not in the habit of talking about myself. We psychoanalysts make it a rule never to let the patients know anything about our private lives. The work is all about them.' He smiled. 'But then, you're not a patient.' Seth had taken a deep breath, turning a steady gaze on Lily as if determined to get through the embarrassment of disclosure. 'My wife died three years ago. I haven't dealt with it particularly well . . . I can't seem to settle to any-thing.' He raised his eyebrows briefly, blinked as he gave a small shrug.

'I'm so sorry. I know how that feels,' she said, adding quickly, 'although it's different for everyone, of course.' She remembered all too well the friends who had assumed how she was feeling after Garret died. They were seldom accurate, grief being such a complicated thing.

He looked puzzled. 'Your husband died? I thought . . .'

'My first husband, yes. Ten years ago.' She told him, in a sentence, about Garret's death, pared down to something almost manageable now. Almost.

'Heavens.' He shot her an apologetic glance. 'Grief is so selfish. You think you're the only person who's ever felt this way, ever suffered so much.'

She smiled. 'Well, I suppose that's true to a certain extent.

261

The pain is the same but there are probably a million ways to feel it.'

The silence was heavy as they both remembered. It had been bewildering as much as painful for Lily. She had felt completely untethered, unable to settle to anything, as if she'd forgotten how to do even the simplest of daily tasks. And throughout that hellish period she'd had the compelling need to cope, to find a way to make things right for the twins and tell her friends she was *fine, really*. A sudden image of Garret's beautiful long-fingered surgeon's hands, always scrubbed so clean and smelling of Betadine, sprang randomly to mind. She had loved his hands.

'I didn't deal with it well either,' she said. 'We don't do death properly in this country.'

He laughed. 'I'm Jewish. Given half a chance we do death more than properly. Sitting *shiva*, it's called. If done to the max we don't shower or shave for seven days, or wear jewellery, have sex, work. We cover the mirrors and all our relatives come over with food and sit about crying with us. It's very cathartic.' He sighed. 'But Anna wasn't Jewish, and I'm not Orthodox. Anyway, I was so angry I refused all the help and comfort that was offered.'

'How did she die?'

She saw his face tense. 'She fell down these concrete steps when we were on holiday and her leg got infected. Neither of us thought anything of it, but it wouldn't heal. She ended up with septic shock. I was in Manchester at the time, at a conference. If I'd been there . . .'

She didn't state the obvious, that he couldn't have known.

She was sure everyone had said the same thing and obviously it hadn't helped.

Seth shook himself, picked up the cup he'd placed on the deck and pushed himself to his feet. Looking down at her, he said, 'But you fell in love again. There is hope.'

Fired up by too much coffee from Seth's swish pod machine earlier, Lily settled at the kitchen table, opened her laptop and loaded a new tape into the Dictaphone. She'd enjoyed her talk with the doctor. He was an interesting man. That he had been through a trauma similar to her own had created a welcome bond in Lily's empty world. Yes, she was living with David and Helen, but neither really talked to her much: they were both so absorbed in their work, mostly silent over supper in the evenings. And the daily phone calls to the twins she had enjoyed in the past had dwindled to nothing. *Sara is busy being in love*, she kept telling herself. *Dillon is still angry with me. They'll come round.* But it was painful, the distance that seemed to be opening up between her and her children. What felt worse was that she couldn't summon enough energy to close the gap.

She pressed 'Play' on the small machine and began to type. The voice, identified in Seth's black biro italics as 'Phil Hookem', spoke low and very fast. Not one of Dr Kramer's successes, by the sound of it, as Phil spent the first five minutes insisting, 'Even you thought I was pretty sane, just having a bit of an episode. And you got me through it, I'll admit that. But it was like you were a shoulder to cry on, somewhere safe I could come each week to offload, save Janey having to listen.

I never got all this bollocks—' He coughed, which was followed by an embarrassed 'Excuse me, not bollocks, Doctor, but the going back to the past seemed a waste of time for both of us . . .'

Lily's neck began to ache. She was not taking her own advice about the separate keyboard and all the muscles in her shoulders were stiffening up with the daily hours in front of the computer. She went upstairs to lie flat for ten minutes and closed her eyes, but almost immediately she heard a strange noise that seemed to be coming from downstairs – a sort of scrabbling, as if someone were searching for something.

Heart pounding, she tiptoed across the room and out to the head of the stairs. Silence. She knew it couldn't be either David or Helen as her brother-in-law was in Buckingham, delivering a table to a client, and her sister had called her twenty minutes before and said she was sitting on a bench outside her office with a prawn sandwich.

Telling herself she must have imagined it – this wasn't her house, after all, so she didn't know all its foibles – Lily continued downstairs, her feet bare and soundless. As she reached the hall and turned towards the kitchen, silence still prevailed and she laughed at herself, although instinct told her something was not right.

The figure – thin, tall, wearing a long-sleeved faded yellow T-shirt and black jeans – had his back to her as he munched a biscuit from the open red and white tin canister. In his other hand he had a phone . . . *her* phone. She knew it by the distinctive sunglasses and blue palm tree on the cover that Freddy had bought her as a joke.

'Hey!'

The figure spun round, dropping the phone on the floor with a clunk.

They stared at each other. Lily didn't recognize him immediately. Her heart was banging so hard in her chest she felt almost faint.

'Aunty Lily,' Kit said, his voice sounding as shocked as she felt. 'What are you doing here?'

'I could ask you the same thing,' she said, sitting down on a chair with relief. 'You scared the life out of me.'

'Thought the place would be empty,' he said a trifle sullenly as he stood over by the kettle, shifting from foot to foot.

Lily was horrified. The last time she'd seen her nephew was seven years ago, at her father's funeral. At the time he'd been in rehab for a month and was looking pale but reasonably healthy, his manner thoughtful and sad – he had loved his grandfather.

Today he was like a ghost of the beautiful curly-headed boy she remembered. His intelligent grey eyes were haunted, his skin pasty and scarred by acne, his blond hair lank with dirt as it fell around his neck. She watched him bend to pick up the mobile from the slate tiles and lay it on the table.

'How did you get in?'

He raised his eyebrows. 'A key?'

She was embarrassed. It was Kit's house more than hers and she had no right to question him.

'I'll make some tea,' she suggested, getting up. He didn't refuse the offer, just stood there blinking rapidly and scratching a sore on the back of his hand.

'Don't tell Mum I came round,' he said as she poured boiling water into two cups, pressed a spoon into the teabags, lifted them out and dropped them into the sink, then splashed milk into the brew.

'Why not?'

He moved away along the counter, as if he were scared to be too close.

'What did you come for, if you knew no one would be home?' Lily pushed his cup towards him across the work surface and went to sit down. 'Sugar's there.'

Kit heaped two large spoonsful into his tea, stirring it vigorously, his actions nervy and quick.

'Sit,' she urged – he looked as if he might fall down at any moment. Kit hesitated, then dropped into a chair across from her. He didn't look at her.

'Why don't you want Helen to know you came round?' she asked again.

When he still didn't answer, she said, 'Kit? Please, talk to me. You can stay here if you want.'

His eyes, when he finally lifted them to hers, were glassy, as if he'd zoned out. It was a minute or two before he answered. 'Don't you know? I'm banned. Mum doesn't want me here. It was Dad who gave me the key.'

'So why did you come?'

Kit fidgeted in the chair as he picked at a splinter of wood on the edge of the table. 'No reason,' he said after a minute, his face softening suddenly, offering a flash of the old Kit, the vulnerable child, not this edgy, sullen addict.

Her heart broke for him. She reached across and laid her

266

hand on his. For a second he let it rest there, then pulled his own away abruptly.

'Do you need food?' It was a pointless question, knowing what he'd really come for. Helen had told her that David dropped off food each week, although it didn't look as if Kit ate any of it: he was skin and bone.

He didn't answer, his hollow eyes darting about the room. *Had he been about to make off with my phone?* she wondered.

'I'm trying to get to Scotland, Aunty Lily,' Kit said, getting up, fixing her with his nervy, blinking gaze, which seemed to be getting more anxious as the minutes ticked by in the quiet kitchen. 'Kirsty – that's my friend – her dad's dying and she really needs to see him.' He produced a charming smile, dragged up, Lily supposed, from some far-forgotten life. 'We'll take the bus, but neither of us has the money . . .' His look became pleading. 'She'll be devastated if he dies without her saying goodbye.'

Even delivered as it was, with a convincing desperation, Lily had lived in London too long to buy her nephew's tale for a single second. She had been regularly stopped by the homeless addicts there, who'd spin her tragic stories about hostels to pay for, funerals and sick relatives in Scotland, coach journeys – always Scotland. A dying mum in Brighton, for instance, would elicit far less cash.

She hesitated. *Would it hurt, just this once?* Kit was an addict. That wouldn't change if she didn't give him money. He'd just get it from somewhere else – maybe rob an old lady, break into a house, commit a criminal act. Wouldn't it be better for the money to come from her?

Kit saw her hesitation and drove home his advantage. 'I know you think I'm spinning a line so I can get money for drugs. But I'm not using any more, I swear, Aunty Lily. I'm clean, look at me.' He spread his arms wide as if this proved anything. 'Me and Kirsty are off all that now.' His accent had taken on the patois of the street, the educated grammar of the Oxford graduate long gone.

Do I believe him? She had no idea what to look for. She knew there was something about pupils being pinpoint or dilated, but she couldn't remember which it was, or whether the substance the person was taking made a difference. And, anyway, Kit kept shifting about and blinking so much that she wouldn't have been able to check. He obviously wasn't well, but couldn't the nerviness and anxiety, the scarecrow looks, equally be a sign of withdrawal from drugs as of taking them? She dithered as her nephew watched her intently, wanting desperately to believe he was telling the truth . . . And coming to the conclusion, finally, that he was not.

In the end, she didn't have the heart to refuse the boy – man, in fact. Kit was now thirty-one, no longer a boy, although he didn't seem to have grown up somehow. As if the drugs had arrested his development. But now, as he stood in front of her, he was also slightly frightening, the violent intensity of his gaze unnerving. She sensed he was on the edge and that the smallest thing could tip him over.

'Hold on a sec,' she said, and made her way into the hall, where her bag was hanging on a coat hook by the front door. She took out forty pounds. *Too much? Not enough?* She folded the notes in half and went back into the kitchen, handing them to him.

The relief on his face removed any doubt as to why he needed the money. Stuffing it into his back pocket and immediately glancing towards the door, her nephew was clearly anxious to get away now he had what he'd come for.

'Thanks, thanks so much, Aunty Lily,' he said quickly, and leaned forward reflexively to hug her, then apparently changed his mind. Up close he smelt rank with a sharp almost chemical odour coming off his body. 'Please . . . please don't tell them I've been here.'

'Why not?' She didn't understand. If David had given him a key, why was it so imperative his parents didn't know about his visit?

'You won't, will you?'

'I can't promise, Kit.'

He stared at her for a moment, perhaps deciding whether it was worth a fight, then shrugged and turned away, hurrying towards the hall. She heard the front door bang behind him and let out a long sigh of relief.

CHAPTER 32

Helen could not believe what she was hearing. 'You gave him money?' It was after supper and she was exhausted after a long week. David was filling the dishwasher, getting a soap tablet from under the sink, placing it in the dispenser inside the machine's door. She stared at her sister as Lily handed her a mug of tea. 'Are you completely mad?'

Lily did look sheepish. *Give her that*, Helen thought, as she watched her sister collect her own mug and go back to sit in her chair on the other side of the table.

'I thought ... He was very convincing. And I decided he was on drugs anyway, so perhaps it was better for me to give him a few quid than let him steal it from someone else.'

David straightened up and Helen saw him staring at her sister, his mouth twisting as he picked up a tea towel and began to dry the glasses – the stems too long for the dish-washer.

'How much did you give him?' he asked.

Lily's face was flushed with embarrassment. 'Forty. I—'

'How *could* you?' Helen interrupted her. 'How could you interfere like this?' A sudden fury took hold of her and she stood up, stamping round the table till she was standing over her sister. 'Have you any idea what you've done? Kit is a *drug addict*. Of course he's convincing. He's clever, always was, but he doesn't know how to tell the truth any more. All he knows is that he needs his next fix. And you've just given it to him on a plate. You might as well have filled the syringe and injected it into his bloody vein.'

She could feel tears of rage in her eyes and swallowed hard.

'Do you understand? *Do you*, Lily? That money could be killing him right now.'

'Helen . . .' David's voice was soft, trying to calm her, but she wouldn't be calmed.

'It's not just about the money. You've let him think he can come back here now, invade our home. Let him think you'll give him what he wants.' She took in a sharp breath as a thought occurred to her. 'Did you let him in? Although he's quite capable of breaking in if he thought there'd be anything to steal.' Something inside her collapsed and she felt suddenly too tired to be angry. She backed away from her sister, went to sit down again. 'We never leave money around now. All our valuables are locked away in the attic. Kit knows that. I thought he'd given up trying.'

She caught Lily's glance at her husband and saw David's almost warning look in return.

'What?' she demanded. 'What's going on?'

David came and sat down with them, still holding the tea towel. 'I gave him a key, Helen.'

'What? You did what?'

'I know what we agreed, but I was scared when he wasn't in the flat the other week and the place was locked up. What would happen if he couldn't stay there any longer? Where would he go?'

Helen wanted to smack her husband for his misplaced compassion. They were on opposite sides of a hellish fence: David trying to save Kit with kindness, Helen believing in tough love. 'He'd go where all good drug addicts eventually go: the gutter,' Helen snapped. 'And maybe, just maybe, being there will finally bring him to his senses.'

Lily and David were staring at her, but she couldn't tell if it was disgust on their faces or pity.

'I should have told you,' David said. 'I'm sorry. But I knew you'd be furious and I didn't think he'd use the key.'

'Ha. No, of course he's not going to use a key that lets him into a house with all sorts of possibilities for obtaining money for a fix. He'd never do *that*.' Her sarcasm soothed her, made her feel almost powerful in a situation over which she had absolutely no control. She glared at her husband. 'I should have warned you, Lily, but I didn't realize he had a key, did I?'

'I'm so sorry. This is all my fault,' Lily said.

Helen saw that her contrition was genuine. But it didn't help. It felt like a conspiracy all of a sudden. Lily here when she shouldn't be, interfering, siding with David, perhaps even in cahoots with him about how to treat their son. And judging her for her lack of compassion. 'You think I'm just letting him go to hell, don't you?'

'No, of course I don't think that.' Her sister sighed. 'Listen, I got it wrong. I didn't know what to do. I'd never seen Kit in that state before. I was genuinely shocked. He was skin and bone—'

'The trouble with you is you're so naive, Lily,' Helen interrupted, not wanting to hear any more details of her son's condition. She herself had not seen Kit for over a year and the guilt gnawed. 'This Freddy business. If you'd been a bit more on the ball, hadn't had your head in the clouds, assuming the best of everyone, you wouldn't be in the situation you're in today. Freddy's as much of an addict as Kit, for God's sake. It's just you can't see the marks on his skin.'

She knew she was being spiteful, and saw the hurt registering on her sister's face with some satisfaction. Later she would feel mean, but right now it was good to make someone else suffer a version of the distress she experienced on a daily basis whenever she thought of her son.

'Helen,' David was frowning at her, 'that's unfair.'

She raised her eyebrows. 'Is it really? Surely if Lily had spotted Freddy's habit sooner, she could have protected her money. And got him some help.' She wouldn't look at her sister.

'It doesn't always work out that way though, does it?' David said, and she knew he was referring to the endless 'help' they had offered their son. The regular visits with Kit to see their kind old GP, which had got them nowhere. The three sessions in rehab at huge expense, Kit relapsing each time within

273

weeks of coming out. The rows, promises, lies, hope . . . None of it had done the slightest good in addressing their son's addiction.

'No,' Helen said wearily. 'No, I suppose it doesn't.' She met Lily's eye. 'Sorry.'

Later, when she was lying in bed in the darkness, wound up to the hilt with the evening's discussion, adrenalin defying her need to sleep, she said to David, 'I want you to get the key off Kit the next time you see him. Promise?'

David, whose breathing told her he was almost asleep, said, 'I'll try.'

Helen sat up. 'No, that's not good enough. You must get it or I'll have to change the locks. I can't have our home wide open to a bunch of drug addicts. Because it's not just Kit, is it? It's anyone he might be hanging out with at the time. We'll come home one day and find the whole place has been cleaned out.'

It was easier to focus on the practical aspect of the key, of lost possessions, than on the state of their son. There was no more discussion to be had on that subject anyway. She and David had talked – cried – themselves to a standstill about him. And it hadn't changed a thing.

'Maybe we should get new locks anyway,' she heard her husband say softly. And she knew then that he was as freaked out by Kit's appearance as she had been. Freaked out by the thought of their son standing in the kitchen in the family home, in *his* home, where he had spent his entire childhood.

CHAPTER 33

It was a Saturday in early June as Freddy once again made his way towards the Portomaso complex and Shirley's apartment. He and Shirley had spent the previous day in the capital, Valletta. She had insisted they take a *dgħajsa* across the Grand Harbour and visit the war museum in Vittoriosa. Do the tour. Freddy had not objected. It made a change from the long afternoons on hot restaurant terraces, when both became stultified with rich food and too much wine. A strange form of hell for Freddy, one that anyone else would consider a most enviable existence, but which he saw as a frustrating lacuna in his life that would soon – God willing – be over.

He and Shirley tended to keep their conversation general, talking about all things Maltese: the food, new hotel developments, wines, government, local gangsters and tourist sights. Or American politics: Shirley was fiercely Republican but loathed both main contenders for the following year's presidential election alike. They had no friends in common to gossip about – in fact Freddy had no friends at all except for Shirley, unless you counted the various bar and café staff he chatted to on a daily basis. They had no work or family to distract them. The days were very long, or so it seemed to Freddy.

But when they were on the traditional water taxi, the chatty Maltese boatman rowing them across the harbour in the sunshine, tanned forehead beading with sweat, began telling them at length about his five children and sick mother, about how hard it was to make ends meet. A transparent attempt, thought Freddy cynically, to extort a larger tip.

'You have big family?' the boatman asked.

Shirley had smiled benignly as she replied from beneath her broad-brimmed straw hat, 'Oh, yes. We have four children and eleven grandchildren.'

The boatman seemed thrilled with this news, his face breaking into a huge grin.

'Ah, you are very blessed, Sinjura.'

'We are indeed,' Shirley said, taking Freddy's hand as they sat on the narrow wooden bench and gazing lovingly into his face.

Freddy found the smile frozen on his lips. It was a joke, he got that, but the look Shirley gave him brought him up short.

The boatman handed them out, Shirley having obliged with a very generous tip that brought blessings raining down upon her head long after they'd walked away along the quay. Neither spoke for a while, just took in the beautiful butter-coloured stone of the ancient, elegant buildings of the Grand Harbour glowing in the sunlight.

276

'So how do you like being a grandfather of eleven?' Shirley said eventually, with a teasing purse of her lips. But the look she gave him implied she wasn't sure if she'd offended him.

Freddy laughed it off. 'I always think it odd that it's seen as such an achievement to have lots of children who subsequently have lots more.'

'Did you never want any yourself?' she asked, her expression suddenly serious. They had reached the small entrance to the museum above the harbour, but they hesitated on the step.

Freddy hated this question, so often asked. He couldn't tell people the real answer. He never had, not even Lily. But the very thought of having a child in his care filled him with dread. Suppose the brutal instincts of his father manifested themselves in him? A malign genetic inheritance that made him subconsciously ape his father's sadism. Wasn't it a fact that often the abused abuse, even without meaning to?

Uninvited images, accompanied by the old blood-draining fear, invaded his thoughts. Coming home from school and seeing the furniture in the sitting room above the pub pushed ominously to the side, a wooden chair placed in the centre, knowing what was to come. He never had any idea what he'd done to deserve punishment, but it was pointless to ask, because the more he asked, the heavier the beating. Freddy's main goal, after a couple of terrible humiliations, was not to wet himself. It helped, somehow, to focus on this, to shut his young body down, screw it tight until his father had had his pleasure.

There had never been a single second in his life when he

could imagine himself needing – because it did seem like a need his father had – to do this to a child, a person, even an animal. But he wasn't going to put any child's safety at risk, just in case he was wrong. That was why Lily's family was so perfect. His past relationships with women had foundered on his unshakeable resolve never to have children. But with Lily, he could be a stepfather to two adults over whom he had absolutely no control.

At the thought of Dillon, his heart contracted. He'd blown that relationship now. Even if Lily decided to trust him again, Dillon – and therefore Sara – certainly would not. And this might be the straw that broke the camel's back when it came to them getting back together. No mother wanted to choose between her children and the man she loved.

'I think I'd be a hopeless father,' he'd said to Shirley. 'Don't have the patience.'

And they both laughed and left it at that.

The dusty, drab militaria in the museum depressed Freddy and left him cold. The underground shelter – raked stone, chilly, dark, confined, airless – made him want to scrabble for breath. But Shirley was lapping it up, chatting for hours with the young Maltese student from whom they bought their tickets. Freddy's mood remained uneasy. He never voluntarily remembered: it was only if his thoughts were triggered, as had happened earlier, that the images escaped the locked box of childhood. But on the rare occasions when they did, it always took him a while to recover, to fully assimilate the fact in his adult brain that the room, the chair, the smell of the old wooden seat . . . that first hot slice of pain and the agonizing wait for the second – and, of course, his father – no longer existed for him.

Later, Shirley insisted on making him supper. Freddy was relieved not to have to go out again. How he missed those evenings with Lily when he had made her a spicy fish soup or a rich bolognese, then sat in their elegant white kitchen with the view over London, laughed together about the day, listened to blues – maybe Robert Johnson or Howlin' Wolf – on his Bose and sipped a delicious red. Their life had been magic. He gave a sigh of disappointment, as he drank his second gin and tonic, that Shirley was not his wife.

Shirley, by her own admission, was not a great cook. The chicken breast was overdone, the olive oil and rosemary potatoes undercooked, the salad dressing sharp with too much vinegar. But she'd prepared it with care and Freddy wasn't complaining one bit.

'There's going to be a storm,' Shirley said, looking towards the windows as they cleared away the dishes.

The night sky was rumbling ominously, a cold wind blowing through the still-open doors onto the balcony. Shirley lit two fat pink candles on the coffee table and brought through a tray upon which stood a pot of fresh mint tea, pale-green china cups and saucers, two small brandy balloons and a box of champagne truffles she said she'd got in Duty Free the last time she'd flown.

It felt odd sitting inside on the pale, squashy sofas. Normally they sailed through to the balcony and the loungers, even at night. Freddy gazed at the numerous photos of Chase dotted about the room and had the uneasy sense that Shirley's husband was watching him. *I should slow down*, he told himself, glancing at his drink. But what had he got to lose? There was no one to care whether he lived or died except this American widow, with her honeycomb hair and bold gold jewellery.

Shirley sat down next to him, brandy glass cradled in her palms, a faraway look in her eye. 'This is what I thought I'd be doing with dear Chase,' she said softly.

There seemed nothing to say to this, so Freddy just gave her a sympathetic glance. The storm was gathering force outside, the rain now pounding on the tiles of the balcony. 'I'd better close the windows,' he said, getting up.

He stood for a moment in the blast of wind and rain, hands clutching the glass doors, assailed by a feeling of such dull emptiness that it elicited a groan. Closing them quickly, he took a steadying breath before turning back to Shirley. 'Quite a night.'

She raised her eyebrows, patting the cushion beside her. 'Hey, what's the matter? You look stricken.'

He tried to laugh. 'Oh, you know. My life's a wreck . . .'

'Stop that. I won't have you sinking. It's just a glitch, hon. We all have them.' She smiled encouragingly, reached for his hand as he sat down. 'Chase always said, "If you have despair you might as well put your head in the oven."'

Very cheering, thought Freddy. *You're such a wag, Chase.* To Shirley, he said, 'Your Chase knew a thing or two.'

They both listened to the storm.

'Are you thinking of going back to the UK?' she asked, not relinquishing his hand, her voice nonchalant.

'Not sure.' Shirley still had no real idea why he was hiding out in Malta and he obviously wasn't going to tell her. 'I don't have a job, now the business has gone bust.'

'Couldn't you find work here? I know the government has just announced a movie fund, and there's always lots of movies being shot here, because of the weather.' She paused. 'I'm not sure what exactly you do, Freddy. How would you describe your work?'

He forced a laugh. 'Good question. I used to be a sound engineer, but I haven't done that in years, not since I got my own studio, and no one would employ me as one now. I suppose you could call me a businessman or entrepreneur. I set stuff up, raise money . . . network. I'm good at networking, Lily always says.'

Shirley's face lightened. 'Well, that's a marvellous skill. I've got this friend, Julian, a British producer, TV shows mostly, I think. He's lived here for years, on and off. He'll know who to talk to. I could introduce you.'

'Thanks.' *Maybe that's the way forward*, he mused drunkenly. *Find a job here, where no one knows me, make some money . . .* For a moment he envisaged Lily living there with him, pictured them doing up Nanna Pina's flat, making it properly habitable. He had done little beyond a cursory clean of the place and still slept on the sofa – the bed was rock hard and reminded him too much of his grandmother – with a duvet, pillows and the cheap scratchy cotton covers he'd bought in the local discount store. It wasn't home, just a staging post, but could it be?

Shirley had got the bit between her teeth now and was

banging on about location work and Valletta being the European Capital of Culture in 2018. Freddy tried to look enthusiastic, but his brain was befuddled and he was barely managing to keep up.

A deafening clap of thunder overhead roused him from his torpor, making them both jump. It was followed, almost immediately, by a violent electric-blue flash that lit up the sky, then another booming clap.

'Heavens!' Shirley exclaimed. 'You won't be able to go home in this.'

'Oh, I'll be fine,' he assured her, not relishing the prospect at all.

'Nonsense. You'll be soaked through. You can stay in the spare room . . . I insist.'

More brandy and maybe an hour of desultory chat later – Freddy had no idea of the time – Shirley led him through to the back of the condo and opened the door to his bedroom. Like the rest of the place, it was decorated in neutral cream and immaculately tidy, with built-in wardrobes, nondescript seascape prints on the wall and a double bed, already made up with smooth cream linen, a blue and cream striped quilt folded across the foot, an assortment of blue and yellow cushions at the head, as if she were expecting company.

'There's water on the nightstand and I have a spare toothbrush,' she said. 'You'll have to sleep in the buff, unless you want a pair of Chase's pyjamas?'

Freddy did not.

*

He slept like the dead, the wide divan mattress and cool sheets a very pleasant change from the cramped leather sofa in his grandmother's apartment. It was still dark outside and his head was banging painfully when he surfaced to the disorienting touch of a hand stroking its way down his naked hip and over his thigh. He was immediately awake.

'Hey,' he heard Shirley's voice, soft in the darkness.

Rolling onto his back, he felt the silk of her nightdress against his arm.

'Thought you needed a bit of cheering up,' he heard her whisper.

'Umm ... Listen, Shirley ...' He stopped, gently pushing her arm away. 'Not sure this is a good idea.'

Silent and clearly undeterred, Shirley drew closer, her hand sliding deliberately across him till it found what it was searching for. He heard her sharp intake of breath and then her body was pressed to his, the silk gliding seductively across his skin. With shame he felt himself harden quickly as her fingers began to move rhythmically – and expertly. It had been a long time.

Without a word, her breathing now fast and jagged, she pushed back the duvet and brought her mouth down on his erection, her lips soft, tongue flicking against the tip. Freddy no longer thought, no longer cared. He just gave in to the pleasure. After a few minutes he took her silk-clad body and raised her up till she was astride him, her thighs surprisingly strong as she held him between her legs. He lifted her gently until he was inside her and she cried out, dropping to his chest, her nipples hard through the silk. He could smell the faint scent of coconut on her hair, taste himself on her mouth. It lasted only a few minutes before both of them came, letting out loud, animal groans.

When Freddy woke next it was morning and he had his bed to himself. There was the pungent scent of coffee on the air as he poked his head out of his room and slipped into the bathroom to brush his teeth. His head was still banging and he saw in the bathroom mirror his chin stubbly dark, great bags beneath his eyes. He was sure Chase's razor was somewhere in the cupboard under the cream-painted basin unit, but that might be a step too far, given the goings-on of the previous night. Although he wasn't sure at this juncture if Shirley's visit had even been real. He sincerely hoped it had not, prayed it was just a fevered dream brought on by anxiety and too much brandy.

He washed his face vigorously with cold water, picked up the pink brush that lay on the shelf and attempted to tame his tangled hair. Frowning as he regarded his reflection for the last time, he took a deep breath and prepared to face his hostess. Thoughts of Lily he pushed far to the back of his mind.

Shirley was sitting on the balcony, a cup of coffee on the small bamboo table, reading the *Times of Malta*. She was dressed in a pair of navy linen shorts and a sleeveless coral T-shirt, her hair sleek, her makeup tastefully minimal to suit the time of day.

She jumped when Freddy materialized beside her, but that was the only sign that she might be embarrassed by the events of the previous night. Folding the paper, she swung her feet off the lounger and stood up, a perky smile playing around her mouth. 'Freddy! Did you sleep okay?'

Sleep? he thought. *Cheeky cow*, but he said, 'Like a log. Your bed is way more comfortable than the one at the flat.'

He had not explained to Shirley the true extent of dilapidation in his grandmother's home, and certainly not invited her there, although she had hinted a number of times that she would like to visit.

Shirley laughed and flung her arms wide, her head thrown back, indicating the vista beyond the balcony. 'Isn't it just marvellous this morning? All glittery from the rain and so clean and fresh. We should have a storm more often.'

She was right: the air sparkled, the Mediterranean light crystal clear as it bounced off the aquamarine sea. Freddy breathed in, wishing himself a million miles away. *Should I say something? Wait for her?*

'I could murder a cup of coffee,' he said.

CHAPTER 34

'Heavens, you're soaked!' Seth said as he opened the glass doors to Lily. She had ridden over, braving her sister's bicycle for the first time and discovering that it was, indeed, 'as easy as riding a bike'. But what had seemed a dry, if cloudy, day when she set out had suddenly turned wet, the rain instantly heavy. Now her thighs were sodden, her jeans clinging to her legs.

Seth ushered her inside. 'Lucky I lit the stove.' He frowned, eyes on her sopping jeans. 'I've got some tracksuit bottoms in the back. You'd better take those off and we'll hang them by the fire. You'll catch your death if you sit in them.'

The last thing Lily wanted to do was change into the doctor's tracksuit, but she had little choice and didn't bother to protest. Seth left her alone to change into the grey cotton trousers, but she was aware of him only feet away on the other side of the open partition and cringed with embarrassment.

Later they sat with cups of his favourite jasmine green tea in front of the fire, Lily's jeans draped on a fold-up chair near the heat.

'What should I have done?' Lily asked, desperate to talk to someone about Kit. 'He's my nephew – I've known him since he was a baby.'

'Did you give him a lot?'

'Forty.' She had thought it was mean at the time, but now it sounded like a vast amount, Helen having told her the current price of a heroin wrap could be as little as ten pounds.

Seth didn't seem to condemn her. 'It's hard when it's someone you're close to.'

'I thought it was better coming from me.' She sighed. 'And David takes him food every week. He even gave him a key to the house, so Kit can let himself in.'

'Sounds like you're all supporting his habit in some way.'

'Not Helen. She was livid.'

'She's right, I'm afraid, although it seems cruel. You and David are just making it easier for Kit to survive as an addict.'

'I'm not sure I could have refused. He was a bit threatening ... I don't think he'd have attacked me or anything, but his desperation was almost palpable.'

They were both silent for a moment.

'Addicts can be very convincing. And most of us tend to believe people rather than not.'

Lily pushed the thought of Freddy to the back of her mind. 'So you think David should stop taking food round?'

'Yes. Your nephew will most likely be trading it rather than eating it anyway.'

'He certainly didn't look as if he'd had a square meal in decades.' She felt suddenly so sad. 'He used to be such a beautiful, funny boy. And clever. He was at Magdalen, got a first in biochemistry by the time he was twenty.'

'So what happened?'

She shrugged. 'No one seems to know. I mean, my sister can be tricky, especially with me, but she's been a brilliant mother, and David a wonderful father. Kit had a very stable upbringing.'

'Something must have triggered it. Something he couldn't cope with.'

'He's never said. I can't bear to see him like this, though. Or see what it's doing to Helen and David.'

'People do turn their lives around sometimes, Lily. To me the ones who do are heroes. The willpower needed to resist an addictive substance is huge. Especially when they know they need to harness that willpower for the rest of their lives.'

Lily asked, 'But what makes them do it – turn their lives around?' Freddy's face swam before her eyes.

'If I knew that, I'd be rich.' Seth frowned. 'They have to want to, that's key, obviously. Often it's getting to rock bottom. One day they wake up to the realization that it's change or die. Then it depends on the help they can access.'

Lily said, 'A gambling addict, for instance . . . I mean, gambling's not like drugs.' She had thought she'd asked the question casually, without any special emphasis, but she saw Seth's dark eyes fix intently on her face.

'It is like drugs, Lily,' he replied quietly, 'in that the need to gamble is just as intense, apparently, as any heroin hit.'

Lily bowed her head. 'But it's easier to give up, surely? It's not like your body is being physically affected by an actual substance.'

Another look from Seth, this one curious. 'I know it should be easier to give up a habit rather than a substance. But, oddly, it's not. Perhaps because the gambler can go undetected, sometimes for a long time, until their debts reach tipping point. But it can make them physically ill, too. Stress, depression, suicide even ... The effects are potentially just as devastating as a heroin habit.'

Lily's throat contracted and she looked away. It still seemed impossible that the man she loved was unable to stop himself destroying everything that meant anything to him, was open to mental health issues and self-harm.

'I'm sure you know most addicts are trying to escape from emotional pain of some sort. Blocking out past trauma. Low self-esteem issues ... a whole variety of complex reasons. There's often a hereditary component.'

None of these seemed to apply to Kit or Freddy. Freddy certainly didn't have low self-esteem, and he'd always told her he'd had an uneventful childhood, his parents both kind and supportive. Although his mother had died when he was fourteen from cancer.

'Like losing a parent when you're young, maybe?' she asked, desperate to work out what had pushed her husband to the edge.

Seth shrugged. 'As I said, it's very complex, Lily.'

Lily realized she must stop. He was still looking at her intently. She wanted so much to tell him about Freddy, but he was her employer: it might cause all sorts of awkwardness in the future if she did. She got up quickly and went to see if her jeans were dry. They weren't, of course, merely warm and damp rather than cold and damp. But she wanted to leave before she said more than was appropriate.

'You can wear my tracksuit pants home if you can deal with the embarrassment,' Seth said, laughing.

'I think I'd better,' Lily said. 'I don't want to interrupt your work any longer.'

'I welcome any diversion, I'm afraid.' He got up. 'I'll go and get some more tapes.'

Freddy's presence hung in the air between them, even though Seth knew nothing about her husband, beyond that he and Lily were separated. Yet he seemed to know everything. Those dark eyes of his were like a laser beam, probing into the depths of her soul.

He handed her another bag. 'I was wondering, could you put all the clients on a spreadsheet? With a date, file name, length of therapy and whether they were one of my patients or someone else's? Those details should all be on the tape boxes, if you can read my scribble.' He grinned. 'Just makes it easier when I come to writing it up, and then I can add other stuff as we go along.'

'Of course,' Lily said, after a moment of hesitation brought on by having never, as far as she was aware, even *seen* a spreadsheet, let alone created one. *Helen will know what to do*, she thought, as she gave the doctor what she hoped was a confident smile.

*

On the ride home she wobbled wildly when she had to signal a turn or when a car passed too close, randomly clicking the gear-shift up and down, not knowing what she was doing, the chain clunking in protest. So when the tears of despair began to wet her cheeks, she had no hands free to wipe them away. She felt, since her conversation with Seth Kramer, as if her life before Oxford had been a complete lie. Every single memory of her love affair with her husband was now tainted with what she saw clearly as his addiction.

Until this moment, she had managed to view what had happened as a glitch, a temporary circumstance that would soon right itself. A financial problem – however serious – not a traumatic emotional one. It was almost as if the meltdown had had nothing to do with Freddy, was just a very unfortunate series of events visited upon them all. Putting the disaster at a safe distance was the only way she'd been able to cope.

But Seth's words had brought home the scale of the problem. It was as if someone had dumped a burning hot weight in her lap. She could no longer ignore it. *People do turn their lives around*, Seth had said, but he'd said it in a way that implied it was not often and not easy, the exception rather than the rule. Was Freddy brave enough? Was he strong enough? Did he *want* to change? She had no idea and, what was more, she didn't have a clue what lay behind his destructive behaviour. Absence, rather than making her heart grow fonder, was making Lily doubt that she had ever really known Freddy March at all.

CHAPTER 35

Neither of them had mentioned the sex. The morning after that first time, Freddy had waited for her to bring up the subject. It seemed the polite thing to do, and his obvious compliance meant he could hardly pretend he was offended. He wasn't offended anyway, it was just something that had happened, a one-off. He was too lonely – too dependent on her generosity – to stop seeing the American on the strength of that one night.

But it turned out not to be just one night. He and Shirley began to settle into a pattern. By anybody's standards it was an indulgent one: expensive lunches, too much wine, evening cocktails, occasional gambling. And then, a couple of times a week, Shirley would suggest it was too late for Freddy to go home.

He should have cared. He should have been ashamed of himself for his betrayal of Lily, not to mention the systematic dismantling of his self-esteem. *I am a gigolo, I am a gigolo, I am a gigolo*. He would repeat this over and over, trying to cudgel his fallen morals into life. But he couldn't find it in himself to be guilty. He remembered his film mates back home quoting the thirty-five-mile rule, 'What happens on location stays on location,' or some such self-serving bullshit for infidelity, and had berated them for it. But his previous life felt as if it were a million miles away. He couldn't relate the sex he had with Shirley to anything remotely real, let alone Lily.

And Shirley let him gamble. The weeks before meeting her, he had had to brace himself, struggling every single day not to give in to his desperate yearning to slip into one of the many casinos around the bay area and feel those smooth chips between his fingers again. But now he had it on a plate: whenever he wanted to gamble she was willingly by his side. It was no longer his painful secret, just a way of passing the time. And she insisted he keep his winnings, so he was stockpiling money, gambling with hers. Sex was a small price to pay. Freddy thought it was her clever way of stopping him having to find work. Or, worse, go back to London. They never talked about the future, unless it involved a discussion about trying a new restaurant for lunch or taking the ferry ride to Sicily.

Is she in love with me? he asked himself more than once. But Shirley was hard to read. She was sociable, easy company, interested in the world beyond the sunny balcony, but she rarely spoke about anything personal except her beloved Chase, keeping Freddy and everyone else at arm's length. He always slept in the spare room, Shirley making sure he was comfortable – a favoured guest – before wishing him a chaste goodnight. She never kissed him, held his hand or made any physical move during the hours of daylight. She barely even flirted with him. Then she'd be there, in the middle of the night, pressing against his nakedness, clad in a series of silky smooth negligees, offering her body for him to use as he pleased. And in the morning there would be hot coffee and toast, a fried egg on hand, plus cheerful smiles and titbits of local news to enjoy in the sunshine.

Freddy found it baffling, and a bit scary. It was as if he were being drawn into a soothing, irresistibly luxurious spider's web, from which it would be harder and harder to extricate himself if he didn't make a move right now.

'My friends are in town,' Shirley announced one June morning, after another night of snatched intimacy. The sex, Freddy noted, always made her look particularly polished and perky. Her hair, this morning, was shiny-gold, her blue eyes very bright, her lips boldly glossed.

'Marty and Jill. Old, old friends from back home. Marty used to sail with dear Chase.'

She handed him a basket lined with a white napkin and filled with knotted white rolls. They were sitting inside, the sun already too hot for comfort. Shirley had laid the table with her usual care: pots of marmalade and honey, a plate of sliced ham, a slab of butter on a blue saucer, a small ceramic jug filled with warm milk.

'I'm dying for them to meet you.'

Freddy nodded, his heart sinking.

'I thought we could all do lunch today, at Pescarino. I know they just adore Italian.'

294

How has she described me to her friends? he wondered. *Friend? Boyfriend? Walker? Lover?*

'I'd better go home and find a clean shirt then,' he said with a smile.

She laughed, and for the first time Freddy saw a faint blush beneath her tan.

As soon as he was free of the building and on his way back to his grandmother's flat, he found himself like a child set free from the classroom at break. He wanted to sing at the top of his voice. But the thought of Shirley's friends brought him up short. *Can I really go on like this?*

Although he was no nearer to paying back creditors such as Lau Heng, maybe he could talk to them, make some long-term deal, now time had passed and his parlous financial state was a matter of public record. They would only be angry if they thought he was hiding money from them, ignoring their debt while living high on the hog. Certainly Barney, although obviously not thrilled by the amount he was owed, might be reasonable in the light of the studio's demise and Freddy's personal bankruptcy. And Lau Heng was not, Freddy thought, a vindictive man. If he believed Freddy was respecting his debt, doing what he could to repay him, he might settle for future earnings. There was no mileage in going after a man who didn't have a pot to piss in.

I should go home, he thought, as he neared the flat. *If I stay here much longer, I'll destroy both myself and Shirley.* Because it was clear that she was getting more attached by the day, even involving her friends now, pinning him down to some sort of public relationship. *Deceiving her like this is unfair*, he told himself firmly. *She deserves better.*

Wearily he opened the door. He would shower and change, go back and meet her friends, then maybe talk to her later tonight, when they were alone. His thoughts elsewhere, he was not immediately aware of the figure propped up on the sofa in the dim light of his nanna's sitting room, the bald head lolling forward. But the sound of his entry must have jogged the man awake, because he jumped, Freddy jumped, and then they both froze.

'Dad . . .' It was almost a question. His father looked like a ghost of his former muscled self. Despite that, as Vinnie Slater began to struggle to his feet, Freddy felt his bowels turn to water.

Fully upright, Vinnie faced his son, hands on his hips. His mean blue eyes were now pale and watery, his skin purplish from the emphysema, cheeks sunken, with deep furrows etched from his nose to his chin. But he straightened his shoulders and gave his son a sly raise of an eyebrow. 'Thought I'd surprise you.'

Freddy was unable to reply. The sight of his father, even in this decayed state, was reducing him, making his body tremble all over as it had when he was a boy. His instinct was to turn tail and flee.

Vinnie was obviously unsteady on his feet and having trouble getting his breath, but he stood his ground. 'Wanted to spend some time with my son before I die,' he was saying, as Freddy moved reluctantly into the room. 'And I thought, No fucking chance he's coming to me, so I'll have to get my arse in gear and go to him.' He gave a short snort of laughter, coughed painfully, and shook his head at Freddy. 'Look as if you've seen a ghost, son. Sit down . . . Been a long night, has it?' A leer replaced the laugh.

Freddy, still trembling inside, sat down on one of the two kitchen chairs, as far from his father as he could get in the small room. 'What do you want?'

After another painful spasm of coughing, Vinnie said, 'Not going to offer your old man a cup of tea? I'm parched, got up at four this morning to catch the sodding plane.' He chuckled. 'Gave me a wheelchair at the airport. Didn't ask for one. Obviously reckoned I was about to conk out.' His words were interspersed with short, snatched breaths.

Freddy filled the plastic kettle, switched it on, mechanically reached for a cup and the tin that contained teabags, opened the tiny fridge for the milk, which he sniffed to check it wasn't on the turn. Handing his father the tea, into which he'd stirred two teaspoons of sugar – a default memory from his childhood, he didn't even ask – he retreated to his seat at the table. 'I've got nothing to say to you.'

Vinnie raised his eyebrows, sipped his tea. Freddy didn't go on and there was a stand-off between the two men in the silent room.

Freddy realized he didn't know how to relate to the person he called 'Dad'. He'd walked out of the house on his sixteenth birthday and never returned, only bumping into his father in and around Leicester during the years, post-school, when he'd worked tossing burgers in a Wimpy Bar, as a porter at the Royal Infirmary, behind the bar in the Merry Monarch. Vinnie always made a point of tracking him down, either at work – humiliating in front of his colleagues – or in the dismal bedsits he rented. He came to bully him, to demand he come home, although why he wanted him home Freddy had no idea, since he made no bones about how much he'd always disliked and resented his son.

Tension distorted the silence, broken only by his father's grating cough.

Freddy said, 'Is death making you sentimental, then, Dad?' The sarcasm felt daunting, even though the figure in front of him was a pathetic old man whom Freddy could have dashed to the floor with a single swipe of his hand. A similar challenge when he was a boy had triggered days of terrifying mind games from Vinnie, culminating in a sadistic near-death assault.

His father's answer surprised him. 'I'm not given to senti-ment, as you know . . .' Here Vinnie paused. 'But not having long makes you think.' He stopped again, his breath raspy and elusive. 'I wanted to make things right with you, son. I know I haven't always been kind to you.'

Freddy felt his mouth hang open. *Is he apologizing?* He gave a short laugh. 'Understatement of the century,' he said.

Vinnie nodded slowly. 'I know, I know . . . I deserved that. Different times.'

'There was never a time when beating a child to a pulp and enjoying it was acceptable.' He heard his voice, surprisingly light, almost flippant, as if he were scared to put more emphasis on his words.

'You were a difficult boy.' Vinnie shrugged. 'But I never enjoyed it, you can't accuse me of that.'

298

Freddy saw a spark of the old malice reflected in the watery eyes. *So much for the apology.* He got up. 'No point in talking about it, Dad. If you want forgiveness, then you've come to the wrong place.'

But Vinnie suddenly looked frightened and feeble. 'Look, son, there's no need to be like that, is there? Can't you let bygones by bygones, give an old man some peace?'

Incredulous, Freddy stared down at him. 'You just don't get it, do you? What you did to me as a child is beyond forgiveness. Beyond belief, in fact. And why should you care anyway? Don't tell me you're scared of hellfire and damnation?'

He'd been joking, his father a famously ranting atheist. So when Vinnie didn't immediately scoff at the idea, Freddy's eyes widened. 'You're afraid of God? *Seriously?* Since when?'

Vinnie just shrugged his thin shoulders again.

Freddy remembered those shoulders when they had been ten times the size, bulging with muscle and hate, towering over him on that sacrificial chair. 'Ha!' he said. 'I like it. My father, afraid of the Almighty! Makes me want to believe in Him myself, someone who can bring about such an astonishing miracle. Makes me want to hug Him.'

'Stop that.'

'Remember the vitriol, Dad? The piss you took when Mum wanted to go to church?' he said softly. 'She begged for a priest when she was dying.' For a moment he saw his mother's emaciated face, yellowed and skeletal from the cancer, heard her crying softly. 'I remember,' he said quietly. Freddy turned on his heel, still shaking, and made for the bedroom where he quickly packed some clothes in his canvas holdall.

He realized he was actually frightened that his father would stop him leaving, although in Vinnie's present state the idea was ludicrous. He strode back into the sitting room and made for the front door, barely glancing at his father, who was slumped, once more, on the sofa.

'Fred, Fred, come back.' Vinnie was struggling to his feet again. Wobbling as he stood, he reached for the back of the sofa and steadied himself. Through tight, laboured breaths, he managed to say, 'I came all this way for you. I'm not well, you must see that. If you leave you might never see me again.' He broke off to lean on the table, bent over, head down, air rasping in his throat. 'I need you to understand.'

Seeing him so reduced, his now reedy voice whining with self-pity, was almost more nauseating to Freddy than the historic savagery. He had no pity for his father, only pity for himself that he couldn't have the fight he'd rehearsed so often in his dreams, in which he beat the living daylights out of Vinnie and made him beg for mercy, reducing him to tears as Freddy had so often been as a child. Seeing the old man so diminished, through no agency of his own, made him feel cheated. 'You aren't even sorry.'

Vinnie straightened up, his eyes clouding as he stared at his son. And Freddy saw the previously pleading look change in an instant. He almost recoiled as his father's voice became suffused with age-old contempt.

'Still the little victim, eh?' Vinnie harrumphed, coughed. 'You and your whining mother . . . I tried to put some mettle into you, son. Tried to make a man of you.' He coughed again, gave a harsh laugh. 'Seems I didn't do much of a job.'

'No,' Freddy said quietly. 'No, you didn't. But if being a man means taking sadistic pleasure in beating a child half to death . . . if being a man means being like you, Dad, then I'll pass.'

'Where are you going?' he heard his father's querulous voice as he closed the door on his grandmother's flat. As he flew down the stone stairs, two at a time, he knew he would never go back there.

He arrived at Shirley's apartment breathless, trembling with shock. He felt like a terrified boy again, the lifetime of effort he'd expended to make himself forget, to build a carapace over that shaking, blubbering child he so despised, seemed to count for nothing now. And he found himself asking over and over the question he'd avoided for decades: *Where were you, Mum? Why didn't you protect me? Why didn't you stop him hurting me?*

'Freddy? Are you okay, hon?' Shirley's face was full of concern as she opened the door, taking in his distressed appearance, the small bag he held. She looked particularly glamorous today, he thought, her sea-green silk shirt, white jeans and elegant gold-chain necklace – all carefully chosen in honour of her friends, no doubt.

She pulled him into the kitchen. 'You look as if you've seen a ghost. Whatever's happened?'

Freddy tried to speak, but all he wanted to do was cry.

Shooting a glance through the door towards the balcony, where Freddy could hear her friends chatting and laughing, Shirley moved closer.

'Hey,' she said, taking him in her arms, 'hey, it's okay . . . it's okay, I'm here . . .' muttering soothing words he barely heard as she drew his head to her shoulder and held him like a mother would.

Choking back his tears, terrified that if he let go now he would crack into a thousand pieces, he felt his chest fluttering with the smallest, softest breaths he would allow himself, not letting the air go too deep and tap into where the darkness lay. And after a few minutes he felt the urge to cry receding, the threatening chaos once more forced back into the box that had contained it his whole life.

Shirley stroked his hair, brought her face up to his, kissed him gently on the lips, her blue eyes searching, trying to reach his pain.

Freddy pulled back, taking her hands in his and squeezing them gratefully. 'God, I'm sorry, Shirley. I'm so sorry. Thanks . . . Listen, I'll explain later,' he said, nodding towards the balcony.

'Are you sure you're all right now? Why don't you go freshen up, hon, give yourself a few minutes? They're on their second gin, they won't notice a thing.' She smiled and pushed him towards the bathroom.

CHAPTER 36

It had gone on all day, the lunch, everyone, particularly Freddy, getting drunker and drunker as the hours passed. After Marty and Jill had finally gone back to their hotel, Shirley settled in beside Freddy on his lounger on the terrace in the dark. It must have gone midnight and he was in that blank, regretful phase of drunkenness, where the fun part of inebriation has worn off, the hangover not yet kicked in, but another drink is a horrible thought and the dread of pillow spin stops you attempting to lie down.

'You were a big hit,' Shirley whispered, her head nuzzled coyly into his shoulder. 'Jill thought you were so funny and *sooo* cute. She just adored your showbiz stories.'

He heard her give a contented sigh. Jill, he thought – a chirpy, straightforward woman with a sensible grey bob and a warm smile – *had* liked him. But Marty's rather persistent, not-so-subtle questions – about Freddy's work, his background and his plans to stay in Malta – had signalled suspicion.

The man, a tall, thin, patrician type with a weather-beaten face, mane of white hair and an arrogant bearing, had spent a lot of time extolling the virtues of Shirley's Chase in calculatedly extreme terms. What an awesome friend . . . exemplary husband . . . remarkable sailor. What a cut above the average, a person of stature. Very much missed. On Marty had gone about Chase Solaris. The subtext being: Who the fuck do you think you are, you *worm*, trying to fill this giant's shoes? The subtext being: *Gigolo*. Or so Freddy, paranoid and rattled by his encounter with his father, gleaned from Marty's conversation.

He didn't even try to defend himself. He did feel like a worm, a sponger, a gigolo. It was what he'd probably have called someone like him in similar circumstances. Shirley tried to big him up, tried to get him to repeat the stories he'd told her about all the famous people he'd worked and hung out with. But that only seemed to make matters worse. With every tale Freddy obediently dragged up from his past, Marty's expression became more cynical, more disbelieving.

'You're a serious player by the sound of it,' Marty had said, not without a hint of sarcasm, at one point late in the afternoon, when they were strolling back, replete with crab linguine, veal Milanese, lemon sorbet, espresso and amaretti biscotti, to Shirley's condo after lunch in the marina. 'I can't imagine you'll be in this backwater long.'

Shirley and her friend were up ahead, talking nineteen to the dozen, not listening.

'Oh, I love it here,' Freddy said, to wind him up. 'My mother was Maltese.'

304

Marty cast him a sidelong glance, perhaps concluding that this explained a lot.

'Shirley's a wonderful woman,' Freddy added with enthusiasm.

'She sure is, Freddy. But vulnerable too.'

'Vulnerable?' Freddy assumed a look of mild puzzlement.

'You know . . . a widow, all alone. She's been so lost since Chase passed.'

'So she says. I think it's a wonderful thing, having a long and loving marriage like theirs. We should all be envious.'

Marty couldn't have been sure how to take this because he didn't answer for a moment. Then he said, his voice very low, with only a hint of warning, 'Listen, I don't know what sort of relationship you two have, and I don't want to, none of my business, but I owe it to Chase to keep an eye on Shirley, make sure she's good.'

'She's very lucky to have a friend like you, Marty,' Freddy said, smiling genially at the American, leaving him nowhere to go with his questioning. It was a small victory. But, in truth, Marty was right, and Freddy knew it. He also knew that something had changed today. Shirley's motherly concern, her pleasure in introducing him to her friends, her protection of him in the face of Marty's suspicion, it felt newly proprietorial. Whatever she said – or didn't say – it was clear she expected more than he would ever be able to give her.

'Come to bed,' she said now, as they sat squashed together on the lounger, a chilly breeze suddenly blowing up from the sea. 'It's getting cold out here.'

It was an invitation, not the usual suggestion to turn in.

Shirley took him by the hand and led him into her room. It was the first time he hadn't slept in the spare room, been visited silently in the night for sex. Freddy felt instantly uneasy, awkward in this new mode, but she didn't given him time for qualms, pushing him down on the bed as she leaned over to kiss him and began to unzip his jeans.

That night she was voracious. None of the silently covert seduction of past encounters. Freddy, drunk and worn out by the events of the day, wanted only to sleep, but Shirley was getting her money's worth. She kept him awake for what seemed like a very long time, her appetite unquenchable as her body writhed with his, her cries and groans reaching a hopeful – to Freddy, at least – crescendo, then dying down, mounting again as she moved to straddle him, or pushed him down between her legs, then brought her mouth dangerously tight around his erection. They were soon both slick and wet with sweat, the dim light from the bedside lamp casting grotesque shadows of their antics. He wondered if this was how a prostitute might feel as he longed for it to be over.

The following morning, with the cerebral thump of a hangover from hell, Freddy lay in Shirley's bed with a cringing feeling in his gut. The tempting smell of coffee wafted through to him and Shirley could be heard singing softly in the kitchen, no doubt preparing another perfect breakfast. But he knew all this was over. It had gone too far.

'I have to take my father home,' he lied to her over breakfast. 'He's too ill to go by himself.' He explained the previous evening that his distress earlier in the day had been because of a fight with his father, although he didn't mention the reason, or anything to do with the past.

She was full of sympathy. 'I'll take you both to the airport.'

He thanked her, told her no. It was agony watching her worried face across the table, knowing how much she had invested in him. He felt like the worst bastard on the planet. Lily, now Shirley . . . Freddy didn't want to be that sort of man.

'You'll be back soon?' she asked.

'I hope so. But Dad is basically dying.'

She didn't push it: she was too mature, too polite for that, but her blue eyes were full of hope as they kissed goodbye. He could see she was waiting for more assurances than he could give her.

She'll forget about me soon enough, he told himself as he stood by the bus stop in the Mediterranean sunshine, waiting for the bus that would take him to the airport, feeling like a fugitive all over again. But he hated what he had done to her.

The hotel Freddy had booked online earlier, as he waited at Malta International for his flight home, was modern and ugly. But it was also dirt cheap, a chain with a summer promotion right by Gatwick Airport. His room was basic, a dull cream and brown, but clean enough. Nobody bothered him, the revolving-door stream of tourists – most there for a night, tops – meant that the staff was not really concerned about getting involved with the guests. The thunderous clap of jets passing overhead every couple of minutes, inadequately muted by what should have been better soundproofing in such a new building, was his only companion.

307

In his last-minute exit from Malta six days earlier, Freddy had booked for two weeks, although he hoped to stay for a shorter time. He had a plan, and to this end had carried out a vast amount of research as he sat alone in his hotel room, often working manically late into the night at his laptop, fuelled by disgusting instant coffee, sachets of which the maids replaced every morning on the tray inside the brown MDF cupboard.

So the plan now was to raise enough money – he was sure he could find someone with the vision – to open a small recording studio in a provincial city. Not Manchester, which was awash with media servicing, as were Leeds and Liverpool. But Nottingham, for instance, Warwick or Sheffield, which held a documentary festival every year. All had thriving universities popular with students hungry for media experience. A studio in one of those cities would be perfectly placed and probably much in demand. Investors would see the sense. And with a suitable building it needn't cost too much to set up.

Of course, there was the not insignificant problem of his bankruptcy: he couldn't be a director of a company, couldn't even open a bank account. But if he set the business up with someone like Max Blackstone on the masthead instead of himself, with Freddy doing all the work, it could be win-win.

Maybe he'd find an existing studio, take it over. Lily could help, do the design – she was good at that – while he brought in the clients. His thoughts began to fly. Maybe it would have a small flat over it where they could live together until things picked up . . .

The lethargy Freddy had felt in those long weeks in Malta seemed to have dissipated as soon as the plane touched down on English soil. Ideas and energy were pulsing through his veins again, plus an absolute determination to succeed. But he wasn't ready to brave London yet, not with the possibility of running into his peers, his ex-employees, his social group. And, worst of all, his creditors. They wouldn't have gone away.

Tonight, having consumed a toasted cheese sandwich and a couple of glasses of whisky at the functional hotel bar, Freddy found himself lonely and longing to speak to Lily. It was harder, now he was home, to resist calling her. But he did resist. He had nothing to offer her right now, only promises. And he knew the first thing she would ask was, 'Have you stopped gambling?'

Freddy hadn't set foot in a casino in the week he'd been home. Proud of himself, and once again determined that he would quit for good, he knew that he had run out of options. He was in the last-chance saloon. If he wanted Max's help, wanted to get back with his wife, then his habit had to be totally expunged from his life. He had even checked out the Gamblers Anonymous site. The nearest meeting was seven miles away, which would require an expensive taxi. But he didn't really need a meeting. It would be a bunch of no-hopers droning on about their sad lives. He wasn't like them: he could do it on his own, prove his father wrong.

Vinnie had left upwards of ten messages on his phone in the days since their meeting, all begging his son to come back. Freddy had answered none, but when the calls stopped he was haunted by the image of his sick father lying helpless in the Maltese flat, knowing nobody, too ill to summon assistance. *What if he dies there?* he asked himself. *What if he dies and his body rots and nobody finds him for years? How will I feel?*

He couldn't answer his own question. All he knew was that he wanted never to see the man, dead or alive, *ever again.*

To stop himself ringing Lily, Freddy, lying alone on the cold, clean hotel bed in that dreary room, thought of calling his friend Fish. He hadn't spoken to him in weeks, only a brief chat when he'd first escaped to Malta to tell him what was what. But Fish represented his gambling self. His friend, although recognizing Freddy's problem and frequently trying to explain the difference between his own love affair with casinos and Freddy's obsession, had never once refused the offer of an evening at the tables. 'It's up to you,' Fish said. 'I can't stop you, so I might as well join you, keep an eye.'

There was no one he could call, Freddy realized miserably, no one, at least, to whom he could really tell the truth.

PART III

CHAPTER 37

Something had begun to shift in Lily. It was as a result of talking to Seth. The doctor, although she had not yet revealed her situation to him, had made her realize she was dealing with something much more frightening in Freddy than she had previously thought. Was her husband hiding some past trauma from her? Something so bad he couldn't speak about it? She had never met his parents, his mother long dead and his father, Vincent, no longer able to recognize his own son. But he had clearly loved them. As she kept going over in her mind her husband's behaviour since she had first met him, she knew that what he'd done this year wasn't in the realms of normal. It was wild, self-destructive, she accepted that. And his ability to hide it all from her and everyone else was epic.

Yet, despite what the naysayers said, Freddy had run an extremely successful recording studio for nearly a decade, a feat in itself. He'd had money, that wasn't in question. And

his love for her, albeit intense, had not felt mad or patholog-
ical. He had been highly functioning, successful, and popular
with almost everyone. How could that be the behaviour of a
seriously damaged man . . . an *addict*?

But life went on. She was establishing a rhythm with her
work, her Friday visits to the doctor, long walks in the parks
and meadows around the city – it had been a beautiful June.
She would take her sketchbook on her walks, do thumbnails
of people on the bus or in the park, then work them up into
pen-and-ink portraits at home. She was getting quite a portfolio together, relishing the time she had never had in her
frantic London life to indulge in her lifelong passion.

Her love for Freddy had in no way diminished, but it wasn't
exactly being fuelled by his silence. Without being able to see
him, talk to him, feel his kisses, see his eyes light up with
something she said, she sensed the edges of her obsession
wearing thin. She wasn't sure what she would do if he didn't
come back. But she was beginning to realize she might almost
survive without him.

The time had come, she knew, to make decisions. She
couldn't wait for ever without any sign that her husband was
even alive. And things were coming to a head with Helen.
Yesterday, for instance, her sister had completely lost it. A
mistake by David – putting a grey wool cardigan of Helen's
into a hot cotton wash and shrinking it – was blamed on Lily.

'For Christ's sake,' Helen had exploded when she'd got
home from work, obviously tired after a long day. 'Can't you
wake up and take a bit of care for once in a while?'

Lily hadn't had time to defend herself before her sister

went on, 'But then you've always had everything you want, of course. You probably can't even imagine that it matters, having to buy a new sweater.' She held the offending garment up for Lily to see, the wool matted, uneven at the edges, shrunk to half its normal size. 'This was one of my favourites. How hard is it to check before you throw it all in together? Honestly, if you can't be bothered then leave it alone. Let me do the bloody wash.'

Used to her sister's temper, but lulled into a false sense of security in recent weeks by the truce to which they'd both tacitly agreed, Lily was surprised by the venom in Helen's voice.

'It wasn't me. David did the washing.' As soon as the words were out of her mouth, she regretted them. It sounded petty. And now her poor brother-in-law would get it in the neck as well.

But Helen barely heard. This wasn't to do with the cardigan, as Lily well knew.

'I don't know.' Helen gave a martyred sigh, dropping the sweater back into the white plastic basket on top of the other damp washing, then turned away and sank down on a chair, removing her glasses before rubbing her hands across her eyes. 'I come home exhausted and I find you sitting here without a care in the world, having nothing to do but a bit of easy-peasy typing all day, a cosy coffee with the doctor, some sketching in the park, and I wonder how long you think this can go on, this – this lifestyle of yours. What are you waiting for, Lily? Yet another knight in shining armour – preferably rich – to come and sweep you off your feet as per usual?'

Lily, shocked, didn't have time to reply before Helen,

putting her glasses back on, said, 'You've been here for months now, and – don't get me wrong – I'm perfectly happy to let you stay. But you don't seem to have any sort of *plan*.' Her voice had settled into a pained murmur, as if she were musing on the problem rather than speaking to Lily. But now it rose a couple of octaves. 'I'm just baffled by your lack of ambition. You've spent your whole life lying about drawing, waiting for someone else to do the slog, to look after you in the style to which you've accustomed yourself.'

'What on earth do you mean?' Lily did not want this argument. She was on the back foot, at her sister's mercy.

'Take Mum and Dad, run ragged with your bloody asthma. It was always "Oh, we can't do that, can't go there, Lily's ill, Lily has to rest, Lily has to go to the hospital. Be quiet, Helen, Lily didn't sleep. Be careful, Helen, Lily can't drink milk, can't run, can't have feather pillows, can't sleep in the small room, can't play with next door's bloody cat. Don't overexcite her, Helen. Oh, and Helen, we can't come to the school play, Lily isn't well."'

The cruel mimic of her mother's wispy voice was painful to listen to. Snippets of her sister's resentment had bubbled up in arguments between them over the years and Lily had always had sympathy for her. It must have been a nightmare, growing up with a chronically – often dangerously – ill sibling, who stole every minute of their parents' time. But she had never heard this drawn-out bitterness before.

'To be honest, I might just as well have been invisible for all the attention I got,' Helen went on. 'My only way to get Brownie points was to look after you, and they didn't even trust me to do that. I lived in dread of you having an attack when we were together, because the first thing Mum would say was, '"What did you do to her?"'

Lily was shocked to see tears in her sister's eyes. 'And then you marry Garret and he does everything for you, absolutely *everything*.' She glared at Lily. 'Did you ever pay a bill, raise a mortgage, get the car serviced, worry about your salary? I'd say not. Then Prem picks you up and hands you a cushy job on a plate until Freddy comes along and whisks you off your feet.' She raised her hands in the air in a gesture of disbelief. 'You got past fifty, Lily, without lifting a goddamn finger. So why am I surprised you're incapable of managing on your own now?'

Lily was too stunned to speak. What her sister was saying was unfair on so many levels. 'The asthma was hardly my fault.'

'I know it wasn't your bloody fault,' Helen snapped, implying, nonetheless, that if it were possible for Lily to have engineered her childhood illness, she would have.

'It must have been hell for you,' Lily said, determined not to inflame her sister further.

Helen stared at her as if she were checking Lily's face for sarcasm. 'It wasn't "hell" exactly,' she said eventually, her voice sulky.

'Pretty bad, though, I'm sure. I had no idea at the time, of course. Children always think that whatever happens to them is normal.'

Lily sat down next to Helen and put her arm around her shoulders. She felt her sister stiffen, then relax slightly.

'Listen, I'm so sorry about the past. You've always been so amazingly kind to me, Helen. I don't know what I would have done without you both this summer. You have no idea how grateful I am.'

Helen didn't speak.

'But I've outstayed my welcome and I'll get on to it ASAP. I've got money saved – thanks to your generosity. I can find a flat somewhere.'

Her sister sighed, and shook off Lily's arm in an almost imperceptible gesture. 'That's stupid, you spending money on somewhere when we've a room here. David would be horrified if he thought I'd made you unwelcome.'

'You haven't. But you're right. It's time to move on, decide what I want to do with the rest of my life. Everyone's been telling me so.'

They were both silent, worn out by the row. Lily felt a small knot of panic forming in her gut at the thought of moving out, leaving the safety of her big sister's care. She couldn't pay rent on the meagre income from the tapes: she'd have to get at least three times more transcription work, or find a proper job. But maybe she could do it, reject her sister's cruel assessment of her lifelong dependency. *After all*, she thought wryly, *I have 'skills' now*.

She reached the entrance to Seth's boat. The doctor's head poked out at the sound of her call and silenced her thoughts.

'Am I glad to see you,' he said, holding the door open while she clambered aboard and down the steps into the cabin. He was casually dressed in a faded grey T-shirt and jeans, his normally settled face alive with irritation, his wiry dark hair mirroring his mood as it stuck out at all angles from his head. 'I've been fighting with that spreadsheet you sent me. I can't get the damn text to go down a line in the boxes. I've tried everything, but it just keeps merrily on, making the box longer and longer. It's driving me nuts.' Without any greeting, he led Lily over to his laptop, where the workbook she'd shed blood over was neatly displayed, showing no signs of her own screeching angst while she had been creating it. Seth held out his hand, palm up. 'See?'

Lily peered at the document. 'Ah. You need to go to Wrap Text.' She calmly clicked on the icon on the top of the sheet and the text that Seth had typed re-formed miraculously to fit the original box. She felt ridiculously pleased with herself.

'Hallelujah! Fantastic. I knew you'd know,' he said, clapping her on the back as if she'd discovered the secret of turning lead into gold. 'Write it down, could you? I'll forget otherwise.' He beamed at her. 'That deserves a strong cup of coffee. Or at least I need a strong cup of coffee. You can have tea, if you like.'

She laughed, 'No, strong coffee is what I need too. Been one of those weeks.'

And as she stood alone, Seth busying himself over by the sink with the coffee machine, she knew she'd been holding on until she was face to face with him, desperate to unload her thoughts on someone who might understand. Someone who might clarify them for her. She didn't care right at this minute that he was her employer. If he sacked her, he sacked her. She just needed him to listen first.

'Tell me about it,' he said, handing her a mug of coffee.

Lily sat on the sofa, Seth opposite in the desk chair. Not knowing where to start, she said, 'It's my husband,' and stopped.

He didn't reply, just waited.

She began again. 'He disappeared . . .' The tale, so often gone over in her mind, tumbled from her mouth – she was barely conscious of what she was saying. But telling the doctor rendered her slightly wobbly, Seth's coffee strong and making her shake. Not wanting to face her sister, she had come out without breakfast, then had to walk fast so as not to be late – she hadn't taken the bike in case that was construed as more ligging on her part. Now she ran out of steam and fell silent.

Seth was nodding encouragingly.

'I've been sort of waiting, because I didn't think Freddy was serious about us being apart, not for so long. I thought we'd be back together by now. But . . . I don't know . . . I haven't heard a word from him since April. All my family think I'm insane.'

'For sticking with Freddy?'

'Yes.'

'And do you feel insane?'

'I didn't . . .' She met Seth's eye. 'You can't stop loving someone overnight. But now . . .'

He nodded.

'I didn't want him to go. I wanted us to sort it out together. But he just went off when I was asleep and never came back. Everyone says he's an addict, but that sounds crazy, especially since Kit came round and I saw what a real one looks like. Freddy was just trying to find a way out of the mess he'd got into with the business.' She paused. 'He was really successful before that.'

'So he went because he wanted to deal with his addiction on his own?'

Did Freddy say that?

'He wanted to sort out the financial mess on his own,' she corrected. 'There were people he'd borrowed a lot of money from, people who didn't take it too kindly when he couldn't pay them back. Freddy said they'd get nasty . . . although it seems a bit fantastical to me. He didn't want me to get tangled up in it all.'

'He got into a mess *because* of the gambling, then? Rather than gambling as a way out of the mess?'

Both options in Seth's question sounded just as bad to Lily. *Which was it?*

'Has he always had a problem?'

'I . . .' That day when Freddy had told her about it all was so muddled in her mind. She'd been too shocked to take in the details. 'He said he'd gambled normally before, just it got out of hand in the last year or so.'

'And you didn't know about it?'

Lily shook her head. *God, I sound like the moron wife who thinks the bodies in the basement were just there by chance, not buried by her serial-killer husband.*

'That must have been a terrible shock,' Seth was saying.

She gave a short laugh. 'You could say that.'

The doctor frowned, didn't speak for a moment or two. Then: 'Do you think he's getting help?'

'I don't know, I honestly don't know. But if he's still

gambling, he'll be on the streets by now, won't he? Lying in some gutter.' She could hear her voice rising. 'He doesn't have family like I do, just a father who's got Alzheimer's. But I can't help him if he won't see me.' She stood, paced up and down, then turned back to Seth. 'If you met Freddy, you wouldn't believe any of this. He's such a strong person, so clever and charismatic. Everyone loves him – *you*'d love him.' She stopped speaking because her throat was choked with the sobs she could no longer control and she slumped onto the sofa, burying her face in her hands.

It was only a moment before Seth was beside her. He didn't speak, didn't touch her, just offered her the box of tissues that was on the ledge behind him, underneath the porthole. But his presence was somehow comforting.

'I'm sorry, I shouldn't have dumped all this on you. It's not your problem. It's just none of my friends or family will even listen when I talk about him. They just lecture me on and on about what a bastard he is, how I should never speak to him again.' She blew her nose, then added quietly, 'I know he's not a bastard, but I also know I can't go on like this, in limbo, being his wife and not being his wife ... having no life. Waiting.'

'You have to make your own decisions, not do what other people want.'

She raised her head to look at him. 'You must think me a complete fool.'

'Loving somebody doesn't make you a fool, Lily.' He gave her a smile and stood up. 'Do you want to get a sandwich or something at the Anchor? I'm famished.'

CHAPTER 38

Freddy's mood of optimism did not last. By the second week in the Gatwick hotel he was no nearer to finding a solution to his problems and was going stir crazy, alone in that dreary room. He had acquired a prepaid bankcard and loaded it with some of the cash he'd stashed from the casino visits. It was a start, but it wouldn't get him a rental property, a job, or his wife back. And the more he read the lengthy business plan he'd bashed out on his laptop for a recording studio in Sheffield, the more ludicrous it sounded.

For three whole days he didn't leave the room, barely got out of bed, didn't shave or wash, didn't eat except KitKats and nuts from the minibar, didn't even look at his phone or his computer. He shot the bolt, put the Do Not Disturb notice on the doorknob and rejected all pleas from the chambermaids to service the room, from the minibar staff to check the fridge. Images of his father kept intruding into his waking thoughts and into his dreams on an endless loop.

The message from Vinnie Slater was crystal clear and always the same: *You are worthless.* No amount of name-changing, no amount of distancing himself from the Leicestershire pub and his father (even lying to Lily about him), no amount of accolades for his recording studio, no amount of hobnobbing with high society and frequenting the most fashionable watering holes in the world was enough to erase that powerful, lifelong message: *You are worthless.*

Freddy had reached rock bottom. He had no energy left for another bout of invention now his previous incarnation had been exposed and dismantled. Medicating himself at the tables involved more money than he had. He was finished.

He wished he could just fade into oblivion because he wasn't brave enough to kill himself, he knew that. Too many of his friends had strung themselves up in hotel rooms – on the heated towel rail or the hook behind the door. One had even blown his brains out on Christmas morning while his family were downstairs opening presents. Freddy had been shocked and baffled by their desperation – they'd all seemed to have so much to live for. He understood better now, but still he didn't have what it took to end his own life. So he lay there, nothing existing beyond the darkened, airless room except the sound of the planes' muffled roaring overhead, his body so inert, so numb, that he might as well have been dead.

'Mr March? Mr March, are you all right?'

Freddy, waking from another fitful sleep, heard the banging.

'Mr March, please can you open the door? I need to come in.' The male voice was insistent. Freddy threw back the covers. He felt dizzy as he staggered across the room in his sweaty T-shirt and boxers.

There was more banging, this time heavy and threatening. 'If you don't open up, I'm going to have to call Security,' the voice said.

Freddy released the sprung-metal loop and the door flew open, surprising the overweight, middle-aged man in a cheap suit who stood in the corridor next to a slim blonde woman in her twenties – one of the chambermaids, he assumed.

'Mr March?' the man said, stepping back. 'I'm Jason Crawford, the hotel manager.' He attempted a smile, but was clearly dismayed by Freddy's appearance, looking him up and down with barely disguised aversion. 'My staff were worried. You haven't been responding. Are you ill?'

Freddy brushed back his hair, aware that his beard must look pretty ferocious by now. 'I'm so sorry,' he said, with his most polished accent. 'I think it must be the flu. I literally haven't been able to lift my head off the pillow. I don't even know what day it is.' He looked around, as if the featureless corridor might give him a clue.

Mr Crawford's face relaxed slightly. 'Would you like me to call a doctor, Mr March? You really don't look at all well.'

Freddy smiled. 'That's very kind, but I think it's passing. I feel a bit better this morning. Is it morning? I'll attempt a shower and some breakfast and see how it goes.'

The manager nodded. 'Right. Please call down if you need anything.' He hesitated. 'I'm not sure how long you plan to stay with us?'

'Nor me. It's been a bit of a nightmare. I had a flood – the

325

water tank in the attic burst, drenched the whole place. But things are moving, my builder tells me. I shouldn't need to be here much longer.' Implying he lived somewhere nearby, he prayed Jason Crawford hadn't checked the register and noted the fraudulent Sussex Square address he'd used.

But the man nodded sympathetically. 'You're welcome to stay as long as you like, sir. I'm so sorry about the flood, nothing worse. If you feel strong enough to sit in the lounge for half an hour, Tina here can freshen up your room for you.'

By the time Freddy got rid of them and shut the door, he was feeling as if he might faint. He lay down again on the fetid, rumpled sheets and took stock. There was only one course of action open to him.

'Freddy?' Max sounded delighted to hear his voice. 'What the fuck? Why didn't you return any of my calls, you lazy bastard?'

Freddy laughed, a hysterical bubble of relief bursting through his chest.

'You still in Malta?'

'No, in a grisly Gatwick hotel.'

'You just got in?'

'Been here a few days, checking the lie of the land.'

'And? What's the plan?'

Freddy sighed.

'Did you get a job? Where are you going to live?'

As if it were that easy, Freddy thought bitterly.

There was silence for a moment.

'Well, it's good to have you back. I must have called you a million times.'

This was true, but Freddy had had nothing worthwhile to say to his friend. 'Listen, Max—'

'Come and stay. We need to talk,' Max interrupted.

Freddy swallowed hard. 'Seriously? Can I? That would be so brilliant.' He knew his voice sounded pathetic, almost childishly eager, but to know he could get out of this place, be among the living again, see his friend . . . It made him want to cry.

'Hey, don't be weird, man. Of course you can stay. See you tonight? Julie'll be over the moon.'

CHAPTER 39

Dillon sat, long legs cramped, in the back seat of his sister's rubbish-filled Peugeot on their way up to Oxford. There were long tailbacks going into the city on a Saturday morning and he was sick to death of watching Ted reach over to squeeze Sara's thigh through her dress and her returning smile; Ted moving his hand along the driver's seat to rest on Sara's bare shoulders, rubbing his thumb up and down her neck as she nuzzled backwards to receive his caress; Ted leaning in to peck the tip of Sara's ear, and her silly giggle in response.

'Christ, guys,' he objected, as they sat stationary in a jam that stretched ahead as far as the eye could see.

But neither seemed fazed: they both just laughed and continued to eye each other lustfully.

'Don't be grumpy, Dillo.'

Dillo? Where the hell did she get that from? he wondered, immediately suspecting Ted. 'I'm not grumpy. I just don't want to watch.' And, in fact, he wasn't feeling particularly grumpy today, for the first time in ages. He'd actually been on a date last night – the first after a wasted summer feeling sorry for himself. But it was officially over with Gabriela and he told himself he didn't give a fuck about her. *Shallow bitch, first sign of trouble and she was off*, he repeated silently whenever her face invaded his thoughts.

The last time he'd spoken to *her* instead of her bloody machine – more than three weeks ago now – he had finally challenged her. He was sick to death of hearing her make feeble excuses for not being able to talk to him, not being able to come home. Sick of hearing the phoney '*querido*' she slipped into the conversation whenever she heard him getting upset.

So he'd taken a deep breath and asked her straight out, 'Is it over, Gaby? Just tell me, for God's sake. Tell me right now.' And instead of pretending that he was being paranoid and ridiculous, as she had on every other occasion he'd put the same question, Gabriela had gone silent for what seemed like a year, then said coyly, 'I think so.' Not much of a response, but enough for Dillon, who had killed the call without even saying goodbye, his whole body vibrating with rage.

In the weeks that followed, as boredom and loneliness threatened to overwhelm him, he had eventually uploaded his profile on to Tinder. Marilynne was almost as pretty as the photo online, taller than Gabriela – although that wouldn't have been hard – slim, blonde hair to her shoulders and dark-eyed, wearing a short red dress with a narrow belt at the waist. He'd been so nervous as he entered the bar that he'd been about to bail, bike home as fast as his feet could pedal, when he'd recognized her perched on a bar stool and knew she'd clocked him. *Too late*, he'd thought. *Here I am, and here is Marilynne. I must make an effort.*

The evening wasn't a disaster. They'd both got drunk enough to relax. She was talkative and flirty, as her photo had suggested, but there was no spark, and when she suggested, round about nine o'clock, that they get something to eat, the prospect of sitting opposite the girl and listening to her bang on about herself – which was all she seemed interested in – made Dillon lose the will to live. Still, it was a start and he knew that a chink of optimism had pierced his previously murderous mood.

This was the first time Dillon had been allowed to meet his sister's boyfriend properly – the other time just a glimpse through a café window when Ted had picked up Sara after a coffee he'd had with his sister. The man was pretty much as he had expected: long-limbed, laidback, thick-haired, tanned, charming and perpetually – irritatingly – good-natured.

Now, glancing round at him, Sara said, 'This is going to be weird, you know. Mum marooned in Helen and David's house. Sort of embarrassing, under the circs. I feel bad we haven't been up all summer.'

Dillon felt bad too. 'I'm sure she's fine.'

'Really? I'm sure she's not at all fine. Why would she be?'

'Okay, but we've both been angry with her and there wasn't anything we could have done to help.' He was actually dreading the birthday lunch Lily had arranged for him and Sara.

Ted was silent, as if his only function were to grope Dillon's sister.

'Except visit. Show support.' Sara paused, then added, 'Well, we can't be angry with her any more. And remember, you two, don't mention the war.'

'You mean Kit.'

'I mean Kit *and* Freddy.'

His mother looked different. Not as thin as before, tanned, no makeup, her hair – always so fashionably cut by that May-fair hairdresser friend of his stepfather – now flopping and tinged with a few grey strands. She was dressed in dark cargo shorts, a sleeveless white T-shirt and leather sandals. An outfit she would never have worn in her sophisticated Freddy March days. But she looked healthy and . . . younger, he thought.

Dillon hugged her tight, suddenly very pleased to see his mum, despite his previous reluctance.

'Hey, happy birthday,' she said, looking at him with so much love he felt almost embarrassed. 'I've missed you.'

His aunt gave him an awkward peck on the cheek, then David shook his hand, mumbled something he didn't catch. There was silence as they all stood about the kitchen smiling at each other, no one knowing quite what to say. Sara was right, he thought. None of this was 'fine'.

'This is a really cute home you have here, Helen.' Ted came to the rescue. 'You've done a great job.'

It wasn't a 'cute' house, not even remotely, and Dillon had no idea what Ted was talking about, but his aunt responded to the American's flattery with an uncharacteristic softening of her customary grump. 'Come outside. I'll show you the garden,' she said, tactfully beckoning her husband to follow and leaving Dillon with his mother and sister.

They all seemed to breathe a sigh of relief to be alone together. Sara moved to stand next to their mum and put an arm around her shoulders. 'How's it going?'

'Fine. I've got a job, as you know, and Helen and David haven't chucked me out yet.' She spoke with a laugh, but Dillon could see it wasn't very funny.

He and Sara nodded. 'That's great,' he said, wincing at his false cheer.

Another silence descended. He thought his mum looked suddenly bewildered and he felt a moment of panic. 'And the typing?' he asked quickly.

'Good. I'm getting there . . . Lots of mistakes still.' She gave another small laugh.

'What's the shrink like?' Sara asked, also looking tense.

'He's nice. Very easy-going. I like him a lot.'

'Good, that's really good, Mum,' he said, knowing he sounded like a total dick with his condescending tone. This was a nightmare. He didn't know what to say to his own mother. He hadn't wanted Ted to come, he'd wanted it to be just family and had sulked for the first twenty miles of the journey when Sara had pitched up with him. But now, as the American strode back into the kitchen followed by Helen and David, all animatedly talking their heads off about when to prune the roses and which sorts of pears stewed best, he was incredibly grateful that he had.

*

The lunch his mum had laid out on the patio table looked fresh and delicious. It included a platter of jointed cold chicken, avocado and tomato salad, sliced beetroot, romaine lettuce – both of the latter from the neighbour's garden apparently – a bowl of buttery new potatoes, a small jar of dressing, a cut-glass jug filled with iced water, and the wine cooler containing a bottle of chilled rosé. She had placed a bouquet of pale pink roses in the centre of the table.

After the salads had been cleared away, Lily brought out a blue china plate holding a magnificent pyramid of cupcakes. Each was decorated with soft swirls of red and white butter-cream icing, a red cherry and a candle. It looked great. Dillon leaned in to his sister and they blew on his 'One, two, three', just as they always had. He tried to enjoy the moment, but nothing was right about the day and he was transported back to happier times when they had been in this house for Kit's birthday and sat at this very table in the sunshine. He remembered his cousin's face with its strawberry-blond curls, so alive in the glow from the candle flames. He glanced at his aunt and their eyes met, as if she knew what he was thinking. But no one had mentioned Kit all day.

Things would have jogged along in this vein, Dillon thought afterwards, each of them making a gargantuan effort to create a jolly birthday mood, but Sara had ruined it. It wasn't her fault, it was the sort of remark anyone could have made after a glass or two, and *should* have been able to make, if his mother weren't being so stubborn. But his sister didn't remember her own advice and mentioned the war.

'Did Freddy know Miles Fanning, Mum? I had his wife as a

patient the other day and I was sure Freddy mentioned him recording something at his studio.' Miles Fanning was a revered jazz trumpeter, now in his seventies but still going strong.

His mum frowned and didn't reply immediately, and there was an awkward pause as they ate their cupcakes and drank their tea. Dillon glared at Sara, who mouthed, 'What?' Ted pulled a face and nudged her; his mother saw it; David got up and grabbed the teapot; Helen raised an eyebrow; a child squealed in a nearby garden. Nobody spoke.

'For Christ's sake,' his mother's voice exploded into the silence. 'Why are you all looking at each other like that? Did somebody die? Or is it *Freddy*? Are we not allowed to mention my dreaded husband's name any more?'

'Mum—'

'Don't "Mum" me, Dillon. You're talking to me as if I'm a recalcitrant child and I'm sick of it. You'd think Freddy had taken a chain-saw to half of London . . .' Dillon watched her mouth purse, her eyes dart from him to Sara and back again '. . . instead of having a breakdown.'

'Is that what you think he had?' Sara, always braver than Dillon, asked.

Lily glared at her. 'Does it matter? Does it honestly matter what happened? I mean, do you see Freddy here? Do you see me texting him, hear me talking to him on the phone? Have I implied we're getting back together?' A pause. '*Have I?*'

Helen grunted. 'Come on, Lily, calm down. Sara didn't mean anything by it.'

But Lily wasn't going to calm down. Dillon watched his

mum push her chair back, the metal feet screeching violently across the patio stone, and stand, arms crossed tight across her body. Sweeping a furious look across all of them, she went on, 'I'm doing my best here, in a situation I'm sure you'll agree is not easy. But none of you seems to believe I can cope. Look at today. It's been like a bloody wake, not a birthday. Helen thinks I'm a spoilt brat. Dillon does nothing but blame me for his miserable life. Sara has avoided me all summer as if I've got the plague.' He saw angry tears in her eyes. 'In fact, neither of you have been near me since the spring.'

Dillon was just about to say something when his mum went on, 'What do you all expect me to do? I can't change the past. I can't click my fingers and make everything okay again.' She swallowed, 'But please, please, can you start treating me as if I'm a normal human being again, and not some God-awful pariah you have to tiptoe around? Give me some credit for being in charge of my own life.'

She shot them all another withering stare before turning on her heel and walking, head held high, into the house, her sandals swishing on the concrete. Neither Dillon nor his sister had had time to speak.

'Wow,' said Ted, blowing his cheeks out.

'Wow, indeed,' Helen retorted, also getting up.

'I suppose we have been a bit unfair to her,' Dillon muttered to no one in particular, glancing at his aunt, then towards the house. He was hurt by his mother's words, but he also felt guilty. He had been avoiding her.

Helen shrugged, picking up the plate on which a lopsided pile of cupcakes still remained.

'At least she sounds as if she's over Freddy,' Sara said, voice also low. 'I'd better go and see if she's all right,' she added, getting up and letting go of Ted's hand.

'No,' Dillon said. 'I'll go.'

CHAPTER 40

Max and Julie Blackstone's house was in the heart of Notting Hill, minutes from the Tube station and Holland Park Avenue. A rambling detached house with a paved area for cars in front, a large garden and terrace at the back, the Blackstones had filled it with modern art: everything from the rampant verdigris stag that greeted you as you came through the front door to the curved wave shape made from glued-together black vinyl records – 78s, 45s and LPs – in the well below the staircase, and the mosaic of Usain Bolt on the sitting-room wall next to the fireplace. The décor was a bit worn – neither Julie nor Max was particularly fussy about things being pristine, despite all their money – and the house had a relaxed, lived-in feel, with plenty of light and comfortable sofas, big towels and a kitchen with wooden dressers and a red Aga rather than the fashionably chilly marble, steel and white interiors favoured by many with similar wealth.

It was late in the evening of Freddy's arrival in London. Julie was curled up on the sofa with a glass of red wine, and Max was pacing about – he was never still for long – with a bottle of Peroni swinging by the neck from his right hand. He was filling Freddy in about the progress of his various investment projects since they'd last talked.

Max had thrown some steaks onto the barbecue earlier, while Julie was concocting a huge salad, and they had sat on the terrace in the light from four yellow garden candles until it began to drizzle. Freddy felt a wave of exhaustion as he lay back against the plump cushions on the sofa opposite Julie. He closed his eyes, his hands clasped loosely over his belly, his ankles crossed.

It was bliss to be there with his oldest friends after months in the wilderness. He had always got on with Julie. Down-to-earth and intelligent, she was a vivacious redhead with a rounded, voluptuous figure who took no prisoners. The money Max had heaped upon her seemed to have made little difference to her soul, even if it had to her lifestyle. She still held to her northern Labour roots, still spoke with a soft Darlington accent, still made beady deals on holidays and flights, cars and clothes – no thousand-pound designer dresses for Julie, although she could well afford them.

'Haven't you told Freddy about the food trucks?' Julie's voice penetrated his doze and he opened his eyes to see her face alive with enthusiasm.

'What food trucks?'

Max grinned. 'Ah, yes, I was getting to that. A new departure . . . bit of a gamble if I'm honest.'

Freddy waited.

'Okay.' Max set his empty beer bottle on the mantelpiece and went to sit next to his friend. 'We thought . . .' he shot his wife a glance '. . . we thought it was about time trendy London got to experience some north-east delicacies.'

Freddy pulled a face. 'Such as?'

Max chuckled. 'Which is what most people would say. Not a region exactly famed for its food, right? But I'm telling you, things like pan haggerty, saveloy dip, singin' hinny . . .'

'Not even sure what they are,' Freddy said.

'No! Well, you have it from us that it's proper soul food, eh, Julie?'

Julie nodded and took over. 'We think people have had enough of the same old same old: burgers, burritos, pasties and fusion stuff. They're in every food market, every festival and fair now. Along with stalls that peddle murky salads with tofu and kale, yams and suspicious sprouting things we've never heard of.' She shook her head in bewilderment. 'Why on earth would you want to eat the likes of chia seeds or amaranth, unless you have the digestive system of a camel?'

Laughing, Freddy said, 'So you're going to give them soul food from the north?'

They both nodded.

'We're not Geordies, but the food will be labelled "Geordie". It's a recognizable USP. We'll be doing proper tasty, easy-to-eat hearty snacks,' Max said. 'Give you a coronary if you ate it all the time, man, but for lunch on a nithering November Tuesday, you can't fucking beat it.'

'These'll be trucks on the street, will they? Or just at markets and festivals?'

'We're starting with five, putting them round the Shoreditch area, Borough Market, the South Bank. There's loads of competition, but our food will make a punter's mouth water.'

'Won't the trendies be freaked out about their waistlines?'

'Ours'll be healthier versions – less fat, less sugar, all that bollocks. But tempt them with a saveloy dip and a cherry cola? We'll have them by the short and curlies, calories be damned.'

'Maybe.' Freddy thought about it, then nodded slowly. 'People are always looking for the new thing.'

'Say what you really think, Freddy,' Julie said, the expression on her round face suddenly focused. 'No bullshit.' She picked up her mobile from the coffee table between them and began to scroll through photographs. 'We've gone for northern cheesy – the trucks are old bread vans.' She began to hum the music from the Hovis commercial as she came round to sit next to Freddy and flick through a series of images on the screen of dark green vans with a serving hatch open along the side.

It was only after Julie had gone to bed and Max had poured Freddy a cognac in a small brandy balloon that his friend moved closer and lowered his voice. 'You heard all the stuff about the new business. Well, I'd like to involve you.'

Freddy's heart skipped a beat. *A job?*

'But . . . you know what I'm going to say, man.' Max shifted on the cushion till he was facing Freddy, his arm across the back of the massive sofa.

340

Freddy did know. Returning Max's look as steadily as his tired eyes would allow, he said, 'I haven't gambled a single penny of my money since I left London in April. Not a single penny.'

Max didn't immediately cheer for joy, instead he continued to stare at his friend. 'You didn't have a single penny. Does that count?'

'I had enough. You don't need much for stake money.'

'Okay . . . That's good, then.' His tone was cautious. 'But now you're back, are you intending to get help, make sure you stay away from the tables? I know you think you can do it on your own, but I'm telling you, Freddy, you fucking can't. No one can.'

Freddy didn't say anything, just took a sip of his drink and felt the liquid burning pleasantly in his throat.

'I'm not going to give you money just to see it fill the pockets of some casino gangster.'

'Give me money for what?' Freddy sat up.

'I'd like help with the food trucks. PR stuff, marketing, networking . . . the stuff you're brilliant at. Me and Julie were thinking of a glitzy launch mid-September. We'd love all those celebrity mates of yours to pitch up.'

Freddy closed his eyes for a second. 'I can do that,' he said, before his face broke into a huge grin. 'I can totally do that, Max.'

His friend held up his hand. 'Wait a minute. There's still things to discuss. For instance, what happened to your gambling debts? Presumably they aren't covered by the bankruptcy.'

Freddy sighed. 'No. Not people who'd bother the Official Receiver with a shortfall, unfortunately.'

'Have you been in touch with them, negotiated some pay-back situation?'

'How can I? I haven't got a fucking bean, Max. That's why I disappeared. I'm just hoping they'll forget about me.'

Max gave a cynical snort. 'Very likely, that.' He was silent for a while and seemed to be considering something. He stood up, paced around, then came back and stood in front of Freddy as he sat on the sofa.

'Okay. Listen to me. I said I'd help if you could prove you'd stopped gambling for a decent amount of time. You've lied to me before on this score, I know, but you seem to be telling the truth this time. So . . . if you tell me what you owe to the ones who'll cause the most trouble, I'll pay them off. A loan, mind. I'll expect it back when you've made your next million.'

Freddy was about to speak, but Max held his hand up again. 'I haven't finished. As I said, I'd like to use your nous on the food truck project – if you're interested – and obviously I'll pay you for that. But I can't risk being associated with someone who racks up debt with loan sharks and gangsters. You need to get professional help for your habit, Freddy.'

At that precise moment Freddy would have agreed to walk the length and breadth of the Sahara Desert barefoot if his friend had asked him to. He was overwhelmed, stunned by his generosity. The most he'd hoped for was a bit of support in some new venture. 'Would you really do that, Max? Pay off my debts and give me a job? Oh, my God . . . I can't believe you'd . . .' His eyes filled with tears.

Max was embarrassed. 'Okay, okay, don't go and cry, you soppy bastard, or I will too.' He glanced away, looked back.

'So do we have a deal, then? You'll keep your side of the bargain?'

'I'll sign on to Gamblers Anonymous in the morning.'

'Don't just sign on. Go to the meetings, Freddy. Keep going.'

'Keep going and going,' Freddy echoed firmly.

Max held his hand out and gave him a hearty shake. 'Fucking good to see you, man. I've missed you.'

CHAPTER 41

The morning was hot and cloudless. In the garden, Lily was working, her laptop perched on the rickety wooden table, barefoot, wearing sunglasses and David's battered straw hat against the glare. Being outside made it hard to concentrate, though, and she found her mind wandering. Thoughts of previous summers with Freddy – driving to the Italian lakes, swimming in the pounding surf at Biarritz, shopping in the covered Marché Forville in Cannes, where a sea bass cost more than the national debt. She closed her eyes, let her hands fall from the keyboard. It was too hot to work, too hot to think.

Lily had been looking for somewhere to live. She was still embarrassed by her angry outburst at the twins' party a week ago – which she had only partially made good with her children – and guilty that she'd allowed them to believe her relationship with Freddy was well and truly over. But maybe it was. Maybe she knew, deep down, and her brain was just refusing to acknowledge the painful truth.

Until she knew for certain, she felt she had to follow up on her assertion that things were under control. She felt like the proverbial rabbit in the headlights, though. The minimum rental in the area was seven hundred a month, for a miserable box of a 'studio'. Plus there would be a deposit, then the ongoing utilities. She could just about afford it now, with the money she'd saved, but she wouldn't be able to afford it for more than a couple of months without securing a better job first. And it would surely be grim, basic . . . lonely.

But Helen and David were going away the day after tomorrow for their annual walking holiday in the Salzkammergut. They would be gone for two weeks, staying at the same *Gasthof* in St Gilgen – on the Wolfgangsee – where they'd summered for the last ten years. So at least there was a short reprieve: she would have the place to herself.

Her sister, with the end of the academic year almost upon her, had been giddy with the prospect of the three-month break – even taking into account departmental meetings, clearing after the A-level results and the new book she intended to research. She had been easier to live with, less combative. Almost, and Lily hesitated to use the word, *cheerful*, their argument about Lily's lifestyle not referred to again. But it wouldn't do to settle back, Lily knew. Helen's moods could turn on a penny. She had to have something sorted before they got back.

A shadow fell across her face and she opened her eyes, blinked, thinking it was David.

'Hi, Aunty Lily.' Kit stood beside her. She could smell the rank whiff of unwashed clothes coming off him.

'Kit! You startled me.' She closed her laptop, immediately apprehensive. Silhouetted against the sun, she couldn't see his face clearly. 'Sit down. Can I get you some tea? A drink?'

She was ashamed of her nerves. *This is Kit*, she told herself, but wondered at the same time how she might go inside to make tea, taking her laptop and phone with her, without embarrassing them both in the process.

'Nah, I'm okay at the moment,' he said, pulling out a chair on the other side of the table and sitting down. 'I thought you might be here,' he added.

'Did you?' Had he been watching her?

'Well, stands to reason. You work from home.' He glanced at the computer.

'You got me into a lot of trouble last time,' she said. He appeared healthier than he had before, she thought. Tanned, maybe a little less gaunt. But his eyes held the same haunted, nervy expression, as if he were constantly prepared for flight. 'Your mother went ballistic, blamed me for giving you money. And your dad got it in the neck for the key.' She knew David had taken the key back weeks ago. Had Kit been intending to break in today? It wouldn't be hard.

He smiled. 'Yeah? Sorry about that.'

'Why have you come?'

Kit, playing with a red elastic band he had round his wrist, shrugged, didn't look at her. 'Umm ... I wanted to talk to you, Aunty Lily.'

346

Kit's use of 'Aunty' felt like a hangover from childhood. The twins had dropped the term with Helen and David years ago.

'About what?'

Her nephew hesitated, then turned the full charm of his beautiful grey eyes upon her, inclining his head slightly to the side, almost as if he were intending to seduce her.

'Umm, I know they're going to Austria on Saturday. Dad told me. And I thought maybe I could crash here while they're away . . . maybe get some help.' He offered another appealing smile, which sat uneasily on his ravaged features. 'You said last time I was here that I could stay if I wanted, and I'll never get clean if I hang around the squat. People come and go at all hours, use the place to score, shoot up . . . The police don't come within a mile.'

Lily didn't know what to say.

'I wouldn't be a bother. I could sleep on the sofa . . .' The boyish pleading was hard to hear.

'You know I can't do that, Kit.'

'But,' he leaned forward, eyes wide, 'it's my only chance, Aunty Lily. I'll never get away from them otherwise. Please, please, think about it. You won't know I'm here, I promise. Just until they get back . . . No need to tell them anything.'

Her heart wanted to believe him. How wonderful would it be to help her nephew kick his habit, bring him back into the family? For a second she imagined Helen's grateful smile. But her head balked at the idea of being responsible for someone who was so volatile and manipulative. So sick.

'I can't. It would be betraying my sister. I can't do it.'

Kit leaned back in his chair. She could see the muscles in his cheek twitching, his eyes blinking double time.

Glancing down the garden, he pointed to the magnolia. 'Do you remember the camp me and Dill had under the tree? God, I loved that place. It felt so safe, so . . . mine.'

Lily couldn't help smiling at the memory of her son and his hero cousin, little boys – one blond, the other dark – crouched for hours beneath a construction of blankets and towels balanced on fruit boxes and sticks. Kit had been the master builder, a genius at creating a cosy, secret world from which all adults were firmly excluded. Dillon had wanted never to come out.

'Those were the days,' Kit was saying, his eyes never leaving Lily's face. He'd seen the softening of her features, she was sure, and wanted to drive home his advantage. Or was she being cynical? Did the man really want to change?

'If you want to come home,' she said, 'you'll have to ask your parents. This isn't my house.'

'But you know what Mum's like. She'll never let me back in unless I can prove I'm clean. And I can't get clean unless I get away from those people.'

'Have you tried methadone?' she asked.

He shook his head. 'Won't work for me. Remember, I'm like you, an asthmatic.'

He may be a drug addict, but he's not stupid, Lily thought, remembering Helen's euphoria when her son got his doctorate so young. She had no recollection at all of him being asthmatic.

'Do you really want to stop, Kit?' she asked.

His face suddenly became animated. 'God, yes. Of course I do! Do you think this is any sort of a life? Do you think living in a shithole surrounded by violence and pain – death sometimes – is what I had in mind for myself? What anyone has in mind for themselves? Aunty Lily, we've always had a bond, you and me. You got me. Please, please, help. Give me the chance to prove myself.'

There was silence for a moment. Why, if he didn't want to give up, was he begging this favour of her? It didn't make sense.

'You're asking too much of me, Kit. You need professional help, people who understand how to bring someone down off drugs. You can't do it on your own, on your parents' sofa. It would be hell.'

He gave a mirthless snort. 'More hellish than my current existence? I doubt it.'

She could see he was beginning to fidget, to jiggle his right leg up and down on the patio stones, to scratch his neck so hard that his fair skin turned bright red.

'I'm not going to one of those fucking prison camps they call rehab. Those people don't understand a fucking thing about drugs. They're just making shedloads of money out of freaked-out middle-class parents like mine. It doesn't work, Aunty Lily. I've tried, believe me. It's a fucking joke.'

His voice had risen a couple of octaves and he was clearly getting agitated. Lily just wanted him to leave.

'I'll talk to Helen,' she said eventually, regretting the words as soon as they were out of her mouth.

Kit burst out of his chair, flinging his arms wide, his head back. 'That's no fucking good! She won't listen. She never listens. She hates me.'

To her horror, Kit came over and threw himself down on the patio, wrapping his arms around her legs and laying his dirty head in her lap. 'Please, please, Aunty Lily. You're my last chance.'

Recoiling, Lily pushed him gently away. Kit flopped back on his haunches, hands hanging loosely by his sides, his face dull with despair and, Lily thought, a burning resentment. He got slowly to his feet. ''Kay.' He turned away but still didn't leave.

His shoulders, poking through his thin, grubby white T-shirt, made his skinny figure look especially vulnerable and Lily's heart broke for him. She got to her feet, laid a hand on his shoulder. 'Kit, you know I'll help you in any way I can . . . But I can't let you stay here without telling Helen and David.'

He swung round, knocking her hand away. 'I get it,' he said, his eyes full of anger. 'Can you lend me some cash then? As you can see, I'm fucking desperate.' His voice was cold, withdrawn.

For Christ's sake, she thought. *What do I do now?* The prospect of having another strained argument with her nephew was too much for her. She just wanted him to go before he turned on her, let the resentment written so clearly on his face bubble over into something more frightening.

'Wait here.'

She couldn't have been inside more than three minutes, but when she came back out into the bright sunlight, clutching three ten-pound notes, her computer and mobile had vanished, along with her nephew.

Stung with disbelief, Lily ran out to the front of the house in her bare feet, painfully negotiating the gravel drive, shouting Kit's name over and over. The street was empty. There was no sign of him anywhere. Just a quiet, hot midday silence, broken only by a silver Ford purring past, the lady from across the road emptying some bottles into her recycling bin, an orange cat prowling slowly along the brick wall that separated Helen and David's garden from the pavement, his coat glinting in the sunlight.

She didn't know whether to be angry with Kit or sad for him. But she was absolutely furious with herself. 'Gullible idiot.' She spoke out loud to the empty back garden, the empty table to which she'd returned, hoping somehow she'd made a mistake and he would still be there. How could she have been so stupid when she absolutely knew that he would take them if he could?

It was a disaster on so many levels. First, she would have to spend money she didn't have on a new laptop and phone – she wasn't insured, having defaulted on the direct debit payments back in April. Second, she would have to explain to Seth Kramer that the confidential information contained in the files she'd been transcribing was now in the hands of a manipulative drug addict. He'd been so clear that the personal details should be guarded with her life – it had made her laugh at the time. Third, she would have to face Helen and tell her how she had been conned, giving her sister further proof of her gullibility, her general uselessness. And fourth, suppose Freddy were trying to call her and she didn't have her phone?

Not knowing what to do, she stood there, shivering, cold even in the heat, as if she had been assaulted. *I've been mugged*, she told herself, *by my own nephew*. Was the conversation just an elaborate ruse to get money off her again, or better, a laptop and mobile phone? Could he really be so manipulative? Had he planned the whole thing, knowing his aunt would be a total pushover?

She snatched up her sunglasses and went inside, locking the garden door firmly, then slung her bag over her shoulder, pushed her feet into some canvas shoes and set off for Seth Kramer's boat. She had to tell him about the files.

Seth raised his eyebrows as Lily, out of breath from the walk, red-faced and sweating, blurted out the sorry tale of the lost data.

'Sit, please. I'll get you some water.'

Lily waited in trepidation for him to comment.

He perched opposite her on the desk chair, handing her the glass. It was baking on the boat, the sun beating on the roof, the open portholes inadequate, even with the long doors pinned back at the entrance – she didn't know how he stood it. Seth looked tired as he took off his tortoiseshell specs and gave both lenses a rub with the bottom of his faded navy polo shirt.

'I don't imagine the files will be seen as valuable. There's nobody famous. And they weren't actual therapy sessions, just interviews . . .' He stopped, took a breath. 'But I used their full names. I'll have to inform them.'

'I'm so sorry.'

'Your nephew will probably just pawn the computer as quickly as he can, won't he? It's the cash he's after.' Seth looked away, didn't speak for a while, considering the implications. 'Have you told the police?'

'No,' she said quickly. 'I can't, he's my nephew.'

The doctor raised his eyebrows. 'He's stolen from you, Lily.' He gave her a searching look. 'What does your sister say?'

'I haven't spoken to her yet.' She squirmed at the thought of Helen's inevitable anger and the blame that would no doubt land square on Lily's shoulders.

'It won't help anyone to turn a blind eye, you know. And if he's arrested, he'll be able to tell them where he fenced the computer. You might get it back.'

Lily didn't reply, the ramifications churning through her mind.

'You're just enabling him, Lily,' Seth was saying. 'Kit will expect you to do nothing. You're his aunt, of course you won't tell on him. So his actions have no consequences. And in a day, a week, however long it takes to shoot up the drugs he bought with the laptop cash, he'll be back at the house, pestering you for more. Are you prepared for that?'

She started to protest, but she knew Seth was right.

'I don't want him to be arrested.'

Seth sighed. 'I know. It seems harsh. And Kit is very vulnerable. But you can't let him ride roughshod over you.'

There was silence. Lily could feel a tickling trickle of sweat slide down her back beneath her T-shirt. 'Do you think the whole thing about him staying at the house in order to get clean was a ruse to get me onside?'

Seth shrugged. 'I think it's odd that he didn't wait to drop in till after his parents had left. Then there might have been a legitimate reason for not telling them.'

Lily thought about this. 'Maybe he does want to quit. Maybe I should have said he could stay.'

Seth cocked his head, gave her a disbelieving smile. 'Where did you get such a soft heart, Lily?'

David shook his head. 'I'm so sorry,' he said.

Lily was at the house when her brother-in-law came home, ahead of her sister, thank goodness. She had been waiting since returning from the boat, stomach in knots, head aching from the heat, for several hours now. She was no longer worried about the computer and phone – although she felt naked without her mobile: it was Helen's reaction that terrified her.

'It was my fault, David,' she said, as they both sat down at the garden table in the hot evening sun. 'I should never have left him alone with my stuff. I knew it was a risk, but I didn't want to embarrass us both. And, to be honest, I didn't think he would do that to me.'

David gave a long sigh. His frayed striped cotton shirt – one of his work shirts – was stained with sweat, his craggy face flushed, the usual wood dust dulling his unruly hair. Lily had made them both tea, and he had gulped half the contents of the mug almost before she had put it on the table.

'You assume, because he's family and clearly fond of you, that he'll behave like the rest of us. But Kit is capable of anything when it comes to getting a fix.'

'He asked if he could stay here when you and Helen are on holiday. He said he needed a safe place if he was ever to get off the drugs.'

David nodded wearily. 'That's familiar.'

'He's said that to you too?' Lily, shocked, felt betrayed all over again. 'But why? If he doesn't mean it, what does he have to gain?'

Her brother-in-law looked at her askance. 'What did he gain from you?'

'So he played me till my guard was down?'

'Oh, I don't know. Maybe as he says it he believes it. Don't forget this is one smart boy. Even with the drugs he's ahead of most of us in the IQ department.'

They sat in silence.

'What will Helen say about the police?'

David considered her question. 'Don't know. She'll be upset, of course, angry.'

'With me, no doubt.'

He looked surprised. 'With you? Why? You haven't done anything, Lily. You're the victim here.'

'I was gullible and now he's got his hands on enough cash to kill himself.' Putting words to her fear did not seem to help. But ever since Kit had vanished with her computer, the image of his dead body, white and still and so young, had haunted her.

David did not reply, his gaze directed towards the rose bushes that grew along the fence. The creamy-gold blooms were thick and plentiful, glowing richly in the evening light.

'David, I'm sorry, I shouldn't have said that.'

He gave her a sad smile. 'Don't apologize. You're only saying what we all know, Lily. Kit's life has hung in the balance for years now.' He started to say something then stopped.

Lily leaned forward. 'Kit said his life was hell and he hated it, David. I know you'll say I'm a fool, but I honestly believe he wants to quit.'

'Well . . .' David didn't go on, and Lily realized he didn't want to burst her bubble. Maybe he needed, just for a minute, to believe it again himself.

'Hi, I'm home!' They heard Helen calling from the house. Then she burst onto the patio, ripping off her grey suit jacket and waving it in the air. 'Woo-hoo, I've finished! I'm free!'

She threw herself onto a garden chair and beamed at Lily and David. 'Such a great feeling. The whole summer ahead and not a single spotty student in sight.' She laughed. 'Not that they have as many spots as they used to, with all those smoothies.'

Lily's heart contracted as David grinned and reached over to give her hand a squeeze. But Helen had already sensed something was up. Her gaze shot from David to Lily and back again. 'What's going on?'

'It's Kit,' David said after a moment, and Lily watched her sister's face fall.

'He came here when Lily was working in the garden. She went inside for a minute and he ran off with her phone and computer.'

Eyes on Lily, Helen frowned. 'Tell me exactly what happened.'

Lily obliged, watching her sister's face darkening with

every word. 'I had to tell Seth Kramer,' Lily finished, 'because obviously there's confidential data from his patient interviews on my computer.' She took a breath. 'He said I should inform the police.'

Helen raised her eyebrows. 'And did you?'

'No, no, of course not.'

'There's no "of course not" about it, Lily. He stole from you. You should call the police.'

Both she and David must have registered shock, because Helen went on, 'Don't look at me like that. He's a thief. He should be punished.'

'What good will that do, Helen?' David asked after a moment. 'They won't pay any attention. He's a known addict. It was only family he stole from.'

Turning in her chair, Helen's eyes were fierce. '"Only family"?' She sighed with frustration. 'Do I really have to repeat myself, David? Do you still not get it? After all this time?' Her mouth twitched angrily before she added, her words deliberately slow and loud, as if her husband were hard of hearing, 'Your mollycoddling is *helping* Kit take drugs. You're *keeping* him addicted.'

Before either of them had a chance to respond, Helen had turned her ire on Lily. 'And you're the same. Your ridiculous *naïveté*. After all I've said to you about addiction, about Kit's behaviour, you still chose to believe him? It literally takes my breath away. And now you're living here, he thinks he has *carte blanche* to pop in whenever he needs another sub.' She dropped her head into her hands for a second, then raised it again. She had not finished. 'What do I have to say to make you both *understand*?' she shouted across the table in the still summer evening. 'Until you start treating Kit like the addict he is, he will never, *ever* get off heroin.'

'I'm sorry,' Lily said softly.

David said nothing.

Tears in her eyes, Helen glared at her sister. 'Ring the police. Report the theft. Stop meddling, Lily. And for God's sake, stop pandering to our son.'

CHAPTER 42

Freddy had to pinch himself when he woke for the first time in the small two-bedroomed flat above a pub on the corner of Charlotte Street, near Tottenham Court Road. It was a recently acquired addition to Julie Blackstone's extensive property portfolio. The flat had been renovated recently and still smelt of paint, plaster dust and rubber from the sisal carpet underlay in the bedroom.

'You can have it for six months,' Julie had said. 'Then I'll have to charge you rent. But until that building next door is finished I won't be able to let it to anyone. You're doing me a favour, keeping the place warmed up.'

Freddy knew he wasn't doing Julie a favour. The building work, admittedly, was a total gutting and reconstruction of a block of flats, but there were plenty of people out at work all day who wouldn't have minded the racket and the dust for a reduced rent. The flat was gorgeous, beautifully finished and furnished with Julie's usual rigour and good taste. He was a very lucky man.

'I'm hoping Lily will be with me,' he'd told Julie. He didn't want her to think he was taking advantage of her generosity.

She had frowned. 'Max said you two had split up.'

They were unpacking the new sofa, stripping off the plastic and cardboard wrapping from the slate-grey cushions, Freddy lying on the newly sanded floor to cut the twisted layers of tape strangling the wooden feet.

'No,' said Freddy. 'We just had a bit of a break.' He stood up and brushed dust from his jeans, then crumpled a handful of sticky brown tape and plastic and put it into the bulging black bin liner in the corner of the room.

'So how is she? *Where* is she? I rang her a few times after it all kicked off with the studio, but she didn't call back.'

'I don't know where she is.' He felt suddenly ashamed to admit it.

Julie looked puzzled. 'So you're not in touch.'

'Not since April. I thought it was for the best until things settled down.'

'And she's twiddling her thumbs somewhere, waiting for you to ring? *Really*, Freddy?' Her tone was cynical.

Freddy shrugged. 'I hope so.'

'After months without even a phone call? And she agreed to this peculiar arrangement?'

'Sort of.'

Julie's expression was scornful. 'I'd tell Max to go fuck himself if he did that to me.'

Freddy thought Julie was overreacting. Always a card-carrying feminist, his friend was quick to blame men for every perceived shortcoming, justified or not. 'I treated her so badly, took all her money, I wanted—'

'So what is she living on, if you took all her money?' Julie interrupted, arms folded, clearly baffled by his admission.

'I imagine she's staying with Prem, her friend who owns the desk and chair shop in Marylebone. You've met her at various parties – Indian, very beautiful. Lily used to work there, so she's probably got her old job back.'

'Right. Oh, that's okay then, leaving her to sponge off her friends. I'm sure Lily's loving that.'

'She . . .' He stopped, irritated by the lecture. 'Listen, I didn't have any choice at the time. But I can make it up to her, now you and Max have given me another chance.'

Shaking her head, Julie turned away and began settling the sofa cushions, plumping them and patting them smooth, pulling off the white safety tag on the bottom of the seat, until she was satisfied. 'Well, good luck with that, Freddy. If I were Lily, I wouldn't even have the conversation.'

For the two weeks since his arrival in London Freddy had jumped in with both feet, immersing himself in Max's food-truck venture, keen to prove to his friend that his considerable investment would pay off. It was work, as Max had known, to which Freddy was perfectly suited. And without the heavy responsibility he'd shouldered while owning his business, Freddy found he was enjoying himself, networking to the hilt as he got in touch with all his old friends and acquaintances.

He had something to peddle, a business, although small, that he wholeheartedly believed could work.

He had been nervous of those first few days in the thick of it. He knew his reputation had taken a heavy blow that spring. But he realized, too, that every one of these people moved in a fickle, fly-by-night industry – here today, gone tomorrow – and were only too aware that it could just as easily have been them in Freddy's shoes, spending their summer as a guest of the Official Receiver. They honestly didn't care, as long as they weren't the ones that Freddy owed money to. And they liked him, welcomed him back like a long-lost son. That is, those who noticed he'd gone in the first place.

Plus ça change, thought Freddy, now, as he lay in bed and looked up at the white, freshly painted ceiling and the frosted-glass half-moon light shade above his bed. He felt relaxed for the first time since . . . well, he couldn't remember. Years, maybe, back when he'd first met Lily, when things were still under control. This was his chance, he told himself. A clean slate. A job. Somewhere to live. Yes, he owed Max and Julie a fuck of a lot. But he would see them right. He had done what he had promised his wife he would do. So now the last piece of the jigsaw could be put in place: Lily.

Freddy had been temporarily disheartened by Julie's reaction to his recent behaviour, but he was certain Lily still loved him. A few months' separation wouldn't be enough to change that. The thought of losing his wife was unbearable. The prospect of their reunion had kept him going through his strange exile in Malta – Shirley notwithstanding.

She was still calling him. Freddy knew he must have the

conversation, let her know he wasn't coming back. But talking to her would mean more lies about his father, more evasions. He just wanted to pretend none of it had ever happened. He wanted to start over as a new man, a sparkling fresh, perfect husband; a man who didn't gamble, who kept down a good job, who wasn't profligate or in any way reprehensible. A man Lily could be proud to love.

Freddy was sure he could make this happen. He hadn't properly committed to Gamblers Anonymous yet, as he'd promised Max he would. He had tried, pushing open the glass door to the community centre in a street behind the British Museum and sitting at the back of the white room on a moulded plastic chair, a paper cup of coffee in his hand. He'd listened to a woman named Deborah recount how she'd stolen money from her boss, how the electric rush up the back of her neck – 'It was better than sex', she said – had made her gamble again and again until her life was in ruins. A well-dressed man in his sixties offered Freddy a friendly hand to shake, told him his name was John. But the trepidation Freddy felt in that atmosphere of confession was too intense, convinced every second as he was that someone was going to point at him and ask him to do the same. He waited politely till Deborah had finished, then quickly got up and left.

This was not honouring the bargain he'd made with Max and he vowed he would go back – he owed that to his friend. But he was not like the depressing people in that room. While he was under Max and Julie's roof, for instance, he'd had no desire to gamble whatsoever. And now he was on his own, he had Lily in his sights. No, he didn't have a problem: he had just temporarily lost control at a time in his life when things were going awry for his business. *A natural reaction*, he told himself as he practically ran along the pavement, away from the centre and towards his new home. *I'm no more an addict than Max, who never puts his phone down for five seconds.*

Looking around the flat one Friday morning, he decided he was finally ready to contact Lily. The place wasn't completely finished: the tiles in the bathroom weren't grouted, the washing machine had yet to be delivered and he hadn't bought any throws or cushions to brighten up the sofa. But he felt it was somewhere he could bring his wife, somewhere they would be comfortable as they started their life again – they could choose the cushions together.

Screwing up his courage and trembling with anticipation, he dialled Lily's number. It rang. And rang. No answer message option. But then Lily never answered if she didn't know who was calling. She wouldn't be familiar with his number now.

Deflated, Freddy stood by the French windows onto the tiny balcony, clutching his phone and gazing at the hotel opposite. The street was already busy although it was barely nine fifteen, a large party of Asian tourists emerging from the hotel and standing on the pavement, heads bent to their mobiles. *Should I email? Text her?* he wondered. But that seemed way too casual, almost cheeky, after three months of silence.

Unable to stay still, his mind wired for his mission, he snatched up his jacket, checked for keys, then raced down the two flights and out onto the street. It took him barely fifteen minutes to walk to Marylebone High Street and Prem's shop. Standing for a moment by the window, he peered inside, past the large black desk chair on display, to see if Lily were there. He couldn't see her, but she might be in the back. Taking a deep breath and pushing open the door, he strode in as confidently as he could, remembering the first time he'd done so and seen Lily, standing there like a beacon of hope.

Prem was sitting behind the desk at the back of the shop, looking as stunning as ever, her glossy dark hair pinned in an elegantly loose knot on the top of her head. She looked up at the sound of the bell, her face clouding as soon as she saw it was Freddy. Getting up and coming round the desk, she stood and waited for him to speak, arms crossed, making no move to offer the usual kisses of greeting. The showroom was empty so early in the day, and they had the place to themselves.

Freddy found himself intimidated.

'What do you want, Freddy?' she asked.

She knew perfectly well what he wanted. 'I'm looking for Lily.'

'She's not here.'

'Does she work here, though?'

'No.'

'Could you tell me where she is, please?' It irked him to have to beg like this. Lily was his wife.

Prem raised her eyebrows imperiously. 'Why would I do that?'

Freddy faltered.

Before he could say another word, Prem's expression

darkened. 'Do you honestly think I'm going to make it easy for you to ruin my friend's life for a second time, Freddy March?'

'Come on, Prem. I'm only asking where she is. You know I can find her on my own. Lily's not a child. She can make her own decisions.'

Paying no attention to his request, Prem went on, 'Have you any idea how absolutely destroyed she's been since you left?' She gave a derisory laugh. 'No, of course you haven't, because you haven't bothered to phone her and find out. You've been living it up, apparently – people have seen you – conning a new set of innocents out of their millions, no doubt. And without a single thought for poor Lily, abandoned virtually without a penny to her name. Frankly, it takes my breath away that you have the nerve to come here as if nothing has happened, and demand my help.' She stopped, breathing hard from her rant. 'Get out of our lives, Freddy. Just leave us alone. And don't try to contact Lily. She's moved on.' Prem turned and went back to the desk, dismissing him with her silence.

Shaken, Freddy left the shop and wandered down Marylebone High Street in the morning sunlight. *Moved on?* He was aghast. Lily would never move on so soon. And who had seen him so-called 'living it up'? He had barely been out in the evenings since he arrived at Max's, except that Turkish place on Julie's birthday. His heart contracted at the thought of Lily hearing he was having a good time without her. No doubt whoever it was who'd seen him would have taken great pleasure in spreading the news.

He couldn't decide whether Lily was staying with Prem and her husband, Anthony, or not. She'd given nothing away. Standing in the street, he called Lily's mobile again, with the same result. Where else might she be? He began to hurry towards Bond Street Tube.

Anthony opened the door to the Fulham house, dressed in grey jogging pants and a sweaty white T-shirt, his face flushed. He looked surprised to see Freddy, but smiled and ushered him inside. The house was calm and quiet, as always.

'Just got back from a run so I'm a bit whiffy, I imagine,' he said, walking through to the cream-painted drawing room decorated in modern Scandinavian style – clean lines, natural fabrics, functional – and way too tidy for Freddy's comfort. Freddy watched as he picked up a bottle of water from the mantelpiece, took a long gulp and wiped his mouth with the back of his hand. Anthony was tall and lean, darkly good-looking, a man who gave little away and was often silent in company. But Freddy knew him to be witty and wry when he relaxed. They had always got on in the past, Freddy eternally grateful for the support Anthony had given Lily when her first husband had died.

'This is a surprise,' Anthony said when Freddy didn't speak.

'Yes, sorry to barge in like this.' *No point in beating about the bush*, he thought, taking a deep breath. 'I'm looking for Lily.'

'Oh. She's not here.'

'I thought maybe she was staying with you?'

'No. She's been with Helen and David since . . . since you split up.'

Freddy wanted to say *We didn't split up*, but Prem's words were still ringing in his ears and he kept silent.

'Are you . . .' Anthony stopped.

'I just want to talk to her.'

The other man raised his eyebrows but said nothing as he took another swig of water, his eyes never leaving Freddy's face.

'Listen, thanks,' Freddy said.

'Don't hurt her again,' he heard Anthony say as he turned to leave. His tone wasn't threatening, just adamant.

Freddy turned back. 'I've been an arse, Anthony, I'm fully aware of that, but I'm on track again now. If she'll have me, I hope we can make a fresh start.'

Anthony pursed his lips. 'As I said, Freddy . . .'

The journey to Oxford was interminable, the train seeming to drag its heels deliberately. Freddy had this feeling, now he had committed to the journey, that if he didn't get there immediately and find Lily, he would be too late. He took the number 500 bus from outside the station, down Banbury Road, then walked the rest of the way to his sister- and brother-in-law's house.

When he arrived he saw that both cars – Helen's Saab and David's Ford van – were parked on the gravel drive. He didn't fancy another mauling, the front door slammed in his face, so he waited down the street, trying not to look like a criminal casing a joint. *Helen and David should be at work on a Friday lunchtime.* And then he remembered it was the holidays and Helen, at least, would not be going to college.

It was another hot day, and Freddy had had only two black coffees all morning. He was lightheaded, dehydrated, and beginning to feel ridiculous, wishing he'd just texted Lily from London instead of stalking her like this. Closing his eyes and leaning against a tree, he almost missed his wife as she walked past on the other side of the road, a canvas bag over her shoulder, her stride purposeful.

Seeing her again after so long made Freddy's breath catch in his throat. He watched her, taking in her cream linen shorts falling just past her knee, her loose navy cotton top, the silver bangle she always wore, the scuffed plimsolls, the smoothly tanned legs, her hair falling shiny and chaotic around her neck. She looked different, more . . . He couldn't name it.

Prem's words haunted him as he set off behind her. He didn't know why he didn't call out now Lily was clear of the house, but he didn't. Was he scared of confronting his own wife? Or was it more that he wanted to drink in her presence, enjoy her before the onset of recriminations, perhaps, or worse, outright rejection? He found himself following her through all the twists and turns of her walk, intrigued as to where she was going, whom she was about to meet.

After a while he saw Lily cross a small brick bridge onto the other side of the canal and walk left towards one of the narrowboats parked on the far bank. He saw her stop and call out and watched as a dark-haired man emerged from the rust and black boat. Standing on the bridge, he couldn't hear what the man said, but he saw Lily's warm smile, heard her laugh as she climbed aboard and disappeared into the interior.

Freddy felt bile rise in his throat, his knees weakening as he leaned over the sun-warmed parapet, swallowing hard. *Who the fuck is that?* he asked himself, having a mad urge to run down there and yank his beautiful wife out of the stranger's clutches. *What if they're going to . . .* The thought sickened him so much that he had to walk quickly away.

CHAPTER 43

Helen and David had left for Austria and Lily was thoroughly relieved. Her sister had not forgiven her for refusing to report the theft to the police, and the days before the holiday had been tense between them. But Lily just couldn't do it. The stuff was gone: there was no getting it back now. And whatever Seth Kramer and her sister said, Lily couldn't see how her snitching on Kit would change a single thing for the better.

She had spent too much money and time getting another laptop and phone. But Corey Ryan, a friend of David's, had set up the new computer one long, hot afternoon in his messy shop on Marston Road, firing questions at her about passwords and iCloud back-up, mail accounts, Bluetooth and network preferences until her head ached.

Lily knew that while her sister was away she should be looking for more work and somewhere else to live – she could not spend the summer with Helen while they were both at home all day: there would be a massacre. But the heat was making her lazy. She decided to think about that particular nightmare next week, treat this time as a sort of holiday. She would focus on it then, when Seth would also be away, making a short visit to his sister in the Dordogne.

Today, however, as Lily set out for the boat around lunch-time, she realized she was nervous about seeing the doctor. Things had got a bit embarrassing between them – to say the least – the other night, when Lily had gone round to his house for the first time.

She had called Seth to update him about the new computer, and to ask him to send her back the typed up client interviews and spreadsheet she had originally sent him, so that she could reinstall them on her laptop. The weather had broken and a summer storm raged outside, the house echoing and chilly as she sat at the kitchen table in the semi-darkness. She had drawn all the blinds – which Helen and David never did – but she was still alert to every sound, nervous that her nephew might be hovering outside, watching the house. 'You can always call the police,' David had told her – looking slightly sheepish at the suggestion – when she expressed her concerns about Kit. But she wasn't reassured.

'Great, so you're back on track,' Seth had said. 'Computer hassles are such a stupid waste of time.'

She had agreed that she was indeed 'back on track', but in fact she felt far from being so, her mood edgy and depressed, the joys of having the house to herself quickly palling in the dark, miserable weather. It was at such times, when there was nothing to distract her from her thoughts, that she would get out her sketchbook and draw. But that night she'd been too restless and the pencil had sat idly in her hand. All she'd wanted was to hear Freddy's voice, to feel the reassuring warmth of his body close to hers.

When she mentioned during the call that Helen and David were away, Seth had asked her over. Instinctively, she'd been about to turn down his offer – she was so unused to socializing these days – but there didn't seem any sensible reason why she wouldn't go.

'It's pouring. Do you have a car?'

'I have Helen's.'

'Right.' He'd given her his address. 'It's just off Walton Street. Shouldn't take you more than ten minutes.'

Seth's house was semi-detached, in soft yellow brick with a half-basement and steps up to a red front door. Inside was stylish, a bit messy, with long windows stretching the height of two floors looking out onto the back garden, real wood floors, mostly abstract art on the walls.

He'd shown her into the kitchen, where soft blue walls, a distressed-oak dresser and table, and grey-blue units created a calm space. A bottle of red wine stood on the table, alongside cheese – a soft goat, Cheddar – on a patterned earthenware plate, a packet of heavy-duty charcoal crackers and a bowl of cherries.

Seth had looked slightly abashed by the spread. 'I wasn't sure if you'd eaten.'

She hadn't and was grateful for the food.

They'd taken their wine upstairs when they'd finished

eating, sat at either end of the big sofa in the sitting room, in front of the gas-log fire. Neither had referred to Freddy or to her nephew, and it was a blessed relief to sit with someone and talk about other things, such as art, books – his house was crammed, floor to ceiling, with all kinds – cutting the grass, parking in Oxford, the holidays coming up.

Lily drank way too much. She knew it, but she didn't care. In fact she didn't care about anything any more. If her life was a mess, she would sort it out. Or she wouldn't. She was tired of worrying about it.

'You can't drive home,' Seth said when Lily finally realized how late it was and got up to leave. He waved the empty wine bottle that was sitting on the coffee table. 'This is the second. I won't let you.'

Lily's protest was feeble. Although the storm had passed, Helen and David's empty house, with the lurking presence of Kit in every tiny sound, held no appeal in the darkness.

They had stood at the door of the spare bedroom. Seth had found towels, directed her towards the bathroom, closed the curtains for her.

'Sleep well,' he said, giving her a smile as he reached out to remove a small feather that had somehow got attached to the sleeve of her green cardigan. It was an oddly intimate gesture, which triggered in Lily a desperate need for comfort from someone, even if it wasn't Freddy. Without thinking, she put her hands on Seth's shoulders and drew him close, bringing her mouth to his and kissing him full on the lips.

For a brief moment he responded, his mouth warm against her own, and it felt like such a relief to be wanted again. But

374

then he pulled back, removed her hands gently. She could see confusion in his eyes, a rare thing in someone always so sure, and when he spoke his voice was shaky. 'We can't do this, Lily.'

'Why not?' she demanded.

'We've both had too much to drink.'

'Isn't this what people do when they're drunk?'

He laughed softly. 'I suppose, but I'm not going to take advantage of you.'

She felt a shaft of disappointment and leaned against the wall, befuddled now, just wanting to sleep. Seth guided her into the bedroom.

'Will you be all right?' he asked as she stood swaying by the bed. But Lily was beyond speech. Waiting till Seth had closed the door, she ripped off her clothes and fell naked between the cool cotton sheets.

Seth had seemed unfazed when she finally emerged, shame-faced, from the bedroom the morning after. She'd found him in the kitchen, making coffee. Taking one look at her, he'd handed her a cup without speaking.

'God, I'm sorry,' she'd babbled, plonking herself down on a stool by the work island – she was feeling queasy, her head thick. 'I don't know what came over me. I promise I don't usually behave like that – it's mortifying. Too much wine and . . .' She'd waved her hand, dismissing her own blather.

'Toast?' he'd asked with a smile.

So they had sat in his sunny kitchen, drinking coffee and eating toast with the honey he'd been given by his friend in Sussex, talking in their usual fashion about everything . . .

except the kiss. It made her cringe all over again to relive the moment.

Now she paused before crossing Banbury Road on her journey to the canal. She had the sudden impression that she was being watched, that there was someone behind her. She spun round. But the pavement was busy with people going about their business, the road full of Friday traffic, and she told herself she must be imagining it. *Suppose Kit is following me?* She shook herself, crossed the road, resolving to stop being so ridiculous. But she was relieved when she arrived at Seth's boat: the feeling of someone behind her had not gone away.

Lily still felt a little self-conscious as she and the doctor went for their usual Friday afternoon lunch at the pub across the bridge – always his treat. Outside was crammed with people so they sat inside, which was cooler anyway. To dispel her nerves she searched for a topic of conversation and ended up telling him about the odd sensation that she was being watched.

Seth frowned. 'You don't seem the paranoid type.'

'So you think it's my imagination?'

'Hmm . . . not necessarily. Maybe someone *is* watching you.'

'Thanks! Just what I needed to hear.'

'But unless you're a spy or a criminal of some sort . . .' He grinned, pushed his glasses up his nose. 'Is there something you're not telling me, Lily? A shady past, perhaps?'

Lily found herself blushing, remembering the fantastical threats of which Freddy had warned her: men pitching up at the flat, lying in wait to duff him up, breaking his – or, indeed, her – kneecaps. She was embarrassed to have believed him now.

She saw Seth noting the blush, but he looked away, obviously not wanting to embarrass her further. 'Those people my husband pissed off . . . He was convinced they were following him.'

'Maybe they were.'

He gazed at her with one of what Lily teased him were his 'therapy stares'. They seemed to reach beyond her willingness to reveal things. 'It must have been hard, being with someone so out of control.'

Lily frowned. 'He never seemed out of control though. Freddy always had a plan.' She thought for a moment. 'But yes, when it all started to fall apart he must have felt pretty unhinged.' She glanced at Seth. 'You don't really see it clearly at the time. At least, I didn't.'

'Do you still love him, despite it all?'

'I'm not even sure who I loved.'

There was silence between them. Seth took another sip of his lager. A dusty shaft of sunlight coming through the window burned hot on Lily's back. She felt peaceful in the doctor's company, the problem with Freddy a lifetime away.

Lily did not see him until he was standing directly in front of her. Her mind had been elsewhere as she wandered along the canal in the opposite direction to home – she didn't feel like going back to the house yet. It was late afternoon and she was hot and a bit wobbly from the two glasses of wine

– one more than usual – she'd consumed, responding to the awkwardness she'd felt at seeing the doctor again.

'Lily?'

She jumped at the sound of her name, her heart almost stopping when she realized who it was. Holding her hand to her mouth she stared up, the sun behind him haloing his head in light. She wondered for a split second whether this was another of her flights of fancy, a mirage.

He laughed. 'You look as if you've seen a ghost.'

'Freddy?'

'As I live and breathe.'

'What are you doing here?' She could barely get the words out, her breath trapped in her throat so that she was having trouble swallowing.

'Looking for you.' She felt his hand on her bare arm. 'There's a bench over there. Shall we sit down?'

He led her across a wooden walkway into the recreation ground beside the canal. Lily, still uncomprehending, kept staring at him. When they were seated, she turned to him. 'Why didn't you ring?'

'I did, but you wouldn't have recognized my number.'

'A text then. Just to warn me.'

'I . . . I didn't know if you wanted to see me, Lily. I thought it would be easy to ignore a text or an email.'

She didn't reply. Did she want to see him? She knew she had wanted to, so much so that she'd thought there was nothing to live for if she didn't. But now he was here . . . She could feel part of her resisting him, aware that he had already shattered her peace of mind. His presence put her on edge.

'*Do* you want to see me?' he was asking.

The look on his face was desperate, his body, so close to hers, both familiar and very alien.

'Were you following me?'

He nodded sheepishly. 'I thought Helen and David were home ... the cars. I didn't want another lecture. Prem and Julie have already bent my ear about what a bastard I am – all of which I know.' He paused. 'Told me I don't deserve you. How I should never darken your door again.'

Lily couldn't help smiling, imagining Prem's fierce loyalty, Julie's northern bluntness rolled out in her defence. But Freddy's face had fallen.

'Prem said you'd moved on, Lily.'

'Did she?' she asked, knowing suddenly that Prem, for reasons she couldn't actually know, was partly right. Her heart would not slow down. She was hot and thirsty from the wine, and the chips she'd eaten. She still couldn't believe he was here beside her: the memories of him that had invaded large parts of her days for months seemed more real – and a lot less alarming – than he did. *Go away*, she thought.

Freddy fell silent. Lily, knowing him so well, could hear him worrying. 'Where have you been?'

He sighed. 'In Malta, in Nanna Pina's flat. Hiding out, being pathetic. I got back a few weeks ago.'

'And the bankruptcy stuff?'

'All done. I'm now officially a bankrupt, *persona non grata* to the financial establishment. I will be for a year ... longer in many people's minds.' There was a short pause. 'But it feels okay. Better than the terrible worry that I might be about to become one.'

'Are you safe from the heavies, then?' She'd asked the question almost jokingly, Freddy's life taking on a slightly unbelievable hue now she had been separated from it for a while.

He nodded. 'Max bailed me out, Lily. Not only that, he's given me a job on one of his projects, and Julie's let me have one of her flats while the building work next door goes on . . .'

Freddy went on talking, but Lily wasn't really taking in any of what he said. Feeling jumpy, waiting for him to put her on the spot and not ready to respond, she turned away, longing for a cool glass of water, the quiet safety of her sister's kitchen.

'That's great . . . I'm pleased for you.' She got up, and as she did Freddy leaped to his feet as well.

'Lily.'

She stared at him. 'Listen, this has all been a bit of a shock.'

'But . . . you're pleased to see me, aren't you?'

Lily watched him brush his fingers through his dark hair in a gesture with which she was achingly familiar. 'To be honest, I don't know what I feel right now, Freddy.'

Clearly crestfallen, Freddy reached out to take her hand, but she moved it to rest on the strap of her canvas shoulder bag.

For a moment they stood, neither moving, staring at each other.

'I know you're angry with me, Lily. Why wouldn't you be? But I said I'd be back when I'd sorted things out and here I am. If you're not in love with me any more I'll do as your friends ask and leave you alone.'

When she didn't answer, he persisted, '*Do* you still love me?'

A walker went past in shorts and a floppy sun hat, a stick in his hand, a daypack on his shoulders.

After a long silence during which the tension flowed from each of them like a live current, she said, 'It's not that simple, Freddy.'

'Isn't it? Why not?' His voice exploded into the still of the afternoon. 'Listen, I've got somewhere for us to live, a job, no debt – except to Max. I absolutely swear I'm not gambling, and I never will again. I've started going to GA. Please, Lily . . . Please give me another chance. I know I've let you down as badly as anyone could, but I love you so much.'

Lily heard the words and knew she should be pleased. But she just felt a strong desire to get away from her husband and have some peace to think. 'I can't deal with this. '

Freddy, passionate as always, repeated his question. 'But you do still love me, don't you, Lily? Just tell me you love me and I'll leave you alone.'

'Of course I still love you. But that doesn't mean anything else.' She suddenly felt angry at his presumption, turning up, invading her space, thinking he had only to declare his undying love and things would go back to where they were before he had betrayed her.

But Freddy's face took on a look of utter relief. 'You still love me,' he said, almost to himself.

'It doesn't mean anything else,' Lily repeated firmly, having the urge to put out her hand, to physically hold him off.

'On the contrary, Lily. It means everything,' he said, giving her a huge grin.

Freddy walked with her over the next bridge, back towards home. He said nothing, and neither did she, but she could feel his thoughts burning between them, heard through the silence his desperate desire to pin her down, to get from her some definite sign of commitment.

When they came to Banbury Road, they stopped.

'I'll get the bus back to the station,' he said.

'Okay.'

'Can I at least call you?' he asked dully, the fight seemingly evaporated in the face of her silence.

She nodded, couldn't speak.

After an awkward pause he leaned in to kiss her cheek. She felt his lips, soft on her skin, inhaled the familiar hint of cardamom from his shaving soap, and her heart lurched. 'Bye, Freddy,' she said, turning quickly away.

As she walked down the side street she knew his eyes were following her, just as they had earlier in the day, and she felt a powerful and unwanted impulse to turn and retrace her steps back to Freddy's side.

CHAPTER 44

Freddy sat in the packed and stuffy carriage back to Paddington in a fug of bewilderment. This hadn't been what he'd had in mind when he'd set off for Oxford that morning. He was baffled by Lily's response. If she'd been angry with him he'd have understood, but she didn't seem angry, just sort of detached. Not like Lily. And while he was with her he'd felt as if he were somehow too much, too loud, excessive . . . She'd seemed to be fending him off. It had been horrible. And yet she'd claimed still to love him.

That man she'd met up with, could he be the problem? Thinking back over her replies, Freddy realized she hadn't actually answered his question about whether she'd moved on or not. A spear of jealousy twisted in his guts. He'd wanted so badly to ask her about the boat man, but he'd known it was the wrong thing to do. If Lily had thought him jealous . . .

Fuck, fuck, fuck, he thought miserably. *I made a complete bollocks of the whole thing.*

Freddy waited till eight that night before phoning her. He literally couldn't hold off a minute longer. On the way home from the station he'd had a burning need for the medicating sights and sounds of the casino, the click of the chips through his fingers, as if the roulette wheel were hooked through his inner core, reeling him in like a fish who'd lost the will to fight. It was so painful that he wanted to cry out right there, alone in the street. But the image of his wife's face, those hazel eyes so full of doubt, the feeling of her cheek against his lips was enough – today at least – to drive him back to the Charlotte Street flat.

Lily did not pick up for three or four rings and he'd begun to give up hope, when a suspicious voice said, 'Hello?'

'It's me.'

'Hi.'

'Listen, earlier . . . I'm so sorry. I shouldn't have barged in on you like that, without any warning. It was so insensitive. You looked as if I'd alarmed you.'

Silence.

'It's okay.'

'Is it?' He heard her give a small laugh and the sound released a long-held breath through his body. 'Say what you're thinking?' he asked.

Lily didn't reply at once. Then she said, 'I'm thinking I don't want to be rushed, Freddy. You did alarm me. I didn't feel you had any right to pounce on me like that, expect me to declare

384

my love when you haven't been in touch at all for more than three months.'

'We did agree . . .'

'There was no agreement, Freddy. I wanted us to get through it together.'

'But I told you I needed to do it on my own.'

'Yes, you told me. But I didn't agree. You just made love to me, then walked out leaving a miserable note. There was no agreement.'

'No, okay.' His memory of the time was sketchy now, but he knew his emotions had been racketing about his body with a mix of anxiety, shame, paranoia and too much black coffee, too many gins in a bar on the way home. He had no idea what he'd actually said to Lily. 'I was pretty crazy at the time.'

She didn't reply.

'Do you think you can forgive me, Lily?' he asked. 'Move past all that crap? It's a huge thing to ask, but we had such a great thing going between us. If I'm not gambling, then . . .'

'What frightens me is that I didn't even know. You say we had a good thing going, but surely if that were the case you wouldn't have had a problem, or I would have known about it.'

'I was too clever at hiding it.'

'Even so.'

'I'm not gambling now. I swear.'

'You'd have said that before, though, wouldn't you, if I'd challenged you?'

'Yes, but . . .' He didn't know how to convince her. Everything she'd said was true.

'The thing is, Freddy, I've had some first-hand experience with addiction in the shape of Kit this summer. He's been round a couple of times when I've been alone here – much to Helen's annoyance – and he's manipulated me, told me all sorts of tales he probably believes while he's saying them, about how he hates being an addict, how he's going to give up drugs for ever. He's *really, really* going to give them up this time . . . and I believed every word. Only to discover it's the same old lies he peddles to everyone. So when you say you've stopped gambling, forgive me for being a bit cynical.'

'It's hardly fair to compare me to Kit. He's a bloody heroin addict.'

Silence.

'A roulette table or a syringe full of smack, it's all the same. I understand that now,' she said.

Freddy felt indignant, but he held himself in check, knowing his relationship with his wife hung by a thread. 'So, what can I do to convince you, Lily?'

'I don't know.'

Freddy thought she sounded sad. 'Can I visit you in Oxford?' he asked, keen to get off the subject. 'Or you visit me here? Pop down on the train, see the flat. It's small but it's really nice, Lily.' He nearly added that he knew they could be happy there together, but again he bit his tongue.

'Okay, I might.'

'Will you ring me, then? I don't want you to think I'm hassling you. I did rush in today, I'll admit it. And I understand what you're saying. I mean, why should you suddenly trust me?'

Silence.

386

'Oh, Freddy,' he heard her say, and then he realized she was crying.

'Lily? God, I'm so sorry, Lily. I'm so, so sorry. I wish I could hug you.'

'I wish you could, too,' Lily said quietly, through her tears.

First thing on Monday morning Freddy went round to Max's office in Goodge Street, two minutes' walk from his flat. The offices, above a key-cutting shop, were small and poky. Max had been in the same premises for over twenty years now and apparently had no intention of upgrading to the sort of show-off space many would expect from someone with his level of success. He said he was superstitious. 'I worry that if I leave my business will go tits up,' he'd told Freddy in the past. 'Sort of grounds me, this place, reminds me of where I came from.'

Freddy had talked to Lily once more since Friday night. He had hovered about all day Saturday, praying she would call, wanting to keep to his promise not to hassle her. He found it agony, sitting on his hands, just waiting; it wasn't in his nature to be patient. By nine o'clock he had virtually given up, and that was when Lily rang. She sounded a little drunk, and he imagined her sitting with a glass of red wine at Helen and David's kitchen table, the door open to the garden and the summer night.

She hadn't said much, but there were no recriminations this time. She told him about the light on the roses, about her typing job, the sketches she'd done in the park. Said that her sister and brother-in-law were away. He explained about the food-truck venture, told her about the tiles in the bathroom, and that the newsagent on the corner – one he used to frequent in the past – had changed hands. They had basically chatted in much the same way they always had. And it meant more to Freddy than any passionate declaration of love.

'Where are we, then, on the launch?' Max was asking now, as they sat in his top-floor office.

'Okay. I know you were thinking September, but I've had this idea. The London Film Festival kicks off the first week in October and I thought maybe we could piggyback on that. The town's full of celebrities, festival-goers, and the students are back. They're constructing a huge pop-up cinema in Embankment Gardens and we could pitch to put one of our trucks there, maybe borrow the venue for an hour or two before the screenings start for a quick glass of bubbly and a speech. Something along those lines.'

Max's look was encouraging, so Freddy went on, 'It's late notice for this sort of thing, but I've got some contacts at the BFI and at American Express, who are sponsoring it. I'm sure I can fix something up.'

They talked on for another hour at least. Max was having trouble with the recipes, Julie insisting they must be healthy, Max insisting the point of Geordie food was that it was not. By the time Freddy emerged into the July drizzle, he felt slightly dazed. So determined was he to prove himself, he was promising stuff to his friend that he hoped to God he could deliver. His whole life rested on making the marketing and launch of the food trucks successful and he was already beginning to feel the old knockings of pressure churning in his stomach – and the urge to soothe that anxiety.

*

There were fewer than six people in that morning's GA meeting. Not enough for Freddy to feel comfortably anonymous, even seated in the back row on the chair nearest to the door. But no one bothered him, beyond a few polite hellos. He recognized Deborah from before, but the well-dressed John was absent. Today it was a young guy, not more than twenty-five, Freddy guessed, who was sharing his problems with the group. He seemed too young to be in such dire trouble, but when Freddy thought back, he realized he had been gambling long before that. But there had been no FOBTs in those days, the nightmare fixed-odds machines on which this youth, trembling before them, had lost thousands he didn't have in a frighteningly short space of time.

Freddy had copied his father back then, with regular punts on the horses. It wasn't till he got to London that he experienced the superior hit of the roulette tables. But even they had been recreational back then: he had never had a problem going home. Nor would it ever have occurred to him to steal – as the man in the meeting had – in order to gamble. Back then . . . He still resolutely refused to see himself as like those sad people at Gamblers Anonymous, blaming his recent fall from grace on the intense pressure he'd been under, one way and another, the hit an irresistible form of escape. It wasn't stealing, as such, just borrowing – he always meant to return the money. And he would.

But that part of his life was over. Lily had said she might come down later in the week. If he could just see her again, hold her . . .

CHAPTER 45

Seth Kramer had put Lily in touch with a psychotherapist friend of his, Janice Stevenson, who was interested in hiring her services for a paper she was writing. But she had put off making the phone call, her mind increasingly distracted the more contact she had with her husband.

They were phoning each other every night now, and had been for most of the week. Freddy had expected her to come to London – she'd said she might – but she kept putting it off.

Lily knew, despite what she'd protested to her family, that as soon as she and Freddy were alone together she would be lost. Theirs was a passionate relationship, had been right from the start, and it was such a long time since they'd made love. The look in his eyes, the kiss on the pavement in Banbury Road – swift though it had been – had reminded her body almost painfully of that.

But could she go back to Freddy and start over as if nothing had happened? Did she even want to live in London again, after her peaceful sojourn in Oxford? Had she really missed that crazy social round, the pressure to look good, the long evenings in the company of people with whom she had little in common, the noise and pollution of the big city?

When she thought of the alternative, however, of turning her back on Freddy March for ever, she had her answer. But the answer was equivocal. She was scared of him. Or, at least, scared of loving someone who could create such mayhem, then hide it so effectively. But the instant lure of his company, the way Lily's body tingled at the thought of his touch, the cosy ease of their chats, all of these were stacking the scales in Freddy's favour, drawing her slowly back in. She was almost shocked at how little she was prepared to resist Freddy's onslaught.

It could be for a few months, she told herself, as she walked back from Sainsbury's on Friday morning with food for her sister and brother-in-law's return at the weekend. *I could insist on a trial period. I've nothing to lose, after all. Helen will be pleased to be rid of me. I can still work for Seth, take the train up every week. And if it's clear that things aren't right between us, I won't be any worse off than I am now.*

Lily unlocked the front door, feeling more at peace with herself than she had for a long time at the decision she'd come to, even a little excited. In the kitchen she began unpacking her shopping bag, loading the perishables into the fridge. Then she went through to the sitting room to retrieve her laptop from the coffee table. The room was still in darkness

– she hadn't yet drawn the curtains back. She noticed an unpleasantly acrid smell as she stumbled against something on the floor in the half-light. Then her eye caught a movement on the sofa and a small cry escaped her lips.

The recumbent figure gave a low groan and she jumped back. Kit. Her nephew was curled on his side, hands pressed between his drawn-up knees, eyes closed, his greasy head resting on one of the orange cushions. For a moment Lily, trying to still her frantic heart, just watched him as he slept. In the weeks since she'd first encountered Kit again, he had become a cipher in her mind: a drug addict, a threat, a source of friction and pain. But sleep rendered him innocent again.

Gently, she touched his shoulder. Kit jerked awake, sitting up in one continuous movement, his eyes wide and staring, his face, previously so undefended, now instantly wary. He looked filthy and smelt worse. 'Aunty Lily,' he said, blinking furiously, leaping to his feet.

She should have been angry, given that the last time she'd seen him he'd caused her so much disruption, but she felt only compassion now: he looked so pathetic, so young. 'Shall I make you tea . . . some toast?'

Kit, hugging his arms around his body and shivering, although it was a warm day, shook his head, then changed his mind. 'Tea'd be good.'

He began to cough as he followed her through to the kitchen – a dry, rasping sound painful to hear, then hovered by the back door while the kettle boiled, as if securing his escape.

'Where are they?'

Lily frowned. 'Away, in Austria. But you knew that.'

Kit seemed befuddled.

Glancing at him, Lily realized he looked ill – now she could see him in daylight. Not just the usual druggie pallor, his pasty skin was flushed, his eyes red and he was taking short, shallow breaths. 'Sit down,' she said. But he didn't move. 'Please.' Approaching him slowly, in case he overreacted, she took his arm and led him to a chair. He didn't object, and as soon as he was sitting he folded his arms on the table and dropped his head onto them. Lily pressed her hand to his forehead. He was burning up.

Abandoning the tea, she tried to rouse him. 'Kit, are you okay?' No response. 'Kit? *Kit* . . . Listen, you're not well. You need to see a doctor.'

He raised his head for a second, eyes unfocused. 'No, no doctor. Leave me alone. I'm okay. Not seeing a doctor,' he muttered, before slumping back onto the table.

Lily didn't know what to do. Helen and David must have a GP, but she had no idea who it was. And if he wouldn't go to the surgery, how could she make him? She rang Sara, but her daughter's mobile went to voicemail. Seth was still in France. Dithering, she checked the side of the fridge for the GP's details and found a dog-eared list of names and numbers, but with no explanation as to who they might be.

She tried to rouse him again. 'Kit?' She rubbed his back firmly. 'Kit, come on, you need to wake up. You're ill. We have to find a doctor.' She tried to get him to his feet, putting her arms under his and pulling him up. The stench of ammonia coming off his clothes was nauseating at such close quarters.

'Fuck off,' he said, jerking free with surprising strength, swiping his arm haphazardly in her direction. 'Leave me the fuck alone.'

Lily eventually managed to struggle with her nephew back to the sofa and make him as comfortable as he would allow. She propped him up on pillows to help with his cough and covered him with a light throw because, although his skin was burning hot, he was shivering and mumbling that he was freezing. She held a glass of water to his lips, desperate for him to drink something, but each time he swore at her and pushed it away. Rambling now, muttering words she couldn't make out, which sounded angry and scared, she realized Kit was way beyond sitting in a doctor's waiting room, or lying there until she could find a doctor to visit the house. He needed to go to hospital right away.

She sat on the narrow bench in the back of the ambulance as it blue-lighted its way through the lunchtime Oxford traffic to the John Radcliffe, cold with terror that Kit would die. Adam, the paramedic, had taken one look at her nephew, then hustled him onto a stretcher and into the ambulance, an oxygen mask clamped to his pallid face. But he wouldn't answer her when she asked what was wrong with him. 'He'll be okay as soon as we get him to hospital,' was all he would say.

Her phone rang as they drove up the slope to the entrance. She thought it was Sara, for whom she'd left a message half an hour ago, and picked up immediately, the deafening noise of the siren making it hard to hear who was calling.

'Hi,' said Freddy's voice.

'Oh, hi,' Lily said, disappointed he was not Sara, then immediately relieved she had someone to talk to about the situation.

'I just had a meeting in Reading. I'm at the station,' Freddy was saying, 'and I thought I might keep on going and take you out for lunch. It's only half an hour to Oxford . . .' From the uncharacteristically tentative way Freddy spoke, she could tell he was nervous of her reply. 'If you're not—'

'I'm with Kit, in an ambulance, going to the John Radcliffe,' she interrupted. 'I found him asleep on the sofa when I came back from shopping and when I woke him he was burning up, disoriented. Then he just collapsed. I couldn't rouse him.'

'Has he overdosed? Taken some dodgy smack, maybe?'

Lily climbed down from the ambulance as they arrived in the bay and the paramedics began dragging Kit out, letting down the wheels of the gurney and pushing him through the swing doors into the emergency department. He did not seem to be moving as Lily hurried alongside. 'Does heroin give you a fever and a cough?'

'Don't know much about it. But no, I wouldn't think a fever and cough was typical.'

'I thought maybe he'd got flu or something, but this is way, way worse. He's really ill, Freddy.'

'Listen, I'm on my way. I'll be there in an hour, max,' she heard him say.

'No, no, that's ridiculous. I can manage.'

'On my way,' he repeated, and hung up.

By the time the triage nurse had finished checking Kit he was barely responsive, unable to answer any of her questions, his breathing now very fast and shallow, his face bluish against his usual pallor. She went to fetch the doctor. After examining Kit, the man, who introduced himself as Nick – in his early thirties, fair, his blue scrubs straining against his plumpness – looked at Lily with a puzzled frown. 'Is he . . . Where did you find him?'

'Long story. He's my nephew, his parents are away. But he's a drug addict, he doesn't live with us.'

The doctor nodded – he'd seen it all. 'Do you know what he's taken?'

'No. It's usually heroin, I think.'

Nick nodded again. 'Is he allergic to anything? Antibiotics, for instance?'

Feeling completely useless, Lily answered, 'He said he couldn't take methadone. He's got asthma. But . . .' She suddenly wondered if Kit had made that up.

'So, penicillin?'

'I don't know.'

Looking weary, the doctor began giving instructions to the nurse for an X-ray, tox screen and a string of other tests Lily was only familiar with from watching the odd medical drama on television.

'We'll have to admit him,' Nick told her. 'I suspect your nephew has pneumonia.'

'Do you think he'll be all right?' Freddy asked later.

He had arrived, as promised, within the hour and Lily found herself ridiculously pleased to see him. They had spent the next hour or so standing and sitting about while Kit was being processed, cleaned up as much as was possible, his stinky clothes replaced by a pressed hospital gown, and carted off to the intensive care unit. Now they sat side by side with tea and a sandwich at one of the metal tables outside the M&S café on level two, late in the afternoon. The area was in shadow and Lily felt shivery in her thin cotton top. 'Depends how he responds to the antibiotics, apparently. Pneumonia can be a killer. The nurse said his immune system will be shot, with his rough lifestyle. She said it's too easy for addicts to pick up infections.'

Lily felt Freddy's arm go round her and she closed her eyes. 'Please don't let him die, Freddy.'

'Kit's tough, Lily. He must be to have survived this long.'

'Helen and David will be devastated.'

He squeezed her close. 'Let's not think like that. Just remember how incredibly lucky it was he came to you when he did. If he'd been on the streets he probably would be dead by now.'

Lily nodded. She had phoned her sister several times and only managed to get hold of her fifteen minutes ago. They had been walking all day in the hills above the lake with no signal on their mobiles. Helen had been silent as Lily explained what had happened. It was the phone call, Lily knew, both she and David had dreaded every single day of their life. But she hadn't envisaged being the one who would have to make it.

'Maybe this'll be the turning point,' Freddy was saying. 'The smack will be out of his system by the time he's discharged.'

'Out of his system, but not necessarily out of his head.'

'No,' Freddy agreed. 'If he's still looking for a way off the planet, it won't make the slightest difference.' He reached across and took Lily's hand. 'You did exactly the right thing, Lily. You saved his life.'

She gave him a smile. 'I'm not sure he'll thank me.'

CHAPTER 46

'Are you going to stay?' Freddy asked his wife, watching her pale, exhausted face as they stood outside the ICU. It was after midnight and they had spent the hours pacing the hospital corridors, drinking too much caffeine, watching the sleeping figure of Lily's nephew, all strung up with drips and monitors in the high white bed. He had opened his eyes a couple of times as Lily sat by him, but they were glazed and blank. He hadn't spoken or reacted at all to his aunt's presence.

'Dr Benjafield says he's stable at the moment,' Lily replied. 'He says to go home, get a few hours' sleep. They'll ring if there's any change.'

'So will you?'

Lily shrugged. 'I'm not sure. What if something happens when I'm not here?'

'They've said they'll call you.'

She nodded. 'I wish Helen and David would hurry up. I feel so responsible.'

'When does their flight get in?'

'Eight fifteen, Heathrow. They're flying from Vienna – it was quicker than Salzburg, Helen said.'

They stood staring through the glass at Kit's sleeping figure. Freddy thought he looked more peaceful now, the previous facial twitching and restless limbs quieted by sedation. He barely knew the boy, Kit's addiction having been well under way by the time Freddy came on the scene. But he had met him a couple of times in one of Kit's short rehab windows and liked his quick mind, his wicked take on life.

'What shall I do?' Lily looked up at him, her light eyes bewildered. He pulled her into his arms and she rested with a sigh against his chest. Her closeness, the smell of her hair, the familiar contours of her body were heaven to Freddy, even in such difficult circumstances.

'He'll probably sleep now, won't he? Maybe you should go home for a bit.'

Lily stood back, pushing her fringe off her forehead. She gave a slow nod. They stared at each other, both knowing the question neither was able to ask.

'I don't want to leave you,' Freddy eventually said.

'I . . .' She looked away.

'If I come back with you, I'll sleep on the sofa, obviously,' he added, and was pleased that Lily's second nod meant that she was willing for him to stay, and sad that she still seemed almost nervous of him, as if he were a threat that had to be managed.

'I'll be long gone by the time Helen and David arrive,' he assured her.

It was nearly four in the morning, but Freddy could not sleep. He lay on the sofa, covered with a duvet Lily had brought from upstairs, aware that he was not welcome in his sister-in-law's house, and not even sure he was welcome in his wife's life. Lily had gone straight to bed when they got back and had barely spoken a word on the journey home. Now the dawn light was creeping over the roofs of the houses opposite and he finally gave up any attempt at sleep, tiptoeing through to the kitchen to put on the kettle. It was going to be a glorious day, the garden, pierced by the diffuse summer light, shadowy and still, beautiful.

As he gazed out, he heard Lily's footstep on the stairs.

'You couldn't sleep either,' she said, as she flopped onto a kitchen chair.

She looked rumpled and exhausted in her T-shirt and pink-checked cotton pyjama trousers – he remembered them well – her dark hair tangled around her face. He handed her the cup of tea he had made for himself. 'Maybe we should go back to the hospital now, see how he's getting on?' he asked.

Shivering, she clutched the mug in both hands. 'Okay.'

She paused, glanced up at him. 'When I sat beside Kit yesterday, I was so frightened he might die. But I think I was almost more worried about how Helen would react – if she'd somehow hold me responsible – than about Kit himself.' She shook her head, 'I don't mean that. Obviously I love him . . .' She gave up trying to explain.

'The drugs make him harder to love,' Freddy said.

She nodded sadly and got up, stretched, then shivered again, wrapping her arms round her body and he went to her, gathering her close and rubbing her back vigorously through the thin T-shirt.

'Come and lie down with me for a minute,' he suggested. 'You're freezing. I'll warm you up.'

She barely hesitated before turning and walking ahead of him into the sitting room, where they lay down on the worn old navy sofa like spoons, her back against his stomach, his arm across her, the duvet pulled tight around their shoulders. Lily, hands clasped under her chin, pressed her icy feet against his legs and laughed softly as he winced. He readjusted the pillow beneath their heads and gradually felt her body relax against his.

'Don't let me go to sleep,' she said.

'I won't.'

When they woke it was nearly eight-forty-five and they tumbled off the sofa in a panic, Lily rushing through to the kitchen where she'd left her mobile. There was no message from the hospital, or from her sister, apparently, but she pounded up the stairs to get dressed. Freddy washed his face and rinsed his mouth at the kitchen sink, drying himself on a tea towel as nothing else was available, then went to check his appearance in the hall mirror, eyeing his stubble and the dark bags under his eyes regretfully. *I look ninety*, he thought, stretching his mouth open, baring his teeth and widening his eyes to wake up his face.

Lily was jumpy as they drove to the hospital. 'Don't come up,' she said, as she parked and began fumbling for change for the machine. 'Helen will be here soon.'

'Not for an hour or so,' Freddy pointed out. 'They won't be out of the airport yet.'

'Still, no need for you to hang around.'

He felt dismissed and tried not to mind.

She gave him a brisk smile. 'Listen, I'm so grateful to you for being here, Freddy. I don't know what I'd have done without you yesterday.'

Her thanks seemed a sop: she *was* dismissing him.

'I'd like to just come in and check he's okay, if you don't mind.'

She bit her lip. 'All right.'

'Don't worry, I'll make sure I'm not here when they arrive. I'm not dumb.' He knew he sounded peeved and regretted it as soon as the words were out of his mouth.

But Lily didn't seem to notice. 'Fine.'

Kit was still asleep. He stirred only briefly at the touch of Lily's hand and her murmured greetings, then turned his head away on the pillow, as if the intrusion were too much.

Freddy waited while she went to find a nurse and check her nephew's progress.

'He's stable. The nurse says he had a good night,' she reported back, her face alight with a relieved grin. 'She said they might move him out of the ICU later.'

Freddy watched Lily's eyes fill with tears. 'Thank God . . . Oh, thank bloody God, Freddy,' she said, and reached out for him, squeezing her arms round his waist and dropping a quick kiss on his stubbly cheek.

Which was exactly how Helen and David found them.

Freddy stood by the bus stop outside the hospital, angry and smarting from the way his sister-in-law had treated him. He told himself he understood. The journey must have been a version of hell, wondering what they might find when they got home. And obviously he wasn't their favourite person right now. But still. Helen had greeted Lily, asked anxiously about Kit, pushed past them both to get to her son's bedside. But not once, after registering it was Freddy, did she so much as acknowledge his presence. David had patted his arm in passing, raised his eyebrows in a form of welcome, but Helen had addressed all her remarks to Lily, as if he simply didn't exist.

So Freddy had left them to it. *I'm still her husband*, he thought resentfully, as he boarded the bus to the station. *If Lily is happy to have me around, then who are they to disapprove?*

CHAPTER 47

Sitting in her bedroom in an attempt to avoid another tense family supper, Lily rang Freddy. It was day three of Kit's stay in hospital and they had talked a couple of times since Freddy's ignominious departure from the ICU. She knew he was upset by Helen's treatment of him, but her sister was treating Lily no better.

Freddy answered immediately, but his tone was hardly enthusiastic. 'How's it going?'

'Kit's better. They say he's not in danger any more, except from himself, perhaps.'

'And how are you?'

'Not great. Things between me and Helen are grim.'

However much Lily tried to sympathize with, and support, her sister, she seemed to say the wrong thing every bloody time. Her very genuine concern about Kit just appeared to irritate Helen.

'Is she angry about me?'

'More baffled that I could still love you.'

There was a silence at the other end of the phone, and Lily realized what she had just said. There had been no equivocation that time.

Before he could speak, she rushed on, 'It's my relationship with Kit that really upsets her. Not that I have a relationship with him. But she seems to think I've stepped in and interfered, made things worse somehow. I'm being made to feel this is all my fault, Freddy, although I know perfectly well it's not.'

But Freddy didn't want to talk about Kit. He said, 'I'm so glad you still love me, Lily.'

His words, spoken in such a gentle, respectful tone, brought tears to her eyes.

'Will you come to London?' she heard him ask.

'When?'

'Now.'

Lily laughed, but felt an uncontrollable surge of joy. 'No, not now, stupid. It's nine o'clock at night.'

She heard him sigh. 'Tomorrow then?'

'Okay. I'll come tomorrow.'

David was alone in the kitchen the following morning, just after six, when Lily padded downstairs to make a cup of tea. She had spent the night thinking about her conversation with Freddy and the implications for all of them. But dithering was no longer an option.

Her brother-in-law, mug on the table in front of him, looked up as she came in and she saw he had been deep in thought and knew pretty much what he must have been thinking about.

'Early for you,' he commented.

'Yeah, not sleeping so well these days. I'm sure neither of you are, either.'

He smiled. 'Still, the worst seems to be over.'

Lily sat down opposite him, not bothering to make any tea, and lowered her voice. 'I'm going to London to see Freddy today.'

David raised his shaggy eyebrows a little.

'I'm thinking of giving it another go with him.'

There was silence for a moment. 'Okay. I'm sure Helen's told you what she thinks of that idea.'

'In no uncertain terms,' Lily agreed.

'You know she only wants what's best for you.'

Despite Helen's constant sniping, Lily thought he was probably right. 'What do you think, David?'

His face crumpled into a considering frown. 'I like Freddy. I think he's got a good heart . . .'

Lily waited for him to go on, but David just shrugged, pulling his mouth down at the corners.

'You know the score, Lily. You're not a fool.'

Not exactly a ringing endorsement, but what did she expect? It would be a lot worse when she told the twins. Even though they, too, had liked Freddy, really liked him.

'Will you keep the job with the doctor?' David was asking.

'Yes. I can do most of it online, then come up once a week, once a fortnight . . . see how it goes.'

He nodded slowly. 'Two pieces of advice. One, always earn your own money. Two, keep that money separate. Goes for any relationship.'

Where I went wrong last time, she thought wryly, *on both counts.*

'So you're leaving today? Helen didn't say.'

'No, I'll be home tonight.' Although she was pretty sure she wouldn't be. 'I'll text if there's any change of plan,' she added, bringing an amused look to David's face. 'You'll take care of Helen and Kit, I know. I'm not doing such a great job of it anyway. Time to get out of your hair.'

'You're not running into Freddy's arms because of Helen, are you?' David was clearly concerned. 'She's only taking it out on you because she can. You know what she's like.'

She shook her head. 'I need to resolve the thing with Freddy one way or the other. If it's a mistake, I'll go to Plan B.' Although, as they were both well aware, there was no Plan B.

'That's the spirit,' he said, reaching across to give her hand a brotherly squeeze.

Freddy met her at Paddington and they walked down past Lancaster Gate into Kensington Gardens. It was cloudy and close, the threat of rain lurking on the horizon. They didn't hold hands, as they used to, but walked together as friends might, across the park with no particular destination in mind. And talked. That was the thing with Freddy: they were never short of things to tell each other, things to discuss.

'Seems decades since we lived here,' she said, when they sat down on a bench under the trees along the wide avenue that led to the Albert Memorial.

'It's only a summer.'

'I know, but a lot has happened.'

Freddy looked sideways at her. 'Tell me about Oxford. Who did you meet?'

'Who did I meet? No one. I wasn't exactly in the mood for socializing, Freddy.'

Freddy grinned. 'Okay, I'll 'fess up. Obviously I saw you, when I followed you, get onto the boat with the dark-haired man.'

Lily laughed. 'Right.' She felt like teasing him and didn't say any more. But the image of that night in his house, the kiss, however brief, intruded on her thoughts and she looked away.

'Come on, Lily, who was he?'

'Dr Kramer. I work for him. I told you about him. You weren't listening.'

'Ah,' Freddy said, although he didn't look entirely relieved. 'You didn't tell me he lived on a boat. I thought he was a shrink.'

'He is. He writes on the boat, shrinks at his house in Jericho.'

'You were in the pub with him for hours.'

'So?'

Freddy grabbed her and pulled her to him, his mouth finding hers in an anxious, frenzied ... *jealous* kiss that set Lily's head whirling and made her gasp for breath. Laughing, she sat back. 'Whoa.'

Freddy was looking at her questioningly, as if he wanted marks out of ten.

Ignoring his silent appeal, she said, 'Seth's brilliant. He's been so patient with my rubbish typing although, I must say, I'm pretty damn good now.'

'God, Lily. You shouldn't be typing for a living.'

She stared at him. 'You really don't get it, do you? I didn't have a Max Blackstone offering me a lucrative job and a flat.' She heard the echoes of her sister and stopped before she said something she regretted. The spurt of anger faded as she looked into her husband's troubled eyes.

Freddy dropped his head into his hands. 'How are we going to get past what I did to you, Lil? No apology will ever be enough. You must say it all, let me have both barrels, so that I know just how hard it's been for you since I left.'

But she couldn't be angry to order.

'Funny,' Lily said, 'Helen accused us of being "middle-class poor". She was basically saying that people like us always have someone to bail us out. It didn't feel like that when you walked out, Freddy. But of course I knew I could rely on Helen and David, or Prem and Anthony – the twins, finally – to make sure I didn't land in the gutter. And Helen really helped me, told me exactly what I should do, even found me a job. It's been depressing, but it's hardly like being genuinely homeless, being on benefits, with no one to turn to who had more money or nous than me.'

'I'm sorry, Lily. I told myself you were better off without me, but I never considered the detail . . . what that might mean.'

She got up, standing in front of him and offering him her hands. 'Okay. I could harangue you till the cows come home for how you behaved. But you seem to be well aware of your transgression. So let's agree that you were a total shit and try to move on. Otherwise there's no point in us being together, if all I do is give you a hard time.'

He looked incredulous. 'You're giving me a massive get-out-of-jail-free card? I hardly deserve that.'

'I'm not saying I'll forget. I'm not saying I won't be angry sometimes. I'm just saying I'll try.' She eyed him intently. 'But if you gamble, Freddy March, all bets are off. I mean it.'

He nodded, couldn't help smiling at her choice of words. 'I'm not gambling, Lily. Believe me, I'm really not.'

Something had loosened between them and they set off towards Bayswater Road holding hands. Then after a while, Freddy put his arm round her shoulders. Lily felt she was moving in a sort of dream. This wasn't real life. Real life was her nephew in hospital, her distressed sister, her typing job, her worry about money and where to live. But here she was, in Freddy-world again, where none of that was relevant. A part of her felt uneasy. A bigger part began to relax into it, to let out a huge sigh of relief.

It was mid-afternoon before Freddy opened the door to the Charlotte Street flat. They had taken the 94 bus into the West End from the park and had lunch in a small café on Beak Street, where they'd sat on stools in the window and eaten Iberico ham and rocket sandwiches on crusty sourdough bread and little Portuguese custard tarts – it had always been one of their favourite haunts.

'What do you think?' Freddy said anxiously, as they stood in the middle of the sitting room of the small flat, having done the brief tour of the two bedrooms and tiny bathroom.

It was what it was, Lily thought. Smart, bland and uncomfortably new, designed for the top-end rental market. Not homely, but then Freddy had barely been in three weeks. 'It's great.'

'You don't sound sure.' He seemed desperate she should like it.

'Just a bit new, I think. But Julie has done a good job.'

Freddy's features relaxed. 'Yeah, I know, a bit like a hotel suite at the moment.' He laughed. 'I'm scared of eating anything in case I spill ketchup on the furniture.'

They stood looking at each other and Lily felt her heart flutter. He raised his eyebrows. She smiled, feeling almost shy. Within seconds they were in each other's arms. Laying his cheek against hers, dropping soft kisses on her skin, Freddy lifted her off her feet and carried her through to the bedroom. As he laid her gently on the plump duvet, which smelt box-fresh, he whispered, 'Are you okay with this?'

Lily didn't answer, just brought her mouth up to his and kissed him until neither could breathe. It was a sort of heaven to be in his arms again. All her concerns about their relationship melted away as they began to make love and she felt his warm, bare skin meet hers, breathed in his clean scent, looked into his deep brown eyes, now focused on her with an intense longing she had thought she'd never see again. Lily wanted to get so close that she was part of him and him of her, her body alive to his touch, his lovemaking so sensuous and other-worldly, it was as if she were in a trance, floating above herself.

After they both came – she for the second time – rather

than pulling apart and flopping back on the pillow as they would normally, she refused to let him go, but lay against his hot skin, almost frightened to let even the cool evening air come between them.

'Will you stay tonight?' Freddy asked, as she stood naked in the bathroom, peering at the shower mechanism. He reached across her and turned the chromium knob until water spurted from the huge showerhead, dousing her hair and making her gasp.

'Right for hot, left for cold,' he told her.

'Maybe I should.'

Freddy ran his hand down the length of her bare back as she stepped into the shower stall.

'I'm sure Helen and David will be thrilled to have a night to themselves.'

He was gazing at her, holding the glass door half open. 'Live with me, Lily. Don't go back.'

Through the water and the steam, she met Freddy's eyes. She was aware of the powerful pull he'd always exerted on her. It was her choice, but still she felt as if she were being gently herded down a narrow path. She pushed away her reluctance. Of course it would be strange at first, in this borrowed rental, with a man she must get to know all over again, embracing his passions, his sociability, his high-octane work. She had got used to another sort of life, a quieter, more measured rhythm that she had come to enjoy, were it not for the uncomfortable dependency on her sister and brother-in-law's goodwill. But her head was no match for her heart.

CHAPTER 48

It was two weeks since Lily moved back in. Freddy had tried to make the days into a second honeymoon. He'd taken his wife for romantic dinners; stood on the Norman Foster bridge, gazing at London from the river before an hour at Tate Modern; organized tea in a Thermos and a blueberry muffin in the park; cooked relaxed suppers in the flat, with the hum of the Soho street wafting up through the open windows; drunk exorbitantly expensive cocktails at the Charlotte Street Hotel. All things they had done before, when it had been good between them. Freddy wanted to remind her.

They both worked during the day, Lily setting up her laptop on the small oak-veneer dining table in the sitting room, the kitchen behind her, separated by a shiny, off-white marble work surface. He didn't stay while she was typing and listening to the tapes, but took himself off to a café or to Max's office, where he had the use of Julie's desk – she was rarely there.

It was such a thrill to be with Lily again. Just sitting on the sofa in the evenings, talking, or holding hands in the street made his heart want to burst with joy. It was how it should be. But Freddy was still nervous. Naively, he supposed, he'd thought things would go back to the way they used to be between them. But the truth was that he sensed a distance, a wariness in his wife. Not all the time – her lovemaking had been intense and abandoned, both of them having a constant need to stroke, to kiss every inch of the other's body, to make the sex last and last as if they feared by stopping something would break. And afterwards the tenderness in her eyes made it clear how much she loved him.

Nonetheless, he worried. *Will she stay?* he kept asking himself in the moments when she wasn't in front of him, when his fragile confidence in her love began to wane. He felt he needed her now more than ever before, his hold on his new life so tenuous. Lily had always grounded him – until that time when he had been beyond grounding by anyone, of course.

She has to learn to trust me. I have to learn to trust her, he told himself. Max had said as much: 'It'll take time. Don't push her, Freddy. Isn't it enough that she came back?' He'd grinned. 'Julie would have seen me at the bottom of the sea first.'

He knew this, but he was impatient. Other things were worrying him too. His briefly perfect return had quickly soured as the obligations of his job piled up and the pressure to make Max's business work began to feel like an uphill task. He didn't want to tell Max, because his friend was so passionate about the trucks and it wouldn't do to seem defeatist,

415

but Freddy had received bored feedback – the worst, even negative would have been preferable – from the people he needed to enthuse for the marketing and publicity. More food trucks? had been the general response. He *had* to make this a success: his whole future – Lily, reputation, money, home – depended on it.

Then there was his father. The hospice to which Vinnie had apparently been admitted on his return from Malta had contacted him the day before. They had left a message saying that if he wanted to see Vinnie alive, he should come at once. Which was not going to happen, of course. But the image of his father lying in a bed, gasping for breath as his corroded lungs finally packed up, was not a pleasant one.

Lily could sense his tension, but he couldn't bring himself to tell her. She still thought his father was a nice middle-class actuary from Nottingham, suffering from Alzheimer's. If he told her Vinnie was dying, she would want to know why he didn't visit. She would definitely want to come too. Never in his life had he spoken about what his father had done to him, and he couldn't imagine doing so now, not even to his wife.

And, to cap it all, Shirley had pitched up. Coward that he was, Freddy still hadn't told her that he wasn't coming back to Malta. She phoned him regularly, left messages asking for updates about his 'poor father' – messages he had relentlessly ignored, assuming she would quickly catch on. But only this morning, when he and Lily were out getting coffee before she went up to Oxford to see the shrink she worked for, Shirley had texted: *I'm here, hon! Dying to see you. Met your friend Riz in Malta, he told me all about your awesome project. Ring me xxx*

Freddy, taken by surprise, knew he had looked shocked because Lily had immediately asked what was wrong.

'Oh, nothing,' he'd replied, 'just some bad news about the launch venue. The bastards won't make up their bloody minds.'

She had inevitably asked, 'Which bastards?' and he had been forced to make up more lies to add to the already heavy burden in his life.

That fucking moron, blabbing his mouth off. What was he doing in Malta, anyway? Freddy wondered. Although Riz was one of those people who turned up like a bad penny. He called himself an 'entrepreneur and film-maker', but no one, to date, had ever seen evidence of either. Yet somehow he knew everyone and went everywhere. Including, apparently, Malta. What the fuck should he do? Suppose he bumped into Shirley when he was out with Lily? Central London was a very small place.

After Lily had gone to catch the Oxford train, Freddy sat – still in the Rathbone Street café – making phone calls and responding to nearly forty overnight emails and texts. He was on his third Americano, and was already beginning to feel unpleasantly hyped. Things were looking up on the food-truck front – despite his impulsive lie to Lily earlier. The film festival seemed willing to loan the space in the pop-up tent for a couple of hours on a Monday morning – not the most sexy slot, but beggars and all that – and also to consider a food-truck presence in Embankment Gardens for the late-night shows, although where and when had still to be negotiated.

Good news indeed. But this morning there was a more pressing problem. Freddy knew he had to deal with it today, while his wife was in Oxford, or not at all.

Shirley rose from her banquette seat in the hallowed centre circle at the Wolseley, her face wreathed in smiles. She looked tanned and smart, attractive in a royal blue sleeveless dress he hadn't seen before, with heavy gold jewellery, a cream and blue silk scarf loose around her neck. Every inch the rich widow.

'My, aren't you the elusive one!' she exclaimed, once they had kissed each other's cheek and Freddy had taken the seat opposite her.

He'd been prepared for this. 'I know, I know. It's been manic since I came home, what with Dad and the new project. It got to the stage where I was embarrassed to contact you after so many missed calls.'

Shirley didn't look like she believed him, her pencilled eyebrow raked at a slightly cynical angle, but he ignored this and ploughed on. 'So you met Riz? What was he doing in Malta?'

'Some business thing. I never quite got to the bottom of it. He talks so fast and seemed to think I knew more about the movie scene than I do.'

'Riz all over.' Freddy laughed.

Shirley's face took on a serious expression. 'Tell me about your father, Freddy. Has it been a nightmare for you?'

'He's in a hospice now. They say he hasn't long. It's a horrible way to go, not being able to breathe.'

Shirley reached over to hold his hand. 'Poor you.'

Freddy, glancing anxiously around, hoped there was no one who might have seen the gesture: it was way too intimate. Unfortunately there was always someone he knew in the restaurant.

They talked about Malta, her flight, her London hotel, the weather, until the two portions of kedgeree and spinach had been delivered, the Chablis poured.

Now Shirley was gazing at him intently. 'Freddy ... I thought ... We had such a great time together in Malta, no?'

Freddy nodded, squirming at the recollection of those strange nights, recalling unwillingly the softness of her silk negligee sliding over his erection.

'I don't know ...' Her eyes were misting alarmingly. 'I thought it was more than just a casual thing ... for both of us.' She reached for his hand again, making no attempt to start her meal, the food lying untouched in the large white bowl. 'It wasn't me you were running away from, was it?' she went on, a catch in her voice.

Before Freddy could reply, a heavy hand descended on his shoulder and a loud male voice exclaimed, 'By Jove, it's the Fredster! Where the hell have you been, March?'

Turning and snatching his hand free from Shirley's grasp, he found the familiar figure of Cosmo Gough-Browne beside him, attired in a tailored suit of cream linen, blue shirt and MCC tie, carrying a Panama. He was clearly on the way to a cricket match.

'Am I finally to have the honour of meeting She-who-must-be-obeyed?' Cosmo held out his hand, appraising Shirley as he introduced himself. 'He's kept you very quiet, my dear.

419

But you're a brave woman, taking this fellow on,' he joshed, punching Freddy in the back. 'You know you can't trust him an inch? He's taken more money off me than the bloody tax man.'

Cosmo wheeled about at the sound of his name from across the restaurant. 'See you at the club?' he said to Freddy, giving Shirley a gallant salute with his hat before sailing off to greet his lunch companion.

When Freddy turned back, Shirley was looking down at her food, hands clenched in her lap. When she raised her eyes, he could see the cold suspicion as clear as day. *Fuck him*, he thought, knowing that Cosmo felt he could say these things with impunity since Freddy's bankruptcy. People like that – who had never had to worry about money – loved to frown upon financial irregularities.

'What did he mean?' she asked.

'Cosmo?' Freddy tried to laugh, 'Oh, we've had the occasional casino night together, that's all. And he's a rubbish gambler, loses a lot. Absolutely nothing to do with me. But don't worry, he can take it. He's incredibly rich.'

Silence.

'Like me, you mean?' Her voice was so quiet he could barely hear her.

'No – God, Shirley . . . no!' Freddy was horrified.

She raised a well-shaped eyebrow. 'Seems like I've been a bit of a fool.'

'I . . .' He stopped. There was no point in explaining.

'And your father? Is he really dying?'

Freddy took a steadying breath. 'I never lied to you, Shirley.

I told you my life was a mess and I was broke. I told you I was married.'

'But you also let me make love to you, Freddy. Was that just expedience?'

'No, of course not,' he replied, but he had hesitated for just a fraction too long.

Her mouth set in a tense line, she began to gather up her brown leather Chanel bag from the banquette with a quiet dignity, wrapped her scarf more tightly round her neck and pushed the corner of the table as she eased herself upright. Freddy stood too, moved aside to let her pass.

'Shirley . . .'

'You can get this, I assume?' she said, indicating the uneaten lunch with a sardonic smile that never reached her eyes.

Freddy sat there, face lowered, flushed with shame, not daring to glance either side and see the inquisitive stares from the neighbouring tables. He should have felt relief. Shirley was gone. But instead he just felt utter contempt for himself, and the familiar ache of worthlessness, so carefully instilled over the years of childhood by his father, until it was his default position.

On his way home, he walked past one of his old dens, the shiny black metal portico with its flourish of a silver logo acting like a beacon in the crowded London street. Freddy didn't hesitate, just strode towards a moment that he knew would block the recent humiliation with Shirley entirely from his mind.

CHAPTER 49

'You know what she's going to tell us.' Sara, for once without Ted clamped to her side, was raising an amused eyebrow at her brother.

Dillon frowned. It was teatime and they were waiting for their mother at a table in the Delaunay deli, the Viennese-style café beside the bigger restaurant in the Aldwych. 'That she's moving out of Helen and David's?' His mother had sounded quite tense when she'd called to make the arrangement to meet up, but he'd assumed that was because of the whole Kit thing. She'd told him things were very tricky with his aunt at the moment.

'No, dummy.' Sara rolled her eyes. 'That she's having an affair with the doctor-on-the-boat, of course.'

'Don't be ridiculous, Sas.'

'Well, what else could be so important that we both had to see her as soon as possible? Something she couldn't tell us over the phone.'

Dillon thought about this for a moment, nodded slowly. 'You think? So soon?'

'He's widowed, Mum says, and she really likes him. They spend a lot of time together. Makes sense, no?'

His sister was nodding her satisfaction. But Dillon wasn't sure he was ready to make friends with another potential stepfather. He hadn't got over the last one. Before he could reply, Sara looked past him and waved. He turned to see his mum making her way through the tables and thought she looked lovely in her red summer shift dress and sandals, a tasselled leather bag over her shoulder.

They ordered – Sachertorte, two chocolate éclairs, tea – while Lily questioned them about what had been going on in their lives. She seemed bright – maybe a tad over-bright? – and talkative, but he felt the unexplained reason for the summons sitting heavily in the air between them. He wished she would just get on and tell them. Predictably, it was Sara who finally lost patience. 'Okay, Mum, so why did you want to see us so urgently?'

His mother's mouth twisted and he could feel her tension. Dillon watched as she took a deep breath and felt his own heart speed up.

'Right. Well, you're not going to like what I'm about to say.' She fiddled with the handle of her teacup. Then she looked him straight in the eye. 'Freddy and I are getting back together. In fact, we *have* got back together.'

The stunned silence was broken by Sara, who said, almost under her breath, 'What?' As if she didn't understand what her mother had just said.

423

'You can't be serious.' Dillon was more bewildered than angry as he and his sister stared open-mouthed at her.

'I know you'll be furious. And I know why. I know you'll think I'm mad or weak or both. And perhaps you're right. But I'm going to give it a few months and see what happens.' Her gaze flicked between them, her hazel eyes willing them to understand. 'Freddy isn't gambling any more. He's getting help. And Max has given him a job, a flat, paid off some of his debts.' She dropped her head for a moment, then raised it again, her expression determined, her words no longer containing the previous hint of apology, as she said, 'I still love him.'

Sara was shaking her head, her face puckered in disbelief. 'Oh, Mum, *really*?'

'I've thought about this long and hard,' Lily went on. 'I'm keeping my job, keeping my money separate. If it doesn't work out ...'

Neither he nor Sara responded. Dillon didn't know whether to cry or laugh. Did his mother really expect them to be happy? Expect them to welcome that man back into the family, after all he'd done to them?

'Say something,' his mother begged.

'Your life, Mum,' Sara said, shrugging.

Lily was staring at him. 'Dillon?'

He knew he had to respond, but his bafflement and rage were choking him. Eventually, through clenched teeth, he echoed his sister. 'Yeah, your life.'

His mother did not look relieved. He hadn't intended she should.

'It's your business,' he went on, 'if you choose to be with someone who's treated you so badly.' He bit his lip. 'But honestly, Mum, don't think for a single second that I will have anything to do with Freddy March. Not now, not next week, next year. Not *ever*.'

Sara raised an eyebrow, whether in agreement or censure at his rant he didn't know, didn't care.

His mother was silent, just nodded wearily. 'I didn't expect you to be pleased, either of you,' she said softly.

'It isn't about whether we're pleased or not,' Sara said, her voice gentle, as if she were talking to a child. 'As I said, it's your life, Mum; you can do what you like. But we are worried about you. Quite reasonably, don't you think?'

Lily nodded again, blinking back tears. 'Of course. I understand.'

But Dillon, in awe of his sister's ability to keep her cool, had the sense his mum was waiting for them both to thaw a little and begin to see it from her side. Maybe imagine there might be a time in the future when they could all be one big happy family again with Freddy bloody March. That was not going to happen.

CHAPTER 50

'So how's London?' Seth asked as they sat in canvas chairs with mugs of green tea on the small deck of his boat. The sun had come out and it was one of those warm, perfectly still August afternoons, when the world seems to be happening somewhere else.

'Noisy.' She smiled. 'You forget when you don't live there for a while.'

'I never have. I came here when I was a student and I've never left. Bit sad.'

'I used to like it.'

'But not any more?'

She shrugged. 'Freddy has to live there for his work.'

Seth didn't answer, just gazed at some ducks having a scuffle on the water, over by the far bank.

'It's good to be here,' she said, feeling almost sleepy in the peaceful afternoon sun. They didn't speak for a while.

'And Freddy?' Seth seemed about to say more, but didn't.

'He's not gambling, if that's what you mean.' Lily heard the defensive tone in her voice. But it had been hard telling everyone that she was back with Freddy. At the miserable tea with her children the previous day, Dillon had got up, not even finishing his chocolate cake, given her a cold kiss and walked out. He'd hardly spoken a word, except to say he wanted nothing to do with Freddy. Sara, who'd stayed behind after Dillon had gone, had been more measured, but no keener to make Freddy part of her life again. It pained Lily to think of the damage to her relationships – with her son in particular – that her love for Freddy had wrought.

Prem had obviously seen it coming, and had done a lot of resigned sighing and shaking of her head as she delivered muttered warnings – like David – about separate bank accounts and keeping her job. Lily could deal with that. But Dillon . . .

'He'll settle down,' Freddy had said. But Lily wasn't so sure, and neither, she could see, was her husband.

'That's good,' the doctor was saying. 'He's got help, then.'

'He goes to Gamblers Anonymous . . .' Then she added, 'I'm enjoying it, being with him again.' She realized her tone was equivocal, guarded, that she didn't go into detail about the last couple of weeks, as if Seth might mind that she had gone back to Freddy. Which she knew to be ridiculous. But it had been magic. And also manic: there was this constant pressure to show Freddy how happy she was. Today, just sitting quietly in the sunshine with Seth Kramer felt like a blessed relief.

'I'm pleased for you, Lily. It's never easy, coming back from a problem like that in a relationship.'

Lily looked at him, 'But you can, can't you?'

'Do you mean yourself or Freddy?'

'Me. I can move past what he did, can't I? People do . . .'

Seth considered her question. 'If you can both be honest about how you feel, free to speak your resentments when they pop up. It's pretending things are perfect that's the killer.'

Which is exactly what I'm doing, Lily thought, resolving to stop the forced honeymoon in its tracks and impress upon her husband that she loved him without things needing to be endlessly sublime.

'I said we had to draw a line. If I keep narking at him about what he did, it'll never work.'

Seth raised an eyebrow. 'Very generous.'

She caught a look of real affection in his eyes, concern, too. The 'but' she had sensed was to follow never materialized, however, and Lily changed the conversation back to work. She knew it was pointless trying to make people see what a good man Freddy was, pointless explaining that her love for her husband was not misplaced. The proof would be in the pudding.

Helen opened the door slowly to Lily's knock. Her face was expectant, almost eager, but when she saw her sister her expression fell. Lily had texted that she was coming up to Oxford and would drop by to fetch some of her stuff, but had got no reply, so she'd walked over to the house after seeing Seth.

Helen didn't say a word in greeting, just stood back for Lily

428

to enter, then closed the door and led the way into the kitchen, where she crossed the room to put the kettle on, still without a word. She was dressed in baggy black tracksuit bottoms and a long-sleeved maroon T-shirt, her short auburn-grey hair untidy and in need of a wash.

'What's happened?' Lily addressed her sister's back, the silence leaden.

Helen turned and gave her a puzzled frown, as if she were surprised Lily was still there. A small burst of apprehension made Lily shiver. 'Helen?'

'He's gone.' Her sister abandoned the attempt to make tea, which had got no further than picking the kettle off the stand and placing it on the work surface. She leaned forward on the kitchen table, propping herself on her hands as she stood, head bowed.

'Gone?' Lily's heart contracted. 'Kit?'

Helen looked up, her expression sardonic. 'Of course Kit.'

Lily frowned. 'He left?' she asked, hoping that it wasn't worse news.

Straightening up, Helen gave a long sigh. 'Yup. Disappeared in the night. Two days. He was only here two days.'

Lily saw the tears and Helen's desire to hide them by turning her attention to the kettle once more. Lily went to her and pulled her into an embrace. 'Fuck. I'm so sorry. He'll come back, surely he will.' Even to Lily's ears, her suggestion sounded naive.

Helen didn't reply, just buried her head on Lily's shoulder, and for the first time in as long as she could remember, her fierce, self-contained sister was racked with sobs, clinging to

Lily as if her heart would break. Lily felt tears in her own eyes. *The cruelty of hope*, she thought, as she held Helen in her arms.

When Helen finally pushed her away, her tear-stained face was set in angry lines. Wiping her wet cheeks with her fingers, she glared at Lily. 'Why did you bother to save him, Lillian? What was the fucking point? If you'd just left him to die we'd all have avoided a whole heap of heartache. Including Kit. He doesn't want to live. He's been trying to kill himself for nearly a decade now.' She let out a small snort. 'Strange, he used to be so good at everything. But dying seems beyond him.'

'Don't, Helen.'

'Don't what?' She pulled a tissue from her sleeve and gave her nose a vigorous blow. 'Mention the D-word? You'd rather I pretend everything is hunky-dory, would you? That one fine day my son will walk through that door, looking like he used to, all cherub curls and big grey eyes, and tell me he's cured?' Her voice broke, eyes filling with tears again. 'I watched him lying in that bed, Lily, and I prayed and prayed with all my heart that he would live. I put every ounce of energy I had into that prayer, all day, all night.' She gave a short laugh. 'Be careful what you wish for, eh? The universe delivers.'

'You wouldn't want him dead,' Lily said softly.

Turning the full force of her fury on Lily, Helen, her face twisted in pain, almost yelled at her. 'Really? You think anything – *anything* – could be worse than the way I feel right now? *Do you?* He lay in that bed and promised me over and over, "I'll never touch a grain of smack again as long as I live,

Mum." I promise, promise, promise,' she mimicked, in a grating, girly voice.

Lily searched for something optimistic to say, found nothing.

'And you know what?' her sister said with a sick grin. 'I was so damn stupid. Even after everything he's put us through, I actually believed him again.'

Silence fell as Helen filled the kettle and slammed the lid shut.

'Where's David?'

'Where do you think?' Helen snapped, as she splashed milk into the two mugs. 'Out looking for him, of course. Keen as mustard to get the boy back, is our David, so we can go through the same old hideous charade all over again.'

Helen's bile was making Lily feel ill, as if actual poison were being released into the kitchen air. 'I'm so sorry,' she said, having no idea how to comfort her tortured sister.

When Lily got back to the flat that night, it was after ten. She had stayed with Helen till David came home, then felt it would be better to leave them to their grief. Freddy was waiting for her, the room softly lit, a spread laid out on the glass coffee-table: bowls with various dips, seeded crispbread, almonds and olives, baby tomatoes, strawberries – it was one of their favourite meals of old – with two sparkling new wine glasses next to the plates, knives and napkins.

He welcomed her as if she'd been away for a year, holding her close, kissing every inch of her face and neck. 'God, I've missed you.'

She pushed him away, laughing at the tragic look on his

face as she sank down on the sofa, kicked off her sandals and let out a sigh of relief.

'You're very late,' he said, his look almost uncomfortably intense as he poured her some wine. 'Good doctor keeping you busy? I texted you.'

She explained about Kit and that her phone had run out of juice.

'It was always possible he'd do that,' Freddy said, throwing himself beside her and laying his head on her shoulder for a moment.

'How was your day?' she asked, not wanting to talk about her nephew any more. There was literally *nothing* to say.

'Great. Yeah, really good. Things progressing on the launch front. Had lunch with a friend from Malta, generally bonded with half the Wolseley.'

'Nothing new there. Which friend?'

'An American called Shirley. She and I used to hang out a bit, do the tourist trail.' He pulled a face, 'It was bloody lonely without you, Lil.'

'Bloody lonely without you, too, Fred.'

His phone rang and, still chuckling, he answered it.

She heard the faint sound of a woman's voice and watched as her husband's face went very still. All he said was 'Thank you·... Yes, thank you ... No, it's fine ... I'll be in touch.'

'Who was that?'

Freddy turned to her, his expression unfathomable. 'That was the nursing home. My father's dead.'

CHAPTER 51

The news was hardly unexpected. He had imagined the even-
tuality a thousand times since he'd seen Vinnie in Malta. But
the relief he'd hoped for felt more like panic. A cold, breathless panic building in the pit of his stomach. Lily had her
arms round him, her words full of sympathy and love, but
his instinct was to shake her off and run out into the summer
darkness, be on his own. He took deep breaths, trying to get
a grip on himself.

'Will you have to organize the funeral?' she asked.

'No.'

'Who will, then?'

'The home. I'm sure they do it all the time.'

'But—'

'I'm not going.' Freddy was barely keeping control. He
pushed Lily off and got up, aware of his wife's baffled look.

'Not going to your father's funeral?' She sounded

incredulous. 'But you must. I know it's hard when you love someone, but you have to go, Freddy.'

Pacing the floor in the small flat, he turned to her. 'He's dead, Lily. He won't give a fuck.'

Clearly shocked, she got up and came to where he was standing, took both his hands in hers. 'Look, it's a terrible thing, losing your dad. I understand. And I know you were close before the Alzheimer's. But you'll really regret it if you don't go.'

Freddy avoided those loving eyes. His heart was pumping double time, as if he'd just snorted a long line of coke. 'With all due respect, Lil, you don't understand.' He pulled away.

She stood her ground. 'Explain then.'

Freddy didn't answer, just leaned against the window frame, looking down on the crowd of people still milling with pint glasses outside the pub. He wanted to yell at them to fuck off.

There was a touch on his arm. 'Freddy . . .'

It was all he could do not to flinch. But she sensed it anyway and he heard her walk slowly back to the sofa.

'When did you last see him?' she was asking. 'Did you know he was so ill? Was it the Alzheimer's?' On and on she went, her words like needles in his skull. 'I'll come with you, Freddy. It won't be as bad as you think. I can help you arrange things. You need to be there.'

And suddenly he lost it. The carefully maintained silence he'd imposed on himself since he was a small child, the stoicism, the carapace behind which he'd hidden his feelings from every single person he had ever met – even Max and

Julie, even Lily – erupted violently through his body with the force of a nuclear explosion. He felt his soul shaking from the very depths, and experienced an out-of-body moment where he watched from above the tall, dark-haired man in jeans and a blue shirt, twisted in agony on the floor below, an unearthly sound rumbling in his throat.

'Freddy!' Lily was beside him, but he didn't want her. He didn't want anyone. No one had helped him back then, no one could now. 'Freddy, please.'

He pushed her off and stood up as words – incoherent, even to himself – suddenly poured from his mouth, tears streamed from his eyes, his skin wet with perspiration, his breath coming in painful gasps.

'Come on, sit down, try to breathe,' Lily was saying, and he felt himself being led gently to the sofa and made to sit.

For a moment he could do nothing but struggle for air, clasping his wife's hand, like a drowning man. When he began to talk it was barely above a whisper, small phrases forced between his lips. Even now, the words seemed dangerous, like sacrilege, to the conditioned Freddy.

'He was a monster. An absolute monster,' he began. 'He wasn't . . . I was only young . . . It never . . . When I heard his voice . . .' He took a few steadying breaths. 'I used to shake so hard I could hardly stand . . .'

Lily's eyes were wide but she said nothing.

'He had this chair. When I came home from school . . . when he was angry about something . . . or nothing . . . the chair would be in the centre of the sitting room, all the furniture pushed back. He would make me choose what he

435

would hit me with. They were all displayed ... on hooks behind the kitchen door. A riding crop, a bull whip he'd cut short, a wooden paddle, a leather shoe ... like he was proud of them.'

Lily's face was still with horror.

'It didn't make much difference. It was *how* he hit me that mattered. He was a sadist, he *relished* it, Lily. His eyes would actually bulge and glitter with pleasure, he would be covered in sweat. The more violent he was, the more he got off on it.'

Freddy's voice became steadier as he began to recount his secret.

'Christ, Freddy. Where was your mother?'

'Mum? I don't know. Out somewhere. But she couldn't have stopped him. He hit her too.'

'She never said anything to anyone? What about the bruises?'

'You don't understand. She wouldn't have dared. He'd have killed her.' He swallowed. 'He was crafty. He'd wait till the marks from the last time had faded. But he broke my arm once, twisting it back, and cracked my ribs more than once – the chair was hard ... I can still smell the chair seat ... old wood ... sweat.'

Silence.

'Nobody ever wondered how you got hurt?'

Freddy shook his head. He remembered his mother's face when she came back after one of Vinnie's attacks. *She knew.* But if there was sympathy in her eyes for her son she never said anything, never did anything, never even tried to protect him.

There was more silence as Lily presumably digested what he was telling her.

'I was never good enough for Dad. He would play mind games with me, sometimes for days, weeks, torment me with the prospect of a beating. Make me wait. Anticipating being hurt is worse than the pain itself, you know. Sometimes I wet myself just hearing his feet on the stairs, coming up from the pub.'

'The pub?'

'My father was a publican. Not an actuary. I didn't grow up in Nottingham. We had a pub in Leicester, the Three Bells. He wasn't called Vincent March either, his name was Vinnie Slater. My father, Vinnie Slater: a brute, a bastard and a villain. But, oh, so popular with his shady clientele.'

'You changed your name? When?'

'In my twenties. I was scared he'd find me. I reinvented myself. Lost my Midlands accent, my name, my background, anything that linked me with my father.' He gave a sigh. 'But I couldn't remove him from my head, of course.' Freddy looked away: he couldn't bear the pain on his wife's face. 'I'm glad he's dead. I wish I'd killed him myself, but I'm way too much of a coward.'

'I can't get my head around this. You used to talk about him, the Alzheimer's, the home ... So that was why you didn't want me to meet him.'

'There was a man in a home with Alzheimer's. Arthur March. He ran the corner shop where I got a job when I was fourteen, breaking up cardboard boxes and sweeping the floor, unpacking stuff, delivering bits and pieces to old people.

He was a good man, he took an interest in me. Maybe he knew . . .'

His wife was silent. 'Bastard,' she muttered. 'Fucking sadistic bastard.'

'I should have stood up to him. He laughed at me the few times I tried to fight back. I *was* probably laughable to him.'

'Don't be ridiculous. What could you have done against a grown man? This isn't your fault, Freddy, not even remotely. For Christ's sake, the man sounds like an animal.'

Freddy thought about when he had last seen Vinnie. Less an animal, more a pathetic, whining shell of a man. Blow and he'd topple over. 'He paid in the end,' he said. 'Gasping for your last breath must be the worst form of torture.'

'Not bad enough, by a long chalk,' Lily retorted. 'He should have had his balls cut off, been publicly condemned, rotted the rest of his life in jail.'

Freddy smiled at her fierceness. *Why was I so afraid of telling her?* he asked himself. But he knew. Whatever she said, and however much he believed it to be the truth, he still retained the image of himself that his father had inculcated into him from his earliest memory: a spineless jessie.

It was cathartic, though, as if a well of sticky black poison were pouring out of his body, down his arms and off his finger-ends as he talked on and on to Lily, as he recounted the hideous experiences of his childhood and watched the absolute horror on her face. Because part of him had always felt it couldn't have been as bad as he remembered – he must have been exaggerating the fear and humiliation because he was a coward. That was what his father had always asserted

– he was just trying to make a man of Freddy. And he had almost convinced his son, made Freddy believe the mind games and beatings were somehow acceptable, what he deserved. But he saw Lily was shocked into silence, appalled by the abuse. Pained and angry for the defenceless boy he had been, she spat vengeance on his dead father's soul. She believed Freddy. She totally and utterly validated his distress.

CHAPTER 52

The following morning, as soon as Freddy had gone out to a meeting, Lily phoned Seth Kramer and described what her husband had told her.

'God, poor man,' the doctor said. 'It explains the gambling, though.'

'I don't know what to do. I think he should get help, some sort of therapy, but he says he feels better now he's told me, and that bastard father of his is dead.'

'That won't be enough, Lily. He needs to process what happened to him. The feelings won't just go away because he's finally articulated them to someone, although he will feel like a huge burden has been lifted from his shoulders right now.'

'Could you recommend someone good? They'd have to be in London or he won't go. Maybe if I give him the names of a couple of therapists you really rate, he might consider it.'

'It would have to be his choice. It won't work if he doesn't want to go.'

'No, but I can encourage him, can't I?'

There was a short pause from Seth. 'You can encourage him, Lily, but you can't save him.'

Lily frowned. 'I'm not trying to save him.' She was irritated: the suggestion seemed to be almost an admonishment. 'But seeing someone you love in that sort of pain . . . Of course I want to help him. Wouldn't you?'

'I'm sure you already have helped, just by being there, by listening.'

'Please can you email me some names? I'd like to give them to him, anyway.'

'Of course.' Seth paused. 'How are you coping?' His voice was gentle. 'It must have been distressing, hearing about such dreadful violence, realizing your husband isn't who you thought he was.'

It had been, but it wasn't until this minute that Lily grasped just how distressing. Her thoughts had been so focused on processing Freddy's pain she hadn't had time to think of how it had affected her.

'I . . . I don't know. It was so harrowing, Seth. I keep imagining him as a little boy and I can hardly deal with my feelings because I'm so angry with that vile man. He's still Freddy, but now he's opened up all these images of his past . . . I don't know what to think.' She felt tearful. 'I can't work out what it means for him. For us.'

'If you need to talk . . .'

'Thanks. I'm fine, Seth, but thanks.'

441

She didn't feel fine at all, and she sensed from his silence that Seth knew that better than she did. But he didn't press her.

'No need to come on Friday if you're dealing with stuff,' he said.

'No, I'll be there. I've done the latest batch of tapes and I'm meeting your friend Janice while I'm up.' She tried to sound enthusiastic, but although the prospect of more transcription work was not exactly thrilling, she had listened to David and Prem and knew she couldn't do what Freddy was urging her almost daily to do: give up work.

Lily sat across from Prem in the café on the corner of Moxon Street, round the corner from the chair shop, both women with a bowl of chilled beetroot soup and black bread.

'That's horrible,' Prem said, her dark eyes wide with shock as she listened to Lily describe what Freddy had told her the previous night. 'Christ, how do you live with all that terrible stuff and not tell someone?'

'Why do you think he didn't trust me enough to tell me till now?' Lily asked. 'If his dad hadn't died, maybe I'd never have known.' She knew she was being stupid, feeling hurt that Freddy hadn't been able to confide in her. This wasn't about her. But still.

'Buried too deep, I suppose,' Prem replied. 'Don't forget you've known him less than five years. He'd already kept the secret for a lifetime before he met you.'

Lily thought about this. 'I don't understand when he says he feels so ashamed. Ashamed of what? Being beaten to a pulp by a violent sadist? He was a *child*.'

'Sounds like the man fundamentally humiliated him. It's what they do, these abusers, reduce their victims to a pulp so they can control them. Poor Freddy.'

They sat in silence, eating their soup.

'Do you think he'll get help?' Prem asked.

Lily shrugged. 'Seth says I can't make him. And maybe he doesn't need it. Maybe telling me will be enough.'

Prem raised her eyebrows. 'You don't believe that, Lil. This sort of damage is a couple of years' worth of shrinking, believe me.'

That night, Freddy didn't come home till gone two o'clock. Lily had spoken to him earlier in the evening, and he had said he'd be late: he was having dinner with a man he needed to schmooze for the launch. He hadn't given any more details.

Now Lily lay in bed trying to believe him. But waiting for Freddy in the dark reminded her of all the old times when she'd done the same, times when she had stupidly never doubted him, or ever questioned the subsequently fluent narrative of his evening. Times when he had, in fact, spent the night in the casino, losing every penny they had.

She was almost asleep when she finally heard his key in the door. He didn't turn any lights on in the sitting room, but there was always adequate from the street lamp right outside the window – the flat was never completely dark. She listened to the soft thud of his shoes hitting the floorboards, the rustle of clothes being removed, a tap being turned on in the kitchen, the splash of urine in the toilet next to the bedroom. She didn't call out. When he tiptoed in and climbed into bed she still didn't speak. Her back to him, she waited for the feel of his body against her own – he always snuggled in. But tonight he did not.

When she turned, pretending she had only just woken, he was lying on his back staring at the ceiling.

'You're very late,' she said, her voice hardly above a whisper.

'Yeah,' he said, yawning, 'Went on a bit.'

She waited for the familiar excuses, but Freddy was silent. Moving across the bed, she put her head on his shoulder as he lifted his arm to accommodate her. His body was chilly.

'How are you?' she asked.

'I'm fine,' he said.

'Did the evening go well?'

'Okay, I suppose. Nothing special.'

He squeezed her shoulder, but she sensed he was answering on autopilot, not really listening to her at all. She wanted to ask him, to speak the words out loud: 'Were you gambling tonight?' But following his revelations yesterday and her concern for him on that count, she didn't feel able to do so. So they lay there until she kissed his chest and rolled over with her back to him again.

'Love you,' she said.

'Love you too,' she heard him reply.

CHAPTER 53

The hospice had sent Freddy a copy of the funeral sheet in the post. He'd been in touch with them: he'd told them he would pay for Vinnie's funeral if they would organize it and that he would not be attending. The woman he spoke to, one Shona Raskin, did not question his decision. Maybe she was used to it. Or maybe she'd known his father.

Staring at the proof that his father really had died and been dispatched, Freddy was relieved to see there was no photograph, which seemed to be the current fashion at funerals, some cheesy shot from the past, before the person was sick and dying. This was one C5 sheet, with a tasteful picture of wild flowers in a meadow at the top, followed by his father's name in bold, the dates of his life, then the time and place of the funeral. It had been held at the crematorium on Groby Road, where his mother also had been cremated. Her ashes were scattered in the garden of remembrance, but with no

445

plaque, no stone, no urn, nothing with which to remember her. At the bottom of the sheet was a prayer:

God of mercy,
    as we mourn the death of Vinnie Slater
    and thank you for his life,
    we also remember times when it was hard for
    us to understand,
    to forgive, and to be forgiven.
    Heal our memories of hurt and failure,
    and bring us to forgiveness and life
    in Jesus Christ our Lord.
Amen

Did they know he was a vicious bastard? Freddy wondered as he read the words of the prayer, taken aback by what seemed like a very apposite and personal communication. He screwed the paper up tight, crushing it in his fist until it was the size of a small plum, then stuffed it into the kitchen bin.

The other letter he'd received in the post that morning was from the firm of solicitors his father had appointed as executors of his will. Vinnie Slater, Freddy read, had left the flat in Malta, plus one hundred and nine thousand, six hundred and thirty-two pounds to his son, the only beneficiary.

The letter and the words it contained felt almost radioactive to Freddy. He found himself pushing it away across the kitchen table, trying to distance himself from contamination. He imagined the cynical smile on his father's face at the thought of Freddy enjoying his money. 'Gotcha! So your old man has some uses after all, eh, son?' And he knew he would never accept a single penny. The house in Malta was never Vinnie's in the first place so he would keep that. But, finding the solicitor's email on the letter, Freddy instructed them to put the money straight into his wife's bank account when it came through, and gave the details. He owed her. It wasn't enough, but it was a start.

The two weeks since his father had died and his secret had exploded into the quiet flat had been rocky for Freddy. The balm of revelation, which had soothed his soul for being heard – made all the more powerful by Lily's sympathetic reaction – had quickly worn off. He was left with a deep insecurity, paranoia and bubbling panic he was having trouble controlling. He felt as if he were literally falling to pieces.

His secret had been the solid platform upon which he had built his life. Freddy March, his new persona, had not been beaten and humiliated, not scared out of his wits, but nurtured and cared for by loving parents. In his telling of the secret his invention had become destabilized, as if a leg had broken off a table, making it wobble and tip. Now he didn't know if he was Freddy Slater or Freddy March, or neither of these lonely spectres.

His instinct was to gamble, of course, and in the first days after his father died, he had not held back. The community centre, with the plastic chairs, the machine coffee, the sorry crew of addicts, was not a serious alternative. He had not, as he was certain Lily thought, been at the tables on the night he'd got home so late: that had been a genuinely drawn-out boys' night with a rather rambunctious PR. No, Freddy gambled in the daytime, when Lily was working in the flat, sneaking into one or other of his old watering holes and setting himself on the familiar rollercoaster again.

But he found it wasn't working for him in the way it always had. Waiting for the buzz, the hit, the high, Freddy was disappointed time and again. Instead of lifting him, it just made his panic worse. And the more he piled up the chips on the numbers, the more extreme the panic became. He was trapped inside his feelings. There was no respite, nowhere to hide. It was making him crazy.

Lily was cooking supper when he got home after a difficult couple of hours with Max. It was early September – less than a month to the launch – and his friend was wound up about the venture. He had sunk a lot of money into it already and there was now an equation to be made regarding advertising expenditure versus outcome – one of the great imponderables in business. Throw vast amounts of money at it so that no one could miss it? Or throw less, letting it build quietly and find its own level? Freddy, true to form, preferred the former, Max the latter. But Freddy's head was too woolly to argue coherently, and Max prevailed. It took some of the pressure off, admittedly, but Freddy was annoyed: he felt Max was selling the project short. They'd had a row, something they never did.

'Spaghetti and meatballs,' Lily announced with a smile as he came in.

One of his favourites. He went over to her at the stove and kissed her cheek. She smelt of mangoes and he buried his face in her hair, inhaling her perfume, the scent soothing his day-long edginess and irritation. Immediately he felt himself to be in a safer, calmer place. She was his salvation.

'Freddy . . .' He watched Lily's face, now serious, as she turned to him, her wooden spoon with traces of tomato sauce held aloft. He didn't want her to speak: he couldn't bear to hear an admonishment, an accusation – his gambling secret seemed to hang above them both, like a neon sign. He'd felt her tension in the air for days now, but knew she had held off in respect for his recent bereavement.

'What?'

'I've got a couple of names from Dr Kramer, well-respected psychotherapists he trusts. I thought maybe you could check them out.'

Freddy frowned. 'You told Kramer about me?'

Lily looked taken aback. 'I didn't think you'd mind. It's his job, Freddy. He deals with people who have your sort of problem all the time.'

But he did mind. He minded very much. The thought of his wife gossiping with that bloody man – whom he was completely convinced was in love with her – about his private, deeply personal revelations made him feel physically sick. 'Who else have you told?' he demanded.

'No one,' she said, too quickly, and he knew she was lying: the blush that had risen to her cheeks was a giveaway.

'Who, Lily? Who have you told?'

She rolled her eyes as if he were being ridiculous. 'Okay, I told Prem.'

'*Prem?* For fuck's sake.'

'She's my friend, Freddy. I had to talk to someone. What you told me was so horrible . . .'

'So, Kramer and Prem. Who else?'

'No one. I swear.'

Freddy realized he was gripping her arm, swinging her away from the stove. He felt betrayed, exposed, humiliated all over again. How dare she? He'd thought he could trust Lily, *of all people*, to protect him. His heart raced, his breath was hot in his chest, his muscles burned, his eyes were filmed and scratchy with rage. He tried to blink it away, but all he could see was his wife talking to that smug fuck of a shrink. They were laughing, flirting, as she poured out Freddy's intimate secrets to be chewed over, passed judgement on. So they thought they knew what was best for him? *Christ!*

He heard her cry from a long way off, another world, as he yanked her up by both arms and threw her violently against the tasteful Parma Grey kitchen wall. There was a crack, and for a second she seemed suspended, then she crumpled gracefully onto the wooden floor.

Silence.

He looked down, bewildered. The noise in his brain had stopped, leaving an eerie calm. Lily was slumped, not moving. Feeling a sick terror in the pit of his stomach, Freddy knelt down beside her.

'Lily?' He shook her shoulder, '*Lily?* Please . . .'

It seemed an age, but she was moving, opening her eyes. *Thank God.* Her expression was dazed as she raised her hand to the back of her head, the fingers coming away wet with blood. Freddy reached out to help her up, but she pushed him away.

'Lily . . . I'm sorry, I'm sorry, I'm sorry – are you okay? Tell me you're okay . . .'

She was struggling to her feet, unsteady, holding out her hand to find support on the work surface. He tried to help again, but she angrily batted his arm off.

'Get away from me,' she said, her voice low and dangerously quiet.

'Please, Lily. Please, I don't know what came over me. I – I was just upset that you'd told people about my dad. It freaked me out, my past being blabbed all over town like that. I'm sorry, I'm so, so sorry.'

His wife stared at him, but he could read nothing in her eyes. They were veiled, blank. She was shaking. Without a word she moved slowly to the fridge, where she took the ice tray out of the freezer compartment. She bashed it on the side, collected the loosened cubes and twisted them into a tea towel, which she pressed to the back of her head. Then she pushed past him and went into the bedroom, slamming the door shut behind her.

Freddy was shattered. *Oh, God, oh, God, what have I done?* The words repeated themselves over and over as he collapsed on the sofa, his hands to his face, heart hammering in his chest. He had hurt Lily. He had hurt the woman he loved. Never in his life had he so much as laid a finger on anyone in anger. He didn't understand what was happening to him.

As he sat there in the fading light, the smell of the meatballs pungent and mocking him from the stove, he wanted to do what he always did: run. Run and hide behind the soothing click of the chips, the bored voice of the croupier, the soft sweep of the rake on the baize, the clack, clack, clack as the ball bounced across the number sections. But he wouldn't leave Lily.

He had no idea how long he sat there, his mind in turmoil, his thoughts fixated on the woman behind the bedroom door. But he was suddenly aware of her ghostly presence across the darkened room.

'Freddy?' Her voice was thick with recent tears.

He leaped to his feet, went towards her, but stopped short of reaching out. He dared not try to touch her. She was in her dressing-gown – the blue one he had bought for her last birthday – her arms clamped tight around her body, her dark hair falling across her pale, tear-stained face.

'Lily, please. Oh, God, I'm so sorry. Are you all right?'

She didn't answer, just indicated the sofa and went to sit down.

When he dropped down beside her she turned to him, pulling her dressing-gown across her bare legs. It was a moment before she began to speak.

'Look, I know how hard it's been for you recently, with your father and then telling me about the abuse.' She swallowed, took a long breath. 'I can't even imagine what you're going through. It must have been utter hell, your childhood.' Another breath. 'But I can't stay here with you.'

Freddy had expected her to say those exact words. But, still, the impact was like a body blow. He held his breath as she went on. 'I know you're gambling.' Her eyes were sad.

'I . . .' He began to deny it, but her expression was resolute. She knew. What would be the point? 'I have, but not . . . only a few times, honestly. It was just a lapse after I heard about Dad . . . I . . .' This wasn't true, of course, but Lily didn't question it.

'It doesn't matter how many times, or when, or why, Freddy. You said you were getting help.'

'I was. I did. I *have* been to meetings.'

'And spoken, got involved?'

Freddy sighed. 'No. Not yet.'

'I thought . . .' She stopped and he wondered what she had intended to say. 'It doesn't matter.'

He felt the atmosphere drain between them. As if someone had switched off the light. Freddy had hated her – and everyone else – nagging him to 'get help'. But he hated it more now that she had given up. He felt tears hot behind his eyes.

'Please . . . please don't give up on me, Lil,' he begged, unable to stop himself reaching out and taking her cold hand in his. She didn't draw back, and he took hope from that. But her next words dashed any hope.

'I'm going back to Oxford tomorrow,' she said softly. 'I love you, Freddy, you know I do. Perhaps too much. And what happened to you as a child literally breaks my heart. But I can't do this any more. I can't live with someone I can't trust, someone who's . . .'

She didn't say the word, she didn't need to.

'I'll get help, I will.' He heard the desperate pleading in his voice. 'I promise I'll go and see one of the people Kramer

453

recommended. I'll make an appointment tomorrow.' He stopped, noting no reaction in his wife's face. 'What happened tonight was unacceptable on any level,' he said. 'I'm utterly ashamed. But it's a wake-up call. I'm not right in the head at the moment. I know I need help.'

Tears were pouring down Lily's face, her mouth puckering, but he was amazed to see that her eyes were still full of love.

'Please, Lily. Just one more chance,' Freddy whispered. But he knew his words fell heavy and rejected in the still night air.

They lay close together, naked and chilly. He held her in his arms, her back pressed against his skin, his hand cupping her shoulder – it was how they always slept. Freddy was awake though, his eyes open, staring into the darkness. He didn't want to miss a moment: he wanted to imprint for ever the feel of Lily's body, the scent of her skin, the soft rise and fall of her breathing as she eventually drifted into sleep. Imprint it so that he could carry her with him, always.

CHAPTER 54

Lily was huddled miserably in Seth's kitchen. She had left London early, before seven, the atmosphere so painful between her and Freddy that she ran along Charlotte Street towards the Tube as if she were escaping a tsunami. Her husband had been mostly silent as she packed her case; he hadn't asked her to stay. But his expression showed such devastation that she felt an overwhelming reluctance as she dragged herself from his farewell embrace.

Dr Kramer handed her a cup of coffee.

'Should I have left him like that?' she asked him, accepting the white china mug, but setting it down on the scrubbed-oak surface without sipping. 'He's such a mess. I'm worried what he'll do.'

'You mean you're worried he'll harm himself?' Seth asked, pulling his own stool closer to the island and sitting down, facing Lily. He was dressed in a pressed blue shirt and black chinos and looked tidier and more formal than he was on the boat – he had already seen one patient that morning, he'd told her, and had another due in an hour.

'I don't know. Freddy's an optimist, but even he says he feels crazy at the moment. And what happened last night was so out of character. He's the gentlest of men.'

'He has the numbers I gave you?'

'Yes. That was what the row was about. He was furious I'd told you.'

'He felt betrayed,' Seth said.

Tears filled Lily's eyes. 'Freddy trusted me with the most important secret in the world and I let him down. I should have asked before talking to you. But I never thought. I told my friend too. It was so horrible, I just couldn't deal with it on my own.'

The doctor nodded.

'I'll never forgive myself if Freddy does something.'

Seth shifted in his seat, his expression suddenly firm. 'Lily, you are not responsible for what Freddy does or doesn't do.'

She stared at him, bewildered. 'But I am. I'm his wife. He's facing the worst crisis of his life and I walk out on him?'

'You're not helping by being there. You protect him, foster his denial. It's called "collusion".'

Irritated at what she considered Seth's patronizing tone, she replied tartly, 'I know what collusion is and I haven't colluded. I've been totally straight with him.' That wasn't true, she thought as she said it, but she had meant to be straight with Freddy. It was just so hard in the face of his need for things to be perfect.

456

'Just by going back to him, you're tacitly approving.'

'But he promised he'd stopped gambling and was going to GA.'

'And if he was, that might have worked in the short term. But only in the short term, Lily. This man has been systematically traumatized in a horrific way from a very young age. No amount of self-help groups – useful as they undoubtedly are – could even scratch the surface of his pain.'

Lily felt the tears and made no effort to stop them. Accepting the square of kitchen towel that Seth tore from the roll by the sink, she wiped her eyes. But the tears kept coming.

She raised her face to the doctor. 'What will happen to him?'

'I don't know. I hope he'll get help.'

'And if he doesn't?'

Seth Kramer shrugged. 'There's nothing you can do. You gave it your best shot.'

His reply seemed almost callous to Lily. Cast her husband to the wolves, basically. Wash her hands of the whole affair.

'I still love him. I really do. Even after everything that's happened.'

Seth's face was soft with compassion. 'If you love him, then leave him to find the help he needs.'

It was cold on the boat, although it was only early September and the days had been very warm. Seth had been kind, as usual, offering lunch, offering supper, offering a bed for the night, but Lily had refused them all. He was obviously busy and she was intruding on his life. In the end he had persuaded her to stay on the boat.

'It's ridiculous paying for a hotel,' he'd said. 'I won't be going there for the next few weeks. I've taken on too many new patients now the summer is over and I don't have the time to write.'

Lily wasn't sure she believed him, but she was too discombobulated to argue. And the last thing she wanted to do was throw herself on her sister's mercy again. Not after all Helen's dire warnings about Freddy. The humiliation would be more than she could bear.

So Seth, after his last client left, had walked with her to the canal. He'd shown her where the wood was for the stove, how to work the chemical toilet. He'd given her the keys to the large padlock on the main door and helped her make the bed – the mauve-and-grey-patterned duvet cover was very much a man's choice, and made her smile.

They had sat together in the dying light, sharing a bottle of red wine he'd brought from the house. But Lily knew she wasn't very good company. The wine tasted too strong in her throat and she was having trouble focusing on what the doctor was telling her about a book he had just finished by a long-dead Dutch writer. Her head still ached despite the paracetamol she'd taken, and was tender to the touch where she had hit the wall the previous night, a constant reminder of what her husband had done.

Now she was in bed at last. But, although she was so tired she could hardly think straight, sleep eluded her. She lay on her side, tense in the unfamiliar setting, listening to the sounds of the water lapping against the boat, the shouts from a party of people crossing the bridge nearby, the occasional tramp of footsteps along the tow path. The duvet cover felt scratchy – maybe it was new: Seth had said he seldom slept on the boat – and the foam mattress fitted into the wood surround was harder than Lily was used to. There was a smell of wood and oil and damp, and a faint whiff of bleach from the loo.

Lily had felt lonely before. After Garret died she had thought she would die too, she missed him so much. But she'd had the twins at home, Prem and Anthony down the road, the chair shop with all the various clients . . . Then Freddy. For a moment she thought back to a holiday in Umbria one summer, the year after their wedding. Her family: Freddy, Sara and Stan, Dillon and Gabriela. Long evenings of laughter under the massive oak tree behind the house – always some friend or acquaintance of Freddy's staying for a night or two to enliven the party – candle flames playing on their tanned faces, the empty wine bottles, moths and fireflies dancing around their heads. She had wanted those evenings never to end. Even this summer, after Freddy had deserted her and her life lay in ruins about her feet, she'd had her sister and brother-in-law to turn to.

Tonight, though, Lily did not feel lonely. She felt, instead, completely alone. All she wanted, like a persistent ache, was to be back in the Charlotte Street flat. To rewind the clock and hear Freddy's laugh again, to look into his brown eyes, to feel his soft skin against her naked body, to smell the lingering waft of cardamom shaving cream in the bathroom, to put her hand in his as they strode through the London streets . . . To allow him to weave a 'perfect' life together.

But Lily knew, as she lay staring at the slatted blind of Seth's boat, she could no longer afford to love him. Freddy had cost her almost everything she held dear in her life. Dillon was barely speaking to her and Sara had stepped back from her mother's chaos. She hadn't spoken to either of them since the Delaunay tea. Lily's forced stay with Helen, and what her sister saw as 'meddling' in her nephew's plight, had tested their relationship almost to breaking point. Prem was openly frustrated with her. She was homeless and broke.

Ring any bells? Lily asked herself, finding it almost funny, comparing her disastrous love for Freddy March to Kit and Freddy's addictions. But there were painful similarities. And the knowledge that Freddy could hurt and destroy her – just as Kit's heroin and Freddy's roulette wheel had ruined both their lives – in no way diminished her love for him. It should have, but it didn't. She still wanted Freddy with every cell, bone, drop of blood and breath in her body. But, unlike them, for Lily the spell was broken. Freddy had gone too far. She would never go back.

CHAPTER 55

He searched for the number on the doors in the north London street, checking his phone to make sure he'd got the details right. The weeks since Lily had left had been a numb sort of hell for Freddy. Sleepwalking through his life – the endless phone calls and emails, drinks and dinners and parties, schmoozing and boozing and negotiating . . . the food-truck launch itself – he had found his only real focus, every minute of every day, was the shocking thing he'd done to Lily. What he'd done and the uncontrollable rage he'd felt as he did it. He had completely lost sight of who he was.

I'm a survivor, he told himself daily. *I don't need help. I'll get through this by myself. I always have.* But one windy, wet Sunday morning, in the middle of October, he had finally understood that he might not. The launch was over – a niche success. Max was delighted. There was no work to focus on, no party to go to, no emails that couldn't wait till the morning. No

Lily. He had gone out to get a paper from the corner shop – Mr Patel, who had taken to calling him 'dear', reminded him of Arthur March. But as he was walking back along the pavement in the rain, he saw his father coming towards him. Not his father as he had last seen him in Malta, but his father when he was still bulked with muscle and rage.

Staring in horror at the approaching figure, Freddy felt suddenly dizzy, his heart racing nineteen to the dozen. He realized he was sweating and wiped his clammy, shaking hands on his jeans. He heard his paper drop, felt his breath wheezing in his chest. A young woman in jogging pants and a pink hoodie touched his arm, said something he didn't understand. He pushed her away. He was sure he was having a heart attack, dying, right there in the street.

A second later the man – who was not, of course, Vinnie Slater – moved past him, casting only a cursory glance at Freddy, now bent over the gutter and retching. But with a familiar sort of inevitability, which didn't even feel painful in the moment, Freddy, as he straightened up, saw he had wet himself.

'It sounds like a panic attack,' the nurse on the NHS helpline had suggested later, her tone sympathetic. 'Have you been particularly stressed lately?'

And Freddy, with a sudden flash of understanding, saw he had been unbearably stressed his entire life.

The door, when he found it, seemed an improbable address for a respected psychotherapist. Although it was a shiny maroon with a stylish pewter knocker in the shape of a dolphin, it was sandwiched between a betting shop – the final

462

irony – and a sandwich bar, which had two metal chairs and a table on the pavement outside. But he rang the bell anyway. A moment later a male voice answered, 'Top floor, be careful on the stairs.'

Freddy saw what the voice meant. The stairs were steep and winding, but carpeted in what looked like an expensive sisal runner, lit by a skylight on the landing above.

Already so nervous he thought he might puke, Freddy hesitated at the sound of the voice, on the brink of turning tail. He'd already cancelled one appointment.

Then a head poked over the banisters. It was that of a man about ten years older than Freddy, balding and lean, with very blue eyes in a tanned face. *He looks*, thought Freddy, *more like a sailor than a therapist*. But the man smiled as Freddy reached the top floor and held out his hand, offering a firm shake. The smile was both wise and kind, and Freddy took a deep breath. *Maybe with this man*, his instinct told him, *I can be safe.*

EPILOGUE

It was a sunny Saturday morning in early December, three months since Lily had said goodbye to Freddy, her head bloody, her heart broken. They had not spoken since. Lily was leaving the flat she now rented in Summertown – a pleasant two-bedroom ground-floor apartment, with a small, neat garden, in a pretty cul-de-sac. She was en route for the 500 bus that would take her to Oxford station.

She had stayed on Seth's boat for a while after breaking up with her husband – almost five weeks – and it had been an intensely solitary time. She had turned in upon herself, stripped bare, for once, of the distracting turbulence that had recently been her life. But, aside from the odd stab of searing loneliness that made her want to cry out, she had found the time strangely peaceful.

Every morning, early, she would get out of bed, pull on a sweater and jeans and pad through to the sitting area, where she'd light the wood stove – she was becoming quite an expert. Then she would make herself a cup of coffee with Seth's state-of-the-art machine and, clutching a blue tin mug full of the powerful brew Seth favoured, she'd sling the tartan blanket from the sofa around her shoulders and open the glass doors onto the deck.

It had been a beautiful autumn, and at that time of day the sun would be tipping the horizon, its rays piercing the pale layer of mist that often rose from the field beside the canal and hovered over the still water. All she was able to hear were the birds. It was so beautiful, so utterly peaceful, that it sometimes brought tears to Lily's eyes. She would lean against the side of the narrowboat, her bare feet cold on the dewy decking, and sip the warm coffee, her heart slow, her breath calm, her mind enjoyably empty.

Then, three weeks after her arrival on the boat, an email from 'freddymarch@hotmail.com' had landed in her in-box. His message had been short, almost formal, but her heart had raced, nonetheless, when she saw it was from him.

Dearest Lily,

I am writing to let you know that I have given Helen and David's address to the solicitors, Markham and Ryde, who are dealing with my father's estate. (I don't know if you're still living there, but I'm sure they'll forward it, if not.)

I have asked Bill Markham to transfer the money left to me in my father's will to your account. It amounts to £109,632, and will go some way in repaying my debt to you.

It might not arrive for a few months – you know how long probate can take – but let me know when it does.

I hope you are doing okay. I struggle, but I'm sure you'll be pleased to hear I've finally been brave enough to get some help!

Much love to you, as always, Freddy xxx

It had taken Lily a moment to catch her breath, all the old emotions Freddy engendered gathering raw around her heart as she read his final line. She'd pushed them firmly away, concentrating on the practical content of his message. *He could so easily have kept the money, gambled it away*, she'd thought.

She'd known she was pleased, as Freddy suggested, that he was getting help. But she had been surprised to find she was not tempted to respond to the email, beyond thanking him for the money. The thought of hearing more about his personal life, of being sucked back into his chaos, of feeling too much for him again, had sent a piercing shaft of anxiety through her gut.

The money was hugely significant in her parlous financial state. Her heart had leaped at the sum. It meant she could borrow enough, until probate was finalized, for a deposit on a decent rental – from Seth, perhaps, or Prem. It was getting chilly on the boat as winter approached, and although the doctor had insisted she stay as long as she liked she knew she would relish a place on solid ground, with central heating and a loo that didn't wobble and smell of bleach.

Today, as she waited for the train to arrive, Lily was nervous, but also excited. Not nervous because she was seeing the twins and Ted. Her relationship with her children had begun

466

slowly to mend over the autumn. They were still careful with each other, and nobody referred much to the recent past, but Lily felt they were a family again. The anger on both sides had gradually dissipated now that Freddy was no longer in the picture.

As it had, indeed, between Lily and her sister. She had been to supper with Helen and David only last night. Kit was still AWOL, still an ongoing cause of distress. But since the summer and Kit's most recent rejection, her sister and brother-in-law were finally on the same page about their son. David, reluctantly, had stopped taking Kit food, cleaning up after him, giving him keys, monitoring him. They both seemed to have resigned themselves – as much as would ever be possible – to the status quo.

No, Lily's nerves this morning were of a very different nature.

'Is this it?' Sara grinned at her mother as they pushed open the door to a small gallery in a narrow lane off the Broad. The four of them seemed to take up a lot of room in the quiet space – Ted particularly, with his loud voice and relentless enthusiasm. Lily greeted the blonde girl, Zoë, who sat behind the desk in the corner.

'How's it going?' she asked, casting an anxious glance around. On the right-hand wall were displayed fifteen of Lily's colourful pen-and-ink portraits. Blues and pinks and yellows, pale green and dark green, blacks and greys, the lines wove through the small, intricate drawings, the faces startlingly alive and full of character.

Zoë grinned, pointing to the pictures. 'See?'

And Lily did see. Dots. Red dots. Seven of them. She had sold *seven* of her drawings. The fact thrilled her.

It had been Seth who'd insisted she talk to Rebecca, his friend who owned the Oxford gallery. Lily had done a pen-and-ink drawing of the boat, *Mairzy Doats*, as a thank-you for letting her stay. He'd been delighted, and asked to see some of her other work. Lily had been reluctant, her father's words still ringing in her ears, even thirty years later: 'You have to be brilliant to make it as an artist, and you're not brilliant, Lillian, not by a long chalk.' But Seth's obvious enthusiasm had finally won her over.

'Awesome,' drawled Ted, examining the art close up.

'Wow!' Dillon grinned, putting his arm around her shoulders and squeezing her affectionately.

Sara laughed. 'God, Mum. These are fantastic. Why didn't you do this years ago?'

Lily smiled, but didn't reply. It didn't matter that she hadn't done it years ago because she had, finally, created some breathing space, some time to call her own. She missed Freddy, sometimes cried for him, but she didn't miss hanging on to the coat tails of his crazy, whirlwind existence – being consumed by him. No, these days Lily was in charge of her own fate. And she found she was hugely enjoying the opportunity to make her life exciting . . . all by herself.

ACKNOWLEDGEMENTS

The Gloria Steinem quote is taken from her book *Outrageous Acts and Everyday Rebellions*, second edition, published October 1995 by Holt Paperbacks (first published by Henry Holt & Co., New York, January 1983), quoted by permission.

As always, huge thanks to Jane Wood and the team at Quercus in the production of this book.